TI
MUF
LISI

CHRIS MERRITT

THE MURDER LIST

bookouture

Published by Bookouture in 2018
An imprint of StoryFire Ltd.
Carmelite House
50 Victoria Embankment
London EC4Y 0DZ
www.bookouture.com

ISBN: 978-1-78681-394-7
eBook ISBN: 978-1-78681-393-0

To my family and Mase

PROLOGUE

Saturday, 21 July 2012

This day will change him forever, though he doesn't know it yet.

Detective Inspector Zachariah Boateng laces up his trainers on the stairs. Pats his pockets: wallet, keys. All set.

'Let's go, Dad, come on!' Amelia bounces on tiptoes. 'Can I have it now?'

Zac raises his eyebrows.

'Please,' she adds, her smile revealing the little gap between her front teeth. She extends a palm.

Fishing in his wallet, he produces two pounds fifty. Sixteen years in the Met Police and he's a pushover for a nine-year-old.

'Back soon, love,' he calls down the hallway. His wife, Etta, raises a mug of tea in acknowledgement, phone clamped to the side of her face. Miles Davis's trumpet drifts in from the living room. Through the kitchen window he can make out Kofi, their five-year-old, punting a football in the garden.

Pulling the front door to, he squints in the sunlight. The air is already warm, heat coming off the pavement. Amelia skips ahead, singing to herself.

'Not too far, Ammy.'

Watching her, he remembers the tiny bundle Etta handed to him in the hospital. That first day, he held her as if she were made of glass. A time will come when she doesn't want to be seen with him, when the highlight of her Saturday is no longer their ritual of pocket money and sweets. *Enjoy this while it lasts*, he tells himself.

The morning is still, quiet. Ahead, Amelia turns off the road, confident on their well-trodden route to the newsagent at the top of Peckham Rye Park.

'Stay where I can see you…'

Turning the corner, he glimpses a flash of her yellow dress disappearing around the next bend. Relax, he thinks. She knows where she's going, it's only one street away. Maybe he'll pick up a weekend paper. Do they need milk, or—

Sound rips the air.

Crack. Crack. Crack.

Zac freezes. No mistake: a handgun, 9 mm. He starts running.

Crack, crack.

'Amelia!' He can't see her up ahead.

Crack.

Zac's body tells him to get away. Police training and a Father's instinct propel him towards the noise.

Crack.

Louder now.

'Amelia! Where are you?'

A motorbike engine revs hard. Shouting, screaming.

He reaches the main road and turns, scanning, frantic. No sign of her.

'Amelia!'

The newsagent. Two people are outside, staring.

'I'm a police officer.' He pushes through, smashes the door open with his shoulder.

The young man at the counter is motionless. Face down on the floor, three small entry wounds in his back, blood pooling around him.

A gasp from the next aisle.

'Please God, no,' he whispers.

There she is, on her back, feet splayed. Eyes shut, breathing quickly, a red stain expanding rapidly in the centre of her yellow dress.

'Get an ambulance,' he yells through the open door. 'Call a fucking ambulance!'

Kneeling next to her, he presses one hand on the wound and feels warm liquid oozing over his skin. His throat constricts.

'Shh...' He cups her head in his other hand. 'It's going to be ok, Ammy.'

Her eyes open a fraction. 'Daddy.'

The blood isn't stopping.

'I'm here.' He pushes down harder and she moans. 'Help's coming, baby.'

'I've called 999.' A woman from outside stands in the doorway.

'Check his pulse.' Zac nods at the young man's body. What the hell happened here?

'Daddy, I'm tired.'

Losing consciousness, getting colder. He clamps both hands to the wound now. 'Come on, Ammy, stay awake.'

Her eyes shut and flicker open. 'I want to sleep.'

'No!' he barks. 'You've got to keep your eyes open, do you understand?' Zac hears the desperation in his voice. Her only chance is to stay conscious. Keep her talking.

'What happened, Ammy? What did you see?'

Her breath is slowing now. 'Man.'

'A man?'

She drifts again, eyes closing. When they open, her gaze is unfocused.

'Ammy! Look at me.'

Tilting her head, for a second she's with him. Then lost again. She draws a long breath.

His hands are soaked, slippery. Leaning over, he turns a cheek to her mouth and looks down her chest. Waits. Counts to ten. No air, no movement.

Puts two fingers on her carotid artery.

No pulse.

Scrambling to his feet, he lunges past the shop counter, searching for the box. Please, God, let them have a defib here. Please.

Behind the counter the older Bangladeshi owner is slumped on the floor, his blood splattered over the cigarette boxes stacked in the open cabinet above him.

'Jesus Christ.'

And no defib box.

'He's dead.' The woman stands and steps back from the young man, her trouser legs dark where she's knelt in the puddle of blood.

'Check him too.' Zac nods down to the shop owner.

Racing back to Amelia, he kneels again and begins compressions. Both hands, fingers interlaced, his body weight bearing down on her. Pumps hard, counting aloud. On twelve some ribs crack. He keeps going. *Twenty-nine… thirty.*

Zac pinches her nose and tilts her chin down. Covers her mouth with his own and breathes into her slowly. Her chest rises and he watches it fall. A second breath. His hands are trembling as he returns to compressions. Thirty more. Harder. Two breaths.

She doesn't move.

'He's dead as well,' the woman calls.

'Help me!' shouts Zac. 'Press on the wound here. Seal it off. Ammy, come on.'

The woman kneels next to him and pushes on Amelia's abdomen. 'You know her?'

'She's my…' His voice cracks. 'My daughter.' Tears are falling onto her body. He keeps pumping his hands over her chest. But she feels cold now. Thirty more. Two breaths. Wipes his eyes on his sleeves. Keeps going.

Nothing.

'Please,' he mumbles, gathering her in, clutching her tight to him. 'Ammy, don't…'

Facial muscles straining, tears flowing, he barely makes a sound.

The siren comes too late.

FIVE YEARS LATER

CHAPTER ONE

Saturday, 17 June 2017

The pawnbroker's shop on Deptford High Street offered 'Payday Loans, Cheques Cashed, Gold Bought'.

Zachariah Boateng lifted the tape marked 'POLICE LINE DO NOT CROSS' to allow Detective Sergeant Kat Jones through. He hated these places: sharks preying on the weak. Up to five hundred pounds instantly? Then pay back five thousand for the privilege. Must be lucrative, selling money to desperate people in a recession. But their presence here was not a good sign for business.

A passer-by had called it in an hour ago, around 7 a.m. Twenty minutes later he'd been woken, as senior officer in the duty team. Pulled on a shirt and suit trousers. Scribbled a note for Etta and Kofi – both still asleep – and jumped in his Audi. Down the road from their home in Brockley, he'd picked up a sleepwalking Detective Kat Jones from her New Cross flat. She was in jeans and a leather jacket, her dark brown hair in a loose ponytail. Jones nodded silent approval at the Ray Charles track he put on. Five minutes later they'd arrived.

Scene of crime officers were already at work, spectral figures shifting around the shop in all-white hooded suits, faces masked. Boateng knew the drill: he and Kat had donned overshoes, masks and latex gloves.

He glanced around the front door. 'No sign of forced entry here. Alarm wire and locks are intact. Same over there.' He nodded to the internal door on the right. In front of them, a counter bisected the room, glass screen extending to the ceiling.

'Back door?' suggested Jones.

'Probably. Much more discreet.'

Behind the glass a white suit moved aside, affording a full view of the body. Jones recoiled: her first murder case.

'Come on.' Boateng laid a hand on her shoulder. 'Let's go through and pay our respects.'

He identified forensic pathologist Mary Volz by the wisps of grey escaping from her hood.

'Morning, Dr Volz.'

'DI Boateng.' Identifying him was probably easier for Volz: there was only one black inspector working murder cases in Lewisham.

'This is DS Kat Jones. She's just joined our team.'

Volz inclined her head. 'And this was Ivor Harris.'

The first thing you noticed wasn't the man. It was the hammer. Embedded in his caved-in skull, its claw and handle sticking up from matted hair like bizarre animal horns. Head forward, Harris was sitting in a chair. Plastic ties at his wrists and ankles said not by choice. His face was heavily lined, with a chain smoker's sallow skin – he was probably forty but looked fifty. Silver gaffer tape covered his mouth. Patches of blood had soaked into the cheap carpet around him.

Boateng examined the wound. 'Penetrating trauma?'

'Leading to intracranial haemorrhage, I'd expect. Perhaps a release, in the end.'

'Meaning?'

Volz gently lifted Harris's hands, curled over the arms of the chair like a bird's claws. 'Two fingers amputated. On each side.'

'How?'

'Mechanical blade of some sort. It's gone clean through the bones. There's signs of blunt force trauma to the back of his head too.'

'Knocked out?' suggested Boateng.

'Could explain how he ended up tied to this chair. The restraints affect rigor mortis slightly but I'd put time of death around two, two and a half hours ago.'

'Does an alarm give a time of entry?'

'The system was deactivated at 5.27 this morning.'

'CCTV?'

'Disabled. Tech guys are examining it now.'

'Anything else so far?'

'You don't need me to tell you we're dealing with a perpetrator of considerable physical strength to put a hammer through someone's skull.'

'Thank you, Doctor.'

Volz resumed her work on the body as they stepped to one side.

'So…' Boateng turned to Jones. If she was in shock she was hiding it well. A month ago she'd been a Detective Constable in the Cyber Crime Unit. Then she made sergeant – in five years, one of the quickest promotions in the Met – and applied immediately to join Lewisham Major Investigation Team. Jones was just twenty-six and her career was moving impressively fast. In the interview, she had said she wanted to get out from behind a desk and back on the street. This was one way to kick things off.

'First homicide,' he stated. 'What do you think?'

She took a breath. 'Attackers enter and exit via the back door, deal with the alarm and CCTV – so they knew the place, or did their homework.'

'I agree. Multiple attackers?'

'It'd be a lot easier to restrain Harris with two, three guys.'

'Forensics will tell us more. Could've been just one guy if he jumped him out of nowhere. Possible motive?'

'Aggravated burglary, by the look of it.'

'Money. Logical.' It wasn't a bad guess, though he wondered how many aggravated burglaries with murder she'd seen.

'They torture Harris to get him to give up the safe code or some other information,' she continued. 'Except he keeps quiet. Robbers get in a rage and one of them smashes the hammer into his head.'

'Why put gaffer tape over his mouth if you wanted him to talk?' replied Boateng.

'Stop him screaming for help?'

'Maybe.' He scoured the room before raising his voice. 'Anything taken?'

'Petty cash,' called out one of the SOCOs. 'No jewels gone. Safe's shut – we don't think it's been opened.'

Boateng cocked his head. 'So Harris loses four fingers and still doesn't give up the safe's code? Then we've either got the toughest pawnbroker in the world or the least competent inter-rogator. Our attackers gain entry – maybe follow Harris in after he's deactivated the alarm – and somehow disable the CCTV. One smashes Harris over the head and ties him up. Then with a toolbox of torture instruments they can't get the number out of him? Bring a mechanical blade anywhere near me, I'd tell you anything.'

'Could be something really significant in the safe?' ventured Jones. 'And he wanted to protect it.'

'With his life? Well, we'll find out once we open it. But let's follow the financial motivation theory for a second. Why doesn't he use the hammer, or whatever it was that cut off Harris's fingers, to break open these cabinets and grab some gold or watches?'

'Maybe there was a noise, a disturbance or something, and he had to run.'

'Have you heard of Occam's razor?'

Jones shook her head.

'Principle that the explanation with the fewest steps is the most likely. Named after William of Occam, old school. Basically, keep it simple.'

'Right.'

'So, what's most probable? Thieves plan and execute a complex job but only take a few quid in cash? Or they didn't want the other stuff?'

'Why wouldn't they want the valuables?'

'Maybe whoever did this wasn't burgling the place.' Boateng moved through the back door into a narrow alleyway and Jones followed. Outside, a SOCO was photographing small numbered signs placed on the ground to mark evidence. Another white suit brushed powder onto the alarm box. Boateng removed his mask and paused while Jones detached her own, studying the concrete floor as she reconfigured the pieces of information.

'Debts?'

'Go on,' he urged.

'Victim loans money to our attackers, or someone very close to them. Time passes, the interest racks up, it's out of control. He or she can't pay. Harris starts making threats. Debtor doesn't know what to do, resorts to violence to make Harris go away.'

'That's more like it.'

Something in his voice indicated she was slightly off. 'But?'

Boateng scratched his stubble. 'If you owe Harris, why not just run away, hide?'

'He might've threatened their family or something.'

'And what would that tell you about the killer's motivation?'

Jones paused. 'Revenge. Retribution?'

'Fits. Could explain how Harris ends up with a hammer in his head. Also, might suggest just one attacker… much simpler that way. You could get your mates to risk prison time for big money. Not so easy signing them up for your vendetta at a cost of life inside if anything goes wrong. Volz said "considerable physical strength", right?'

She nodded.

'But that alone isn't enough. You'd have to be in a rage to split a man's skull point-blank. Revenge works. There are a lot of easier ways to kill someone. This was personal. Must've been something serious.'

'So we look for Harris's enemies?'

'Good place to start.'

Her eyes darted around. 'Ask his family and friends. Search for previous disputes, altercations – there might be something on record.'

'Probably want to check out his creditors too – flip your debt theory around. Maybe Harris was the one who owed money. If it was a corporate job then we could be dealing with multiple assailants. And we should see who's got form for hammer attacks. Hope you didn't have any plans for your weekend,' he smiled.

Jones returned it. 'Not now.'

Boateng knew she needed no incentives. He remembered the buzz of his first murder case: thirteen years ago, a pimp killed in his own home in Lewisham. Since then he'd been to a hundred more dark places on behalf of the Met. And after Amelia had died five years ago, he'd worked even harder, as if every case he closed made a tiny dent in the truth that her killer had never been caught.

'Same here,' he said. Etta was used to him working weekends. Though the Met had tried to freeze overtime as part of cutbacks, murders didn't fit neatly between nine and five. The key investigative period was the first forty-eight hours after a body was discovered. After that, suspects had time to destroy evidence, go to ground. Then the chance of catching the perpetrator dropped significantly. As a lawyer, his wife based her career on probabilities like that. And she knew how important her husband's work was to him.

Boateng checked his watch. He'd planned to take Kofi to the park for football training today. Maybe even get a run in himself: the slight paunch under his shirt suggested he needed it. If he could get his team into the office and set things in motion this afternoon, he might be home in time to read his son a bedtime story and have a drink with Etta.

'Time we called for some reinforcements.' He reached for his mobile. 'I'll give Connelly a shout. You see if Malik's free. And if he isn't, tell him to come in anyway. Briefing in the station at nine thirty. And when you've spoken to him, get the details of the person who found our body. The uniforms outside will have logged it all.'

'Gotcha.' Jones replaced her mask and entered the shop.

Boateng called Detective Sergeant Patrick Connelly and, after asking his older Irish colleague to abandon the courgettes on his allotment for the day, stood alone with his thoughts for a moment.

Something didn't quite fit.

Go back to basics: psychology. He'd studied the theory and the experiments. Four years' hard slog at Birkbeck, University of London. Evening lectures and assignments in his spare time, getting up before dawn to read. Etta respected his drive for education and Boateng never shirked his childcare responsibilities during that time. He just slept less. The result was more than the letters BSc after his name, the psychology degree on his CV. It was scientific insight into the mind: human motivation and behaviour. And this scene wasn't right.

There was a disconnect in the profile he'd sketched out. Cool detachment to disable the CCTV, planning ahead to bring plastic tags. The guy knew he was going to restrain Harris, intended to torture him, sourced the tools. This was stuff on the psychopathic spectrum. Then the blind rage to smash a hammer into someone's head, right up close. That was anger, in the moment, out of control. But what had given rise to that rage?

An hour ago Boateng had been looking forward to a quiet Saturday with his family. Damn. That was the Job.

CHAPTER TWO

If it didn't seem inappropriate, Boateng would have described the office of Lewisham Major Investigation Team as dead that morning. His MIT colleagues had open cases, of course, but none pressing enough to warrant a Saturday at work. Boateng's own team had been working an attempted murder in New Cross. Knife attack outside a nightclub. There were witnesses, decent forensics and a teenager in Lewisham hospital with a stab wound who could tell them the story. Most importantly, they had a suspect on remand. The rest was essentially paperwork. Not an uncommon incident: violent altercations peaked in the summer months when more people were out and tempers flared in the heat. This new case taking priority was altogether different. There was planning, detail, calculation.

Boateng didn't want anyone on his team who wasn't up for the challenge. No pen-pushers, no jobsworths. Just men and women who wanted to catch people who were making London more dangerous. Those driven to never let a criminal get one over on them. Experience showed these were the coppers who'd go further, who'd always put in the extra shift. The ones who made it personal: us versus them.

Detective Constable Nasim Malik was one such officer. After Jones's call he'd been first in. A faint whiff told Boateng he'd not had time to shower after working out, but at least he'd changed shirts. As usual, his beard was meticulously shaped, a high fade in the short black hair. Malik was a broad-shouldered twenty-four-year-old whose parents had fled Iraq under Saddam Hussein after the Gulf War. Born and raised in Acton, Malik grew up hearing stories of police you couldn't trust on the streets of Baghdad. Balaclava-wearing men who'd shake you down for a few dinars, bang you up for your faith. Execute a man just for his name. At eighteen he'd signed up for the Met to be part of something he believed in: justice that was the same for everyone. Twenty-one years' service made Boateng question if that really existed. But experience had not diminished Malik's motivation and he was reliable and hard-working.

Ten minutes later a muddy DS Connelly arrived straight from the allotment in Herne Hill. Depending on the season, they could expect bagfuls of free veg to turn up in the office. The more the better as far as Boateng was concerned, even if they weren't the staples of West African cooking he and Etta loved. At fifty-two, Connelly was one of the oldest in Lewisham MIT. He was a wiry ex-boxer with a crooked nose and full head of curly grey hair. Bushy eyebrows danced when he spoke, his accent still strong. As a young man in County Wexford, Ireland, he'd chased the ladies until his parents chased him off to London to get a job at sixteen. In Southwark he'd progressed through the building trade, from labourer to plasterer's mate and on, for two decades before deciding there was more job security in the police. That was important when you had three kids. They were adults now and his marriage had long since broken up, but Connelly had found his new home in the Met. And despite his lack of formal education, common sense had carried him slowly up the ranks to Detective Sergeant.

As they pulled chairs around the briefing board, Boateng poured out mugs of coffee. Malik dumped three sugars in his, black, while Connelly had insisted on brewing his own mud-thick tea. The board was practically the only free wall space in their room. They'd moved into the new office two years ago, and while top brass had given orders to be 'paperless', no one seemed to have told the MIT. Computers lay buried under files, notes taped to the walls, boxes crammed under desks. On her first day, Jones had asked how anyone found anything.

'Victim is Ivor Harris,' began Boateng, pinning an A4 mugshot to the board. 'Deptford pawnbroker. Forty-three, unmarried, lived alone above his shop. When Kat and I saw him this morning, he looked like this.' Another photo, from the crime scene.

Connelly and Malik exchanged a glance.

Boateng described Harris's injuries and their theory about who might have wanted to do this to him. He sat down, took a big slug of coffee to give them a moment to process. 'Kat, what did you get on the person who found the body?'

She glanced down at her notebook. 'Rosa Lopez. Female, fifty-seven, market trader. Sells second-hand goods. On her way to set up the stall this morning. Passed Harris's shop, saw the light wasn't on, looked closer—'

'And got one hell of a fright,' interjected Connelly.

'She was pretty shaken up. I had to calm her down. Uniforms gave her the usual info about seeing your doctor if you get nightmares. She's got family at home to look after her.'

'Did she know Harris?' asked Malik.

Jones checked her notes again. 'Said she saw him most days she ran the stall. He was usually in early. They'd sometimes exchange pleasantries, nothing more. Lopez thought he seemed a quiet sort.'

Boateng tapped his pen on the table. 'Any chance she was involved?'

'Unlikely,' replied Jones. 'Physically she couldn't have managed it – on her own at least – and her behaviour was pretty consistent with shock. But they've swabbed her anyway and I can check her alibi for 5 to 7 a.m.'

'Let's do that. Once they've processed the DNA and fibres that'll probably exclude her.'

'Should be ready by tomorrow.'

'Thanks, Kat. Alright.' Boateng stood again. 'First things first. Nas, can you run Harris through our system, see if there's any record on him.'

'On it.' Malik slid the chair over to his desk and began tapping away at his PC.

'There must be CCTV for the surrounding area,' continued Boateng. 'Pat, I want you to check if we've got a camera active on the High Street. Then find out what other surveillance is going on there – banks, council, shops opposite.'

'Grand. Three or so hours beforehand on the footage?'

'To start. Then make it six if we need to. Jackpot's the back alleyway around 5 a.m.'

Connelly smiled, jotting notes. 'You're hoping for the luck of the Irish there.'

Malik pushed back his chair. 'Boss, I've got a hit.'

Boateng spun round. 'Our man?'

'Seems like it, name and date of birth match. But I don't understand… Have a look.'

They gathered round the monitor.

Jones read off the screen. '"You are not permitted to access this file." What's that about?'

Boateng studied the text. He'd seen this once before. 'It means Harris was into something bigger than just running a pawnshop. He was cooperating with us in some way.'

She frowned. 'A protected witness?'

'Maybe.'

'Informer?' suggested Connelly.

'Probably.'

Informants, officially titled 'Covert Human Intelligence Sources', were the murkier side of the Met's work. Forensics could only go so far. And if you were gathering DNA, fibres and toxicology reports, it was already too late. Across all command units, officers relied on agent reporting to spark investigations, raids, arrests – ideally before the crime. Many risked their lives to provide intelligence. But it came at a price, financial or otherwise. With each case, the big guns had to make a call on how far the Met would go to get their tip-offs. Boateng wondered what Harris had been doing in secret. For now, they were in the dark.

'I'll call DCI Krebs. She'll need to authorise it for us. Mean-time, Kat and Nas, can you make calls on the neighbours around Harris? Someone might have heard or seen something this morning, or be able to give us some more background on him. Drop into his flat while you're there. Pat, crack on with the CCTV. I'll try and find his next of kin.' He scanned their faces. 'Let's do this.'

Trudging up the tiled path and steps to their Victorian terraced house on Tressillian Road, Zac felt exhausted. A twelve-hour day, and they hadn't got much further. No clues from the CCTV at the front of the shop, except Lopez approaching the window at 6.57. Not a lot more from the back. There were no cameras in the alleyway, just one belonging to the council on a street leading into it. That produced a few poor-quality frames of a hooded individual in near pitch-darkness entering the alleyway at 5.23 a.m., and leaving at 6.04. Chances were this was their man. Seemed to support the lone attacker theory. Connelly had dispatched twenty-eight seconds of footage to the tech guys for enhancement, but they were still tied up trying to get anything from CCTV inside the shop.

The neighbours hadn't said much to Jones and Malik about Harris; he kept a pretty low profile. Many didn't even know his name. Zac had drawn a blank so far on next of kin. And by the time Krebs had returned from her hundred-kilometre bike ride and begun the chain of authorisation, it was already late in the day. The earliest he could access the restricted file on Harris was tomorrow morning, from the central repository at Scotland Yard.

Entering the hallway, he slipped off his shoes as the smell of jollof rice hit him. Result. Both his Ghanaian family and Etta's Nigerian relatives claimed it as their country's dish. Truth was the Senegalese probably invented it. But that was academic when it came to eating the stuff: his wife made the best outside West Africa.

'Hello, love.' Etta emerged from the kitchen, wiping fingers on her apron, hair tied up. 'How's my hero?'

'Knackered.' He grinned and kissed her, drawing her into his arms. She was curvier than when they'd first got together and he liked that. She'd probably say the same about him, not to mention the grey flecks in his close-cropped hair. They'd met eighteen years ago. He'd gone to give a briefing at the London Bridge law firm where Etta worked – where she still worked – and was so smitten he'd forgotten how to begin his talk. She'd stayed to ask him a question. Legal points turned to personal chat and by the time he left they had a date planned.

She smiled and jerked a thumb towards the garden. 'There's someone who'd love a teammate out there. Food'll be ready in half an hour.'

'Can't wait.' He grabbed his trainers and made his way past the family photos in the hall. Sunny beach holidays mostly: Gambia, Spain, East Coast of America. The formal portrait from his '96 Hendon Police College graduation stood out – Zac alone, rigid in uniform – but Etta insisted on hanging it there. He stepped into the kitchen and through the French doors onto the decking.

'Dad!'

'Who's this superstar in our garden?' exclaimed Zac, wide-eyed. 'It's the future captain of England, Ko-fi Bow-a-teng!'

Kofi giggled and blasted the football to the end of the garden. They chased it together, Zac slowing to let his son get there first.

'Tackle me, Dad,' cried Kofi, dribbling back towards the house.

Zac nipped the ball off him and spun around, shielding it with his body as Kofi ran circles trying to retrieve it. Eventually he grabbed Zac's leg and kicked the ball from under his foot.

'Foul!' demanded Zac. 'Where's the ref?'

Kofi booted the ball between two small trees that served as their goalposts and it clattered into the wooden fence. 'Goal!' he shouted, leaping and punching the air before running a victory lap around the garden.

At these moments Zac wished time could stand still. That they might stay cocooned in this home together, safe from everything bad that lurked out there in the world. That he could protect Kofi and Etta in the way he should have looked after Amelia. Joy abruptly turned to unresolved shame.

'Come on, Ko, let's wind it down now.'

'Da-ad,' he protested. 'I want to keep playing.'

'Hey.' Zac knelt down, eye-level with his son. 'If you're a good boy and brush your teeth properly, I'll come and read you a story in bed.'

Kofi's face lit up. 'Promise?'

'Promise.'

After turning Kofi's light out, Zac headed back downstairs. They had a dining room but preferred to eat at the smaller kitchen table. There, golden chicken thighs were piled atop steaming rice, fried plantain and greens on the side. He put some jazz on low, poured the wine, then planted a huge kiss on Etta's forehead as he sat down. 'Thank you. Exactly what I needed.'

She clinked glasses with him and sipped. 'Tough day?'

Zac nodded, mouth already full.

'Any progress?'

'Not a lot,' he managed through bulging cheeks. Sometimes he told Etta about his work; her methodical brain helped him register an omission or error of logic. In other cases – usually the most violent – it was better to say nothing. She knew which it was now.

'Better luck tomorrow then?'

'Has to be.'

Etta laid a hand on his.

Zac's smile faded as he caught Amelia's photo on the side. 'Five years coming up.'

She followed his gaze to the picture and paused, weighing her words. 'We'll never forget her, but we've got to move on, love.'

'Don't know if I can,' he replied, taking a large gulp from his wine glass. 'When the bastard who did it's out free.' He spat the words.

'Revenge won't do any good.'

'I'm not talking about that,' he snapped. 'I mean justice.'

'Then why are you angry?'

'I'm not, I just—' He stopped, put down his cutlery and took her hand. 'Sorry.'

Etta leaned over and slid her arm round him as they both looked towards Amelia's portrait.

'How was your day?' he said eventually, calm returning to his voice.

'Alright. I went to the gym while Kofi was over at Neon's house.'

'On the estate?'

'It's not that bad, Zac. And Neon's a nice boy. Kofi had fun.'

'I know, I just want to make sure he's safe.'

'Me too. But he's got to play, see his friends. Have a life.' She took a sip of wine. 'We can't protect him 24/7.'

Zac considered this. 'You're right.' He smiled and took up his knife and fork again. 'I should've learned by now – you normally are.'

CHAPTER THREE

Darian Wallace needed money. He was out at two years, half the sentence served. It was a condition of parole that he wore an electronic tag on his ankle. One step outside the ten square metres of his hostel room after curfew and an alarm would go off in a security firm's office somewhere. Made it impossible for him to move around at night with the tag on. Tamper-proof, they'd said. Anything you can think of to remove it, we've already tried and it won't work. He smiled to himself. That was if it had been attached properly in the first place.

Wallace scanned the stadium's exterior. Floodlights were fired up, the air already charged. He'd missed the greyhounds in prison. The Wimbledon track was his favourite, the most predictable. He pushed through turnstiles; no one searched him on the way in. Hundreds of people milled about inside, holding plastic pint glasses, the smell of chips heavy on the air. Sound rose as he emerged onto the grandstand, cigarette smoke thick. Wallace felt a rush go through him, but needed to check his excitement: it wasn't useful. He had a talent for gambling here. Why? Because he understood the dogs, the track, form and trainers. And he knew maths. Couldn't really explain it, he just got numbers. Even when he was a little kid. Saw the patterns. Could've gone to college or even university, but he had better things to do. Like get paid, by whatever means.

Three hundred quid in one coat pocket, something to protect him in the other. Never know when someone might call you out.

Recognise you and try to settle a score. Wallace stood opposite the clutch of trackside bookmakers shouting names and odds, scrutinising the row of electronic boards. He waited. He needed to watch the first couple of races to see how the track was running tonight. People who said the bookies always won didn't know how to bet.

There were four ways to win at greyhound racing: simulations, arbitrage, luck, knowledge. With no computer, simulations from big data were out of the question. Arbitrage meant exploiting differences in bookies' odds so you were guaranteed a win. Effective, but the margins were small. More a long-term strategy, and he didn't have time. For serious money there was always blind luck. That kind of unpredictability wasn't really his style, which left knowledge. An informed guess was reliable if you knew what you were doing, and he did. Wallace was twenty-five; he'd been watching dogs at Wimbledon since he was fifteen. Followed every race during his two years inside. He'd even owned a pair of racing dogs – Blaze and Bambam – but he'd had to put them both down before he went to prison. They'd served their purpose.

Target tonight was three grand. Should be enough, for now. Until he could get back what was his, and sort out the other business. Then he'd be gone.

Greyhound racing wasn't the sport of kings, but there was something real about it for him, compelling. Lacked the glamour of horses, but it was raw: survival of the fittest. He watched the dogs being placed in their traps for the next race. Lean beasts trained to hunt, seek and destroy. Chasing on sight, they needed to be muzzled to stop them attacking each other. None had a choice in life; the system was run by someone else. They just had to fight and make money, or they'd end up in a canvas sack being shot and dumped in a canal. Yup, that resonated.

Wallace studied the programme. The 7.45 was up. Eyes flicked between numbers on the bookies' screens. Supersonic at 7/2; 11/3 at the next guy. Wiggins Flyer 3/1, the favourite Mephistopheles 7/4. Long odds on the outside runners. Betting was closed. He moved closer to see the sand track. The bell rang. A whining motor meant the hare was coming. As it whipped past the box, the traps flung open and six dogs bolted. Crowd roaring around him, Wallace kept quiet, watching the bend. Dogs One and Two by the rails skidded out slightly. And they were inside runners. Seemed outside was better tonight, firmer. Charging down the back straight, Dog Five took the lead from Six ahead of first and second favourites. They held round the final two bends as baying men surged forward in the stands, Five pounding past the line to win. Couple of guys were celebrating. Most were staring at their betting slips or into their pints. Wallace checked the stats: 30.15 seconds for 480 metres. He did the maths. Just over fifty-seven kilometres per hour. Bit slower than usual. He noted it, factored everything in.

Letting the next two races go, Wallace bided his time. Refined the algorithm in his head. In the 8.30, Vince Parry had a bitch called Bullet Tooth drawn in Trap Five. The dog next to it in Six was two kilos lighter and Parry trained outside runners. Most importantly, he knew Parry gave his younger dogs steroids. Wallace made his calculations, then bet a hundred pounds on Bullet Tooth.

Five minutes later he had a four hundred quid profit. Now it was time to get creative. Nothing he liked in the next race; let it go. But 9.00 and 9.15 both looked good. Wallace took the programme and began computing an accumulator bet across the two races. His choice for the first was Double Top, with Mad Bomber in the second. Each-way bets: if both finished top two in their races, a five-hundred-pound stake would let him walk away just over three grand up. If it came off, that'd probably be enough for one night. If not, well, there was always robbery.

Wallace climbed the grandstand to get a better view as the 9.00 set up. Felt a slight stab of adrenalin. He'd never been one to react much, even as a youth. Didn't really get nervous. That wasn't him trying to be hard, it was just fact. Psychologist's report when he was sixteen said that was common in conduct disorder. It was supposed to be a bad thing. Unless you were gambling.

Relief. Double Top had scraped in second. About a snout's length from losing five hundred quid. Wallace watched preparations begin for the 9.15. So far, so good. Part one of the accumulator had come off, just. Now he needed Mad Bomber to finish top two and the cash was his.

Dogs were set in the traps. He took out the programme again, checked his competition.

The shunt was followed by cold liquid spreading down his left arm.

'Watch out, son,' came a voice behind him.

Wallace turned slowly, registered a big skinhead with an empty pint glass, England football shirt stretched over his gut. Glanced down at his own sleeve, the shirt material darkened, sticking to his arm as beer soaked in. The guy was about six three, seventeen stone, and had two mates. Wallace was three inches shorter, six stone lighter, alone. But he already knew size didn't matter. And once you took out the loudest one, the others backed down.

'You spilled my pint,' the guy smirked at Wallace. Jerked his head towards the bar. 'Go get me a new one. Boy.'

That rage grew inside him, ballooning in his torso. Eyes narrowed and jaw set. Wallace's mum, Leonie, was a pacifist. Said she'd seen enough violence in her life – on the streets of Jungle in West Kingston, Jamaica, where she was raised, then in the '81 Brixton riots just after she arrived here as a teenager. Strange then that she'd shacked up a decade later with his dad, Craig, the angry soldier. They must've bonded at first over feeling like outsiders in London, though he was only from Drumchapel in Glasgow. Craig was a worthless piece of shit, but before he left Darian and his mum for the last time, he'd taught his son one thing. Strike first, surprise them, finish it quick. His mum hated fighting, but if you had to, her advice was the same.

'Up next tonight, our 9.15 race. In lane one, Bricklayer's Lad; Morden Electric in two,' came the announcer's voice, tinny through the speakers.

Wallace held eye contact, still facing away from the track. Slowed his breathing. Felt in his right pocket.

'Oi, you hear me?' The guy moved forward a half step, arms hanging ape-like. 'I said buy me another pint.'

Wallace's fingers slid around the handle of his portable angle grinder, index finger flicking the safety catch off. In less than a second he could open up this guy's belly. Or maybe his face.

The bell rang; whining told him the hare had started. Noise and movement grew behind him but Wallace held firm, considering his next move. One more step forward by this guy and he'd have to do something. He glanced left and right at the others.

'Two is out strong from One and Three into the first bend,' shouted the announcer. Mad Bomber was Four.

'D'you speak English?' The guy jutted his chin.

Wallace checked the exit. It was behind the men.

'Now Four and Five running well at the second bend, and Two is there…'

'Fuckin' 'ave 'im,' said one of the others.

Kept eye contact. No backing down.

'It's Five from Two and Four into the third…'

Fingers curled onto the trigger. The disc could accelerate to 19,500 revolutions per minute. Three hundred and twenty-five a second.

'Five holding on from One and now Three is neck and neck with Four at the final bend…'

Go on, Four.

The guy chucked his plastic pint glass down, swayed slightly. Bunched his fists. 'D'you want some?' he yelled.

Wallace pictured him as a big piece of meat, ready to be sliced up. The other two would shit themselves the second they heard the sound of it, saw the blood. In the chaos of this mob he'd be out before anyone realised what had happened.

'And Five takes it from Four and One.'

A smile spread across Wallace's face as the noise died away.

'Nah, man, I'm cool,' he said quietly, stepping back and taking his fingers off the tool in his pocket. He spread his hands out to each side. Saw a security guard move towards the skinhead. Gradually absorbed into the crowd, Wallace turned to collect his winnings.

CHAPTER FOUR

Sunday, 18 June 2017

'Making enough for two?' Etta wandered into the kitchen, tying the belt on her dressing gown. Zac stood at the hob, stirring porridge. He was already showered, dressed in a pink shirt and navy slacks.

'Always.' He grinned, and kissed her. 'That way if you don't show I get seconds.'

She punched his shoulder and slipped an arm around his waist, pulling herself into him. 'When did you get up?'

'About an hour ago. Kofi and I were playing video games. He's still in there.'

'Big day ahead?'

'Reckon so,' he replied, dishing up the porridge and scattering blueberries on top. 'Probably back tonight, sorry.'

'Kofi and I will be at church this evening.'

He didn't respond.

'Come on, love, you know it's important for Mum and Dad that I'm there. It's good for Kofi to see his grandparents. And they have nice gospel music.'

Although he liked the traditions of church, Zac had been a religious sceptic since his late teens. Etta, however, had started questioning beliefs held for a lifetime only when Amelia had died. She'd often asked how a loving father could have let that happen. Zac knew she was talking about God, but applied the words equally to himself. He ate a spoonful of porridge too quickly, scalded his mouth.

'So where are you going this morning?' she asked, pouring coffee.

He looked up from his bowl and swallowed. 'To dig up the past.'

Heading north on Old Kent Road towards Elephant and Castle, Boateng tapped the steering wheel in time to some blues. The sky overhead was cloudless; it would be one of the year's longest days.

Krebs had confirmed yesterday that Harris was a Met informer. Now they needed details. Boateng's destination was Curtis Green Building, the art deco home of New Scotland Yard since late last year. The move to Victoria Embankment had prompted a lot of piss-taking about Met bigwigs just wanting a penthouse bar closer to the Thames. Boateng imagined the roof was a decent spot for cocktails, but this morning he was interested in what lay below ground.

Locked in the basement were hard copies of informant files dating back to 2000, when the Regulation of Investigatory Powers Act had begun. The system was only fully automated in 2015, meaning any sources recruited in those fifteen years had a dossier of paper notes. These were kept in case of future inquiry, like the one right now. Harris had been on the payroll, but who had he shopped in exchange for that money?

Having confirmed ID and deposited his phone at reception, Boateng followed the duty constable along a drab corridor, down the stairs. The uniform barely said two words to him as they navigated the building's underbelly. Probably pissed off about being here on a Sunday. Stopping in front of a large door, the constable tapped a code into the electronic keypad. Curious,

Boateng peered over his shoulder; the display was one that shuffled the numbers each time. A click granted them access.

Lights flickered overhead and illuminated a space the size of his entire office, filled with identical filing cabinets, back to back in rows. Each was labelled with acronyms and code words. Boateng recognised many: MAXIM and GENESIUS – the Met's projects to counter human trafficking and document forgery; SVU – Stolen Vehicle Unit; SIS – Special Intelligence Section. Tough-guy names for operations: VIPER, FALCON, HAWK. This repository housed the sum of civilian lives risked to prevent or detect crime. Most sources were mixed up in dodgy business themselves, hence their access to information. At some point, they'd decided the best chance of surviving was betrayal. Each dossier was trust broken, ends justifying means.

'Flying Squad's over there.' The constable jerked a thumb to the far corner. 'You want 2004. Your man was known as Cobweb. They're alphabetical. Nothing can leave here, so make notes and destroy them before you exit the building. Sir.'

Boateng nodded. He found the file, a thick manila folder with string ties. There was Harris, alias Cobweb. Thirteen years on the books. Recruited by Flying Squad officers – the Met's robbery specialists – in '04 after being caught flogging stolen goods. Harris flipped on his supplier and the arrangement with Flying Squad became regular. Since then he'd helped convict six men and one woman. None of them was known to Boateng; no reason why they would be. Flicking through, he noted each name and key points of the crime. Armed robbery, smash-and-grab jewellery raid, art theft, muggings for luxury watches, a safe deposit box vault job. Much of Harris's work was opportunistic, based on spotting when something came his way that wasn't legit and notifying his handlers. Pausing, Boateng made a list of them too, just in case. He was aware the constable was watching him from the doorway.

'I'm done,' he called over. 'I need a secure terminal upstairs.'

'Follow me, sir.'

The names he'd scribbled down comprised the best guess they had so far at a suspect list. Next step was to email it to his team and let them get searching on the Met's Crimint and Police National Computer databases. With any luck there'd be something for him by the time he arrived back at the station.

Replacing the Cobweb file, Boateng turned and headed back to the doorway. That was when he saw it.

TRIDENT.

A row of filing cabinets, one for each year of the Met's programme to counter gang crime in London, beginning in 1998. Trident developed from an advisory group into an Operational Command Unit, focusing on shootings in black communities. By 2008 it had grown to encompass all firearms incidents in the capital, expanding again in 2012 to cover gang activity more broadly. Gang violence accounted for half of all shootings. And two thirds of gun victims in London were males under twenty-four years old. Like the young man he had found face down in the shop the day Amelia died. Boateng hovered by the drawers marked 2012.

'If you're done, sir.' The constable let the words hang.

'Yeah,' replied Boateng, walking past him and out into the dim passageway. 'I've finished.'

But something told him he'd only just started.

The low-rise block on Denmark Road in Camberwell was unremarkable. Exactly what Wallace needed. A couple of days here would work before he'd have to move again. He glanced up at the balcony. Damp laundry hung from a slack wire. Good. She was in, or nearby. Jasmine Fletcher was his ex. In two years he'd screwed her around, cheated four times and lied more often than not. It ended when he went to jail. No visits, no heart to hearts.

She'd just texted him on the day he had to give up his mobile: *We're done.* She'd made a choice. Had a three-year-old to look after, not his. But Wallace knew she still liked him, drawn to the glamour of a real roadman. Someone who could keep her safe. Now he needed her protection.

Wallace tapped gently on the door. 'Jas?'

'Who is it?' came the voice inside.

'Your special man.'

Pause. 'Darian?'

'Yeah, girl.'

He heard footsteps. Door opened a crack, still on the chain. Half a face appeared, one eye scrutinising him. More make-up than last time he'd seen her, glossy hair in a high ponytail. Looked even better than she had before he'd gone to Pentonville prison.

'What do you want?' Her voice was quiet.

Wallace chuckled. 'Come on, baby, I'm out. Had to see you.'

'We're kind of busy.' She shut the door but Wallace blocked it with his foot.

'Thought you might need some help.' He displayed a wad of notes.

She stared at them.

'If you've got company I'll go someplace else,' he added.

The chain slid back and she opened the door. Wallace stepped inside, duffel bag slung over his shoulder. Kissed her cheek, felt her go rigid.

'Don't be like that,' he smiled, teeth showing. 'Been thinking about you.' He wandered into the cluttered living room, where a small boy was smashing toy cars together on the carpet. 'Hello, lickle man,' beamed Wallace, ruffling the kid's hair. 'Remember me?'

'Course he doesn't.' She folded her arms. 'Why'd you come here?'

He slumped down onto the sofa, peeled off two hundred pounds in twenties and put them on the coffee table. 'Can I stay a couple nights?'

Silence.

'Come on, Jas.' He held open palms up to her. 'Hook me up. I just need a place to crash for a bit, till I sort something out.'

'You tagged?' she said at length. 'I don't want no one coming round at night looking for you. Breaking the door down.'

Wallace pulled up both trouser legs. 'Nope. I'm clean. Gonna get myself a job 'n' that.'

'What kind of job?'

He unzipped the duffel bag. Inside was an angle grinder, mallet, chisels and an electric drill. 'Handyman,' he replied, drawing out a four-inch nail and pressing its tip into his thumb. 'Got trained inside.'

Arms still crossed, she said nothing.

'Two hundred pounds a night?' he suggested.

'Two fifty. Two nights max. And you sleep on the sofa.'

Wallace grinned. 'That's my girl.'

CHAPTER FIVE

'What've you got?' Boateng called as he crossed the room. His team was gathered round Malik's computer.

'Harris was in at the deep end,' replied Malik. 'One or two people he put away are proper nutters by the look of their records.'

'Anyone serious enough to murder him for it?'

Jones glanced up from her notebook. 'Two still in prison. Another dead, cardiac arrest. The female's in a wheelchair after a car accident. Fifth guy moved to the Costa del Sol last year and the UK Border Agency have no trace of him returning since. So unless it was a commissioned job or a relative, they're out. Occam's razor,' she offered, remembering Boateng's advice to keep things simple. Boateng grinned. 'Sixth and seventh both possibles,' she continued. 'No forensics linking either to the scene yet though.'

Boateng appreciated her brevity. 'Which two?'

'Gary Tomlinson, out three years, now works as a boiler repairman. Seems like he's made a new start in life. And this guy.' She indicated the screen. 'Darian Wallace.'

'Wallace got out four days ago,' added Connelly.

'Interesting timing.' Boateng dropped into a chair beside them. Examined the photo on one of the monitors. A light-skinned man of dual heritage stared back. The high cheekbones and lean face gave him a hungry, almost gaunt look. His dark eyes were unreadable, a single teardrop inked under the right one. 'Great work. So what's his story?'

Malik clicked to another document on the computer. 'Twenty-five years old. Born and raised in Brixton. Scottish dad, Jamaican mum. Mum did most of the work, by the look of it. Dad was an ex-soldier, alcoholic, two convictions for assault – did six months in Wandsworth for ABH. Dad was in and out of the home, then left for good when Darian was fifteen. Behavioural problems at school got him referred to an educational psychologist.'

'What did they find?'

Jones lifted up a printout. 'Conclusion: Wallace was bored.'

'Wasn't everyone at school?' Connelly laughed.

Boateng frowned. 'Why?'

'His IQ was estimated at 155.'

Boateng let out a low whistle.

'I'm no psychologist, but that sounds pretty damn high,' observed Connelly.

'Put it this way, Pat,' said Boateng. 'You could run a country with that kind of brain. A hundred is average.'

'Borderline genius,' continued Jones, turning the page. 'Excelled at maths. Took the GCSE at thirteen, then for two years they just gave him the A-level textbooks and let him work alone. Apparently it was the only class where he wasn't disruptive. Psychologist's assessment also found a full house of antisocial personality traits. She diagnosed conduct disorder: lying, rejection of authority and rules, aggression towards others, stealing and destroying property, impulsiveness, low emotional reactivity. Ed psych notes that conduct disorder is extremely rare in high IQ subjects; she'd never seen another case like him.'

'So what happened?'

'Wallace was kicked out of school in the end for fighting. Before leaving they let him sit maths and further maths A-levels on his own. A-star in both.'

Boateng nodded slowly.

'That was in '08.' Malik prodded the screen. 'Next mention is when he decides to rob a safe deposit box vault in 2014.'

'Capital Securities on Holbein Place, off Sloane Square,' Connelly read from a sheaf of paper. 'Early hours on the twenty-sixth of May. Bank holiday Monday, no one around. Alarm didn't go off, so they might've had some inside help. Never confirmed. Our Flying Squad colleagues estimated three million quid's worth of stuff nicked; some of it belonging to pretty important clients, by all accounts. Jewellery, watches, uncut diamonds, gold bars. And that was just what people claimed for, never mind any contraband that wasn't insured. Robbers took the hinges off each deposit box with an angle grinder. Forensics were thin but eventually they picked up two guys for it, including our man Wallace. He was the only one charged though. Five-year sentence, reduced to four for good behaviour, out in two.'

Boateng rubbed his chin. 'So they try to sell the stuff on to Harris, he comes to our lot and the other guy rolls on Wallace in exchange for his freedom. Who was the second man?'

Connelly consulted one of the pages.

'Trent Parker.'

'There's more,' said Jones. 'Our locksmith drilled Harris's safe. He can't rule it out, but looks like nothing was taken. Probably not even opened in the attack. Apart from a load of valuables, Harris was keeping personal records of everyone he'd provided intelligence on. Plus a few individuals he hadn't yet brought to Flying Squad. Maybe blackmailing them?'

'Talk about playing with fire. Any other forensics from the scene?'

'Not yet, boss. They'll call us when they've got something.'

'Alright. Wallace is the priority for now then. Motive, opportunity, timing. Nas, can you get on to the security firm and find out where he is? If he's on parole he should be tagged.'

Malik grabbed the desk phone.

'What happened to the gear from the safe deposit job, Pat?'

Connelly located the relevant document. 'About half of it was retrieved. Parker may have given up his share as part of a deal. The rest, no trace. Both men claimed their loot was found. So Wallace's stash is probably still hidden, since he didn't give it up when they lifted him.'

Malik replaced the receiver and spun round. 'Got the address, boss. Hostel on Talfourd Place in Peckham. Halfway house for ex-cons. Security firm's GPS says Wallace is there right now.'

Boateng stood. 'Stab vests, covert. Pat, bring the Taser. Let's go.' Jones looked tense. He clapped her on the shoulder. 'Stay with me.'

'Boss,' interjected Malik. 'They said he was there yesterday morning too, when Harris was killed.'

'Then he hasn't got anything to worry about, has he?'

The street was quiet as they pulled up in unmarked cars. Boateng sent Connelly to cover the fire escape while the rest of them went to the main entrance. The hostel's front door had a large window in it, a standard feature in these places. He rang the buzzer and moments later an older man appeared in the corridor. Boateng showed his warrant card through the glass. The man pointed at himself, visibly relieved when Boateng shook his head. He opened the door and Boateng whispered thanks, directing the guy back into his room. Once upstairs, he dialled Connelly's mobile and, speaking in hushed tones, brought him inside. The four of them gathered silently outside Wallace's room before Boateng thumped on the flimsy door. 'Darian Wallace, this is the police. Open up.'

Nothing.

'Mr Wallace, it's the police. If you do not open the door to us we will break it down.'

Still nothing.

'Ready, Pat?'

Connelly nodded, Taser in hand. 'Right, go ahead, Nas.' Boateng motioned towards the door and Malik wound up with the Enforcer. One hit smashed the lock, plywood splintering as Malik kicked it wide open and stood aside.

Connelly darted in. 'Clear,' he shouted a second later. 'We're too late.'

'Damn,' whispered Boateng, entering and scanning the room. The furnished space held no evidence that Wallace had been there, save a black transponder unit on the floor. Plugged in, switched on, display lit. He stared at the device. 'How…?'

Connelly re-holstered the Taser as he rounded the single bed. 'Jesus, would you look at that. Cheeky bastard.'

Leaning against Wallace's bed was a moulded prosthetic leg, bandaged to the calf. Attached at its ankle was the grey plastic and black strap of an ex-con's electronic tag.

'How the hell did he pull that off?' Jones shook her head.

She and Boateng were in his car, cutting through back roads as they returned to Lewisham. Malik and Connelly were driving separately.

'Magic, psychology, misdirection and showmanship.'

'Derren Brown,' noted Jones.

'Very good. Believe it or not, that same trick has been done twice before. Once in Manchester, then in the US. Distracted security contractor is on the clock, doesn't want to hang around in certain locations where he doesn't feel safe. Guy on parole is chatting away about this and that, and the employee fits the tag on a prosthesis. Under a bandage or thick socks you couldn't tell if a moulded limb was plastic unless you touched it.'

'I didn't see anything in Wallace's file about an amputated lower leg.'

'Right. He probably strapped his lower leg up round his thigh and sat down, claiming an ankle injury or something. Must've given him one hell of a dead leg. But you've got to admire the creativity.'

Neither of them spoke for a minute as Boateng negotiated the warren of Victorian terraces, taking his usual shortcuts.

Jones broke the silence. 'So what next?'

'We work out where else Wallace might be, and wait for the forensics report on Harris's shop to come through. Was there anything useful in his flat when you guys went there?'

'Not that we could find,' she replied. 'He didn't seem to have much outside work, but looks like he kept what little private life there was separate from his business.'

'That'd be nice.' Boateng chewed his lip.

Jones stared ahead. 'True.'

He'd lost count of how many times work had impinged on his marriage, his children. Child, now. He needed to change the subject.

'So how'd you get into this game then? The Job.'

'Family.'

Boateng glanced at her, nodded. So much for the change of subject.

'My dad was a bobby,' she continued. 'Sergeant in Haringey. I remember the last time I saw him. Seventh of October, 2001. I was ten. He stood there by the front door in his uniform, promised he'd watch *Toy Story 2* with me when he got home, then he left. When Mum told me he'd been hit by a car, I didn't understand. Thought he was indestructible. You know, like a superhero.' She turned her head to the window.

'What was he doing?'

Jones fiddled with a Velcro strap on the vest. 'Chasing some guys who'd just done over a Post Office. Car swung out of a side road as he was running.' She paused. 'I made her take down his photos at home, I couldn't deal with it.'

'You were only ten,' said Boateng gently.

'When I was fourteen, I took an oath on the anniversary of his death. Put some flowers on his grave and swore to do what he did. Join the Met. I wrote the vow in a card and left it with the bouquet. I'd carry on what he was trying to do. Sort of like his spirit was still living through me. Mum didn't want me to. She was still trying to talk me out of it at university.'

'But you wouldn't hear it.'

'No. Sent off the application before I'd even left UCL. Mum got angry. Said it wouldn't bring him back, no matter how much danger I put myself in.' Jones sighed and wriggled in her seat. 'Sounds stupid, but you know when you think you can change the past by doing something that relates to it now?'

'Yeah.' Boateng checked his own reflection in the rear-view mirror. 'I know exactly what you mean.'

'Are we just kidding ourselves?'

'I'm not sure.'

Back in the office, they pulled swivel chairs around Connelly's desk. Boateng dispensed the coffee while the others grabbed pastries out of a paper bag spotted with grease.

'Right.' Boateng clapped his hands. 'This is where we're at. Our main suspect is Darian Wallace. He burgles a safe deposit vault. Harris shops him, Wallace goes down for two years. Comes out on Wednesday, then around 6 a.m. Saturday Harris is murdered. Wallace has absconded from his hostel and is untraceable. There are no other serious leads on Harris and no witness statements or anything else in his shop or flat to suggest who might've killed him.'

'Unless he was blackmailing some of those people he was keeping tabs on?' suggested Connelly.

'True. We need to check them out. Well volunteered, Pat,' Boateng grinned, and made a note on his pad. 'Any other updates?'

'CCTV,' said Connelly. 'Techies say they can't do much with our footage of the guy walking in and out of the alleyway. Maybe a gait analysis, but otherwise nothing. I've requested the footage from nearby streets to see if we can pick him up elsewhere, work backwards. Don't hold your breath. They've drawn a blank on the camera inside Harris's shop. Shows him arriving and sitting at his desk for ten minutes before it cuts out.'

Boateng pursed his lips and let the moment of frustration pass.

'Lopez is in the clear too,' said Jones. 'Family put her at home before she left at six forty-five to walk to the High Street. Phone record confirms it – the mobile she used to call 999.'

'Fine. She wasn't top of my list.' Boateng leaned back in his chair. 'So until forensics give us a smoking gun, the question is "Where's Wallace?" Kat, check the stuff Harris had on Wallace in his safe for any places of interest. Nas, pull recent addresses off his file – family too, if you can find them. Pat, can you follow up the other guys Harris was spying on? The ones he hadn't yet come to us about.'

Half an hour later they still hadn't found Wallace's mother or father, but they did have two potential locations: his last known address from Crimint records, plus the name and flat of a woman – possibly Wallace's girlfriend – called Jasmine Fletcher. His mobile records had shown intense bursts of contact with her over nearly two years, right up until his conviction.

'Pat, Nas, you guys head to his last known address. Kat and I will go and see if Ms Fletcher has any idea where Mr Wallace might be. Don't forget your stab vests.'

CHAPTER SIX

'Just pull the trigger. Go on.'

The boy's hand wasn't big enough to wrap around the grip of the electric drill. Extending it to him, Wallace came off the sofa and knelt on the carpet. 'I'll hold it for you.'

Wide-eyed with concentration, the boy reached out and pushed the plastic trigger. The bit whirred to life, a loud shrill. He giggled, reaching for the drill with both hands. Wallace held it slightly out of reach, chuckling, before presenting it again and letting the boy hit the trigger to release another burst.

'Oi! What you doing?'

Wallace turned to see Jasmine, hands on hips, staring him down.

'Gettin' him started early,' he grinned. 'He could be a handyman like me.'

'That's not funny, Darian, take it away from him. Reece, you know you're not allowed to play with things like that.'

'Let him have some fun, Jas,' protested Wallace. 'It's just a game.'

She leaned forward, raising her voice. 'No one's gonna be laughing when he cuts his hand open, are they?'

'Chill out.' Wallace sucked his teeth.

'Chill out?' she screamed. 'Don't tell me what I can and can't do in my house!'

'It's not your house, is it? It's Lambeth Council's.'

Her face darkened. 'If your mum could see you now… You're a disgrace. Maybe your old man didn't hit you hard enough.'

Wallace shot up and in one stride closed the gap between them. He clamped his left hand over Jasmine's mouth, driving her backwards. Her body thumped against cheap plasterboard. His right hand pressed the pointed tip of the drill bit into her neck. She froze.

'Don't you ever talk about my Mum and Dad. Never.'

Eyes bulging, she searched his face, looking for mercy, humour. There was nothing. She glanced at her son, watching silently from the carpet. 'Please, Darian,' she managed to whisper through his hand. 'I'm sorry. Don't. I didn't mean to say that.'

Wallace relinquished his grip on her face, held the drill out to one side and pressed the trigger briefly, revving the motor. He cracked a smile. 'I'm only playin', babe.'

Jasmine was silent, shaking.

Examining a tiny drop of blood where the bit had pierced her neck, he tutted. 'You've cut yourself, Jas. Here, let me.' He leaned in and kissed her throat slowly. She remained against the wall. Wallace pulled back and his expression softened. 'You know I'd never hurt you or Reece, right?'

'Course not,' she replied quietly.

'Look, I'll put this stuff away.' He dropped the drill into his holdall, zipped it shut and pushed it under the sofa. 'Reece, you don't touch any of that, you understand?' The boy nodded.

Wallace flopped down on the sofa and let out a sigh. 'Jas, gimme your phone.'

She picked the iPhone up from the table and handed it to him without a word.

'What's the passcode?'

'Twenty-one oh-five.'

Wallace frowned. 'Your birthday? That's not very secure, is it?' His eyes flicked to Reece. 'You've gotta think about safety, Jas.'

'Sorry.' She stared at the floor, picking a nail. 'Um, do you want a cup of tea?'

'Yeah, white one,' he said without looking up. 'Cheers.' Wallace tapped in the passcode and opened the web browser. He googled 'Breakdance classes London' and began scanning the hits.

'Sick tune, Zac.' Jones moved her head to the beat as a harmonica solo filled the car. Denmark Hill sped past, hospitals flanking the road. Their destination was two minutes away. 'Who's this?'

'Junior Wells. "Messin' with the Kid". Classic.'

'Need some of that in my collection.'

'He nearly didn't make it. Wells, I mean. Got arrested for stealing a harmonica at fourteen. Thieves were in deep shit in forties America, all the more so if you were a "Negro".' He made quotation marks with his fingers. 'Judge asked him to play in court. Apparently he was so good they dropped the case and his judge paid for the stolen harmonica himself. Set him on the right path in life.'

Jones laughed. 'If only all criminals could be redeemed with talent. Any chance our man Wallace is using his massive brain for good now he's out?'

Boateng turned to her. He didn't need to say anything.

Trent Parker was his name. Snake in the grass. Wallace used to roll with him on the regular. They were tight like brothers. Met at primary school, stayed close and were mixed up in all kinds of shit by their teens. Parker was a white kid from the Akerman Road estate. Small but strong, breakdancer in a b-boy crew called Flying Daggers. He'd done some time inside too, for theft. The safe deposit box job had been his idea. Heard about it in prison. Maximum takings, minimum collateral – the places were unstaffed at night. No weapons, didn't need any violence. Non-domestic target, so even if you were caught your sentence could never be higher than ten years. Plead guilty, reduce it to eight. Serve half, out in four or less. Worth the risk.

Parker came to Wallace for the planning. Said he knew a guy who worked there called Ash. Wallace was tempted by the money. Hundreds of thousands, maybe millions. He'd be able to start a new life someplace else. He'd planned it to the finest detail, and the job went smoothly. There was just one thing he didn't factor in: human weakness. They'd agreed to leave the takings for a year, let things blow over. But Parker had tried to flog his share to that pawnbroker snitch. Then the feds turned Parker on him. There was a code. Parker had broken it. Wallace had to make him understand that.

The ninth website he checked yielded what he wanted. No name, but a photograph of a dance instructor surrounded by half a dozen kids in the studio. Image posted one month ago. He had a new beard, and his face was angled away from the camera, but there was no doubt: it was Parker. Wallace memorised the Bermondsey address, and dumping his unfinished mug of tea on the table, he left the flat.

'This is the place.' Boateng checked his notebook and pocketed it. 'I was thinking, Kat, why don't you lead? Fletcher's about your age, might help engage her. Give me a chance to snoop as well.'

Jones knocked on the door. 'Jasmine Fletcher?'

'Who's that?'

'Sorry to trouble you, Ms Fletcher, it's the police.'

'I didn't call you.'

'Of course, we just wanted to ask for your help.'

'Hang on.'

They heard Fletcher speaking in maternal cadences before a chain slid back and a slim, pretty woman in her mid twenties opened the door. She wore cut-off denim hot pants and a tight T-shirt. There was a small plaster on her neck.

'Could we come in for a few minutes, please, Ms Fletcher?'

She barred the doorway with an arm. 'What's it about?'

'We'd like to ask you a few questions regarding Darian Wallace. You're not in any trouble,' Jones said, smiling to confirm it.

Fletcher glanced from Jones to Boateng, then stood aside to let them in.

'Hello there,' exclaimed Boateng as he discovered the little boy playing with cars in the living room. 'What's your name?'

'Reece.'

'And how old are you, Reece?'

'Five.'

Fletcher sat on the sofa. 'He starts school in September. Can't believe it.'

'Happens so fast,' he replied. 'I have a ten-year-old.'

'Aw, sweet.'

Jones cleared her throat. 'Ms Fletcher, we believe you know a man named Darian Wallace, is that right?'

Fletcher stiffened slightly. 'Did.'

'Sorry to ask a personal question, but were the two of you a couple?'

'You could say that.'

'Did you know that Mr Wallace was released from prison last week?'

'No.'

'I don't suppose you have any idea where he might be, do you?' continued Jones.

'No.'

'Does the name Ivor Harris mean anything to you?'

She shrugged. 'No.'

As Jones explained their interest in Wallace, Boateng scanned the room. The walls were bare except for a mirror and a forty-inch plasma screen with CBeebies on mute. There was a mug on the table. His gaze travelled over the carpet and toy cars towards Reece and alighted on a straight metal object beside the table. Boateng leaned over and picked it up. About four inches long, steel. He waited for a lull in the conversation. Held the nail out to Fletcher.

'Did you know this was on the floor?'

She stared at it in silence for a moment before taking it from him. 'God, the handyman must've dropped that.' She glanced at Reece. 'Lucky you spotted it. He could've got hold of it.'

'Handyman?'

'Yeah, he put up the mirror the other day.' She gestured above the sofa.

Boateng nodded. 'Is your neck alright, Ms Fletcher?'

She instinctively touched the small circular bandage. 'Oh, yeah, thanks.'

'How did you hurt yourself?'

Fletcher blinked. 'Accident in the kitchen. Stupid really. I'm ok.'

Boateng caught Jones's eye and turned his wristwatch.

'Well,' beamed Jones. 'Thanks for your time, Ms Fletcher. If you think of anything that might help us locate Mr Wallace, here's my card. Mobile's on there. Call any time.'

Boateng spun the car around and parked down the street, with a line of sight to the front door of Fletcher's block.

'What did you think?' he asked.

'She was scared, when we mentioned Wallace.'

'Yup. And she was lying.'

'Probably. About what specifically?'

'I think she did know Wallace was out. He may even have been there.'

Jones turned in the seat. 'What makes you say that?'

'You'd notice a shiny four-inch nail on your floor pretty fast. She said the handyman dropped it the other day. But the mirror had a ton of dust on top. I'd guess it's been up weeks – months, even. She must've lied for a reason. Maybe because the nail belonged to Wallace. He seems fond of tools.'

'There's something else, isn't there?'

Boateng continued to watch the street. 'Her breath smelled of coffee.'

'I noticed.'

'Mug on the table had tea in it. Caught a whiff when I picked up the nail.'

'Doesn't prove anything, does it? Perhaps she had tea earlier,' suggested Jones. 'Or a friend dropped by?'

'And maybe her five-year-old drank it.' He raised his eyebrows. 'Plus the injury. Who cuts their neck in the kitchen? She lied to us, and I think it was to protect Wallace. Not because of love. She's scared of him. Body language changed when you mentioned his name.'

'I know what you're saying,' conceded Jones, 'but what can we do about it? There's no proof she committed a crime. Maybe she just didn't trust us – a lot of people don't. Especially in these communities.' She indicated the housing blocks around them.

'Right. That's why we're staying here for a while to see what happens. She might be our key to finding Wallace.'

One hour passed. Then two. Three. No one resembling Wallace entered or exited the block. Though not a long stint in surveillance terms, it was more than Boateng could justify given the speculative lead. It was nearly 7.30 p.m. They checked in with Connelly and Malik: no sign of Wallace at his previous address either.

'We could be here all night,' he sighed. 'Let's call it a day. Not a lot more we can do without the forensics report. Enjoy what's left of your weekend. Plans?'

'My flatmates are heading to a comedy gig in New Cross. Might still be in time to join them.'

'I could do with some laughs.'

She paused. 'If you wanna come along, I'm sure they wouldn't mind—'

'Thanks,' he smiled. 'Maybe another time – recce it for a team night out. I'll drop you off.'

Unlocking the front door, Zac remembered that Etta and Kofi would still be at church for another hour. He felt drained. It'd been two long days working on the Harris murder, without much to show for it. And after his visit to the Scotland Yard vault that morning, there were other things on his mind. Zac made himself a quick plate of scrambled eggs on toast, wolfed it down and took a cold bottle of Brockley Brewery pale ale up to his little music room.

The 1957 King Zephyr tenor saxophone gleamed on its stand. A beautiful creation. He smiled, recalling how he'd begun on a clapped-out sax, courtesy of his first Met pay cheque. His dad had bought a watch when he found a proper job in London, and Zac wanted to commemorate starting work in some way too. He'd no idea how to play the damn thing. After twenty years of jamming and the occasional lesson he was starting to get the hang of it, though the neighbours might not agree.

Lifting the sax, he looped the strap round his neck and moistened his lips, gently touching the keys. Warming up with a few scales and twelve-bar blues, the image of the Trident 2012 filing cabinet came back. He'd been cut out of the investigation into the triple murder at the newsagent. He'd offered all his help, but top brass said he was too close and it was Southwark MIT's case anyway. Their leads had gone nowhere: stalling on witnesses, getaway motorbike stolen, escape route lost on CCTV, no ballistics trace. Some rumours circulating in gangland were picked up by sources, but the intended victim was a junior and few seemed to care. Dead ends piled up until the case was shelved. Zac lobbied tirelessly, but nothing changed. Amelia's death – like the other two that day – were added to the Met's list of several hundred unsolved murders.

The Trident files kindled the faintest hope of something new. Could an informant run in 2012 reignite the case? Chances were slim: the stable of sources would have been pumped for intelligence at the time. Some might be dead themselves, in prison or moved out of London. Pursuing any fresh inquiry through official channels would be impossible. There was no way the Trident team would allow Zac to delve into their work on a whim. He'd have to find another way. That'd be tough, risky.

But Amelia deserved it.

Zac switched his fingering, began to play 'Ain't No Sunshine'.

CHAPTER SEVEN

Monday, 19 June 2017

Every contact leaves a trace.

Boateng recalled this as he walked briskly down the corridor to DCI Krebs's office. He'd first heard the mantra of Edmond Locard, the original forensic pathologist, during basic training at Hendon. Once more it proved true. Connelly had worked late into the night, combing through CCTV footage, risen early and carried on. Councils, businesses, security firms, even a few seconds from the camera inside a bus. With an allotmenteer's care and patience he'd recreated the journey of the figure entering that alleyway behind Harris's shop. From Deptford, winding back through side streets around New Cross, into Peckham, finally arriving at the street of Wallace's hostel. Logic and instinct had told Boateng that he was the prime suspect: there was motive, opportunity, timing, then his absconding from the tag. Connelly's result had given ballast to his theory. The forensics report hadn't turned up Wallace's DNA or prints at the scene, but fibres had been found that could be matched to his clothes, if they hadn't been burned. Now Krebs wanted to go public. That worried Boateng.

Her door was open and he knocked while entering. The office was spacious, neat. Framed commendations flanked a photograph of Krebs with Commissioner Cressida Dick. She was in her early forties, like Boateng, but her career trajectory was altogether different. While homicide and major crime work had become his vocation, Krebs was just passing through on her way up to Superintendent.

'Zac.' She smiled briefly. 'Take a seat.'

At six feet, Krebs was a couple of inches taller than Boateng, with angular features and a grey-streaked bob cut. She projected authority, even sitting behind a desk.

'Good progress on the Harris murder,' she began, putting some papers to one side.

'Mostly DS Connelly's efforts, ma'am.'

'The point is there's something publicly actionable now. We'll call a press conference this morning, get the community involved. Mobilise a million pairs of eyes, all those smartphones. Make it impossible for this Darian Wallace to hide.'

Boateng hesitated. 'I hoped we could keep his name out of the press for another day or two, give us the advantage. More chance of surprising him.'

She fixed him with a stare. 'Our advantage is having everyone across London keeping watch. Ordinary people on the street. Community policing, that's what we're meant to do.'

'He's smart, ma'am. Could go to ground if we do that. Then we never find him, and it's another open case.' He knew she hated those statistics.

Krebs leaned back and cracked her knuckles. 'Let me ask you this, Zac. What do you think he's going to do next?'

'Well, if this is about the safe deposit box job, and he murdered Harris for revenge, Wallace must have the other guy in his sights too. Trent Parker. DC Malik checked the interview transcripts. Parker sold out Wallace and got immunity.'

'So there's immediate risk to life?'

Boateng chewed his lip. He could see where this was going. 'It's not just that,' he replied. 'Half the stash from the vault robbery was never found – £1.5 million. Wallace probably knows where it is. My guess is he'll retrieve it once he's settled his scores, maybe before. If we find him first, we might get the stuff back. Lots of happy customers reunited with their valuables. Great headlines.'

'So what's your plan?'

'DS Connelly is trying to trace the journey away from Harris's shop. Separately we find Parker, put him under surveillance, do the same for the ex, Jasmine Fletcher, maybe even his mum or dad, and one of them will probably get a visit from Wallace. Then we nick him on suspicion of murder. Use the life sentence to lean hard on him for the jewel location, job done.'

'Four separate surveillance operations. Do you have the resources for that?' Krebs arched an eyebrow.

'No, but I was hoping—'

She shook her head. 'There's nothing spare. We're stretched as it is. Five active murder investigations in the borough, three attempteds, including your nightclub stabbing, which I've handed to DS Barnes. And our uniforms are managing thirty-four overspill prisoners in the cells downstairs.'

'I know. I just think operationally the best—'

She lifted her hand to cut him off. 'Sorry, Zac, we're going public. Immediate risk to life. It's that simple. We can't be seen not to. Imagine the headlines if Wallace kills again and we've sat on this. The Met is—'

'But we're not sitting on it, we're investigating,' he protested. 'DS Jones is trying to locate Trent Parker.'

'Meet me in the briefing room in one hour, and have your notes ready. I'll give the big picture, you do the detail. Thank you.' He was dismissed with a curt nod as Krebs returned to her papers.

It'd been a long time. For the two years Wallace had been inside, he couldn't see his mum. And she couldn't visit him. Not because she didn't want to, she just couldn't.

Leonie wasn't well. Vascular dementia. Started with a stroke four years ago, just after her fiftieth birthday. Supposed to be rare at that age, but her blood pressure was all over the place, the diabetes uncontrolled. Eventually something snapped: an artery in her brain. Doctors said that caused an intracranial haemorrhage, bleeding inside her skull. Since then, her memory was shot to pieces. She couldn't ever find the right words and her moods swung. Then he got sent down. Wallace dreaded finding out how she'd declined over the past two years, but he had to see her. There might not be another opportunity. By now the police would've realised he'd done a Houdini on the security tag and would be on the hunt, even if they hadn't connected him to anything else yet.

Wallace signed in on the care home register as John Blake, listing his relationship to the resident as 'nephew'. Grunting acknowledgement of his presence, the receptionist barely looked away from the TV screen displaying BBC London News. Some story about traffic management. Wallace guessed she'd still be in the same room, so he walked through without a word to staff. The less interaction the better. He'd be on camera but that was unavoidable. And soon it wouldn't matter anyway.

He passed a communal area simultaneously playing pop music through speakers while the same BBC news programme ran on a flat screen. Some residents were in wheelchairs, others motionless in their seats. Not one looked as if they knew what the hell was going on. A fat woman in a pink tabard was distributing tea that sat undrunk on side tables.

Jesus Christ, it was grim. Wallace used to hate visiting, and two years' absence hadn't changed that. It was a nightmare vision of the future. When you lost it and had no money, Croydon Council put you here. Throw food down your shirt, piss yourself, shit the bed for a few years and then die. His mum had put up with enough before the stroke; she deserved better than this. Maybe once he'd sorted his unfinished business he could make a donation to move her someplace better. Then again, if she had no idea where she was, it might not make any difference.

The door of room 109 was open. A TV droned quietly on top of the chest of drawers – the news again. Leonie lay in bed, staring out of the window, unfocused. She'd lost weight. She turned her head as he came in.

'Mum,' he whispered, smiling. 'It's me.'

She stared at him. 'Me don't want no bath now.'

'It's Darian, Mum.'

'Yes, yes, nice to see you again. How are the children?'

Wallace approached the bed. 'What are you talking about, Mum?'

'Me got to get on. Cleaning, you know.' She flapped a hand.

Hopeless. This was the strongest woman he knew. Resilient to the crime and violence around her for her whole life. Dealt with stigma and discrimination. Raised a child on her own while working two jobs. Now reduced to confusion that would only get worse. He took her hand in both of his and squatted by the bed rail penning her in. 'Mum, remember me? Darian, your son. I've come back.'

Gradually, recognition spread across her face, shifting from confusion to a flicker of joy before contorting into pain as she began to cry. 'Me thought you were dead.'

'I'm not dead, Mum, I'm here. I wanted to see you,' he spoke slowly, allowing her to keep up. 'I've got to go away again, I'm sorry. And I might not be able to visit for a while.'

'Where you going?'

Did someone call his name? Wallace turned but there was no one in the doorway. Then he saw the TV. His own mugshot filled the screen. His name ran in big letters above the text: *Wanted on suspicion of murder.* A small inlay showed a press conference with a black guy and a white woman at a table, Met Police logo in the background. Time to move.

'Sorry, Mum.' He squeezed her hand. 'I love you.'

No way back past the receptionist glued to the news. Wallace peered through the curtains. A floor below, the garden was empty. Fence at the back. Low wall one side, quiet street behind it. That was the best option.

'Where you going?' she repeated.

He studied his Mum's face for the last time, throat tightening. He pressed a finger to his lips, bidding her silence, then opened the window, stepped up and lowered himself into a hanging position from the sill. Pushed the window shut with one hand and dropped silently to the ground. Hood up, Wallace crossed the patio and slipped over the wall. Now he needed to be a ghost.

Connelly and Malik parked up outside the Riverbank Care Home in Thornton Heath. They'd finally traced Wallace's Mum here after a nightmare runaround from social services.

'Where's this river then?' said Connelly, pushing the buzzer by the entrance. 'Croydon Council should be done for trades description.'

Malik chuckled and pushed the door.

Putting down a copy of *Metro*, the receptionist swivelled his chair to face them.

'Good morning, sir.' Malik brandished his warrant card. 'Metropolitan Police. We're looking for a relative of one of your residents, Leonie Blake. His name's Darian—'

'That guy,' barked Connelly, pointing at the TV.

The receptionist opened his mouth, stared at the screen.

'Have you seen him?' Malik put both palms flat on the counter, leaned in.

'He was just here.' The man glanced down the corridor. 'I didn't know…' He trailed off, gazing back at the rolling news still displaying Wallace's mugshot.

Malik grabbed the register. Ran a finger down today's entries. Leonie Blake, visitor John Blake. Time of visit, 10.25. He checked his watch: 10.32.

'What room's she in?' he demanded.

'109. Down that corridor on the—'

They sprinted.

CHAPTER EIGHT

'Looks like a partial footprint.' Connelly examined a mark on the windowsill and scanned the garden. 'Must've jumped out the window.'

Malik bent over the bed. 'Where did your son go, Ms Blake?'

'Eh?'

'Your son,' he said, louder. 'Darian. He was here, wasn't he?'

'Who?'

'Where did he go?'

'Oh, nowhere.'

'What?'

Connelly gripped Malik's shoulder. 'Not worth it, Nas. I'll call in some backup, check for CCTV and get a description from our man at the front.'

'I'm heading outside,' replied Malik. 'See if there's any sign of him.'

'Leonie,' began Connelly, slowly. He knew from his father's last few years that people with dementia needed time to orientate themselves. 'My name's Patrick, and I'm a police officer. You're not in any trouble. I'd really like you to help me, please…'

Malik rounded the corner, checked the garden wall on its other side. Turned a circle, assessing the options. Four streets leading off the nearby junction. Wallace could have gone in any one of those directions. Most logical option was the closest, the one he was on right now. He jogged up to the first bend, surveyed the road. About a hundred metres off, a bus pulled out to reveal a hooded figure walking away. Jeans, trainers. Matched the description. He radioed it in: name, badge, location, in pursuit. As he ran, he tried to keep his footfall quiet – didn't want to give himself away. The guy was pacing quickly, head down. Within twenty metres, Malik picked up his speed.

'Stop, police!'

The figure turned, began to run. Malik gave chase. Slalomed round some pedestrians.

'Stop!' he yelled again. The guy kept moving, in a sprint now.

Malik was breathing heavily, adrenalin surging. Houses flashed past. He was fit, but pegging it after a suspect like this always produced that hollow feeling in his legs: lactic acid. He kept going.

He heard a siren and slowed down to grab the radio off his vest, give an update on his position. No escape for the bastard now, not with a patrol car on its way. They had Wallace. The siren grew louder, then Malik saw the blue lights.

The hoody broke left into another road, patrol car screaming after him. Malik followed, giving it one final burst. The car pulled up hard in front. Two uniforms scrambled out. One went at the guy, the other produced a Taser from her holster.

'Police officer, stop right now!' she barked. Took aim.

The figure halted, surrounded.

'Hands up. Keep them raised. Nick 'im, fellas,' she called, steadying the Taser. They approached, Malik from behind, the other uniform opposite. They stepped closer towards him, within a couple of metres now. The suspect dropped one hand to his pocket.

It didn't reach his jeans before the probe hit him. Fifty thousand volts crackled down the wire and the guy dropped with a strangled moan, rigid on the tarmac. A one-second burst was enough.

'Arms out,' yelled the woman. 'Arms out now!'

'Cuff him,' said Malik. The male officer did, yanking his hands behind his back. Malik stepped forward, pulled down the hood. 'Oh shit,' he whispered, closed his eyes.

He didn't know which South Asian ethnic background best described the guy they'd just arrested. Right now it didn't matter. There was only one thing he was sure of: it wasn't Darian Wallace.

Jasmine Fletcher stood alone in the living room. Reece was at a friend's. She studied the card.

'Detective Sergeant Kat Jones – Lewisham Major Investigation Team.'

Email. Landline. Mobile. One call away. Fletcher grasped her iPhone in her other hand. She'd seen the press conference highlights, Darian's face plastered all over the news. Wanted in connection with a murder. She knew he had a past – ran with a few guys on the road, got into scrapes. She'd never asked him too many questions when they'd been together. But smashing some guy's head in with a hammer? That was a whole different thing.

She tapped the card against her mobile.

Maybe the police had found him already, since it was after midday and he hadn't come back. His duffel bag was still under the sofa. Some cash was in there, she knew that. He hadn't paid her for the two nights yet. She wanted that money – needed it. Five hundred. Would it be a crime to help herself? After all, he owed her. If she turned him in now, would the cops let her go? If she didn't, then she was part of it. With him.

She slid her thumb across the phone screen. Her heartbeat quickened.

Maybe he was innocent – the police made mistakes all the time. Darian had his flaws, the temper, but he did care about others, deep down. She believed that. Would he really have killed someone? What if there'd been a good reason for it?

Guilty or not, if she made the call to Jones, he'd know it was her – and he'd find her, one way or another. Fletcher closed her eyes at the image of Wallace wielding his electric drill. The feeling of that sharp metal tip digging into her neck. That was minor compared to some of the injuries he'd given her over their two-year relationship. He'd pushed her down the stairs for slapping him in the face during one of their arguments. Imagine what this would lead to.

The screen went black again.

It wasn't only her. There was Reece to think about. His dad had left long ago and she had devoted herself to raising him, whatever it took. She couldn't let anything get in the way of that. No matter what choice she made now, there'd be consequences for Reece. Her son was involved, though he didn't understand. Both of them had been sucked in.

Part of her just wanted to get away from Darian Wallace. But once you met him, there was no escape. You loved him; you hated him.

'Screw you Darian!' she barked aloud, though the flat was empty.

She swiped and stabbed the passcode. Twirled Jones's card in her fingertips. Slowly, she pressed 0 – 7 – 9 – then deleted it quickly. She took a long breath in through her nostrils. Stared at the screen, steeled herself. Typed 0 – 7 –

The door clicked open.

'Yo, you home, Jas?' Wallace's voice was cheerful.

She stuffed the card down her back pocket. 'Yeah, babe, in here.' Locked her mobile.

He swaggered through, taking in the room. 'What you doing?'

Heart pounded against her ribcage. 'Nothing.' She forced a smile.

'Where's lickle man?'

'Playing at a mate's.'

He grinned. 'So we finally got some time alone?' Stepped close, smelled her hair. Clasped her shoulders.

Relax, she told herself.

His hands slid down to her arse. Fingers played at the top of her back pockets, creeping inside. Began kissing her neck. 'I've waited for this,' he whispered.

Probed deeper into the pockets.

She reached behind and took his wrists. Lifted them off her shorts, looked up at him. 'If we're gonna do that, gimme two minutes.' Turning, she left the room.

'Why you making me wait, girl?' he called after her.

Fletcher locked the bathroom door and took out the card. She examined it one last time, then tore it into pieces, flushed the toilet and dropped them into the cascade. When it settled, the bowl was empty. She knelt to check. Stared at her distorted, shifting reflection in the water.

Career-ender.

That's what they called the hardest kind of tackle in football. Pulling it off could be a game-changer. But get the timing and execution wrong and you're red carded, banned from playing. Boateng was about to launch the professional equivalent. Too late to stop now; he was already in the run-up. No margin for error.

Approaching the desk at New Scotland Yard, he saw it was the same constable as yesterday. Produced his warrant card. 'Detective Inspector Boateng, Lewish—'

'I remember you, sir. Source inquiry. What can I do you for today?'

'Did you get my message?'

'No.'

'Called ahead,' Boateng lied. 'Need to see the Harris file again, couple more details.'

'I didn't get any message. If it's not been authorised by the commanding officer, I can't—'

'It has been authorised. By DCI Krebs.'

'Each visit requires separate—'

Boateng held up a hand. 'Look, Constable, I'd love to chat about this but we're in the middle of a murder investigation. We don't have time.' He leaned in, lowered his voice. 'You don't want Krebs on to your boss for impeding our work. She told me the approval carries over because it was an out-of-hours request. Maybe check the small print. Either way, she's taken responsibility.' The guy was wavering, unsure of his ground now. Time to gamble. Boateng produced his mobile. 'But we can call Detective Chief Inspector Krebs now if you want to check. Just introduce yourself nice and clearly.' He proffered the device, let it hang in the air.

The officer shook his head. 'That won't be necessary.' He glanced around, thought about it. Bit his lip. 'Fine,' he said eventually. 'Leave your phone here.'

Boateng deposited the mobile in exchange for a small laminated card.

'Follow me, sir.'

The tiniest of smiles crept up Boateng's face as he took the basement stairs behind the constable. He began counting. One thousand, two thousand, three thousand…

Seventy-five seconds to get to the vault.

The uniformed officer opened it again with the electronic key code and they stepped inside as the lights flickered on. Boateng headed straight for the 2004 Flying Squad cabinet and extracted Harris's documentation under his alias, Cobweb. Began skimming, produced a notebook. Fished in the other pocket of his suit jacket.

'Damn,' he exclaimed. He turned to the constable, who stood in the doorway, arms folded. 'My pen's in the car.'

'I'll have one brought down.' He reached for his radio and called it up. No response, because there was no one else at his desk. The officer puffed out his cheeks. 'You bloody detectives. All those exams and no common sense. Wait here, I'll be back.'

Boateng listened as the footsteps receded. Then, leaving Harris's file out, he went straight to the Trident 2012 cabinet. He estimated he had ninety seconds, if that. He checked his watch. Pulled open the top drawer of three: hand-labelled tabs on dividers, manila folders behind each. Boateng recognised one immediately: *TOTTENHAM MANDEM*. They were arranged by gang name, but not alphabetically. He flicked between the folders. A different code word marked on each. The sources inside a gang, or informing on it from the outside.

The young man who'd been targeted the day Amelia died was thought to be a low-level member of SSP: South Side Playaz. Back then, leads into the gang had gone nowhere. Boateng rifled through the drawer. Nope. Closed it. Yanked open the middle one, read the gang names: *GUNS AND SHANKS; ALL FOR Ps; MURKAGE SQUAD; PECKHAM BOYS*. Not here either. He glanced up at the empty corridor.

Seventy seconds left.

Come on.

Bottom drawer. Original Rudebwoys – no. Tek Nines – no.

Yes. There it was: *SOUTH SIDE PLAYAZ*.

Boateng extracted the single manila folder behind the tab. Read the code name: *NIGHT VISION*. He opened it.

The mugshot of a young black guy was clipped onto an A4 piece of paper at the top of a bundle. He lifted it, scanned the biodata handwritten on a pro forma.

Full name: Clarence Jeremiah Thompson. Date of birth: 8/10/91. An address in Peckham. Recruitment date: 26/2/12. Four months before the shooting.

He checked his wrist: fifty seconds.

Producing the second phone he'd brought – a team spare – Boateng laid out the mugshot and data page on the cabinet, photographed both.

The device beeped and clicked and he cursed. He'd switched it to airplane mode but not turned off the camera sounds.

The image was blurred. Come on, dammit. He refocused, tapping the screen. Clicked again. Pressed the gallery icon to bring up the result. Waited. Why was it so slow?

Thirty seconds.

He peered into the dark corridor. Noticed his hand holding the phone was trembling slightly. But the new photo was clear.

Boateng riffled through the wad of paper inside Night Vision's file: mostly contact notes, some handwritten, others typed. A lot of meetings. These Trident guys had been busy if nothing else. He snapped a few more of the early pages without stopping to assess either their content or his picture quality.

Twenty.

Were those footsteps coming? He wanted to keep reading. He strained his ears, clutching the papers. Couldn't be sure. His own pulse was thumping in his temples.

Fifteen.

Papers inside the folder, biodata on top, photo clipped in. Just how he found it.

Ten.

Folder back in the drawer, closed quietly. He crossed the room.

Five.

Picked up the Harris file and his notebook. Flicked through a couple of pages.

'Got your pen, sir.' The constable strode in, holding the biro aloft.

Pretending to start, Boateng raised his head. Smiled. 'Cheers.' He took it from the officer's outstretched hand. 'Appreciate it.' Looking past him, Boateng clocked the bottom drawer on the

Trident cabinet, still open a centimetre. He scribbled some notes and handed the pen back. Replaced the Harris file. *Please don't let him see…*

'Thanks very much, mate,' said Boateng. Keep your eyes raised.

The constable turned, leading the way out. 'Find what you needed?' he called over his shoulder.

Boateng followed a few paces behind. Coughed as he nudged the cabinet door shut with his foot. 'Yeah. Think I got what I came for.'

CHAPTER NINE

Zac spooned a huge ball of peanut butter into the pot and stirred the simmering red broth, watching it thicken. Domoda: a recipe he and Etta had picked up on holiday in Gambia over a decade ago. The tinkling of a blues piano filled the kitchen. Kofi careened about in his Spider-Man pyjamas, clutching a toy digger. Zac could hear the rise and fall of Etta's voice from the living room, on the phone to a friend. Business as usual in the Boateng household.

Except for one thing: he was crackling with nervous energy. Home was always where he relaxed, no matter what Lewisham had thrown at him. But not today. It wasn't Jones's inability to locate Trent Parker, Wallace's possible next target. If they couldn't find him, it was unlikely Wallace had managed it yet. Nor was it the 'near miss', where Malik had chased a Sri Lankan asylum seeker who didn't speak English through the streets of Thornton Heath, culminating in a Tasering by one of Croydon's finest. That was unfortunate, and there might be questions from on high, but he'd put it out of his mind quickly.

Or rather, it had been displaced by the urge to hide away somewhere and scour the data he'd acquired on Clarence Thompson, aka Night Vision. Zac couldn't stop thinking about him. What did he know about the hit that killed Amelia? If he'd had decent access to the gang, he might have information about why the target was murdered. Maybe Thompson even had a theory about who had done it. Zac knew he couldn't pin all his hopes on this guy. At best, it was a long shot. The only thing he could do was locate Thompson and find a way to speak to him, if he was still contactable. Starting place was his listed address. First thing tomorrow morning. He tasted the stew, added pepper.

Through the wall, Etta's intonation suggested her call was coming to a close and moments later she appeared through the doorway. Zac sipped his beer and resolved not to tell her anything. Could he break away after dinner, call round at Thompson's address? *Slow down*, he told himself. *Plan it out properly*. Besides, he'd already promised Etta they'd watch TV together after Kofi had gone to bed.

'Ah yes.' Taking a dramatic sniff, Etta docked the cordless phone on the granite counter and craned on tiptoes to kiss Zac's cheek. 'Makes me think of Cape Point every time I smell that.' She stroked his lower back, nodding at Kofi, who was loading the digger's bucket with nuts from a bowl. 'Think that's where this one started life.'

Zac pressed his lips into a line, turned to her. 'Amelia was four. She wanted to know who Gambians were. We had to explain the idea of nationality.'

'She said, "Mummy, if your parents are from Nigeria and Daddy's parents are from Ghana, what am I?"'

'"British," you told her. "West African. And you're Amelia Boateng of course."'

'That confused her.' Etta laughed softly but Zac didn't join. She cocked her head. 'You OK, love?'

He nodded vigorously, began tearing chunks of smoked fish. 'Yeah, yeah.'

'Sure?'

'Fine.'

Etta reached for a glass and removed a half-finished bottle of wine from the fridge. Poured, took a sip, murmured her approval.

'Can you take Kofi to school tomorrow morning?' he asked without looking up.

She frowned. 'Tuesday? You always take him in on Tuesdays. I do the earlier shift at the office.'

'I know, love, it's just – there's a meeting first thing tomorrow. Got to be there at eight. It just came up this afternoon.'

'Try and let me know about these things earlier,' she said, irritated. 'I could've arranged it with Chandeep if I'd known by the end of the day.' She glanced at her watch. 'Bit late to ask her now.'

'Could you be on emails?'

'What, while I'm driving the car?' She shook her head. 'OK. You make his lunch, I'll take him in.' Jabbed a finger. 'And you owe me one.'

Zac allowed himself a brief smile in return. 'Thanks.' It felt horrible holding something back from her, but without knowing more, he wasn't even sure what he was holding back. If she thought he was just digging aimlessly around Amelia's death, she'd tell him to stop. Move on. Put it in the past and look forward, like she was trying to do. But if he could tell her he'd got real evidence, she'd want to know. Humans were programmed to seek out certain things. Closure and justice were two of them. He just needed something tangible.

Zac clapped his hands. 'Right, time for all construction foremen to down tools and go to bed.'

Kofi picked up his digger and pointed to the wall clock. 'It's only twenty-seven past eight, Dad. I've still got three minutes.' He grinned.

'If you want a piggyback upstairs then you'd better stop playing now.'

'Yay,' squealed Kofi as Zac bent down and he climbed on.

'Need to get a good rest tonight,' said Zac over his shoulder as Kofi bumped against him up the stairs.

'Why's that, Dad?'

'Important work to do tomorrow.'

It was absurd.

The Smoking Room, and you weren't allowed to smoke. What was the point of paying for a private members' club on Pall Mall if you couldn't even puff the odd cigarette indoors when you felt like it? Susanna Pym was trying to quit. Not good for the image of the Parliamentary Under Secretary of State for Health. The PM would bollock her with both barrels if she was caught fag-in-mouth by some paparazzo with nothing better to do than hang around the Oxford and Cambridge Club of a Monday night.

Tobacco would be just the ticket at this moment though. She wasn't nervous as such, but there was a certain anticipation to her impending encounter. It was why she suggested the Oxford and Cambridge. Not her usual haunt, but ideal for a meeting you didn't want many people to observe. On a Monday night at the O&C you could more or less guarantee privacy in the Smoking Room, with the exception of a dribbling old boy in the corner and one or two 'young members' quaffing happy-hour port. And discretion was essential to the gentleman on his way.

Pym knew that Tarquin Patey had left the army at colonel, having commanded the 22nd Special Air Service in Afghanistan and Iraq. He then founded his own private military company and sold services back to Her Majesty's Government, and presumably whoever else could afford them, mostly using ex-SAS chaps from his former regiment. She recalled the television footage of the Iranian embassy siege back in '80: smoke, grenades and abseiling men in black. Fearsome bunch. But it wasn't Patey's CV that had Pym on edge. It was the job she was planning to offer him. Bit of a gamble, and the stakes were rather high. She glanced at the grandfather clock, laboriously ticking. He should arrive any minute now. She took a large sip of Speyside single malt. As she set the glass down, a tall figure entered, paused, then zeroed in on her with silent recognition.

Patey strode over to Pym's table. The cut of his navy-blue suit was impeccable: probably tailored. He thrust out a hand and the flash of garish lining confirmed her hypothesis.

'Delighted to meet you, Under Secretary of State. Tarquin Patey.' The voice was rich, authoritative.

'Susanna, please.' She motioned him to sit on the red leather armchair opposite. 'Drink?'

'No, thank you.'

'Very well.' She crossed her legs, tried to relax. 'You come highly recommended.' Patey said nothing; evidently it didn't pay to inquire into clients' grapevines. 'I'll get straight to the point. There's someone I'd like you to find.'

Patey smoothed his thinning hair. 'That is one of our specialties,' he smiled. 'Where?'

'London, probably.'

He nodded. 'Who?'

Pym took another sip of whisky and settled back into her chair. 'Did you hear about a robbery three years ago, safe deposit boxes in London?'

Patey shook his head.

'Around three million's worth stolen, mostly jewellery. They caught the thief but half of the items were never recovered. Including a rather precious heirloom of mine.' She unfolded a piece of paper displaying a chunky art deco pendant, silver with inset emerald.

'And you believe this person knows the whereabouts of your piece?'

'Quite. After all, he stole it.'

'Are the police involved?'

Pym grimaced slightly. 'Very much so. They made an appeal for information leading to his arrest this morning. That's why I need your help. You see, the pendant isn't just a bit of jewellery.

Bloody ugly if you ask me, he can keep the damn thing. But there's something inside it that is considerably more important. With… personal implications.' She decided not to mention the memory stick or its contents at this point. 'I need you to retrieve it before the police find him – or worse, he escapes abroad and tries to flog it.'

'Yes, of course.' He studied the photo. 'What's his name, this fellow?'

'Darian Wallace. He spent two years in prison for the robbery and has just been released.' Pym swilled the whisky round her glass. 'That's why I called you. I expect he'll be heading straight for the buried treasure. Perhaps he'll take you to it. There's a mobile number on there, too, someone you can call in the Met if you need a steer on their progress. A friend of mine. They'll need paying, of course, but you can tell them to expense me for any services they supply.'

Patey nodded, carefully re-folded the photograph and began tucking it into an inside pocket.

'There's one other thing,' she said. 'He's wanted on suspicion of murder.'

He froze, hand still inside his jacket. Raised his eyes to her. 'I don't think that'll trouble the chap I'm sending after him. He's dealt with far worse.'

Pym finished her drink. 'I don't want to know.' In her experience, it was preferable to keep above the details. You never knew when they might come back to bite you in the arse.

Patey didn't respond. She imagined his view was much the same when it came to politicians and details. The less they knew, the better.

The Bucket of Blood.

So much of the stuff had been spilled here, the patrons gave the Lamb and Flag pub a new name. Two hundred years ago, blokes beat the shit out of each other most nights, bare-knuckle boxing for cash. A hundred and fifty years before then, a famous poet got done in by hired muscle in the pub's alleyway. The irony wasn't lost on him. For all our modern 'progress', people were still paying for violence. Employing others to fight and take down their enemies. Normally that was why the gaffer needed him. He assumed this job would be no different. At least it gave him an honest wage: day's work for a day's pay. Spike grunted a laugh and took a big mouthful of Guinness.

The pub was lively: usual mixture of Covent Garden tourists, office drones out on the piss and a few awkward dates all crowded in under the low ceilings. He'd arrived first. In the army they told squaddies to get wherever they needed to be five minutes early. Some lads always turned up five minutes before that. 'Five minutes before the five minutes before,' they called it. Spike favoured five minutes before that. Bagged the corner table and sat facing the door, avoiding the 'dead man's chair' opposite. Old habits.

He was halfway down his pint when the gaffer came in, holding a lager. Patey still looked weird in a suit. He was more used to seeing the boss in his Hereford 'uniform' of polo shirt, jeans and Timberlands: exactly what Spike was in now. Suppose if you run a business you've got to look the part.

'Spike.' Patey sat and glanced around, evidently uncomfortable with his back to the door.

'Colonel.'

'You look well.'

'Just done a week BASE jumping in Norway.'

'Christ. Do you have a death wish, man?'

He sipped his Guinness. 'One geezer did croak actually. Cocked up his own chute rigging. Fair play to him though, he died doing what he loved. That's how I wanna go.'

'Well don't go anywhere just yet. I've got a job for you.' Patey produced the photograph, slid it across to Spike. Outlined the brief. Didn't name his client.

Spike pocketed the photo. 'Find Darian Wallace. Get this emerald pendant back,' he confirmed. 'And whatever's inside it.'

Patey rested his elbows on the table, steepled his fingers. 'Correct.'

'What do you want me to do with Wallace? Thames drop-off?' Spike had picked up the phrase in Iraq, where bodies turned up in the river all the time. Made death sound like a form of transport.

His boss recoiled. 'God, no. The client doesn't want any mess, neither do I. Wallace is a murder suspect. If you can see your way to alerting the authorities on his whereabouts once you've retrieved the item, you'll be doing the public a favour.' Patey gave a mock salute. 'Dyb dyb.'

'Sod off.' They both laughed. That was one reason he'd loved the regiment – still did. There was nowhere else you could've said that to a commanding officer. 'Murder suspect?'

'Apparently.'

'Should I be worried?'

'Are you ever?'

'No.' Spike sniffed. 'And suppose he doesn't want to tell me where the stuff is?'

'Then get creative. Baghdad rules. Standard comms, updates as and when.'

'Colonel.'

Patey stood, buttoned his jacket, shook hands and left. His pint was untouched. Spike finished off his Guinness then helped himself to the lager. Waste not want not, especially when he'd be off the beer for a few days now.

Old habits.

CHAPTER TEN

Tuesday, 20 June 2017

'I'm not hungry.' Zac placed a hand over his belly, then took a swig of coffee.

'Eggs?' Etta arched her eyebrows, tipping the pan to show him.

'Gotta leave soon.' It was quarter past seven. He would've happily scoffed a plate of scrambled eggs before work on any other day. This morning, though, he'd woken early with a nausea that hadn't yet shifted. Anticipation. Drinking coffee probably wasn't a great idea, but he had to have something.

'Your loss.'

'I've done his lunch,' he added, nodding to the Batman tin on the granite counter.

Kofi followed his gesture to the lunchbox. 'Batman fights the criminals like you, Dad,' he said, mouth full. 'Except he does it at night so no one sees him.'

'That's right.' Zac stepped over to his son and ruffled his hair, the tight curls soft on his palm.

'You're a caped crusader!' he exclaimed, still chewing.

'Don't know about that,' said Zac quietly.

Etta turned, coughed theatrically, eyes wide. 'What have I told you about speaking with your mouth full, young man?'

'Sorry, Mum.'

Zac winked at him. 'See you later on, mate.' He kissed Kofi on top of his head, hugged him close.

The boy stuck out his tongue in disgust. 'Get off, Dad!' he laughed.

'You're very precious to me.' Zac stood back, studied his son. Kofi looked up from his cornflakes, confused by his father's unusual show of emotion at the breakfast table. Mornings were normally all business: get up and out. Cuddling was for the evenings, bedtime, weekends. Zac realised Etta was watching him too.

'Hope your meeting goes well, love.' She reached out a hand to him and he briefly squeezed it.

'Yeah, thanks. I should go.'

Zac could still feel Etta's gaze on him as he hurried through the front door.

Night Vision had been easy to find. Or more accurately, his parents had made him easy to find through their choice of name. There was only one Clarence Jeremiah Thompson in the whole of Britain. The Experian database search had confirmed that yesterday, with matching date of birth, and provided a new address near Kennington Oval. Thompson had moved house since 2012, but he hadn't changed his name. That suggested he'd got away from informing for Trident unscathed. Despite this positive sign, Boateng counted many more unknowns. Anything could have happened in the last five years. He'd not been able to check if Thompson was still on the books for the Met or if he'd been discontinued. A source could be dropped for all sorts of reasons, including the risk they posed to the officers running them. Boateng was unarmed; had to rely on his bare wits. If this developed, he might need to think about some personal protection. Just in case anything went pear-shaped.

He drummed his fingers on the steering wheel, Dizzy Gillespie's 'Soul & Salvation' floating around the car on low volume. Soul.

Salvation. He snorted a laugh as he realised. Maybe he'd chosen the album unconsciously. Did he think this private – what could he call it? – 'inquiry' into the people and circumstances around his daughter's death would bring redemption? He felt that he'd failed twice that day – first to protect Amelia, then to resuscitate her – and there was no way to change those facts. So why this? Why now?

Another part of the motivation surely came from a simple character trait. It was present long before he joined the police, perhaps even helped him select the career: his drive to know, to understand. To use that knowledge to protect and seek justice. But did the drive go further in this case, even as far as revenge? Boateng wasn't yet sure. He'd thought about it countless times, especially just after her death, when he was so often angry. But without the first clue as to who'd killed his daughter, any possibility of revenge was purely hypothetical. That meant he didn't really have to deal in advance with what he'd do, if push came to shove.

He pulled the herringbone flat cap low over his head and cracked the window to avoid steaming up the inside. Tried to relax, focus on his task. He had a good line of sight to the front door of Lockwood House. Took out the team mobile and opened the image of Thompson's mugshot, studied it once more. People came and went. Boateng knew the clock was ticking: his team would need him in Lewisham soon.

Thirty-five minutes later a skinny young black man emerged wearing a Post Office uniform. Same high cheekbones. Identical chinstrap facial hair. Boateng wasted no time. Got out and intercepted him alongside the building.

'Clarence,' he began, spreading his arms to show he posed no threat.

Thompson looked around. 'Yeah…' he replied slowly.

Boateng stepped forward and lowered his voice. 'I'm a police officer. I need to talk to you about the South Side Playaz.' He flashed his warrant card without it leaving his jacket.

'I don't do that any more, man.' Thompson sucked his teeth.

'OK. I just need some information. About back then.'

'Where's the last guy?'

Boateng had anticipated this. A source would always be wary of new contacts, especially with an unscheduled meeting. It took time to build trust. He'd clocked an alias used by the Trident handler from Night Vision's file. 'I work with Nathan.' He saw the recognition in Thompson's face. 'We've got this for you.' He produced a roll of twenty-pound notes from his pocket. Had to use his own savings for it; no way he could explain to Etta how two hundred quid vanished from their joint account.

Thompson paused, nodded. 'Alright, I got ten minutes. Late for work already.'

Boateng gestured towards the car and Night Vision slid into the passenger seat.

'I'm working a cold case. Murder of Draymond King in July 2012.'

'Shit. Now you're interested in that?'

'What do you mean?'

Thompson's eyes narrowed. 'You sure you're working with Nathan?'

'I'm in the same unit, but he's moved on now.' Boateng didn't know if that were true; he was improvising. Hoping his bluff wouldn't get called. 'Like I said, it's a cold case.'

'Only thing cold about it was the feds. Nathan told me not to ask no questions. Cos of the op.'

Boateng didn't know what he was talking about, so kept quiet.

'They was tracking guns and food – crack,' resumed Thompson. 'I told Nathan I wanted to work on the murder, you know, dig around. Draymond was my boy. Whatever mu'fucker done it, I wanted him found. But Nathan said I had to focus on his op. Said there was "too much at stake".' He spat the words. 'They'd deal with the murder later.'

'Except they didn't.'

'Yeah, right. They wasn't interested.'

Boateng's heart was beating faster now. 'So what did you think, at the time?'

Thompson shook his head. 'It's a waste, man. Draymond. Damn,' he sighed. 'Mans thought it was GAS – Guns and Shanks – cos they was bringing in crack as well. Trying to sell to the same customers. But Dray was a younger. No reason why they'd pop him.'

Boateng could follow the logic. 'So you think his murder wasn't gang-related?'

'Nah, man,' said Thompson. 'I don't think. I know it wasn't.'

No safety catch.

That's what he liked best about the Sig Sauer P229. Meant you could get rounds off much quicker. Didn't have to worry about flicking a lever before brassing someone up. He'd known that to be the difference between *us* and *them*. Between alive and dead.

Spike surveyed the components of the pistol laid out on his workbench. Slide, barrel, recoil spring, frame. He set about carefully wiping down, cleaning and oiling each part in turn. Poked a wire brush through the barrel, pulled it back and forth. You didn't want the thing jamming on you with a target in range. Again, difference between alive and dead. Spike had survived the West Side Boys in Sierra Leone, Balkan snipers, the Taliban, al-Qaeda and the Mahdi Army in Iraq. He wasn't about to let some thieving scrote-bag from south London take him down.

Still, shouldn't underestimate this Wallace guy, he'd pulled off a half-decent burglary job and the police reckoned he killed the pawnbroker. That took balls. Had to be prepared for him carrying something. But if Wallace was armed and knew how to shoot, the skills would be rusty. He'd been in prison for two years so couldn't have got any rounds down in that time. A lot of these gang types used converted replicas anyway. Unless you were standing right next to your enemy, they were gash: inaccurate, unreliable. Mostly for show, intimidation. If Spike's kit was a hundred per cent, and he had to draw, he fancied his chances. Taking care of your tools – that's what these street guys didn't understand.

One man who had understood that was the Engineer, a bomb-maker from Baghdad. His explosive devices had already killed around a hundred people by the time they caught him. Spike was part of the Special Forces group that tracked him down. Took four months. Had a few near misses – even lost a man on one failed detention op – but they didn't give up. Eventually they got eyes on the Engineer, holed up in a disused factory. Spike set an explosive charge on the front door and it blew a splinter through his cheek. Adrenalin was going so hard he didn't realise till they got back in the helicopter. Great big cut in his face, bit of wood sticking out. The boys all started calling him Spike after that. More importantly, they'd found the Engineer and the bombs he'd built; probably about two hundred lives saved. Worth a hole in your face.

Shifting the anglepoise lamp over the case trimmer tool, he opened the 9 mm ammo box and took out a round. Locked it in place and lined up the drill bit. Began to punch through the tip of the bullet, ribbons of lead streaming to each side. Hollow point rounds were the better option for his work. They expanded on contact with the target. That meant less collateral damage – useful if you were out in public. And it caused more problems inside the body – worse for your enemy. The Firearms Act 1968 made them illegal in the UK – some human rights shit – so Spike had to manufacture his own. It wasn't that hard. All you needed was a drill and steady hands.

Forty-five minutes later the hollow points were ready. He loaded them into three mags and pushed one into the Sig. Pulled back the slide and drew a round into the chamber. Packed the pistol and mags in a rucksack along with a prepaid mobile, portable charger, GPS, Maglite, camera with zoom lens, Gerber multitool, shove knife, some rope – never knew when you might need that – and a thermos flask of tea. The gaffer had said Baghdad rules, so Spike added a stun gun. Commercial model bought online from Latin America: gave a bastard of an electric shock.

He switched off the anglepoise and went downstairs to the garage. Yanked the cover off his Kawasaki Ninja H2R. A thousand CC beast of a bike. Spike had treated himself to the new edition. Forty-one grand well spent. He unscrewed his usual number plate and selected one from the batch custom-made by his mate who ran a garage. Each was single use only, culled or copied from other bikes. Enough to confuse the police automatic number plate recognition system if a job went tits up and the coppers started investigating, reviewing CCTV. Spike lived in the Kent countryside, so even with ANPR he'd drop off the grid somewhere outside town.

He donned the neoprene face mask and black helmet with tinted visor. The heat in summer was a hassle – or 'nause', as they'd say in the regiment – but worth it to keep your face hidden from cameras. And people, once you got close enough for them to see you.

Destination was south London. First stop, the most logical place to find Wallace. Think like your enemy.

Spike gunned the throttle and the Ninja roared to life.

CHAPTER ELEVEN

Lewisham MIT's open-plan office was busier today. Most of the twenty-strong section were there, working the phones or hunched over their computers, tapping away. Across the room, three detectives gathered around a whiteboard, matching mugshots to CCTV stills. One DC had pushed Boateng yesterday for gory details of Harris's death, but most kept to their own work. Such was homicide in London: even a hammer attack didn't divert his colleagues' attention. MIT personnel had other cases to worry about.

Boateng was grateful for the lack of scrutiny as he entered quietly, hung his suit jacket and cap on the stand. 'Sorry I'm late guys. Stuff I had to do.' He felt awkward deceiving those he trusted. First Etta, now his close colleagues, ratcheting up the guilt. 'My kid,' he added. It wasn't entirely a lie. He held up a bag of jam doughnuts. 'Second breakfast if anyone's interested?'

Connelly put down his biro. 'I'll get the kettle on.'

As the coffees were poured and doughnuts distributed, Boateng sensed the mood among his team was low. There was little chat as Malik, Jones and Connelly rolled their chairs up to his desk. He chastised himself for his freelancing absences: they needed him.

'We were unlucky in Croydon,' he began, scanning their faces. 'But Wallace can't hide forever. And we've done everything right so far.' He noticed Malik's head bowed over his mug, stirring more than necessary to dissolve even his three sugars. 'Nas, I would've done exactly what you did, alright?' The young detective looked up. 'If I could still run that fast.' Boateng swigged his coffee as the chuckles subsided. 'Most important thing is where we are right now, and where we go from here.' Nods. He could feel the atmosphere lightening. 'We're gonna catch this guy, yeah? I don't care if he's Albert bloody Einstein.' He jabbed the desktop with a finger, making eye contact with each of them in turn. 'Sooner or later he'll run out of places to go, or make a mistake. That's when we nick him. The more preparation we do now, the more we anticipate his next move, the more likely we are to find him.' Stating the obvious, but sometimes that was all it needed: for the troops to hear it from him. 'OK, what's been happening?'

Malik shrugged. 'Filling out the damn forms from yesterday. Waiting to hear if he makes an official complaint. Sri Lankan guy's lawyer is gonna have a field day.'

'You did what you had to do in the interest of public safety,' said Boateng. They all knew the line. 'That'll stand up, trust me. Don't worry about it now. Pat?'

'Followed up on the CCTV from Thornton Heath. Care home footage shows it's Wallace, different garb to the pawnbroker's alleyway though.'

Boateng knew what this meant: likely Wallace had ditched his clothes from the Harris murder. Probably burned them. He kept his reaction in check. Now was not the time to dwell on dead ends. 'What happened after he left?'

'Goes over the wall, heads east. Two streets later the coverage drops out.' The Irishman shook his head. 'Then we lose him. Central London, we'd be able to see what he ate for lunch. But out there, it's patchy. And no other traces so far, no patrol reports.'

'Good effort, Pat. Get his description out to Southwark units, ask if they can detour via Fletcher's place regularly.' He tilted his chin up, scratched the stubble. Hadn't had time to shave this morning. 'He's got to go somewhere…'

'I called in yesterday.' Jones sat upright. 'On Fletcher.'

'Good thinking.' Boateng bit into a doughnut, caught the dribble of jam in his other hand and hoovered it up. He was starving.

'Asked again if she'd seen Wallace. Said no, but there was something there. Hesitation. Like she wanted to tell me more about him. She let me in. We had a cup of tea, in fact.' Jones smiled. 'When I went to use the bathroom, I spotted a used condom in the bin. Frustrating, but I had to leave it there.'

'Should've nabbed it,' chipped in Malik. 'Probably full of Wallace's spunk.'

'Inadmissible,' said Boateng. 'Fletcher invited Kat in, but she wouldn't have given her permission to take the condom. If we had Wallace's DNA in her flat though…' He considered this, took another bite of doughnut. 'Maybe we'd get her to cooperate on accessory after the fact.'

'At the very least it tells us we need more squad cars around her place,' observed Connelly.

'Anyway, we bonded a bit. I asked her about raising a kid on her own. Must be tough.' She paused. 'I mentioned working with vulnerable women. Gave her the domestic abuse speech before I left, about how it's not just violence but includes controlling, someone stopping you doing what you want. Didn't make it about her, just talking generally.'

Boateng leaned back in his chair, impressed. 'Nice one, Kat.'

'After I got back here I chased up the forensics on Harris. Dr Volz is doing the full post-mortem tomorrow, and she'll be checking foreign DNA on Harris's body for any trace of Wallace now she's up to speed.'

'Outstanding.' Boateng helped himself to a second doughnut then passed the bag around.

Jones reached for a notebook. 'Then I went into the files on Wallace and the safe deposit job.'

'You've been busy,' he observed.

She glanced up. 'You were out, so we had to find something to do.' Her expression showed she wasn't serious, but Boateng felt that pang of responsibility again, the guilt creeping in. 'I was working on the revenge theory,' she continued. 'So I followed up on the others involved. Parker was tough to track down, took a few inquiries. He's moved house and isn't on the electoral roll. Eventually, I found his new flat, but there's no phone. Best I could do was his workplace, and he wasn't there when I called up. After some sweet-talking they gave me his mobile, but no one answered.'

Connelly slurped his tea. 'Hang on a minute. Others? There was only Parker, wasn't there?'

Jones tapped the notebook. 'Depends whose version of events you believe. Flying Squad detectives who ran the case thought there might've been inside help, since the alarm was disabled. Security guard named Harvey Ash was in the frame, but there was no supporting evidence. Neither Wallace nor Parker named him in interviews. Basically their insider theory came down to the alarm.'

'But Wallace disabled the alarm at Harris's shop,' Malik said, dusting sugar off his fingers. 'He wouldn't have needed someone working there.'

'Maybe he didn't know how to do it back then,' suggested Connelly.

Boateng liked the way his team was thinking. 'Let's back up a second. What do we think Wallace wants?'

'To keep an eye on his mum?' offered Connelly.

Boateng chewed his lip. 'I'm sure he does. But it's risky now, isn't it?'

'To get the hell out of London,' said Malik. 'Leave Britain.'

'More than likely. What does he need for that?'

Malik rubbed his thumb and forefinger. 'Cash. For transport, maybe buy a fake document or two.'

'Right. So he's going to retrieve the stolen jewels, wherever they are.' Boateng reached over, topped up the coffees. 'What else?'

'Payback,' said Jones.

Boateng nodded. 'Also likely. This is a guy whose reputation is essential to him. Classic social psychology. When the status of people with low self-worth is threatened, they're more likely to respond with violence, try to restore that status. For all his smarts, Wallace can't leave London till he's taken care of the guys who betrayed him.'

'I'd say he did that pretty effectively with Harris,' said Connelly, reaching for another doughnut.

Boateng leaned back in his chair. 'So who's next?'

'Parker.' Malik's response was instant.

'And?'

'Ash.' Statement not question: Jones was confident.

'Maybe.' Boateng clasped his hands. He felt better now: coffee and doughnuts had done the trick. 'If there's any chance Wallace will go after Ash, we need to find him too. They're both possible murder targets. Not to mention that either might lead us to Wallace. Pat and Nas, can you trace Ash and go visit him? Kat and I will take Parker.'

Jones flipped some pages. 'He's working at K Studios in Bermondsey. Teaching breakdance.'

Boateng moved his arms in a 'wave', got laughs from the team. 'As you can see, I need some new moves. Come on.'

Crossing the car park, Boateng checked his mobile. There was a text from Etta:

Have to work late but Kofi going to play at Neon's. Can you collect him on your way home? Dinner at 8? I'll cook. E x x

This was his fault. If he hadn't been doing his own thing this morning, Etta would've gone in earlier and been able to meet Kofi from school as usual on a Tuesday. Boateng didn't like him hanging out on the estate. Neon was OK, but his house was chaotic. When his Mum was there, she wasn't always in control. Last year, Kofi had watched a horror movie at Neon's. It was an eighteen-certificate which they'd got from his older brother, himself only fourteen. Kofi had had nightmares for weeks. There was probably worse he didn't know about.

Boateng stuffed the phone into his trouser pocket without replying, pissed off with himself more than anyone.

Darian Wallace stood alone in the cemetery, looking towards Beecroft Garden Primary School. He was concealed between a large stone angel monument and an old sycamore, but pulled his cap down and turned his collar up nonetheless. It was only yesterday his face had been on TV. There'd been no replay of the item this morning. Even though it was just local news and people had short memories, he had to be careful.

He studied the children, a cacophony of shrieks and calls rising from the mass. Three hundred kids on a patch of concrete. Chasing each other, pushing and shoving, playing games. Some on smartphones, a few sitting quietly alone. He checked their faces one by one.

Then he saw him.

Neon Grant was trying to drop-kick a football, but, struggling to coordinate his hands and feet, kept missing. Another young black boy with him was demonstrating. The other kid booted it way up into the air and both ducked as the ball fell, shielding their heads. The whistle blew and an adult came over and had words with them. Wallace laughed, shook his head. Typical teacher. Soon as you reach up, they shut you down.

Not that Wallace had tried that hard. His old man had always told him he wouldn't amount to shit. 'You're naebody,' he used to shout, with whisky-soaked breath, grabbing a handful of Darian's T-shirt, pulling him close. 'D'ye hear? Naebody. Useless piece o' shite.' If he answered back, he'd catch a slap. He recalled one time he'd kept silent, pinned against the wall, and wet himself. The boozed-up wanker had hit him anyway. 'Fuckin' baby.'

Despite this, Wallace knew he was good at one thing: maths. The question was where it would take him. By age fifteen it'd become like a game theory situation from his A-level decision maths module. If he sold drugs, he'd either make a lot of money or go to prison. If he didn't sell them, someone else would make that money, and he might end up inside anyway. He assessed the risk and concluded his optimum strategy was the business end of drugs. Success through education was less likely than being caught dealing. When he had ended up needing to use violence to protect his profits, he'd even started enjoying it. Still, he wondered if there could've been another way.

That's why he'd started tutoring Neon. Teaching him maths. Making amends, maybe. Wallace's mum knew Neon's family through church, and one Sunday Neon's Mum told Leonie that her boy couldn't do numbers. So Wallace went to see him, an hour a week for nearly three years. By the end the kid was pretty good for his age. Wallace started thinking how Neon could get himself up and out of the estate. Take his family with him. If he could just keep mentoring the kid... Then he'd gone down for burglary. Anger welled in his gut. Trent Parker. And that other one, the fat bastard.

He watched Neon and his mate trying to find a way to do drop kicks without the teacher seeing them. Creative, energetic, determined, challenging the rules. They had all the potential in the world. Wallace's decisions had been made; too late to change now. Leopards and all that. Neon still had a chance, though. He needed to speak to the kid. Partly to see how Neon was doing before he left.

But also for his own plans.

CHAPTER TWELVE

The industrial estate was in a run-down part of Bermondsey, enveloped by high-rise housing blocks. Even the late morning sunshine couldn't make it pretty. Still, there were signs of development spreading through anywhere central in London. Supply and demand: the logic of business. Warehouses used three years ago by struggling artists or food packers now housed architects, artisanal coffee roasters and brand management creatives.

Thumping bass became loud funk as Boateng pushed open the door to K Studios. He recognised it immediately: James Brown's 'Super Bad'. Exchanging a glance with Jones, they followed the sound to a room off the reception. A gaggle of boys and girls in their late teens circled a guy squatting on the laminate wood floor. He was small, a muscular upper body evident despite his loose tracksuit. The grade one all-over buzz cut left his scalp visible.

'Your right foot comes around here, yeah?' he explained without looking up. 'Right to left. Then step back with the left and back again across with the right, so you're in like a push-up position. Got it? Right, left, right.'

'I never could manage that,' Boateng grinned at Jones, before rapping his knuckles hard enough on the door to be heard above the music. The whole group turned towards him. Boateng flashed his warrant card. 'Trent Parker?'

Parker froze for a second, still in a press-up, then flipped himself into a standing position in one movement. 'Work on the six-step, yeah?' he told the students, who were unable to hide their excitement. 'Back in a minute.'

They took the low sofas in reception. There was no one else around and James Brown's screams were too loud for the students to overhear the conversation.

'The Godfather of Soul,' said Boateng. 'Good choice. My favourite track by him is "The Boss", though.'

Parker smiled. 'What's this about?' The accent was pure south London. He had lean features, almost good-looking if they hadn't been so rat-like.

'Darian Wallace.'

Parker swallowed.

'Did you know he was out?'

'I heard something like that.'

Boateng leaned forward. 'Have you seen him?'

Parker made a brief choking sound. Might have been a laugh. 'Nope.'

'Why's that funny?' asked Jones.

Parker looked her up and down before responding. 'You lot know. Must've read the file. Man'd kill me.'

Boateng clasped his hands. 'Wallace is the main suspect in a murder investigation we're running.' He used the term 'main' rather than 'only'.

'Murder?' Parker's face became even paler.

'Did you see the London news yesterday?'

'No.'

'Seems he didn't waste any time after his release. Victim was a pawnbroker in Deptford called Harris.' Boateng paused, watched

Parker recognise the name and tense up, shrinking in his seat. 'We think the motive was probably revenge.'

Parker was silent. Ran a hand over his head. Glanced from Boateng to Jones and back.

'Do you know where he might be?' Boateng held his gaze, searching for any sign.

Parker didn't blink. 'Ain't seen him for over two years. And like I said, man might come cut me up after what happened. Did what I had to do. Back then my baby was six months. Couldn't leave the kid and her mum alone. Now I'm just on a quiet thing.' Turned his head side to side, took in the dance studios. 'Do my job, pay my rent, stay out of trouble, away from man like Wallace.'

'That's the main reason we're here, Trent,' said Jones. 'We'd like to offer you some protection.'

Parker sniggered. 'Protection? By you lot?' Slumped back on the sofa, bravado regained.

'We consider Darian Wallace to be highly dangerous,' Jones continued. 'It's standard procedure that in these situations we—'

'I'm not shook, yeah?' Parker stared at her, jaw set. 'Not scared of no one.'

'Nobody said you were, Trent.' Boateng's voice was even. 'But there's no shame having a bit of help sometimes.' He'd known that line to work before on younger guys, pride and machismo stopping them from admitting fear.

'I don't need no help,' Parker snapped. 'Specially not from no Five-O. Take care of my own self.'

Boateng nodded. 'OK. But don't do anything you're going to regret.' Paused. 'That's just my personal advice.'

'I've got a class to teach.' Checked out Jones again. 'Want some new moves?'

'No, thanks.'

They stood.

'Appreciate your time.' Boateng held out his card. Parker let it hang in the air. Boateng placed it on the sofa arm. 'In case you change your mind. Or you see Wallace.'

Parker turned and tried to walk casually but Boateng perceived new tension in his limbs. Seen it a thousand times. Fear.

James Brown's scream pierced the room again.

Bit windy up here.

Spike sipped tea from the lid of his thermos. Not a bad brew. He was in a decent spot, with eyes on Jasmine Fletcher's flat, seven floors down. Shifted position slightly, leaned his back on the chimney. Calculated it from the ground: he'd be invisible here to most of Crawford estate. It was easy enough to get up the block's internal stairs. Fire escape brought him to the roof.

Recon. That's what they called it in the military. Posh word for sitting and watching for hours. But it had to be done.

Colonel Patey's contact in the Met – the one the client gave them – had pulled the file on Wallace off the Crimint system and whatsapped the photos of it to Spike's unregistered mobile. He didn't much care for apps – load of bollocks, mostly – but WhatsApp was alright. Hard to crack: a closed network with decent message encryption. Good enough for this kind of job.

The first page of the file had given Wallace's address in the hostel in Peckham. Pure Delboy and Rodders territory. But when he'd gone there, Wallace's room was kicked open and the place was empty. Police tape across the door, but no coppers. One geezer there was having Polish lager for breakfast. For twenty quid he told Spike he'd not seen Wallace since Friday night. Spike thanked him and issued a simple threat never to tell anyone they'd spoken. Didn't even need to say 'Or…' – the fella got the message, clutching his can and nodding furiously. Might've been reliable, might not. Spike gave him the benefit of the doubt. Made sense that Wallace had vanished if he smashed the pawnbroker's head in. Only a mug would stay in his registered address after that with an electronic tag. Might as well send up a flare. Grunted a laugh to himself.

Think like your enemy. If you're on the run, you can't use a hotel, can't go anywhere central. Gotta stay with someone you trust, off the radar. Use other people's phones and computers. File said his old man was an alcoholic ex-squaddie who'd disappeared off to Scotland. So not him. Mum was in a care home. Probably couldn't go there either. Wallace had no siblings. Next most obvious: girlfriend or ex.

If it were him, Spike thought, he'd go to an ex. Not his ex-wife, she'd turn him in. An ex who still liked him, if that existed. He thought about it. Nope, no such thing. Spike always burned his bridges, somehow. Maybe it felt safer that way. Didn't want to get too close to anyone or stay too long, it made you weaker. Vulnerable to… he didn't know what. Slapped his own cheek; he was getting distracted.

File listed Jasmine Fletcher as Wallace's bird when he did the robbery. So here Spike was in Camberwell, sitting and watching her flat. Recon.

Didn't have all day though. She and a boy had come in about two hours ago with Co-op bags. Three hours later they were still at home. Just needed them to go out again and he could take a look inside the flat. See if Wallace had been there. If not, he might need to use Plan C: widen the network.

Spike peered through the zoom lens at Jasmine Fletcher's window, focused it manually. Nothing going on.

Police car cruised past her building. Skoda Octavia estate. He'd seen the same one twice in twenty minutes now. Call sign in big black letters on the roof: thanks for the confirmation, lads. Too frequent to be their normal beat. Helpfully, one of them pointed through the window towards Fletcher's block. So the coppers were keeping an eye on her too.

A curtain closed in the flat and less than one minute later Fletcher and the kid appeared at the communal doorway to their low-rise block. Started walking south. Spike considered tailing in case she was heading to an RV with Wallace. Possible, but more likely he was in the flat – if he was here at all. He removed the pistol from his bag and tucked it into the small of his back, handle resting over his belt and to the right.

Spike put his ear to the door. Nothing. Nudged it forward with his toe. Slipped the shove knife into the jamb and worked it up, through and down to the lock. Over the catch. Pulled gently towards him. Click. Piece of piss. Right hand reached back under the jacket to his Sig. Left hand teased the front door open.

Messy interior. Normal small kid signs. Listened. Scanned around quickly: living room, kitchen, bathroom, bedroom. Checked the wardrobe and long cupboard. No one here.

Back in the living room, he clocked the sofa. Slight angle to the wall, little compressed circle of carpet where one foot usually rested. Spike lay prone and examined the gap under it. Canvas bag. Probed it with a gloved finger. Tools. Pretty sure they weren't the chick's. And a roll of banknotes, looked like a grand at least.

On the small table sat a half-eaten bowl of cornflakes, a newspaper underneath. He lifted the corner. A cheap magazine lay beneath, face down. He extracted it. Greyhound racing pro-gramme, Wimbledon track. Flicked some pages, saw hand-jotted notes. Bloke's writing. Maths. He was briefly thinking how he was never much good with numbers when he heard something slam.

Spike's left hand whipped back and lifted the jacket as his right drew. Instantly his aim covered the doorway. Slow breaths. Pistol level, arms steady. Nothing happened. He crept sideways, peered through. Front door was still shut. Must've been a neighbour. Damned flats so close together. Replaced the Sig.

Wallace had been here, Spike was sure. And he'd want those tools, they were his MO. So, assuming the cops didn't have him, it was very likely he'd return. Probably after the bird and her kid got in. Which meant all Spike had to do was head back up to the roof and wait. He slid the dog-racing programme back under the newspaper.

The night light cast long shadows across Zac's face. He sat on the top stair, cradling his chin with both hands. Kofi was tucked up in bed, but he wasn't ready to go back downstairs, despite the teriyaki smell coming from the kitchen. He heard the sizzling pan and notes tumbling rapidly from John Coltrane's sax in the kitchen. Play a snatch of Coltrane and you hear chaos. Listen to the whole track and there's order. That's what he needed now: order from chaos.

Talking to Night Vision this morning had sent Zac's head into a tailspin. Could his Met colleagues have put a lid on the murder investigation five years ago to work their own op? Same guys he'd line up next to in the canteen, join for five-a-side football, share a beer with at someone's leaving drinks? Boateng couldn't fathom it.

Thompson had given him a single name, or rather, three digits: 210. It came from a thread on the chatroom page set up by King's mates: Draymond RIP. People had been posting under aliases like Killer Clown and Gatman about how Draymond had been in too deep. Others replied to say those guys didn't know what they were talking about. Some – mostly females – just appealed for the violence to stop. *Enough is enough.* Thompson had found the still-active page on his mobile and showed Zac in the car. Buried among the hundreds of comments, one user with alias IceKing99 had written, *Dats wot u git wen u fuk wid da 210.*

Thompson thought Two-Ten was responsible. He'd suggested that because there was no drug connection, it must have been something personal. But he couldn't say what. Draymond didn't tell him anything before he died, though Thompson hadn't seen him around as much in the few months before. The name Two-Ten was alien. Didn't even know if it was a person, group, place – or all three, like Thompson believed.

'Ready, love!' Etta's voice snapped him out of it.

'Smells good,' he said quietly as Etta placed salmon fillets on heaped noodles. Realised he could have been more enthusiastic. He needed a beer. Automatically, he reached into the fridge for a bottle, cracked it open.

'I already poured you some wine.'

'Alright,' he protested. 'I didn't know.'

'You could've looked on the table.'

'I'll drink both.' Zac scraped his chair back, sat down heavily. Grabbed a half lime and crushed it over his food.

'Hard day?' Etta spun some noodles around her fork.

'Yeah.'

They ate in silence.

'So how was your meeting?'

'Which one?'

'This morning. The early one. Reason I had to take Kofi to school.'

'OK.'

'Who did you have to meet?'

'Can't say, it's about the case.'

She nodded, sipped her wine.

After a while, Etta spoke. 'You know, you don't have to act like this. Whatever it is, you can talk to me.'

Zac didn't respond.

CHAPTER THIRTEEN

Wednesday, 21 June 2017

'Gimme some juice, bitch.' Reece pointed at the carton in his mum's hand.

Jasmine Fletcher slammed it down on the table. 'What did you say?'

The boy laughed, waving toast in one hand. Turned to Wallace for approval.

'Never talk to me like that.' She bent down next to the table, got close to his face, eyes wide. 'You don't use that word to a woman. Least of all your mother. D'you understand?'

'Sorry, Mum,' he conceded, giggling. Looked at Wallace again, received a smirk in reply.

'This has to stop,' Fletcher said, still gripping the orange juice. She raised her voice. 'You come into this house, disrespect me in front of my boy, put bad words in his mouth and dangerous stuff in his hands.'

Wallace winked at Reece. 'Calm down, Jas. Time of the month?'

'Fuck you!' Fletcher screamed.

'Not supposed to say that word either.' Wallace arched an eyebrow at Reece.

Fletcher wiped both hands down her face, calmed herself. 'Look, the only reason you're here, Darian, is cos you're paying.

Two fifty a day and it's supposed to be only two nights. You been here three and you haven't given me anything yet.'

'I wouldn't say that.'

'Dickhead.'

He leaned back. 'You'll get your money.'

'Not good enough.' Fletcher shook her head, limbs taut with rage. 'I want the cash now.' She slapped the tabletop.

Wallace chuckled. 'Or what?' Swigged his tea.

'I'll call the police,' she blurted.

Wallace banged the mug down. He was out of his seat in a flash. Pushing her backwards. Fletcher stumbled, lost her footing and fell. Howled as her coccyx hit the floor. Wallace straddled her on the ground, knelt on her arms. Grabbed her cheeks in his right hand and squeezed hard, concentration on his face. Lips splayed, she made a gargling noise. Wrenched one arm free and tried to hit him but there was no power in the blow. Wallace turned her head to the right and pressed hard with the knuckle of his left middle finger behind her jawbone. The mandibular nerve. She wailed, but the sound was diluted, soft. Reece watched in silence.

'I stay as long as I want.' Wallace hit the nerve again with his knuckle, deeper. Her body bucked under him. Pressed once more. 'Got that?' She nodded furiously, tears forming. He stood, towering above as she lay on the carpet, massaging her face. 'And if you call the feds…' Wallace shot a glance at Reece. 'Then it's game over.' He flopped down onto a chair. 'Ain't that right, lickle man?'

'Game over,' mimicked Reece.

'Sorry, Darian,' she whispered, and wiped eyes with the back of her hand.

Wallace drained his mug. 'Now make me another cup of tea. I'm gonna have a shower.'

*

Fletcher watched him walk out of the living room. The bathroom door clicked shut. Heard him pissing. What was it the police-woman said? Abuse was physical, but it was also about restriction of liberty, often humiliation. Jones told her that a lot of men thought they could tell women what to do. But nobody had the right to control someone else. Fletcher couldn't take this any more. Neither she nor Reece should have to live with the fear of Darian Wallace hanging over them. Money or not, whatever he threatened. The toilet flushed.

'Where's that tea, Jas?' he yelled from the bathroom.

'Coming.' She went over to the kettle, flicked the switch. Heard the shower go on next door. Took her mobile off the counter. Keyed in Jones's number from memory. Deep breath.

DW in my flat now. Jas.

Her thumb hovered over the send icon. She looked over at Reece, kicking his feet in the air under the table and gazing out the window. Enough. Sent. She deleted the message history. Exited and locked the phone, slipped it into her pocket. Noticed the tremor in her hands as she made tea.

The shower was still running.

'Anything?' Boateng looked up hopefully.

'Nothing,' replied Jones, turning back a page and scanning some numbers. A soft ping sounded on her mobile.

'Me neither.'

They sat across from one another in the office, Malik and Connelly at the two adjacent desks.

Boateng swivelled left. 'What about you boys?'

Connelly blew out his cheeks. 'Sweet FA, boss.' Clicked the mouse a few times, pulled up an image of an overweight young man. 'This is our Harvey Ash. I got the picture from a newspaper – they ran it when police questioned him after the burglary. But it's like he just vanished off the face of the earth a year later.'

'Same here.' Malik tossed the document in front of him. 'Not a single member of the public knows a damn thing about Harris or Darian Wallace or any of it. One fella does claim he saw a UFO over Deptford that morning though. What a waste of time.'

Boateng was trying to digest Volz's pathology report on the Harris post-mortem. Jones was reading the same write-up, the idea being that two sets of eyes were better than one. Despite his experience, she probably understood more than him with the biology and genetics of her human sciences degree. Genes were conspicuously absent from the report though – meaning Volz hadn't found Wallace's DNA or anyone else's on Harris. He read the same paragraph a third time, failed to absorb it.

Problem wasn't the science, he got ninety-nine per cent of that. Wasn't his patchy sleep either, though that didn't help. What his brain was really working on was Thompson's lead, same as it had been all night. And he knew multitasking was a myth. Every time he returned to Volz's report, the words Two-Ten came back into his mind. He had to find someone who knew the group, but how? Apparently they were from Brixton. Boateng ran a hand over his face. Needed an in there. Who could he trust?

'Do we have enough to charge him?' Jones asked.

Boateng pressed his lips together, shook his head. 'Motive, timing: yes. Pat's CCTV link to his residence is solid, and we can strengthen it if the others who live there have alibis. But we've no forensics from the crime scene. We have to prove he was there. Right now the only charge that'd stick is skipping parole with the electronic tag scam. Arrest warrant's out for that. We can nick him on suspicion, then either hope he confesses, or some new evidence turns up while he's on remand.'

'Smoking gun?' said Connelly.

'Smoking hammer more like.' Malik looked across the desk. 'Kat, how do you not read your texts instantly? I can never wait.'

She held up the report. 'I'm working on this.'

'What if it's your boyfriend?' A tiny grin twitched at the corners of his mouth.

'I don't…' She cut herself off, flustered, reached for the phone.

Connelly shot Malik a conspiratorial glance.

'Holy shit,' whispered Jones. Rotated the phone screen to them. 'Wallace is in Fletcher's place now.'

Boateng squinted to read it. Stood immediately. 'Crawford estate?'

Jones nodded.

'Right. Nas, get onto Firearms. If there's a spare Tactical Support Team I want them on the ground ASAP. If not, just Armed Response. Kat, give us a couple of local units nearby with eyes on.'

'Lambeth or Southwark? It's on the boundary.'

'Both. And tell them to keep it low-key, let's not spook him before we're ready to go in. Pat, grab your Taser from the armoury. Vests, everyone. I'll tell Krebs and sign out an unmarked pool car. Outside in three minutes.'

Wallace turned off the water and stepped out into clouds of steam. Wasn't going to lie, he'd got a hard-on when he was on top of Jas just now. Had to finish himself off in the shower. Took a while, but there was no rush. He was heading back to Bermondsey later today. Go see his old mate Trent. Fingers rubbed a circle in the misted mirror. Smile spread across his face, imagining the moment he confronted Parker. Stared at the teardrop under his right eye. Maybe room for one more of them to mark the occasion. Or two, when he had time. He'd tell the story when it suited him, once he'd gone and started a new life. Big himself up. Nobody screws with Darian Wallace. See what happens when you do? Took in his grinning reflection as the glass fogged again. He opened a window. It was just a flash of white but he registered it.

Police car.

Cautiously, Wallace craned his neck to see better. Two feds inside, standard. It was the spot that stood out. They'd backed in along the wall by a low-rise opposite, nose forward. Like they were trying to be discreet. Wasn't a patrol, they didn't sit in the middle of estates. No other reason to park up there. And they hadn't got out. So they were waiting for something, someone. Not a snitch, they'd be in an unmarked car. Wallace quickly dried himself, pulled his T-shirt, jeans and hoody back on.

Stomped into the living room, eyes darting around. Fletcher's mobile was gone from the counter. It'd been there before. 'Jas?' he called. No response. Went to the bedroom, tried the door. Locked. 'Can I use your phone?' Silence. 'I know you're in there.'

Wallace went to the front door, peeped through the spy hole. Nothing. Opened it a crack to widen his view. A hundred metres across the tarmac, another police car rolled out of sight. He didn't believe in coincidences. Carefully closed it. Strode over and smacked his fist on the bedroom door: once, hard. 'Bitch! You're fucking dead, you hear me? Dead.' Stepped back, checked his anger. That wasn't going to help him now. Had to get out. Couldn't carry the tools. He scanned the living room. Balcony.

Wallace gently opened the door, lifted a piece of damp laundry on the line. No feds on this side. Picked one of Jas's baseball caps off the plastic chair. Rolled it up, stuffed it in his pocket. Pulled his hood over. Climbed up and lowered himself off the metal railing, dropped one storey to the ground.

Started running.

Boateng cut the blues and twos long before they reached Camberwell, the district where Fletcher lived. There was no music this time. They'd made it from Lewisham in ten minutes at fifty miles an hour. Jones and Malik rode in the back. Connelly worked the radio, in contact with the two patrol cars already in place. Southwark and Lambeth had both offered more but Boateng declined. Too many cooks: they needed skill, not numbers. An Armed Response Unit was prepping in Brixton, ETA six minutes.

The radio crackled. 'Papa Lima Two Five One, this is Lima Delta Three.'

Connelly grabbed the Airwave mic. 'Receiving.'

'Figure seen running on Lowth Road south towards Coldharbour Lane. Appears male, black hoody, jeans.'

Boateng needed confirmation of ethnicity. He asked for the identity code.

'Nine,' came the reply.

Unknown. Boateng chewed his lip, the Croydon Tasering fresh in his mind.

Connelly pushed the mic button again. 'Lima Delta Three, is it our man?'

'Papa Lima Two Five One, uncertain.'

Boateng scanned the areas between the housing blocks on the estate. 'Tell them to stay where they are, Pat, keep eyes on Fletcher's building. We'll pursue.' Connelly did so. Boateng spun the BMW X5 round and stopped sharply. 'Kat, Nas, head over to Lowth Road on foot, we'll box to the south side on Coldharbour.' Car doors clunked shut and he watched them both vault the fence and begin sprinting across the tarmac. 'Get that Taser ready, Pat.' Boateng pulled away, gunning the engine hard in first up to the corner. His exit was blocked by cars stopped at the lights. He swore and hit the siren, but the traffic was nose to tail. Smacked the steering wheel, backed up and edged onto the pavement to find a way through.

Wallace saw two shapes from the corner of his eye. Maybe a hundred metres off, moving quickly. About fifteen seconds to make up on him. He accelerated. Traffic was stopped on Coldharbour Lane at the lights and he headed straight across into the next road towards the hospital. Glanced over his shoulder, couldn't see them yet. Ran to a low wall bordering the car park, hopped across and crouched beside a four-by-four. He'd probably be on camera but there were more important things right now. Stay calm, no time for emotion. Breathe. Plan. Glanced up to the entrance of King's College Hospital. The road parallel to the main entrance was rammed with vehicles, teeming with people. Patients, family, staff. Old and young, coming and going. A mob. Perfect.

He took off his hoody. Removed the cap from its pocket and pulled it low over his brow. Rolled up the hoody, stuffed the ball under his T-shirt and tucked it in. Did his belt one notch tighter. Leaned against the car, eyes flicking from person to person outside. Saw what he needed. Stooped and walking slowly, he advanced on the smoking area. One geriatric guy with a tube up his nose was puffing away, eyes shut, oblivious. Wallace stole up behind him and lifted the dressing gown he'd slung over the bench. Pulled it on and tied the cord around his new belly. Across the path, a patient was being transferred from her wheelchair at the side door of an NHS minivan. Two crutches were stacked against the rear doors. Wallace swiped both and slipped around the far side of the vehicle. Jammed them into his armpits, began limping. Merged into the mass of humanity milling around the steps. Didn't look back as he entered the building. People even made way for him. Knew the giant corridor made an L-shape to A & E on Denmark Hill. Kept moving, now just another body in the crowd.

Jones and Malik had radioed to say they thought Wallace had taken the main road into King's College Hospital. Boateng found it blocked by stationary vehicles on each side and a third line up the middle queuing to park. He swore again, reversed and took the parallel one-way street against the traffic flow. Slalomed an ambulance and two more cars coming at him, hands working quickly to manoeuvre the hefty BMW X5. Connelly had already drawn his Taser and jumped out as they halted, running for the buildings. Boateng cut the engine and followed. Picked out Jones and Malik in their black stab vests jogging between groups of people around the hospital steps. Boateng signalled and made eye contact with them in turn. Each shook their heads. He jabbed a finger towards the entrance, motioning his team inside.

For a second he stood alone, grimaced. Knew it was probably too late.

Wallace emerged from the Denmark Hill doors next to A & E. Three taxis sat outside. They'd be pre-booked but he had to chance it. Shifted himself on crutches over to the first and popped the door.

The driver turned. 'No, mate, I'm here for…' Checked his tablet. 'Mrs Gupta.'

Wallace shut the door without a word. Glanced around, checked the exit. Heard a siren in the distance. Approached the next car.

The cabby put down his paper. 'Mr Henderson?' he beamed.

Wallace nodded. Opened the door.

'I can help,' the driver got out.

The siren grew louder.

'It's OK, I'm good,' Wallace waved him away.

The driver got back in as Wallace threw his crutches inside and slumped into the seat. Opened the robe, checked his jeans pocket. Few hundred quid, the rest was back at Jas's with the tools. Bollocks. She'd got her money after all.

Cabby glanced in the rear-view. 'East Street, isn't it?'

'Yeah.' Good enough.

They pulled out. Wallace sunk lower into the upholstery as a Met Police van screamed past and into A & E. Smiled to himself.

CHAPTER FOURTEEN

'You did the right thing.' Jones laid a hand on Fletcher's arm. 'Took a lot of courage to make that choice.'

Fletcher's cheeks were slick with tears and mascara. Jones gave her a tissue and she wiped her eyes with a shaking hand. '"Game over", that's what he said.' She gave a juicy sniff. 'He's gonna kill me. Reece too. My son.' Another spasm of grief screwed up her face.

'We're doing our best to find him,' Jones said gently.

'Bit fucking late now, isn't it?' Fletcher produced small gasps between her words.

Jones swallowed. 'Sorry.'

Boateng knelt on the carpet next to Reece, who was rolling a toy car back and forth, staring at it. 'Are you OK, Reece?' The boy nodded. Zac got closer. 'It's going to be alright.' He was no longer sure if that was the truth. Wallace, Parker, Fletcher, Harris. Amelia, Thompson, Two-Ten. Him and Etta. Any of it. His head bowed as if pulled by a huge invisible weight. He gazed at a point on the floor, guilt creeping in again. Responsibility for failure was his. He was senior officer on the ground. The arrest tactics had been his call. OK, Wallace must've clocked the squad cars before they arrived, but he'd requested them with no briefing, no plan. Couldn't blame the PCs who just happened to be closest when they'd radioed. The tip from Fletcher was real-time, but that was the nature of police work. Should he have waited for Tactical

Support, held off altogether and staked out the flat? He'd need to explain every choice to Krebs soon. She wouldn't like the bad press one bit.

For now, they were doing what they could. Connelly was briefing the unit from Brixton who remained on standby. Malik was in with security personnel at King's College Hospital, reviewing the footage, trying to work out how the hell their target had vanished. Boateng had underestimated Wallace. The ex-con nearly twenty years younger had outsmarted him, outmanoeuvred them all. Maybe if he'd been more focused…

A knock at the door made everyone start. 'Scene of crime officer,' called a female voice outside. Boateng walked over, checked the spy hole before letting her in. The SOCO was head to toe in black, including her stab vest and gloves. 'Where shall I start?' she chirped, opening the briefcase and removing a camera.

By being less cheerful, Boateng thought.

He turned to Fletcher. 'Jasmine?' She pointed under the sofa. They dragged out the canvas holdall. The SOCO removed, photographed and dusted a mallet for prints. Repeated the process with two chisels, an angle grinder, electric drill and a box of nails. Boateng took a nail, held one up. 'These what your handyman uses?'

Fletcher sniffed. 'I couldn't tell you then, I was scared.'

'And now it's too late,' he retorted. Instantly wished he hadn't. 'Sorry. I know he threatened you and Reece. I'm just frustrated.'

'We all are, Zac.' Jones glared at him.

'You're right. My bad.' Boateng pulled himself up: time for action, not blame. Then his gaze alighted on the angle grinder, a small handheld one. The image of Harris strapped to the chair came to him. Severed fingers. Blood pooled on the carpet under his hands. 'Could you match that blade to a cut on a body?'

The SOCO stuck out her lower lip. 'In a lab, maybe.'

Boateng glanced at Jones, his spirits lifting. 'Could be just what we're looking for.' Took out his mobile and hit Volz's number.

They rode in silence. Boateng driving, Jones alongside. He stared ahead, she sideways at the Peckham shops flashing past. It was just the two of them; Malik was still at King's and Connelly had joined him to take witness statements.

'Do you think it's about empathy, in the end?' she said without turning.

'What is?' He fiddled with the stereo, tried to find a decent station. The speakers hissed.

'The Job.'

'It's about solving crime. And preventing it.'

'Yes, but can you do that if you don't empathise with the victims?'

His eyes flicked to her. 'Is this about Jasmine Fletcher? I know I was a bit heavy-handed, fair enough. But she could've made that call to us earlier, then we'd have our man and she'd be safe.'

Jones snorted. 'The only reason she called us at all is because I bothered to relate to her, build some kind of trust.' She paused, swivelled in her seat. 'Sorry, boss. Didn't mean to—'

'Oi.' He raised a palm at her. 'Speak your mind. I want people in my team who tell it like it is. Within reason,' he smiled briefly. 'Everyone gets it wrong sometimes. I did today.'

'Zac, you couldn't have—'

'The kid. Not even started school yet and what has he seen so far in life?'

Jones knew it was rhetorical.

'I wanted to pick Reece up and take him out of there,' he continued. 'Make sure he never claps eyes on Darian Wallace again. Call it a dad's instinct. Put him and Jasmine Fletcher somewhere safe. But you've got to have limits to empathy. Can't solve everyone's problems. If you believe you can, it just creates more for yourself. Before you know it, you can't do the job any more. I've seen coppers get to that point. Then you don't help anybody.' He adjusted the radio again and music crystallised.

Jones broke the silence. 'I understand why you'd want to protect a child.'

Boateng stared at the road.

'I heard what happened, Zac. Five years ago.' She chose her words carefully. 'Can't imagine what it must've been like for you and Etta. For Kofi. How do you…' She faltered.

'You hope.' His face twitched. 'That one day the person responsible will get what they deserve.'

'Justice?'

He hesitated a second. 'Yeah.'

'They never caught the guy who did it.'

'Not yet.'

'What do you mean?'

He kept looking ahead, but she could tell his eyes were moistening. 'Never give up. You owe it to that person you loved. To the memory you still love, that no one can take away.'

Jones nodded slowly. Boateng didn't need to ask her if she was thinking about her father.

Wallace stood opposite the Colombian café that was also a money transfer and clothing store. Nobody was watching. No CCTV either, far as he could tell. Wallace slung the crutches and dressing gown into the industrial bin and pulled a wooden pallet over them. Headed for the market down the road at Elephant and Castle junction. Descending filthy iron steps towards stalls by the underpass, he felt anonymous again, one molecule in a sea. Sellers hustled under tarpaulins and crude plastic sheeting that did little to block the intensifying sun. Racks of cheap clothing, hats and shoes sat alongside fruit and veg in crates piled between the hawkers. The scents of deep-fried food wafted from kiosks by the underground station. Wallace heard conversations in at least five languages inside a minute. Without a word, he paid cash for aviator shades to cover the teardrop tattoo. Then he purchased a sun hat, new T-shirt and trousers. All in lighter colours than his existing outfit, the one they'd be looking for on cameras. Next he picked up a mobile phone handset, scratched and worn but described by the South Asian man selling it simply as 'used'. Stolen and unblocked most likely. That didn't matter; he wouldn't need it for long, and no one would bother tracking the IMEI now. Bought a Lebara SIM card: one of the hardest to trace. No paperwork for any of it. He had to duck inside the shopping centre itself to find a small rucksack and sleeping bag. Wallace changed in a grubby public toilet, putting his original clothes and new bedding in the pack. Checked his roll of notes: two hundred and eighty-five quid left from his winnings at the track on Saturday night. Enough.

There was nothing in the town hall lobby, nor in the public library. Same in two GP surgeries, a Post Office window, and the big Methodist church. Told himself to be patient. Finally in the community centre, scouring his seventh public notice board, he found it.

Lock-up garage to rent.

Wallace tore a strip with a printed mobile number from the advert, fired up his own phone and called. Two minutes later he was walking towards Old Kent Road.

*

The owner was on time. Older white guy, probably fifties, thin grey hair. Solid-looking. Introduced himself as Derek. 'What d'you need it for then… John, wasn't it?' he asked, twisting the lock and heaving the metal door up.

'Storage,' replied Wallace.

Derek squinted. 'For what?'

'My car.'

They stepped inside. The guy flicked on a single, bare electric bulb. It was still so dark that Wallace was obliged to remove his sunglasses to see properly. Breeze-block walls, bare concrete floor. His prison cell had more atmosphere. But beggars couldn't be choosers. At least there was a plug socket.

'Twenty-five pound a week,' said Derek.

'I'll take it for two weeks.'

'Minimum's a month.'

Wallace clenched his jaw. Recognised he had no power here. 'Fine.'

'Got any ID?'

'Aw shit.' Wallace patted his pockets. 'Must've left it in the car. At my girlfriend's place.'

Derek stared at him. Wallace held the gaze, which drifted to the corner of his right eye, the black teardrop tattoo. The older man coughed, jammed hands in his pockets. 'If you ain't got no ID,' he said at length. 'It's fifty pound a week.'

He weighed it up. 'OK.'

'Plus twenty quid deposit for the key.'

Wallace peeled off the notes from his roll. Didn't bother winding up the rest: there weren't enough.

Derek grasped his cash, counted it and extracted one of two keys on a fob. 'Gimme this back in a month then, 'less you wanna extend. You got my number.' Gave a final glance at the teardrop and moved towards the door.

'Wait,' said Wallace. 'I'll give you two hundred more at the end of the month.'

Turning, Derek sized him up. Nodded, and was gone.

Wallace shut himself inside the garage, unrolled the sleeping bag and lay down. Damn, the floor was hard. Used his old hoody as a pillow. Stared up at the bare bulb, its filament glowing weakly, like it was about to give out. A wave of tiredness washed over him. It was early afternoon, but he felt like he'd been awake for days. Closed his eyes. Would the guy see him on the news, call it in? Maybe, but he'd have to be quick. Wallace wasn't planning to hang around this shithole any longer than necessary. Then again, the old bugger might be so venal he wouldn't go to the feds even if he knew something was up. Like the landlords who know their properties are being used by hookers, hydroponic skunk farmers or ten-to-a-room illegal migrants. Long as the rent comes in, it was hear no evil and all of that. Problem was that Derek no doubt had another key, the spare on his fob, so if he was curious he might come back and check.

Minor. Now Wallace had a place to hide, sleep and plan. Knew what he had to do. Finish his business then get off this island. It started with Trent Parker. For that, he needed new tools. Sixty-five quid in his pocket wasn't going to cut it.

Then he remembered: it was Wednesday. Thursdays were race nights at Wimbledon greyhound track.

CHAPTER FIFTEEN

Spike had begun to doubt himself. As usual he'd arrived early, but now it was twenty minutes until closing time at the gallery and still no sign of his boss. Was he definitely in the right place? Knew there were two Tates in London, and the gaffer had said the one opposite the Spooks. That was Tate Britain in Pimlico. No mistake, be patient. He stood in front of the four-by-three metre canvas, staring. Didn't get it. Just a load of words on a massive board. He could've done that. Checked the tiny information sign next to it. 'Break Point, 1998. Fiona Banner b. 1966.'

'Rather good, isn't it,' remarked Patey, gliding alongside him.

Spike glanced left, pissed off that he'd been caught unawares. They made an odd pair, the boss in his skinny-cut Savile Row suit and Spike in a light fleece, jeans and hiking shoes. Since most other visitors had already cleared off, though, no one seemed to notice.

'What…' began Spike. Tilted his head. 'What is it?'

Patey smoothed his regimental silk tie, its tiny silver-winged daggers the only hint of his previous life. 'It's a scrambled narrative. Illustrating the limits of our comprehension.'

'Scrambled bollocks, more like.' Spike wasn't comfortable here, not his turf. Come to think of it, he wasn't sure when he'd ever been in a gallery outside of a surveillance job. Parents had never brought him to places like this as a kid, why would they? Waste of time. 'Not gonna pay the bills, is it?' as his old man always said of anything other than work. Miserable bugger grafted himself to a heart attack on a building site at fifty-five, died in hospital, and

Spike's mum wasn't too far behind. They never had any money, but their early deaths taught Spike that once you earn some, best enjoy it while you can. Hence his need for the colonel's cash.

Patey gave him an indulgent smile. 'The piece describes a chase scene from the film *Point Break*, where the hero is in pursuit of a robber. Seen it?'

'Don't think so.'

'Well, you see, by flipping the title words around and condensing a textual description of events, the artist conveys the rising psychological pressure our protagonists find themselves under. Before they snap.'

Spike frowned. Was the boss talking about him? He'd never snapped. Wasn't a jellyhead. Never once got PTSD in twenty-two years, and he'd seen a lot of stuff.

'It's not going very well is it?' Patey thrust hands in his trouser pockets, rocked back and forth.

'I had him in the bird's flat,' Spike's voice was a low growl. 'Waiting for her and the kid to head out, then I was going in for him. She must've tipped off the coppers or something.'

Patey glanced around, checked they weren't being overheard. 'You couldn't pursue?'

'I was on the roof of the building. Been there all night.'

'So you've lost him?' Patey snorted. 'Christ, after our contact got us the lead intelligence. That wasn't cheap. I don't need to stress the urgency of this to you again, do I? Our client is particularly keen we action their request double-quick time.'

'I ain't been sitting with a thumb up my arse.'

'I know. But nevertheless, failure to meet our brief is bad for business. Which is bad for your status as a contractor with our firm.' Patey paused long enough for Spike to appreciate this before smirking. 'And the sooner you get this done, the faster you can get back to throwing yourself off buildings or however it is you spend your ample free time.'

Spike cracked his knuckles; pops echoed around the room. 'Got an idea where he might be.'

'I'm listening.'

'Whatever he wants to do, Wallace needs money. Another burglary's too risky, even a mugging, and he's probably run out of people to stay with who might lend it to him. So, he's trying to work out how to get cash. Must be holed up somewhere he can't be traced.'

'Where?'

'No idea. That's not the point. In the bird's flat I found a greyhound racing guide from Wimbledon track. He's well into it. Looked like he knew what he was doing and all. There's a meet there tomorrow night. You always told us think like the enemy, right? If I'm Wallace, I need untraceable money and I know how to bet, then I go down the dogs.'

Patey pulled a face. 'Rather speculative.'

'Well, unless our noble Metropolitan Police Force can supply any more suggestions, there aren't a lot of other options.' Spike let the statement hang.

'Fine. Follow your instincts. I'll speak to our contact.' Patey spun on his heels and began striding towards the door.

'Boss,' Spike called after him. 'What happens in the end?'

'Excuse me?'

'The chase.' Spike jerked a thumb at the canvas. 'This bollocks.'

Patey shot his cuffs one by one. 'He dies.'

'Which one?'

'I forget.'

Etta was sitting up in the little bed while Zac had pulled a chair close beside. Kofi was tucked between them, reading aloud from *The Hobbit*. He finished a paragraph and let the book fall on his lap. Looked from one parent to the other.

'Was he scared? Bilbo Baggins.'

Etta stroked his head and looked at Zac as she spoke. 'I expect he was, love. Everyone gets frightened sometimes, especially when you've got some monsters to face.'

Zac blinked.

'But he kept going, didn't he? Even when he was scared and he had to go into the woods with the big spiders and stuff.'

'Yes, he did. Because he was very brave.' She kissed the top of Kofi's head.

'And if he was really scared he could just make himself invisible with the magic ring.'

Etta lifted the book from his lap, closed it gently. 'But every time he did that it changed him, destroyed a little bit of his life. It's not good to hide from things, whatever kind of monster it is.' She placed Tolkien on the bedside table and stood. 'Time to go to sleep now.'

'Night, son.' Zac reached across and pulled the X-Men bedcovers up to Kofi's chin as he wriggled down. Kissed him on the forehead and switched the reading lamp off. 'Sleep well. See you in the morning.'

Zac took off the saucepan lid. Okra soup simmered inside, their favourite Nigerian dish. Etta's mum's recipe, with salted cod and crayfish. Mrs Adichi's secret was frying the Okra in palm oil before adding it to the broth. Zac was supposed to be losing a bit of weight, cutting out saturated fats and the like. Palm oil was top of the list of banned substances. He took a lungful of the aroma. Dieting was overrated. He stirred it and began to dish up.

As they ate, Etta talked about her day: a new legal aid project they were setting up, gossip that a senior associate was being headhunted by their rival firm, the incredible pulled pork sandwich she got for lunch from Borough Market. Zac listened to it all, knowing that by the end of the meal he would have lied to her once more, disappointed her again. That the distance between them would be slightly greater. Began to hate himself for it. Wondered how long he could keep this up.

'Soup's amazing,' he said, to stop the rumination.

'Thanks. And to Mum. You could tell her yourself on Sunday.' She placed a hand on his. 'How about after this we snuggle up on the sofa with a little cognac? See what's on TV. Watch a film, maybe?'

He met her eyes. 'I'd love to…'

Etta sensed the intonation. 'But?'

'I've got to go out.'

'Zac.'

His forehead and palms felt clammy, the soup's heat and spice only partly responsible. 'Have to meet a contact for work.'

'Can't you delegate some of this stuff?' Her exasperation was clear. 'We've got to have a life, too. It's great that you lead by example and everything, but if you don't relax once in a while you won't have the energy to run a team. Especially in your job.'

'I'm sorry love, I—' He circled the spoon in mid-air, fumbling for words. 'That was the deal I made with my guys. I'd come home early so I could put Kofi to bed and we could eat, then I'd head back out. Go see this guy.'

'For your case?'

Split-second hesitation. 'Yeah.'

She looked hurt, searched his expression. Gave a long, slow breath. 'OK. Don't forget,' she wagged a finger, 'you're taking me out dancing on Saturday night. We've got Kof a babysitter. Can't get out of that one, Detective Inspector Boateng.'

He managed a smile. 'It's a date.'

*

No denying it, he felt a rush of excitement about the encounter. More than four years without a new lead and tonight he might step closer to the truth of Amelia's murder. Just one pace on a long path that could go nowhere, but he was moving nonetheless.

Boateng parked on an outlying street and walked back until he hit the centre of Brixton, where the railway met Coldharbour Lane. Only that morning he'd been chasing Wallace a mile up the other end of this massive road that cut its way through south London. It was a Wednesday but the place was buzzing, drinkers spilling from bars into the streets, shouting over music that pumped from every doorway. The sun refused to go down on the year's longest day.

Approaching Dogstar he could see two men working the entrance, one the giant figure of Samuel Agyeman. The hulking Ghanaian doorman wore a black T-shirt and trousers, a high-vis armband displaying his ID. Agyeman patted down a couple of youngsters and opened the door for them, releasing a blast of sound. Spotting Boateng, his whole face lit up. '*Akwaaba*!' he cried, slapping hands and pulling him in for a bear hug with arms like granite. The Akan greeting literally meant 'you have left and come back'. It was accurate: last time he saw the big man was over a year ago. They'd met eighteen months before that, when Agyeman's cousin had been the target of an attempted murder in Lewisham. Boateng had caught his attackers, dealt personally with the family. Comforted the grandmother with an explanation of events in her native Twi language that he grew up hearing his parents speak. Agyeman said he'd never met a police officer like him. Promised that whatever Boateng needed, whenever, he just had to name it. And he was a man who could supply a lot of things in this city.

'Too long, my friend.' He looked Boateng up and down, jabbed a finger in his belly. 'What happened? Did you forget how to find the gym?' he grinned.

'Easy. Some of us have families. Can't spend every spare hour of the day chucking weights around.'

Agyeman flexed a thick bicep. 'This is part of my job. It's a professional responsibility. And the ladies like it, too.' He laughed loudly, slapped Boateng's palm again.

Boateng removed his flat cap. 'Somewhere we can talk?'

'Come with me.' Agyeman nodded to his colleague. 'I'll take my break now.'

Boateng followed him inside. Trap music thumped out of a sound system. The DJ worked off a laptop in the corner, headphones wedged under one ear. High-pitch autotuned voices laid over staccato snares and basslines that made his whole body vibrate. Was this what young people were listening to? Suddenly he felt older than his forty-three years.

Agyeman led the way into a back room. Took a plastic flask out of the little fridge and shook it up. 'Protein,' he explained. 'Chest workout today.' Bass reverberated through the walls, but at least they were alone.

'Does the name Two-Ten mean anything to you, Sammy?'

The big man frowned. 'Like the numbers two one oh?'

'That's it.'

Agyeman swigged the pink liquid. 'I think they were a gang, few years ago. Small outfit from this area.'

Boateng's pulse accelerated. He was talking to the right guy.

'Don't hear much about them today,' continued Agyeman. 'Mostly the young guns around here now, y'understand? Lot of these gangs don't last but new ones always spring up. Why're you interested in them?'

'It's about a case.'

Agyeman sucked on the drink, narrowed his eyes. 'The finest detective in south London. You don't need me to help with your work, Zachariah. So what's the real story?'

Boateng said nothing. The subwoofer next door was making his hairs stand on end.

'If I don't know what you're after, I'm not gonna put myself in the firing line. Some of these boys would murder each other over a bag of chips.'

Silence. Bass.

'My daughter. I think someone in Two-Ten killed her.'

Agyeman crossed himself, shook his head. He knew about Amelia. After a few seconds he looked square at Boateng. 'Tell me what you need.'

'I want you to find a member of Two-Ten or someone who knew them personally. Set me up with a meeting. Don't give them my name or real job. Say I'm a mate with a business proposal. If they play hard to get, mention that I've got information to trade. For extra reassurance I'll meet on their turf. No undercover cop would do that.'

Agyeman drained his protein shake, proffered a huge hand. 'Consider it done.'

CHAPTER SIXTEEN

Thursday, 22 June 2017

'My office. Now.' It wasn't a request.

Krebs's three terse words by phone told Boateng what was coming. He'd arrived early, hoping to find some development to mitigate the inevitable bollocking. But Krebs was already in and summoned him before he'd even switched on his computer.

'You've lost Wallace,' she stated, hands clasped.

'Ma'am,' he began slowly, 'thanks to careful work by DS Jones, we received a tip-off and had to act immedia—'

'Not good enough.' Krebs pressed her lips into a flat line. 'Sit down.' Boateng did so. 'For Christ's sake, where was Tactical Support, Armed Response? And what were those PCs from the area playing at?'

'There wasn't time to stand up the specialists, ma'am. Wallace could've left the property at any moment. We needed eyes on quickly and the local units didn't have full background, they—'

'You requested patrol vehicles apprehend a murder suspect, dangerous and probably armed, without the complete intelligence picture?'

'We briefed them, ma'am, but it was against the clock and the informant's life could've been at risk.'

'Well, it certainly is now.' Krebs flicked aside a curtain of her bob cut. 'The woman's petrified by all accounts, and she's got a child there. We may have to refer them to the Protected Persons Service. Not to mention us looking like a bunch of incompetents. And I assume you've seen the pictures on social media of your team rampaging through a hospital, scaring hundreds of patients.'

The photos were news, but Boateng was aware of the rest. He said nothing. Berated himself again for not slowing it down, making a different call. Would he have planned better if his mind hadn't been elsewhere? The pang of guilt came again, making him doubt his judgement.

Krebs looked down at him, sighed. Clicked the button of her ballpoint pen rapidly. Boateng had seen Crown Court judges deliver life sentences with more humanity. Finally she spoke. 'What should we do then, Zac? Are you up to this task? Your initial plan to locate and apprehend the murder suspect was logistically unfeasible, and when presented with an opportunity to nick him you royally screw it up.'

'We'll do better, ma'am. Items were retrieved from the flat which include a weapon possibly used in the Harris murder. Dr Volz is examining it today. If it matches, we'll be able to charge Wallace. And my team will chase down every lead on him, double our efforts.'

'See that they do. You've got one more week before I hand the case over to another DI who can close it. They'll lead the investigation, your team can assist, and you can go back to the paperwork on your nightclub stabbing.'

Boateng clenched his fists out of sight. 'Understood.'

'And I want another press briefing this afternoon.'

'Ma'am?'

'I told you before, Zac, community policing. I'll have the *Evening Standard* come by at four and you can brief them on where we are. They'll get Wallace's photo out to a million people across London. It'll be online tonight and in print first thing tomorrow. Probably the best chance of finding him now.'

Boateng tried to hide his exasperation. Failed. 'With respect, our last appeal produced nothing actionable, just a load of crap we had to waste time sifting. Increasing publicity could push him further underground, make him take extra precautions and—'

She held up a hand. 'I'm not interested, the decision's made. Now go back to finding Wallace and when the *Standard* gets here at four you'd better have something new to give them. That's all.'

'Get stuck in, guys.' Boateng laid out the tin trays of meze, kebabs and hot bread on the meeting room table. Marinated chicken and lamb off the charcoal grill, home-made hummus, lahmacan, spiced sausage and stuffed vine leaves. His team gathered round, loading up from the spread. Boateng knew they'd been working flat out all morning. A Turkish takeaway was his reward to them. Experience showed a direct relationship between food and morale. Both were essential if they were to keep going. As he carried in the bags, a colleague had asked what they were celebrating. Boateng ignored the sarcasm.

'Sweet. Cheers, Zac.' Malik already had his mouth full. The others paused, examined the mountain he'd piled on a plate. 'What?' he shrugged. 'I was at the gym this morning.'

'Seven a.m. run to the river at Greenwich and back.' Jones took a bite of kofte.

Connelly inclined his head. 'And I dug the allotment before work.'

The three of them turned to Boateng, who stroked his slight belly. 'Well, I walked at least two hundred metres to pick this up for you smug bastards. So don't give me any stick.' He flashed a grin. 'Alright, what's the deal? Pat.'

The Irishman hoovered garlic yoghurt off his thumb. 'Wallace is one clever son of a bitch. Security footage shows him grabbing a bathrobe and crutches then limping off inside the hospital like Verbal Kint in *The Usual Suspects*. Probably could've walked right past us.'

'We can't have been more than twenty seconds behind him.' Jones glanced at Malik. 'How'd he come up with that plan?'

'Processing speed,' replied Boateng. 'One factor of IQ. Basically he can think faster than normal people. Then what?'

'Gets in a cab outside and off he goes. Just before the Armed Response van turns up. Cab was from the Waterloo Cars firm. Driver says Wallace claimed to be a Mr Henderson on a pre-book. Dropped him opposite East Street. Couldn't tell us anything else we didn't already know. I've pulled up the nearest Southwark council camera at the drop time and we've got him exiting the vehicle.'

'Great. And?'

'We lose him in East Street market, too many people. I've been working outwards from there in ten-minute windows, reviewing tape. But it's a big job. Nothing so far.'

'Good work, Pat, keep going. We'll catch a break.'

'Don't worry about me, boss.' Connelly's thick eyebrows rose. 'When you've spent three months tending raspberry plants every day to get a handful of fruit, you know a thing or two about patience.'

'I'll take your word for it. Nas?'

Malik rested his still-heaped plate on the table, belched into his fist. 'Been in with the techies this morning. Got decent forensics off Fletcher's phone after she told us when he'd been using it. Wallace cleared the browsing data so it took a while, but we got there.'

Boateng leaned forward. 'So what was he doing?'

'Searching for dance studios.'

'Let me guess, he found one in Bermondsey.'

Malik nodded. 'The last website he visited was K – where Parker works.'

'Doubt he's after a breakdance lesson. Question is why he wants Parker.'

'What do you mean, boss?' Jones frowned. 'We know that already.'

'Do we? He could be out for revenge, nothing more. Parker grasses, code of the street says Wallace takes him down. But what if Parker's the one who knows where those jewels are stashed? Maybe he bluffed Flying Squad first time round, led them to Wallace's half.'

'Why would Parker wait another two years to sell them?' Malik crammed chicken into his mouth. 'He was the one who tried to flog some to Harris straightaway.'

'I don't know,' admitted Boateng. 'Perhaps he wanted to get rid of Wallace and he knew Harris was a snout. Set him up.'

Jones stopped chewing. 'The file said they were old mates.'

'Don't take everything at face value.' Boateng noticed her crestfallen expression, felt like a prat. 'Sorry, I didn't mean…'

'It's OK,' she nodded. 'You're right, no honour among thieves.'

'Some fellas I've dealt with over the years would sell their own grandmothers. We can't be too suspicious. Either way, let's check on Parker again this afternoon. What've you got?'

'Been working on the safe deposit box guy – Ash,' she said. 'Not much to show for it though. Pat's right, it's like he just dropped off the planet two years ago. Experian lists four Harvey Ashes in the country. None with current activity fits the demographics of our thirty-one-year-old white British man from Croydon. Last record of anything on that Harvey Ash was a National Insurance contribution paid by Capital Securities in 2014, a month after Wallace's conviction. Tried to find out from them what happened but the company went bust a year ago. Haven't got hold of anyone yet.'

'So why'd he disappear?' Boateng scanned their faces.

'Guilty conscience?' offered Connelly. 'If he was the insider on the vault job.'

'Not guilty,' countered Malik. 'Just scared. Intimidated maybe? Wallace gets a message out from prison, Ash scarpers.'

'I thought maybe he'd gone overseas,' resumed Jones. 'But there's no record of him leaving the country. Could've taken an informal route out, I suppose. Reckon a name change is more likely though.'

'And?'

'Bugger all. Went back through *The Gazette* and Royal Courts of Justice over the whole period since the burglary. They list every official name change. Nothing registered by a Harvey Ash.'

Boateng scooped hummus with his bread. 'It's legal to change your name without using a deed poll. We'll check for anyone matching his profile who seems to appear out of nowhere in mid 2015.'

'Could take a month to go through those records,' Jones protested.

'And that's the easy option. Bigger problem is if he's off the grid altogether.'

'Where would he go?' asked Malik.

'Some place you can live without leaving any trace.' Boateng twirled a plastic fork. 'Commune, island, camp site, monastery, farm… help me out here.'

'Allotment?' suggested Connelly.

'Right, you get the idea. No one can completely become a ghost. Wallace will be thinking the same as us, unless he knows something about Ash we don't. And Wallace hasn't left town yet, despite the cash he had at Fletcher's and more ingenuity than MacGyver.'

'Who?' said Jones.

Connelly clapped a hand on Boateng's shoulder. 'Don't worry, boss. I remember that show.'

'Thanks, Pat. Alright, now get this lot down you and find these bastards.'

*

Etta wrapped her arms around him from behind, rested her head between his broad shoulder blades. Zac was in their sitting room, studying his original James Barnor print. The legendary Ghanaian photographer had depicted his compatriot, champion boxer Roy 'The Black Flash' Ankrah, eating breakfast with his family back in '52. Black and white. Man and woman with their little girl. Zac had bought it when Amelia was three. He'd liked it for being a link to his family past and a vision of their future.

'Been thinking about her, love?' She spoke gently.

'All the time.'

Squeezed him tighter. 'Same here. That's normal, it's five years next month.'

'I know.'

'Zac, is it—' Etta paused. 'You haven't been yourself lately, I just wondered...' She let the half-formed question hang.

He turned to her. Cradled her head in both hands, searched the deep brown eyes. Had to tell the truth. 'I...'

'Yes, love?' She grasped his shirt at the waist, pulled him closer.

'I've—' Zac broke eye contact. Felt the emotion well up, pushed it back down. 'I've had a lot on with this case. Boss is giving me stress about it, we're not making enough progress.'

Etta let go. 'It's OK to say if you're struggling. With Amelia, I mean.' Her tone had changed, harder now. 'We can talk about it, God knows I've needed to. You must as well, you can't keep it all inside. I tried that – it doesn't work. Remember? I'm still dealing with it now, same as you. Some days I'll just think of her and start crying – doesn't matter where I am, what I'm doing. Like I've got no control over it. Round and round, asking why it happened. I don't even know what I believe any more. The difference is that I talk about how I'm feeling, and that has to help.' She let out a long breath, laid a hand on his chest. Lowered her voice. 'You're the strongest man I know, but everyone has limits. And anniversaries make it even tougher.'

Zac pinched his moistening eyes. Eventually he spoke. 'She had so much love. With everything she did. Passionate about saving the planet by the time she was eight. Wanted to fill the garden with trees then climb them all. I think about what she would've been like now.' His voice caught. 'And the woman she'd become.'

'Me too.' Etta's mouth quivered.

He stroked her shoulders and their gaze met. 'She had the best example to follow.'

Etta's forehead fell to his chest, her body shaking with tiny movements.

Stop fighting it.

He let the tears roll.

They stayed like that, held one another.

'Are you hurt, Daddy?' came a small voice from the doorway. Kofi was standing there in his Spider-Man pyjamas.

Zac sobbed once more, smiled. Wiped his nose with the back of his hand. 'Yes. But I'm OK. Come here, son.'

Kofi looked up at Etta as he burrowed into their embrace. 'Is it about what happened to Ammy?' he asked quietly.

Etta nodded, lips pressed tight, then sucked in air. 'Your Dad and I are very sad about it, love.'

'But it was a long time ago, wasn't it?'

'Sometimes you remember things more when it comes around to the date they happened.'

'I'm sad too,' replied Kofi, though Zac knew he was too young to understand at the time, perhaps didn't really know now. All he could see was his parents crying together, and for a ten-year-old boy, that meant something hurt.

Which was right.

CHAPTER SEVENTEEN

Wimbledon Greyhound Stadium was a welcome change. Wallace wasn't made to be on lockdown. Didn't matter if it was at Her Majesty's Pleasure or in a garage off Old Kent Road. One day's solitary confinement in that breeze-block cube and he was going nuts, staring into the darkness, punctuated by slivers of sunlight framing the metal door. Tried to think of reasons he was inside with no vehicle in case the owner came back, but Derek clearly had more important stuff going on. With the sun up it was too hot to sleep properly and there was nothing else to do except lie low until the dogs brought a chance to get more cash. He did push-ups, crunches and squats, two hundred of each. Lay on the bare floor, drifting in and out of consciousness until a skeleton put a gun muzzle to his forehead and pulled the trigger. Awoke hyperventilating, took a second to work out it wasn't real. Sat up and mopped sweat off his face. Only time he'd ventured out in more than twenty-four hours was to buy a large bottle of water and family-size bucket of fried chicken. He'd been on the alert, vigilant to any signs that the King Rooster staff recognised him off the news, but no one made eye contact. Hat, sunglasses, head down on the Northern Line from Elephant and Castle to Tooting Broadway underground station: same result. Nobody paid attention to him. That was London; everyone in their own little world.

The dog track was sensory overload compared to the lock-up. Chatter, movement, bodies shifting around him. People and noise, cigarettes and alcohol. Money changing hands. Old boys leaning on sticks. Kids chasing each other. A few women with their arse cheeks hanging out of miniskirts. Funny little place. Might be the last time he ever came here. Even if he wasn't planning to leave this island for good, the Mayor of London was knocking down the stadium to give Wimbledon Football Club a new home. Lot of memories here, some big wins. Racing his own dogs, Blaze and Bambam, till he had to kill them. They'd gone on to a better place, a higher purpose. RIP. Wallace surveyed the grandstand, soaked it all up. Then he blocked out everything except beasts and track. He'd studied the programme, developed his strategy. Built up slowly off a fifty-quid stake with a couple of each-way bets. Picked a winner in the 8.45. Switched between bookies, avoided the guy he took two grand off last time. Now he had seven hundred pounds and counting. All good. Kept half an eye out for the skinhead from Saturday. Without weaponry he had nothing except bare wits if anyone started on him tonight. Not ideal.

Next race was up. Muscular, long-limbed greyhounds stalked in front of him, paraded by trainers in white coats. Wallace unrolled some notes, began calculating.

Bunch of mugs. Pissing money away on dogs that didn't have a clue what was going on, legging it blindly round some sand after a rag. Muppet with a mic jabbering away like it was the most exciting thing he'd ever seen in his life. Probably was.

Spike stood on the grandstand's top step with arms folded, twenty-twenty vision sweeping the crowd below. Scrutinised each face, dismissed them one by one.

Gaffer had it right: this was a long shot. Even if the target was among this crowd, he didn't have much control. Couldn't just follow him home, wherever that was now: too much chance of disappearing again. He'd need to ambush Wallace, get him alone outside, then he could interrogate. But means to do that were limited. Goons on the turnstiles meant he was forced to leave his rucksack under the motorbike seat in the car park, and with it the pistol. Only tool was his three-inch folding knife, squeezed through security between his arse cheeks. Pat-down covered his arms, sides, legs; after that the bloke lost interest and waved him inside. Too shy or lazy to put a hand in his crack. Perhaps it wasn't the kind of establishment where patrons smuggled in blades.

Spike didn't gamble – with money on animals at least – but reckoned the odds of a result tonight were slim. Had one crucial advantage though: he knew what Wallace looked like, but the geezer wasn't even aware Spike was after him. Pull this off through instinct and he'd be back in the colonel's good books. Old habits proved right. Reliable Spike: he gets the job done. That'd mean decent pay cheques on a regular basis over the foreseeable. Military pension wasn't enough to cover a mortgage plus BASE jumping and kit like his motorbike. Money for the things to enjoy life while he could. On top of that, he hated failing. Screwing up. That's what his ex-wife had called him: 'screwed up'. Always gone, never around, no time for anyone except himself. 'Cold-hearted' – she used to like that one too. She blamed their wrecked marriage on him, his 'failure'. Spike disagreed with her. Depends on your measure of success.

There.

Eight rows down, far side. Lone male. Spike rapidly checked off the observer's A to H: A, B, C – age, build, colour – were all squared away, fine. D, distinguishing marks, was the problem. Bloke had shades on, couldn't see the tat under his eye. Had to get closer. Spike manoeuvred through sweaty bodies and clouds of cigarette smoke, watching the guy constantly, even when his hiking shoes slid on discarded programmes and crunched plastic pint glasses. Got within about five metres of the target's back at forty-five degrees. Waited.

The geezer was sitting still, just staring, like he was on drugs or something. After three minutes without moving a muscle, he quickly stood and approached a bookie. Gave him a wad of cash, exchanged a few words. Took a little square of white paper, pocketed it and turned. Removed his sunglasses. Teardrop below right eye. Wiped the shades on his T-shirt, replaced them and sat down. After the race he collected a bundle of notes from the bookie, must've been a grand or more. Lucky bastard. Target read the programme for a few minutes. As the next lot of dogs was brought out for the 9.45 he got up and walked inside. Spike followed through the bar and down a long corridor.

Wallace went into the bogs. Spike paused outside, listened. Hand dryer; more than one person. A yellow 'Cleaning in Progress' sign leaned on the wall outside by a mop and bucket. The door swung open and someone left. Spike glanced inside. Target was pissing. Alone. Everyone else watching the 9.45. Checked his watch: 9.43.

At Hereford barracks, his first sergeant in A Squadron used to say SAS stood for 'Speed, Aggression, Surprise'. He unfolded the knife, held it backhand, the grip concealed against his right wrist. Pulled up the cleaning sign outside the door and entered.

Closing his eyes, Wallace exhaled as his urine stream swelled to full flow, spattering off the tin, gurgling into the drain. He heard the door close. Bliss. He'd been desperate for a slash but needed to wait because the 9.30 looked good. Parade had confirmed his algorithm choice. The dog had come in second, eight hundred return plus his three hundred stake. He'd picked up the winnings and could finally relieve himself.

First thought as he felt the tip of a blade press his side was that the skinhead had turned up again, found him. Followed closely by a second: that lumbering clown couldn't have come up on him silently. Third thought: this was someone serious. All in less than a second. Body frozen, he opened his eyes.

'Darian Wallace. Hands on the wall. Face forward.' Voice was calm. Clear, not posh. Southern, not London. Undercover feds? They wouldn't use a knife to arrest him. This was something else. He raised both arms slowly. The jet of piss dried to a dribble.

'Do what I say.'

Wallace couldn't see the man's face. He was right behind him, but far enough off to be out of reverse headbutt range. 'OK, you're the boss.'

'We're going for a walk.'

'Can I put my dick away?'

'Keep your hands where they are.' The man reached round and quickly swept Wallace's arms, legs, torso, belt, arse crack.

'Enjoying yourself?'

'Left hand only. Put it away.'

Wallace fumbled, steered his cock inside the fly. 'Alright, big man, you not interested in that then?'

'Do yourself up.'

Wallace chuckled, relaxed his body. Then he spun fast as he could right, deflected the blade and swung a haymaker with his left fist. The guy ducked it and Wallace lurched forward off balance before a blunt object snapped his head sideways and he fell. Vision went blurry. A solid, wiry body pinned him, one knee on his chest. He smelled the stink of piss next to him in the trough. Iron grip on his neck was choking, pain seared through his face. Took a second to register the back of the blade on his top lip. It dug into his septum and nose cartilage. Jesus, it was agony. The guy's breathing had barely changed. Head throbbing, the white sparks in front of his eyes began to clear. Must've been an elbow that floored him. Despite the blow, Wallace could think straight enough to realise the way out of this was not force. 'Alright, fuck's sake, man. Take it easy.'

'Get up.' That grip lifted him to his feet, blade still pushing the septum, forcing his head back. 'Don't try that again, do you understand? Out the door and right. To the car park. Walk.'

Initial shock gone, Wallace tried to think as they marched along the dim corridor towards the exit. The guy was in step behind him and lowered the knife to his kidney area before anyone else appeared. A roar came from the track – 9.45 over. Think. Their route out had to pass through the bar. Blade jabbed the hollow of his back as they moved, felt razor sharp. He needed time to plan. 'What's this about?'

'My employer wants something you stole.' The man's voice was low. 'You're going to tell me where it is. Then we can all go home and have a nice cup of tea.'

Safe deposit job. Wallace mentally scanned through the stolen items. Which ones? Who had they robbed that would employ this nutter? Actually, that was the scary part. He wasn't mad at all. He was a pro, behaving like this was a normal day. Maybe it was. Soldier? Didn't matter who was paying him. Work that out later. Just had to use his brain to get out of this right now.

They slowed to enter the crowded bar. Dozens of people milled about, queuing for beer and chips or gazing vacantly up at race results on bright screens. Wallace's eyes darted around, searching for information, anything. Stools around a pillar. Walking stick. Tray of shots on the bar. Safety notice stuck to the wall with a floor plan. Announcer listing the 9.45 result through speakers. Dogs lying on a rug, unmuzzled and breathing harder than normal. Maybe they'd raced at 9.30. Owners standing over them chatting. Woman shouting odds into a mobile. Fire alarm box. Drunk man with unfocused gaze holding a Guinness and wandering in front of them. Think, dammit. Wallace's head pounded from the elbow strike. More punters entered the bar from the grandstand.

Then it crystallised. Like a camera lens focusing, pin-sharp. And Wallace knew what to do. One shot, no margin for error. Here we go.

Wallace turned his head left, pretended to look at the new arrivals. Hooked his right foot under a bar stool. Flicked his leg out and tipped it straight onto a dog. Thirty-five kilos of muscle launched itself at them, adrenalin still going from the race. Snapped its jaws mid-air, missed. Man with the knife to his back stepped off just enough. Wallace grabbed the walking stick. Reached out, punched the fire alarm on the wall. Glass tinkled. All hell broke loose.

Fucking dog. Should've seen it coming. Lost physical contact with the target when the avalanche of punters came through. All panicking like a herd of wildebeest. Alarms hammered, ear-splitting. Stewards bowled into the bar with high-vis jackets, directing everyone out. Dogs barked and strained as the owners got them under control. A drunk man flailed, spilled his pint down Spike's leg.

Folding and pocketing his knife amid the crush, he saw the white T-shirt move right. Side door. Spike shoved his way through the crowd, more drinks washing to the floor, another bar stool clattering over. Reached the exit Wallace had taken, marked 'Owner Enclosure'. Shouldered the door open, slipped inside and shut it behind him.

A few bare electric bulbs hung overhead. The space was packed with metal cages, couple of dogs still inside, barking like mad. Spike brought out the blade again in a backhand grip. That way you could slash and stab with the same movement, not just one or the other. Crept between the cages, treading slowly heel to toe for minimal sound.

A door burst open behind him. Spike whipped round, ready to strike. Saw a fat middle-aged bird calling after her dog. He concealed the knife and turned back, kept moving. Heard the clunk of a car boot.

Got you now.

Emerging into the car park, he saw a row of near-identical white vans lined up, some marked with kennel brands or owners' names. Silently he approached, scanning each for his quarry. Heard the murmur of moving bodies processing out on the other side. Put his ear to the vehicle back doors, listened to each in turn. Passed five or six. Stopped. Thought he heard breathing. Slowly reached for the handle, then flung it open and raised the knife. Leaned in. Empty.

'Sir, you need to be far side of the car park, please. It's a full evacuation of the premises.'

Spike wheeled, blade at his back. Three high-vis stewards stood there. 'I'm sorting out my van,' he replied. Nodded inside the back.

'Sorry, mate, got to move now.' They took a step closer, fanning out. 'No exceptions.'

A memory surfaced. Bosnia, '94. Dusk in winter. Three armed guys on a checkpoint stopped his car on the forest road. He was in civvies. They surrounded him and after a few words barked in Serbian, they realised he wasn't local. Obvious conclusion: spy. Made Spike exit his vehicle at gunpoint, took him into the woods. Three against one. But they forgot to pat him down, didn't find the gun in his belt. Only one of the four men came back.

Spike calculated the cost-benefit now. Three blokes versus what might be his last chance to find Wallace. But he wasn't going to kill these men, just incapacitate them. That'd make them witnesses. Three witnesses. What a nause. Thought he could still hear someone breathing. Snatched another glance inside the van. Nothing. Sniffed hard, as if that would help, but all he could smell was dog shit and diesel vapours.

'Alright,' he conceded. Dropped the blade into his back pocket, raised his hands in mock surrender. 'I'll find you,' he called out, and began walking away with the stewards. 'My dog,' he added for their benefit.

None of them noticed the figure who began to crawl from under a van towards the perimeter fence, keeping to the shadows.

CHAPTER EIGHTEEN

Friday, 23 June 2017

Since getting Kofi out to school at quarter to nine, Boateng's thoughts had been consumed by his personal inquiry. When he'd seen Agyeman on Wednesday night, the big man had told him it would probably take a day or two before he could generate an introduction. His call was overdue. On the short drive from school to the MIT base at Lewisham Police Station, Boateng had already checked his phone four times. He knew he needed to curb the obsession; his team would quickly spot it, want to know what was going on. And this was something he needed secrecy to pursue.

Moreover, the hunt for Wallace was demanding his attention. Boateng's own reputation was under threat. Krebs seemed particularly concerned about Wallace. Could it really just be the media spotlight? He resisted the temptation to tap his mobile screen again and turned up the stereo instead.

Jones, Malik and Connelly were already in when Boateng dropped his flat cap on the coat stand before helping himself to the cafetière. He filled his favourite Ghana Black Stars mug from the 2010 World Cup – the year they reached the quarter-finals and were denied a place in the semis by a last-second handball – and dropped into his chair. Took a sip.

'Christ, who made this?' he exclaimed.

'Guilty.' Malik raised a hand. 'Iraqi rocket fuel for you, boss.'

'I'm not complaining.' Boateng reached for the milk.

'I am,' chipped in Connelly. 'About the lack of any CCTV images of Wallace coming out of East Street. Must've taken some back roads.'

'Right. What's your plan, Pat?'

'Get footage from the main thoroughfares around it within thirty minutes of the cab drop-off, then run the lot through FRS.'

Boateng had known the Met's bespoke Facial Recognition System to produce spectacular results, albeit only occasionally. Storing over three million images, the IBIS Face Examiner could pick out a convicted criminal from a sea of people. *Minority Report* stuff – assuming you gave it the right film to work with and your target was more or less facing front on. Last year the Met even trialled it as a live-feed system at Notting Hill Carnival – Europe's biggest street party – with some success. Still needles in haystacks, but worth a go here.

'Good shout,' he replied. 'Nas, I'd like you to give Pat a hand with that today. Also get Wallace's mugshot out to homeless shelters. He's got to be sleeping somewhere. What about our breakdancing friend?'

Jones spun her chair to Zac. 'We dropped in on Parker yesterday. Still giving it the hard-man routine, doesn't want our help. Also claims he's told us everything he knows about Harvey Ash and the jewels. I wasn't convinced – it was all too neat. But soon as we pressed him, he tried turning on the "charm" with me again. Said the only protection he needed was the Durex in his pocket, asked if I wanted any of it.'

'Prick,' interjected Malik.

Jones glanced his way, gave the young DC a little smile. 'Nothing I haven't dealt with before.'

Boateng could believe that. Still, he wondered whether Jones should report it; the Met was hot on recording sexual harassment incidents now. About time. He'd seen too much of it in twenty years. He'd have a private word later, didn't want to embarrass her in front of the others. 'Good job, guys. There's only so much—'

He was interrupted by the vibrating mobile on his desk. Snatched it as a reflex before the first ring even finished, but saw it was Volz rather than Agyeman. Excused himself and stood to take the call, wandered over to the window. A minute later he returned with a broad smile. 'Volz has matched the blade on Wallace's angle grinder to the wounds on Harris's fingers. And there was some blood in the mechanism too. Harris's. Now we've got something to tell the *Standard* before they go to print at noon. Wallace isn't just a suspect any more – we can charge him with the Harris murder.' Across the desk from him, Connelly and Malik low-fived. Boateng swigged his coffee. 'That should cheer Krebs up.'

Three hours later, with the Irish-Iraqi duo ensconced in the video room running footage through FRS, Boateng and Jones were alone at their desks, combing Experian for new individuals who cropped up mid-2015, just as Harvey Ash disappeared. GB Accelerator IQ was a more powerful database but their access had been cut after the Met failed to renew its subscription. It was damned slow progress. Each name had to be cross-checked with both immigration and deed poll records to be eliminated as candidates for a reinvented Ash. All 100,000-plus of them. There was bulk processing of course, but it was still serious desk work. Modern policing. Some days you were on the streets chasing a suspect, but most of the time you were at a computer, crunching data, analysing information.

'Looks like we might be at this all day,' observed Boateng.

'OK by me,' said Jones. 'Beats chatting with a breakdancing perv.'

'Sorry about Parker.'

'Don't be, it's not your fault.' She stopped typing. 'Want me to work overtime on this?'

'Yeah, if you can. Please. I'll get Krebs's sign-off, pay you time and a half.'

She leaned back in her chair. 'Thanks. Didn't have any big plans tonight anyway.'

'On a Friday night?' Boateng knew millennials didn't like to be tied in too much, but even so.

'It's been a long week.'

'Come on.'

Jones hesitated. 'Alright, my date bailed on me. Told him I was fifty-fifty with work anyway, I think that made up his mind.'

'His loss.'

She smiled. 'Wasn't that bothered about the guy anyway. What about you?'

'Promised my son I'd take him to the park for a kick around before dinner.' He paused, remembered that Kofi was going home from school with Neon this afternoon and needed picking up from there. 'There's gonna by one pissed-off ten-year-old if I don't show by six thirty. And I could use the exercise.' He patted his belly.

Jones laughed and they returned to their computer screens, continued searching.

A bell tinkled as the hardware shop door creaked open. Wallace stepped through, inhaled thick odours: machine oil, paint, lumber, fertiliser.

Glancing up from his Quran, the elderly Pakistani shopkeeper smiled. 'Good day to you, sir.' He gave a tiny bow from behind the counter.

Wallace clocked the holy book immediately. A sixth of the inmates with him at Pentonville followed Islam. One guy even told Wallace he 'looked Muslim', whatever that meant. Invited him along to their study group. In a darker mood, ruminating on forgiveness, Wallace went. Concluded he still didn't believe in any supreme being. But a few words of Arabic he'd picked up went a long way with other Muslims, built trust. In this case, it might be enough to stop a call to the police. Another lesson from prison. Some would call that manipulative; to Wallace it was just logic. He removed the hat and sunglasses. '*As-salaam aleikum.*'

'*Wa aleikum as-salaam.*' The shopkeeper closed the Quran, stowed it above his head. 'Muslim?'

'*Al-hamdulillah.*' Wallace nodded.

'What can I do for you?' he asked gently.

Wallace scanned the shelves. 'Kitting out my business, need a few tools. Some big jobs coming up. Got an angle grinder?'

'Oh, yes, sir. This way.' He walked down one aisle to the end where a wooden board displayed the selection hung by nails.

Beautiful, terrifying machines. Wallace spotted his favourite, the Bosch cordless. Portable, compact, powerful. 'I'll take this,' he told the shopkeeper. 'Diamond blade?'

'Not as standard, sir, but I have them.'

'Gimme two.'

A diamond blade at 325 revolutions per second cut through anything – iron, concrete, never mind bone. Pretty much the planet's hardest substance. Scientists measured that on Mohs' scale. It was all about scratches, leaving marks. One material scores another and comes out unscathed, it's harder. And nothing scratched diamond. Wallace used to think the same applied to people: the harder you were, the fewer things in life made a mark on you. But it turned out that wasn't true. No matter how hard you thought you were, some stuff left its trace.

Years ago, the psychologist at school said he had a 'pathological disregard for others' feelings'. In most cases that was true when Wallace hurt someone. At best he was numb, a blank slate. Worst, active pleasure. After years of taking beatings off his Dad, he remembered the first time he'd stood up for himself, struck back. Not at his old man, that would've been a death sentence. It was at school, age thirteen. Bigger kid in his class kept calling him dirty, cos his uniform was second-hand. Wallace told him to watch his mouth, and the kid punched him in front of everyone, hard. He lay on the deck with a bloody face, humiliated. Didn't fight back then – he waited. Knew the route the kid took home. Days later Wallace hid behind a wall and cracked the kid over the head with a rounders bat he'd stolen. Remembered the thrill, the satisfaction of seeing him drop unconscious. Kid spent a month in hospital after that. And though no one could ever prove it was Wallace, the guy never called him dirty again. Wallace preferred to use his brain, but sometimes violence was the only way to protect yourself or get what you wanted. Not surprising it didn't take him long to go the next level. And once he'd got there, it became second nature.

But what no one told him about taking a life was that your mind replays that moment, over and over again. Regardless of why you killed them. Without warning, the slightest thing could remind you of it, take you right back there. At those times, he felt something like fear. And that was just in the day. At night he had no control over the images. They'd been coming more frequently over the last few weeks. He didn't know why. Grim Reaper or whoever it was. Bag of dry bones armed with a pistol, putting the muzzle to his forehead. Wallace pleading with it, begging like a pussy. Other times saying nothing, pathetically resigned to the single outcome of each nightmare: a slow trigger-pull, a bang that wrenched him awake.

'Sir?' A soft voice brought the room back. 'What is your line of work, if I may ask?'

He coughed. 'Handyman. You know, odd jobs.'

'Ah, jack of all trades. I was just considering the size of tool you might require.'

'This one's good.' He stroked the small angle grinder like a pet. 'How much is that with two diamond blades?'

'It's £134. Anything else?' The little man folded his hands.

Approaching another group of hanging tools, Wallace's mouth curled into a grin as he pointed to one. 'Is that steel?'

'Yes, sir, single piece, twenty-two ounces. Very powerful.'

'Good. Gimme a claw hammer as well then. And a bag of plastic ties.' Wallace peeled notes off a thick bundle. 'Cash OK?'

What a nause.

Spike crushed the teabag to bursting point against the inside of his mug. He was still royally fucked off about the greyhound track. Angry with himself. Chucked in some milk, two sugars: NATO standard. Stirred it and sent a teaspoon clattering into his kitchen sink. Took the brew over to his Panasonic Toughbook, set up on the dining table. Chunky old thing, but it was nails. Functioned in any environment, even Iraqi deserts or Afghan caves. Drop it off a building and it'd still work. He grunted, realising that could've been a description of himself. Except the laptop was probably more reliable than him on current form. Spike hadn't told Colonel Patey the outcome of his trip to the dogs. Was hoping he could rectify the gigantic balls-up before he had to check in. Find Wallace some other way.

Once his rage had subsided, early this morning, Spike had to admit the little bastard had played a blinder. Couldn't have got out of it better himself. But with his experience, Spike should've foreseen the problems. Tested and checked. Recce'd the place twice as thoroughly. Found an exit that didn't go through the bar. Or dealt with the wanker more effectively in the bogs. Done him a broken ankle. Belfast-style kneecap maybe, stop him running off. All those tactics had counterarguments, obviously. Bottom line was that Wallace had escaped. Again. Pretty soon, serious questions were going to be asked.

He sipped his brew and fired up the web browser. Private window. It'd still leave a trace, but like WhatsApp, it was good enough for now. Typed in Darian Wallace, filtered to results from the past week. Scanned the hits. One was a page he'd already seen on the Met website, a public appeal. The anonymous Crimestoppers number along with it for those without enough balls to leave their names. Same shit. Then a new article from the *Evening Standard*. He clicked in and read that Wallace had just been formally charged with Ivor Harris's murder in Deptford. That meant the coppers had proper evidence. They'd be stepping up the search now too. Bollocks.

Hang on.

Spike grabbed his unregistered phone, flicked through to the scanned Crimint files on his target. If he did stiff the pawnbroker, it was probably revenge. Checked the original conviction. Wallace went down while some other little scrotebag called Trent Parker walked free for giving evidence. After two straight Houdini acts, Wallace had to be sticking around for something important. Hopefully jewels, that was the brief. But maybe he was gunning for the snitch too. If that was true, then if he found Parker, Wallace would come to him. Spike gulped his brew. Tasted better now than when he'd first made it.

Thirty minutes later he was squared away. K Studios in Bermondsey. Photo on the website matched the Crimint mugshot of Parker. Dancing. Spike shook his head; he wasn't one for dance floors. At Play nightclub in Hereford, he preferred standing still with other lads from the regiment in 'SAS Corner'. Just putting away the pints, checking out the talent. Couldn't stop even once he got married. Maybe that was part of the problem. Lifting a glass was the only movement you needed to make. Sooner or later a local bird who wanted a bit of blade would come up to him. Wouldn't mind some of that now, it'd been a while. Oi, focus. After the job.

His limited-edition SAS Breitling read 2.12 p.m. On the bike he'd be back in south London by three. Recce the studio, get eyes on. Hurry up and wait, as they say in the army, then follow Parker home from work. Jobs a good 'un.

The policy briefing on NHS waiting times was predictably dull, but there was no chance of Susanna Pym nodding off in the post-lunch 'graveyard shift'. Her attention was well and truly captured. Just not by the mid-ranking civil servant droning away in front of her. The chap was clearly relishing his audience with a minister, had probably prepared for weeks. He would've been rather dismayed if he'd been able to see behind Pym's desk. What she hoped looked to him like deep concentration, thoughtful consideration of his brief, was in fact the act of reading from a tablet on her knees.

Darian Wallace's mugshot stared back at her from the screen. The *Evening Standard*'s website carried a brand-new article saying the Met had now charged him with the murder of pawnbroker Ivor Harris. Her hands felt a bit clammy; fingertips left a sweaty residue on the screen as she scrolled down. Police were well and truly on to him now. And she knew the stats: over ninety per cent of murders these days were solved. Did that make it more or less likely she'd get the pendant back? No bloody idea. The memory stick contained within it was encrypted pretty damn well, which gave her some confidence. But encryption was only as good as a hacker's ability to penetrate it. And there were people out there who could. That was why she'd tried to restore some control to the situation by hiring those military fellows to find Wallace first.

At the Oxford and Cambridge Club on Monday, she hadn't mentioned a memory stick, fearful it might leave her vulnerable to exploitation herself. That wasn't the point of the stick and its contents, quite the reverse in fact. But that was always the gamble in politics – in life, perhaps: how much should you tell others in order to get what you want? Colonel Tarquin Patey was a smooth operator, but she didn't completely trust him.

Nevertheless, now the ante was upped on the Met's hunt for Wallace, every piece of information she had might offer a slight advantage for her side. Like it or not, she was lumped together with Patey and his private soldiers now, her fate tied to their performance. How had she ended up here? The whole business had started out as a single mistake, nearly twenty years ago. But if the consequences of that moment became public, it was all over for her. Career down the pan, disgrace, perhaps prison.

The memory stick was her insurance policy against the worst threats of blackmail from the police officer who'd let her go scot-free that day in '99, pretended he hadn't seen her snorting coke in the House of Commons toilets. At thirty-four, one of the youngest MPs serving, her future was too bright to compromise. So, she made a pact with the devil. Agreed to help with the officer's request to push a promotion through for him, spoke to some Home Office friends. But the policeman hadn't gone away after that. He'd come back too many times, demanding more 'favours' be done to advance his interests, and in return offering his assistance. Which she'd taken. Over the years they'd become bound together, requests ebbing and flowing, both in too deep to stop. But she'd managed to record some of their conversations. If he tried to take her down, she'd bring him with her – or threaten to, at least. That was the memory stick's purpose. Therefore, Patey's man did need to know about it, otherwise how could he check it was there when he found the pendant? That was the whole point of the search.

She'd bite the bullet, make a call. Soon as the tedious little man in front of her and his cheap suit had buggered off.

CHAPTER NINETEEN

Five p.m., give or take. Quiet. Schoolkids home, but just before London's offices and shops disgorged their worker ants. Wallace stared up at the horseshoe of brickwork peppered with satellite dishes, balconies full of crap. Metal cages for ground floor entrances, bit like prison. At least these people were free to leave. He didn't have a lot of good memories, but those he could recall were here: Spalding House, Honor Oak Estate. Neon Grant's flat. He tucked the *Evening Standard* under his arm, pressed a buzzer. The door clicked open and he mounted the stairs. Knocked and heard scuffing feet, high-pitched squeals. Neon opened the front door.

'Didn't your mum teach you to ask who it is before you let them in?' Wallace tilted his head.

The boy gave a sharp intake of breath. 'Darian!' His face lit up, enormous grin revealed several missing milk teeth.

'Gotta be careful, you know.' He wagged a finger, returned the smile. 'Your mum in?'

'No, she's at work. She said you went away.' He bent sideways, still gripping the door handle. Not sure if he was allowed to ask, knew he probably shouldn't. Curiosity got the better of him. 'Where did you go?'

'I had to move somewhere for a while,' replied Wallace. 'So, you miss me?'

Neon nodded furiously.

'When's she back then?'

'Six o'clock.'

'And your brother?'

'He's gone out.'

'That's lucky, I've come to see you. What you doing?'

'Playin' PlayStation.'

'Show me.' Wallace glanced over his shoulder as he stepped in, closed the front door. Took the hat and shades off.

Neon wrinkled his nose. 'You smell.'

'Watch your mouth.' Wallace knew he needed a shower, change of clothes. 'Listen, don't tell your mother I've come here, yeah?'

'Why not?' said Neon, scrambling up the stairs on all fours.

Wallace walked up after him. 'Cos she'll want help with her maths too.'

Neon giggled loudly as they reached the top, synthesised noises of a football match rising. Wallace entered Neon's tiny bedroom to see his drop-kicking friend from the school playground sitting there, holding a video game controller.

Wallace sprawled into a plastic chair covered in clothes. 'Alright.' He nodded. The boy stared at his teardrop tattoo. 'I'm Neon's mate. What's your name, cuz?'

'Kofi.'

'Ghanaian bredda! Hanging out with an original Jamaican rudebwoy here. You two don't let no African versus Caribbean beef get in the way. I like that.'

Sitting next to each other, the ten-year-olds exchanged glances, laughed.

'So how's school, Neon?'

'Good.'

'Yeah? How 'bout your grades?'

'Good.'

'You working hard?'

'Every day!'

'My man.' Wallace held out his fist and Neon spudded it with his own. 'What 'bout the maths?'

'Good.'

'Shut up!' Kofi pushed Neon. 'Don't lie. It isn't good.' Wallace's eyes widened; Neon looked down. 'He's sick,' said Kofi. 'Best in our class at maths.'

Wallace felt the swell in his chest. He'd seen this boy come a long way under his tutelage from the timid five-year-old too shy to have a go at anything with numbers. Neon had kept growing in stature and maturity over the two years Wallace had been in prison. Now he was a confident ten-year-old getting top marks in maths. Pride, that's what this feeling was – not something that happened too often. Wallace couldn't resist. 'Two hundred and fifty-six divided by eight?'

Neon shut his eyes, silently mouthed numbers. 'Thirty-two.'

'Yeah!' Wallace grinned. 'Like you said, Kofi, he's a mathematical badman.' The two fidgeted slightly, waiting for the grown-up to tell them what to do. 'Come on then.' Wallace jerked his head at the screen. 'Let's see you play.'

'I want to be Portugal.' Neon bounced on the bed as he selected his team. 'They won Euro 2016.'

'Well, I'm going to be Ghana,' said Kofi proudly. 'Kevin-Prince Boateng.'

Neon tried to grab the controller off him. 'Only cos it's your name!'

Wallace tensed. 'Whose name?'

'His.' Neon pointed. 'Kofi Boateng.' The boys wrestled over the controller, giggling.

Twice he'd heard that surname in the last three hours. Both times in this little part of south London and with a connection to him. Common name in Ghana, but in Lewisham? Twenty minutes earlier he'd picked up the *Standard* at Brockley train station. There it was on page eight. Wanted for murder now.

He'd admired the mugshot they'd found – CCTV of him exiting the cab opposite East Street. Senior Investigating Officer on the Harris murder: DI Zachariah 'Zac' Boateng, from Lewisham MIT. Described as 'experienced'. Wallace stared at the boy, tried to register any similarities. Inconclusive: maybe the kid looked more like his mum.

'Boateng… Think I might have seen your Dad on the telly once. Is he a policeman?'

'Yeah. He's like Batman.' Kofi kept his eyes on the screen, tapping the controller. 'He fights the criminals around here and stuff.'

'I bet he does,' chuckled Wallace. Schoolmates. That meant Boateng junior had to live nearby. Two Boatengs in the same borough, both feds? Unlikely. There were barely any black officers in the Met to begin with. Must be the one. That feeling of pride from moments ago had already dissolved. In its place was a strange sense of inevitability. Split-second flash of a skeleton, a gun muzzle. This boy's Dad was tracking him. And Neon could tell the kid exactly who he was. Kofi might even have heard him shout 'Darian' five minutes ago at the door. Realising the implications of all this, a twitch of sadness hit Wallace. He'd have to do something about it. And his relationship with Neon was over. Wallace had known that already, but now it was definitive.

'And my Dad's good at football,' continued Kofi, locked in combat on-screen with Neon as the little figures danced around, lunged sliding tackles at each other. 'We're going for a kick about later on.'

Wallace folded the newspaper tighter. 'Where d'you guys play?'

'Hilly Fields Park.'

'Yeah, I know it.' Short walk from here.

'By our house.'

'Is it? He coming to pick you up then?'

'Yes.' Kofi stabbed buttons, shot at the goal. 'Six thirty, when he's finished at work.'

Wallace nodded, didn't reply.

After the match had ended 8–8, Wallace got rid of the kids, told them he needed to use the PlayStation. Sent them downstairs to play with the remote-controlled car he knew Neon owned, the one he'd bought for him. Alone, Wallace fired up the console's Internet browser and began searching. Coastal map of the English Channel. Maritime companies in Kent and Sussex that dealt in rigid inflatable boat hire, day charter fees. Calculated speeds and fuel costs for a 180-kilometre trip from London, enough to reach France. Small ports like Gravelines in France, with no customs checks. Looked up shipping lanes, tides, forecasts. Browsed back issues of *Motor Boat & Yachting* magazine, trawled the classifieds and chat pages. Noted down four names, each a south-coast skipper offering his RIB for private hire. Cross-referenced each on Google, built mini profiles. Knew exactly what he was looking for, just a question of turning over enough stones. Boateng senior would be on his way soon; it was six already. Hurry up. Click, scroll, back, double click. Heard the whirring of a tiny engine downstairs, laughter, an argument quickly resolved.

Jackpot.

Steve Miller. Based in Whitstable, Kent. RIB with forty-horsepower two-stroke outboard motor. Six hundred quid a day to hire the RIB with Miller as skipper. Pricey but no deposit needed. Good sign, probably meant few questions asked. And London was within his pickup range. Deciding factor was the piece on a local paper's website saying Miller and his brother went down back in '09 for cross-channel cigarette smuggling by boat. Obviously he'd served his time and was back in business.

Wallace allowed the smile to creep across his face as he stored Miller's mobile number on his phone. Just the sort of bloke he could work with.

Checked the clock: 6.25 p.m. Time to leave.

Downstairs, Wallace stuck his head into the living room. Neon was steering the car, brow knitted with concentration. 'Yo, I'm out. Behave yourselves, yeah?'

'Are you coming back, Darian?'

Wallace hesitated. Neon needed to stop saying his damn name. 'I…'

'Can we do some more maths?'

'Look, I need to travel again, there's something I've gotta finish.'

Neon stopped moving the car, looked up wide-eyed. 'Are you leaving forever?'

That sadness struck him again. *Don't be a sentimental pussyhole*, he told himself. Wallace hovered in the doorway. You could count on Boateng being prompt. Leave now.

'Look, I'll come say goodbye. I promise. And don't tell no one I was here right?' Turned to Kofi. 'Specially not your dad. You both know what happens to boys who tell tales.'

The approaching car engine was his cue to get out. As the Grant's front door clicked shut, Wallace realised he hadn't erased the Google search history.

'OK.' Zac placed his tracksuit top and Kofi's jacket two metres apart on the grass.

'That's not fair! Make it bigger, Dad.'

'Standard width!' protested Zac, before cracking a grin. 'Alright,' he relented, shifting the goalpost out.

'I'm going to beat you today,' asserted Kofi, restless with excitement.

'We'll see about that. Game on!' Zac blasted the ball over his son's head and the boy tore after it. Took a deep breath. It'd been a long week. Devastating, frustrating, knackering. Couldn't remember a week like it for ages. He drank in the scene. Warm sunlight bathed the lower slopes of Hilly Fields Park alongside the cricket pitch. Dog walkers, parents with prams, a few people working out on hanging bars up the hill by the tennis courts. A carefree summer evening. He wondered how many other people here tonight were waiting for information that could change their lives. Agyeman still hadn't called, so Zac's mobile was stuffed in his trouser pocket. Just had to remember not to dive right. Kofi dribbled back and punted a shot; Zac stuck out a leg, blocked it.

'How was Neon's?'

'Alright.' Kofi jogged backwards to receive the ball.

Zac threw it out to him. 'What did you guys do?'

'Played video games.'

'That it?'

His son thought about the question. 'Yeah.'

'Fair enough.' Clapped his hands. 'Play on!'

Kofi approached, shot to Zac's left. Could've saved it, but let the ball go under his body as he sprawled to ground.

'Goal!' screamed Kofi, and flung both arms up in celebration.

Zac collected the ball, ran back. 'Nice shot.'

'Da-ad…' Kofi elongated the word. Usually that signified a request was on its way. 'Can we go to the cinema tomorrow?'

'What if it's sunny? Don't you want to be outside?'

'I want to watch the new *Transformers* with you.'

Boateng knew his response depended entirely on events that were outside his control. 'Let's see.'

Kofi groaned and Zac felt guilty. Just like he had an hour ago, leaving Jones to carry on searching for the ghost of Harvey Ash, lurking somewhere in a database. She seemed up for it though, still keen to prove herself. Long may it continue. He could always go in tomorrow if need be. Jones had dealt with a lot over the past week. Zac was really warming to her – she had drive, intelligence, compassion; the ability to learn and revise her assumptions; toughness under the surface. Everything you needed to be a detective. Provided you didn't burn out and have to leave the pitch for an early shower. He hoped she wasn't sacrificing too much of her private life for the Job.

Racing towards him, Kofi faked a shot, shimmied left and dribbled closer. A burst of vibration hit Zac's right hip and he froze. A ball he'd intended to save shot past him at waist height between the posts. Kofi squealed in delight, sprinting off and sliding towards an imaginary corner flag.

Zac retrieved the ball and drop-kicked it as hard as he could, sending Kofi running. He whipped out the phone, stabbed in his PIN. Agyeman had kept it brief.

Meet me @ 2am corner of Akerman and Loughborough. It's on.

In the shade of a tree, Wallace sat back against the trunk. Gazed down at the father and son kicking a ball to one another a hundred metres off. Like something out of a film, their relationship. An advert for how to be a family. Briefly pictured his own dad, too boozed to ever play football with him, when he was even around. His main sport was fighting; that game had been a bit one-sided when Wallace was a kid.

So this was Detective Inspector Zac Boateng. Zachariah. What kind of a name was that? Like some old guy out of The Bible. He didn't look much. About average height, bit overweight, early spread of a belly on him. Probably forties, grey in his short hair, clean-shaven. Square shoulders, though – might be stronger than he seemed. Not a bad touch on the ball either, must've played as a youth.

Impossible to know what was going on inside though, how his mind worked. Could he be approached, bribed? Some Five-O were like that. Wallace had heard stories in prison of officers who'd say they knew about your crack-cocaine store then offer to keep their mouths shut for cash. This guy looked the decent sort, so the answer was probably no. They said everyone had a price, but watching Boateng deliberately letting his son beat him at football, Wallace wasn't sure that was true. In any case, the stakes were too high now to risk deal-making.

If corruption was out of the question, that always left threats. He knew well how much you could hurt a person through what they loved most in life. That was worse than anything physical. Some would even choose their own death over harm coming to family. Boateng was probably that kind of man. Wallace thought of his own mum, lying in the care home bed without a clue what was going on. He'd seen her for the last time, no way to change that now. She'd been good to him; the only one who had. Bit his lip, scratched at one eye behind his shades. The teardrop wasn't tattoo ink.

CHAPTER TWENTY

You couldn't miss him. Six foot four, twenty stone. Standing on the street corner, checking his mobile. For a clandestine contact, it wasn't exactly low-profile, but there was no choice. Hopes of unravelling the Two-Ten story – off the books at least – rested on Agyeman: if there was a thread to follow in Brixton, he'd find it. Boateng considered his own appearance. Did the flat cap and overcoat he'd grabbed to keep out the night's chill have 'undercover cop' written all over them? Perhaps he should've thought more carefully about it, but his priority had been leaving the house without waking Etta.

This time there were no effusive greetings. Their simple palm slap became a brief clinch before the Ghanaian doorman jerked a thumb over his shoulder. 'This way.'

Walking towards the main road, Agyeman explained that he'd briefly worked at The Jamm way back. Boateng knew the club by name: one of Brixton's late-night venues. Discreet inquiries by Agyeman had turned up a resident DJ who'd spun backing beats some years ago for a rapper 'linked' to Two-Ten. The DJ, stage name Optikon, was finishing his set at 2 a.m., after which they could catch him. Boateng fought back disappointment at the vagueness of this lead. Tried to focus on the positive: it was somewhere to start.

'I didn't say much about you.' Agyeman's voice was low. 'Just that you're a friend of a friend with some interest in the rap scene. Tell the rest yourself, whatever story you want. Just don't make me look like an informer.' He clipped Boateng a punch on the shoulder, hard enough to show he meant it.

Boateng thought quickly as they approached the Victorian red-brick house on the corner, a muffled hip hop beat pounding through blacked-out ground floor windows. Young people milled outside, the air heavy with weed smoke. Could he be a sax player looking for vocalists? Picking his way through empty bottles strewn across the pavement, he concluded that simple was best. 'Freelance journalist' gave licence to ask questions. And he'd used the cover before in police work. This time though, no one had signed it off. 'Freelancing' was the operative word.

Agyeman led the way around metal barriers to the door, queue parting automatically around his colossal frame. Following in his wake, Boateng noticed a group of men staring. One pointed at him, said something to a mate. Perhaps they thought he was a performer arriving with his bodyguard. Better than the unthinkable: someone recognising him from the day job. Would've preferred a low-key approach, maybe via a back entrance, but he was in Agyeman's world now. The big man whispered something to one of the doormen out front, who nodded and waved them in.

Agyeman clapped hands with another bouncer inside; no search. A heavy door shut behind them, streetlamps gave way to darkness punctuated by blue and green beams of light that spun and swept the room from an overhead rig. Boateng was enveloped by sound, swallowed up, eardrums vibrating. The room was crammed with bodies, mostly males in big jackets. They navigated their way forward.

The music cut out sharply, and the crowd bayed and whistled as new figures climbed on stage. A gangly youth in a baseball cap introduced himself, told his DJ to 'run the track'. Bass cranked up again, his man at the turntables scratching a sample that Boateng recognised. Might've nodded along if he wasn't so tense.

Boateng stopped, backtracked. He shouldn't even be here. This whole idea was madness. They hadn't reached the front yet; he could still call it off. Go back home, slip into bed with Etta. She might not even know he was gone. Almost immediately, caution was pushed aside by another voice, louder. The desire to understand what had happened to his daughter. To Amelia. Five years without an answer. Now he had a chance to find out.

Agyeman turned, mouthed, 'Alright?'

Boateng blinked, nodded. His companion fist-bumped a guy who'd just stepped off stage, said a few words and gestured at Boateng.

Optikon was a slightly-built South Asian man in his twenties with thick-rimmed glasses, shaved head and Parka jacket. Boateng extended a hand. 'Roy.'

The DJ shook it. 'Ishaq. Wa gwan?'

'I'm a journalist.'

'What?'

Boateng noticed the young man had earplugs in. Raised his voice. 'Journalist.'

'Ah, is it? Who d'you write for?'

'*Drum.*'

Ishaq looked blank.

'Pan-African lifestyle magazine. Music, news, all sorts. I want to do a piece on the relationship between rapping and gang culture.'

'I'm not in no gang. Got my crew, but we ain't—'

'That's OK.' Boateng held up a hand. 'I was hoping to speak to a guy Sammy said you used to spin for. Rapper who was around Two-Ten a few years ago.'

'Froggy?'

Boateng took a chance. 'Yeah.'

Ishaq fidgeted, rubbed the back of his hand. 'You know that clique don't exist no more.'

'Right. It's more of a retrospective angle. Don't want anyone getting in trouble.' He barked a laugh, aware of his own nerves. Ishaq didn't respond. Time to push it. 'What's his real name? Froggy.'

The DJ glanced over Boateng's shoulder at Agyeman, who was leaning against the wall. 'Who d'you say you were again?'

Boateng swallowed. 'Roy.'

'Roy what?'

'Ankrah. Listen, you don't have to promise anything right now. Ask Froggy if he'll do an interview with me. I can get some exposure for his music if he's still in the game. Or off-record, however he wants to do it.'

'What if we're not in contact no more?'

Boateng produced a wad of notes, counted off a hundred quid in twenties. Rolled them up, angled it at waist height towards the DJ. Leaned in. 'Call this an introduction fee. Same again when you set it up. Tell Froggy I've got funds to pay him.'

Their faces close, the young man pursed his lips, squinted like he was trying to see into Boateng's soul. Sweat pricked Boateng's lower back and armpits. Seemed like the bass was shaking his internal organs. Ishaq took the notes in his left hand and with the right produced a mobile. 'Gimme your number.'

Hurrying back to his car, Boateng's ears were still ringing from the sound system. What had he achieved? He'd left Etta and Kofi in the middle of the night without a word. Driven across south London to dispense a hundred quid for one nickname and the possibility of a meeting. Now he had to creep back into his own home. Could smell the weed clinging to his Chesterfield overcoat. Resolved to leave it in the car boot, get a dry clean tomorrow. Remembered the quote about weaving tangled webs...

Froggy.

The only solid outcome of his nocturnal mission. Sounded laughable, more goggle-eyed geek than associate of a group responsible for murder. But Boateng knew nicknames could deceive and no one should be underestimated. Often kids joined gangs in their early teens, when childhood had barely ended. In communities where they'd grown up, old monikers stuck. He'd come across guys known on the street as Young Pup, Scoot or Haribo who'd stabbed their victims in cold blood over nothing more than a tenner owed or a wrong look.

Whoever this Froggy was, Boateng hoped he'd take the bait.

Shoes off. Tiptoeing up the stair edge, Zac heard Kofi's soft breathing through his open door. The night light cast a milky glow on the landing. Peered into the bedroom. His son was sleeping deeply, mouth open, an arm thrown behind his head. Zac straightened the duvet he'd kicked aside, covered him. Gazed down at his son. Along with Etta, this boy was the most precious thing in his world. He'd do anything to protect him – give his own life if need be. A primal feeling. He knew at some point he'd have to let go, allow Kofi to make his own way. But part of him didn't want to, not after what happened to Amelia.

How many times had he replayed that morning, wished he'd told her to slow down and walk with him, or imagined he'd been there to shield her with his body? His right brain told him the bullet could've passed straight through him and still hit her. Left brain said wrap her up, take the impact and then throw yourself at the attacker despite his handgun. Also futile. Nothing could've made a difference, except not being in that shop. Amelia's death was the ultimate example of wrong place, wrong time. Chance, bad luck, whatever you called it. Even so, Zac wondered if he could ever let himself off the hook, assuage his guilt. The same voice that propelled him towards Optikon an hour ago now whispered that Froggy was the next step to redemption. Reversing the injustice that had been gnawing at the edge of his ego ever since, its bite deepened by his chosen profession. A police officer whose daughter was murdered and whose own force was incapable of solving it. Or perhaps unwilling. The latter was worse, raised too many questions. His brain was already overloaded, and Zac couldn't slow his thoughts down to allow himself some respite.

He undressed outside their closed bedroom door and, turning the handle silently, stepped in barefoot. Held a breath. Crossing to deposit his clothes on the chair, a floorboard creaked under him and Etta turned over, murmured something. He could still pull this off. Just needed to get under the covers without waking her and—

'Where've you been?' she mumbled, voice thick.

He slipped under the sheets quickly, felt her warmth. 'Nowhere.'

'Your hair smells of weed.'

Damn. No other way to explain it. 'Had to go out for an emergency call. Didn't want to wake you.'

'Wasn't sleeping that much anyway. Heard you go out.' She tensed, stretched. 'Who was smoking?'

'Guys in a suspect's house.' More freelancing only piqued her interest.

'Couldn't the duty team have done it?' she mumbled. 'Why'd they call you?'

'Connected to my case, guess they knew it was high priority.' Zac felt his adrenalin stab, willed her not to probe further. A few more questions and her lawyer's skill would catch him out. Had to change the subject. 'You couldn't sleep?'

'Not a lot…' She sighed. 'My brother called earlier, couldn't wait to tell me about his latest conquests. I've given up trying to convince him to slow down and act his age, take some responsibility for his future.'

He knew how Etta felt about her younger brother's playboy lifestyle. Particularly when he was her parents' golden child and she took all the flak. Boateng pressed himself closer to her. 'Don't listen to him, love. Think about something good. We're going out tomorrow night. We'll have a dance, forget all that stuff.' He was including his own issues in that.

She sighed again, said nothing.

'Come on. Can I take your mind off it?' Stroking her stomach, he could sense her relaxing.

'Naughty boy,' she whispered. 'Well, now you've woken me up…'

CHAPTER TWENTY-ONE

Saturday, 24 June 2017

'How you getting on with those eggs, chef?' Zac had to raise his voice over a boogie-woogie piano on the stereo.

'I've done five, Dad.' Kofi held up the last one from the box as proof.

'Nice work. Crack him in with the others then.' He turned thick sausages that fizzed and popped in the pan.

'Can I have some juice, Dad?'

'Ask nicely.'

'Please?'

'First you've got to do the scrambled eggs, that's your job. Then you can drink all the juice you want.'

Kofi sat up straight. 'All the juice?'

'Alright, not all of it.'

Etta looked up from her tablet, laughed. The full English was a Saturday morning routine for the Boatengs. Something Zac's father had adopted quickly in his new country. Claimed you could survive all day on one plate. As a boy, Zac used to help his old man cook a fry-up every Saturday before football. Though his parents had passed on, Zac kept that tradition, and not just because he was partial to the grub. He savoured the four of them – three, now – lazily eating together without school, work, cars, trains or bedtime. Sounded over the top, but to him it was sacred. This morning, however, he was struggling to focus even on grilling bacon.

Optikon had texted first thing, when Zac was in the supermarket at New Cross. Invited him to the Angell Town estate that afternoon to meet Froggy. Zac hadn't expected any news for days. Maybe the suggestion of publicity had appealed to the rapper's vanity; most performers had a narcissistic streak. Perhaps he just needed cash. But the jab of excitement as he read the message rapidly gave way to anxiety about how to manage the encounter: his cover, money, safety. Then came the guilt when he remembered Kofi's request to see the film with him later. It wasn't just what the boy, carefully stirring eggs alongside him, would say in protest. Etta already knew something was up, and this would deepen her suspicion. And there was only so long he could use the Harris case as an excuse for his absences.

Zac had seriously considered telling his wife what was going on. Explaining to her why he'd been out extra early or late three times this week on top of his murder investigation. But something prevented him. Maybe he thought it was safer if she didn't know. Or was the reason more selfish, born from fear that Etta would try to stop him? The way things were progressing, she'd find out sooner or later. Then it'd be worse, because she'd know he'd lied. About where he was, who he'd met. He felt exhausted, hadn't slept well. One eyelid had started flickering, a sure sign of accumulated stress. When he needed concentration most, his racing mind prevented it. More likely he'd slip up, be caught out. Consequences didn't bear—

'Is it ready, Dad?'

Zac started, glanced down at the eggs. 'Bit more.'

'When are we going to watch *Transformers*?'

'How about tomorrow?'

Kofi whined; Etta put down the tablet. 'You said you'd take him this afternoon.'

'I can't.' He prodded the sausages. 'Gotta work.'

'Zac!'

'Sorry. My team's doing overtime with the files and CCTV, I want to help them out. Plus, I have to follow up on last night.' That was true, at least.

She tutted.

'Can we go, Mum?'

Zac could feel her eyes on him, the disapproval. Made him feel even worse. 'Yes, love,' she replied.

He switched off the gas hob. 'I'm sorry. Don't think it'll be like this much longer.' He began plating up the food, hoping he was right.

More sodding recon.

Spike swigged tea out of a cardboard cup. He was sitting outside a café with eyes on the studio. At noon he'd gone in, seen Trent Parker doing a headstand. Bunch of kids round him gawping like muppets. Had to ask about classes himself and take a leaflet so it didn't look weird. Shook his head as he glanced at the flyer. Dancing. People do all kinds of pointless bollocks on civvy street. Thank God he didn't have to go that route. On the security circuit he could still get paid for what he used to do, more or less. Stuff he knew inside out. What else was there? Lorry driving, warehouse packing, guard at the front of a supermarket? Jobs some of his ex-army mates who weren't Special Forces had to do. Leaving school at sixteen like most of them did, there wasn't much choice.

Failure was his greatest fear. Much more than dying. If you died doing something you were good at, that was alright. People respected you. Taliban bullet through the neck, they'd say, 'Fair play to him, he was doing something useful.' Ex-soldier grinding away in a minimum-wage job, developing a booze problem cos he can't pay the bills or his post-traumatic stress disorder gets too much? People call you a loser. He couldn't stand that, so he had to keep bringing in the cash, succeeding at this. And right now, that meant watching.

Spike sawed off a chunk of jacket potato from the polystyrene container. Shovelled it in, followed by a big spoonful of baked beans. More tea. He'd need a piss again soon.

Last night he'd followed Parker home from work. Knew where he lived now. Wallace would come to one of those two places: the studio or his flat. Stick with Parker, he'd find Wallace.

The colonel had said no bodies. But after Wallace had given him the slip at the greyhounds, Spike wasn't taking any chances this time: pistol tucked into his belt, bullet in the chamber.

All he had to do was wait.

It didn't look like somewhere in the country's most deprived ten per cent. Or a district with twice the crime rate of London's average, never mind the rest of Britain. Smart new housing rose around Boateng as he marched to the rendezvous with Froggy. Only the occasional boarded-up unit or shuttered shop front suggested Angell Town's current fortunes weren't what civic planners had intended. Soul music drifted from a distant balcony but otherwise it was quiet, few people about despite the sunshine.

Optikon had given a meeting place and time, no more. Ordinarily in a situation like this, Boateng would've had at least one colleague, comms, covert vest and other equipment. Now he had nothing – except the four hundred quid in his pocket that made him even more of a target. The money needed for this little project was starting to add up. It was coming from his private savings account, but he'd intended to use those funds for a surprise family holiday to South Africa this winter – something that was looking increasingly unlikely with each payment. But that wasn't his main problem right now. If the journalist cover didn't hold with these contacts, he was in deep shit.

Rounding the corner from Angell Road, Boateng saw a group of men behind a cluster of trees in shadow alongside St John the Evangelist Church. He'd thought the location was odd, but when he clapped eyes on the blue bin alongside them it made sense immediately. Knife amnesty points were purposely sited out of CCTV range by the Word 4 Weapons charity to reassure anyone making a deposit of anonymity. That also made them ideal spots for anything else that people didn't want recorded. Boateng spotted Optikon among the five-strong crowd. He couldn't discern many details, since each man was dressed almost entirely in black, hood up or hat pulled low. They looked to be in their twenties. A white face, another South Asian kid and two black guys, the shorter of whom had a huge silver necklace, chunky as the chain leash his staffy strained at. The powerfully built dog began barking as Boateng approached, but it was the Puffa jacket of the taller black man that made his pulse quicken. Too hot to be wearing one.

'Roy!' shouted silver chain as he approached. 'Welcome to A-Town.'

'Alright,' replied Boateng, voice steady. 'Ishaq.' He nodded at the DJ from the previous night.

Ishaq stepped forward, extended a hand. 'Where's my money at?'

Boateng reached into his pocket, drew out a hundred quid he'd separated from the rest, held it out. 'Here you go. Thanks.'

Ishaq took the folded notes. Tipped his head back in what might've been acknowledgement before turning, touching fists with the other four. 'I'm out. Peace, yeah.' Boateng watched him leave, suddenly feeling more alone now his connection to Agyeman was gone. He wondered if he could've brought the doorman as backup.

'Roy Ankrah,' said silver chain. 'How much you gonna pay me for this interview?'

'You Froggy?'

'Some people call me that. How much?'

'Hundred.'

Froggy snorted. 'Three.'

'Two.'

He exchanged glances with the rest. 'Man drive a hard bargain. Two fifty.'

'I've got two. More for a follow-up, or another intro.'

'Give it here.'

Boateng proffered a hundred. 'Half now, half at the end.' He handed over the money, stepped back. Flicked his eyes to the Puffa. 'And publicity for the music if you want it.'

Froggy pocketed the notes, frowned. 'You know what? I googled Roy Ankrah. Ghanaian boxer, innit? The Black Flash. That's a coincidence.'

He'd anticipated this. 'My dad named me after him.'

'Maybe. Ain't no journalist called that though.'

Boateng's mouth felt dry.

'What's your real name, Roy?'

The big man behind Froggy flashed open one side of the Puffa and Boateng glimpsed something at his waist. Small, black, metallic. Stay calm.

'I write under an alias to protect my sources.' He could see them processing this, had to be quick. 'Sometimes people risk a lot, talking to me. Politics, crime, whatever. There are places I report from where those who speak out go to jail, or worse. I take that seriously. Cos I believe it's worth it. Letting readers know what's going on. Stories I want to tell, stuff the world needs to know. Do you know what *Drum* magazine's circulation is in Africa?' He didn't pause for them to guess. 'Two point five million. On top of that you've got a quarter of a million readers in the UK, half a million African Americans. And when communities have got facts, they can start to change things.' Boateng tapped his forehead, leaned towards Froggy. 'The fifth element of hip-hop: knowledge. Education, teaching the youngers. But some authorities want to stop those messages spreading. That's why I go to the people who know what they're talking about.' He was relaxing now, getting into his stride. 'We need someone who can tell the story of life in Brixton, the side you don't see in the organic food shop or the estate agents' windows. Be a voice for the community.'

Froggy cocked his head. 'They read your shit in Ivory Coast?'

'Yup. All through West Africa.'

'So my family there's gonna see it?'

'I have to pitch the article to my editor when it's ready, but yeah, once the story's out there. Either way there's cash in it. Up to you though, whether you want to be off-record or in the limelight.'

Froggy gripped the dog leash in two hands, pulled the muscular staffy to heel. 'Limelight, fam,' he grinned. 'Standard.' The others chuckled. 'What's the story then?'

Boateng took a half step forward, hands spread. Open stance equals lower aggression, that's what the Hendon instructors taught him back in the day. 'In south London there's a relationship between music and street life. Rappers tell stories about what gangs have done and why, in a way that youth can understand. Struggles they face living here. That's why I've come to you.'

The young man looked down at his staffy, sniffing at cigarette butts next to the knife bin. 'D'you know why I'm called Froggy?'

'Tell me.'

'Didn't speak no English when I came from Ivory Coast. Baoulé with my family, and school back home was in French. So I go into the classroom here on day one and start talking French to everyone. Kids was pissin' themselves laughing. That's how I got the name.'

'When did you start rapping?'

'Age twelve. Them days you had Choong Fam in Brixton. "Pain Don't Stop", you know it?'

He shook his head.

'Talks about trying to find some peace in life when there's this pain that just won't go away.'

Boateng swallowed, nodded slowly. That was the reason he was here.

'They was the early days. When I was a youth, grime was just starting and man hadn't even heard of "drill" music.' His mates laughed.

'Got some bars for me then?' Boateng smiled, raised eyebrows. He knew it was a tipping point for the encounter.

Froggy didn't reply, seemed to be weighing something up. Like he might've given too much away already, made himself vulnerable. Boateng kept half an eye on the Puffa jacket. Then Froggy's face cracked a big grin and he glanced around his buddies. 'Shit. Where's Ishaq when you need him? Gimme a beat, cuz.'

His white friend produced a smartphone, swiped and tapped a few times before a tinny drum snare started up, staccato, stabbed with a violin sample. The South Asian guy was filming on his mobile.

Froggy began nodding, wrapped the chain leash around his wrist. 'Yeah, it's Froggy, straight outta Brikky,' he paused a beat. 'Sixteen bars, check it. Man might say I'm crazy, government call us lazy, ca the weed smoke here gettin' hazy, but you know them haters don't faze me. See Froggy hustle in the ends, rolled deep from way back when, keep an enemy close like a friend, ca bare man them bring a skeng. Gotta watch your back for the feds, just clap a man bla-bla dead, better know that path that you tread, 'fore the Five-O lick off your head. When the informer get found, then shh don't make no sound, fill a hole six feet in the ground, with a snake man around A-Town. Brra.' He continued bobbing his head, the crew making long, low noises of appreciation. One fired an imaginary gun into the air.

Froggy had a decent flow but Boateng wasn't sure about the lyrics. Were they generic references to violence or a coded warning for him? Maybe that was just paranoia – chances were it was written before the rapper had ever heard of Roy Ankrah. He waited for the excitement to die down. 'Nice rhymes, you've got skills.' Extended a hand. Froggy stared at it a few interminable seconds, looked up again at the journalist he'd just met and slapped palms, linking thumbs.

'Is there someplace we can sit and talk?' asked Boateng. 'In private.'

Froggy exchanged a glance with the Puffa, nodded almost imperceptibly and turned to Zac. 'Come on, Roy, my yard's just across the way.'

CHAPTER TWENTY-TWO

Long. Saturdays always were: solid classes till half nine. Finally everyone had gone home, but Trent Parker stayed in the studio. Training time. He closed the door, selected a breakbeat track off his phone, cranked up the sound system. Let the drums and organ riff echo around the room. Got warm with some toprocking moves, back and forth, side to side. Watched himself in the full-length mirror, checked his footwork. Thought about that buff girl from his street dance session earlier. Turned up with those hot pants on. Fitter than his baby mum. Worth getting her number if she came again next week. Had to be eighteen, right? Seventeen, maybe. Imagined teaching her all kinds of extra things…

The thud and tinkle of shattering glass wrenched him back.

Must've come from the corridor, since the building was soundproofed. One of the framed photos fallen off the wall? Seemed weird. Then another possibility dawned on him and his pulse quickened.

Parker stopped dancing, walked towards the doorway. Thought he heard movement but the music was too loud to be sure. 'Who's that?' he called. No response. Stepped silently into the dim space outside the studio. Saw the mess of broken glass down to his left. Then his head snapped around and the burst of light in his vision turned to black as his legs buckled.

*

Next moment he was awake, head swimming. What happened? Felt like he was pissed, drugged up. Last thing he remembered was warming up in front of the mirror. Same windowless studio he was in now, except he wasn't dancing. He couldn't move. Seated, wrists tied down. Ankles too. Hard plastic that bit his skin. Belt around his waist held him to the chair. Side of his head started to throb, blood pulsing inside his right temple. Parker looked up to the big mirrors, clocked himself, then the figure standing behind him wearing a white face mask. Tried to say 'What the fuck?' but it came out slurred: 'Whahefu?' Brain started processing. He knew who it was.

Darian Wallace's face came into focus as he lifted off the mask. Teardrop tattoo, lean face, sharp cheekbones, thin smile. 'Thought it would make things a bit more dramatic, you know?'

Parker stared at his old friend's reflection in the mirror, swallowed.

'One ninety-nine from a fancy-dress shop.' Wallace pushed out his lower lip. 'Not bad. Like the Jabbawockeez crew wear. You'd appreciate that, Trent, dancers who choose to hide their faces.'

'Let me go, man.' Parker pulled his wrists against the chair arms. He was sharpening up now.

Wallace chuckled. 'No fun being held captive, is it?'

'Fucking psycho!'

'Let me give you some advice, mate. Don't make this any harder for yourself. You're not in a position to be backchattin' me.'

Parker's breathing was quicker; he fidgeted in the chair, drove his legs against the plastic clips at his ankles. 'The fuck do you want? I'm the one who lost his jewels, his money.'

'Didn't lose your freedom though, did you? Your girl. Your name on the street.' He came closer to Parker, bent down. 'Didn't have to defend yourself against some big fat battyman in the pen. Or anyone else who decides you looked at them funny in the lunch queue when no one's got your back. Man get all kind of shit flown inside by drones.' Wallace lifted his top, revealed a six-inch scar above the hip. 'Including a switchblade, turns out. Some guy tried to do me in, God knows why. He smoked a lot of skunk, probably made him hear things. Might've died if it'd gone any deeper. I was lucky. You did that. Course, things didn't work out too well for that kid. I couldn't risk him having another go, so I got myself on cleaning duty in his wing. Two weeks later he was staring off the fifth-floor balcony outside his cell, high off the smoke again. Didn't see me. I caught his knees from behind, tipped him over. Man landed head first, it was a mess. But I wasn't on cleaning rota for the ground floor,' he chuckled.

Parker was silent.

Wallace's laugh ended abruptly. 'That's before we get to my mum. On her own in a care home for two years. Couldn't see her. She couldn't visit me. Didn't know where I was. You made that happen too.'

There was anger in Wallace's voice, but not as much as Parker had expected. That worried him. He was detached, calm. Distant.

'Had to kiss man's arse, suck up to the screws, do laundry for time. Clean the floors. Go to classes on good behaviour where a psychologist that didn't know me chatted shit. Then I got a year off. And here I am. You should've got out of London while you had the chance, Trent.'

'Where could I go? You know I got no money now. The feds are on me, too – I'm watching my back the whole time.'

'Am I supposed to feel sorry for you? You're a snitch.'

'Darian, I had to. My kid was only—'

'Had to? Jesus Christ. We were like brothers, man. And you betrayed that. Like some Biblical shit. You know what the Old Testament says? Eye for an eye.'

'Please.' Parker felt his resolve weaken. Knew he couldn't escape.

'Code of the street, innit? Nuff man have died for less where we came from. Know what the judge said to me? "I sentence you to five years in prison." Five.' Wallace bent down, and Parker felt his breath on his ear as he spoke, the words more venomous now. 'Well, I find you guilty, Trent Parker, of breaking the law of brotherhood. Know what the price for that is?' He barked a single laugh. 'The Grim Reaper. I sentence you to the death penalty.'

'Don't kill me, Darian.'

Wallace cocked his head to one side, relaxed. 'You know what? I've got an idea. Since you were so good at negotiating a deal for yourself before, I'll offer you one now. How about your life in exchange for the location of that fat prick Harvey Ash?'

'What?'

'I want to know where he is. And if you're lying, I'll come back for you.'

'I don't know where he is.' Parker was blinking rapidly, felt tears pricking his eyeballs.

'Hm.' Wallace frowned. 'See, I find that hard to believe. Your mate who helped you sell your soul for your freedom, send me down, then between you try and work out where I've hid the stash? You're telling me you ain't spoken to him, even though you knew I was gettin' out? Come on.'

His hands flexed. 'I swear.'

Wallace studied him for a moment. Then he walked back to his bag and pulled out a small blue-black object. 'Remember this?' He rotated its safety cover and flicked the switch, releasing a high-pitched whirring. Parker knew exactly what it was. The tool that'd let them cut through metal hinges on the safe deposit boxes. Didn't need a demonstration but Wallace gave one anyway. Knelt down, put it to the floor. Its blurred disc bit into the hardwood like butter before he shut it off. 'I'll give you one more chance. Where's Ash?'

Parker filled his lungs and screamed. Loud as he could. Yelled for help – somebody, help. Wallace kicked over his chair, squatted alongside him.

'Shut up, man. Givin' me a headache. Place is soundproofed, in case you forgot.' He held the angle grinder to Parker's left hand. 'Where is he? I'm not playing.'

Parker was sobbing, his hand vainly jerking around. 'Please.'

'Wrong answer.' Wallace flicked the switch, grabbed Parker's pinky by its tip. Yanked out sideways, sliced it off. Dropped the digit. Parker stared at it for a few seconds in silence. Watched blood running from the stump. Then he began howling, wailing. Couldn't control it.

'Tell you what,' said Wallace. 'I'll leave it here, even call an ambulance for you when I go. Doctors can reattach that shit nowadays. And if not, well, you can probably still breakdance with a finger missing. Let's try again.' He turned the angle grinder on.

'OK, OK!' Parker let out another scream. Retched, held it down. Gasped. 'Just put that thing away.' Gave a long, low moan.

'Where?'

'Crystal Palace. In the caravan park.'

Wallace nodded. Backed away, replaced the angle grinder in his bag.

Parker exhaled. 'Please just let me go,' he whispered. 'I've told you everything.'

'Right.' But Wallace didn't move.

'That was the deal.' His words were choked, desperate. 'What you said, just now. My life for his location, right?'

Wallace reached down, pulled the chair upright. Stood behind him.

'Darian, please.' Parker made eye contact in the mirror, turned his head wildly. 'Cut me loose, man.'

'Alright.' He walked over to the bag.

'Thank you,' mumbled Parker.

Wallace pulled out a claw hammer.

Hyperventilating, Parker watched him cross back towards the chair. Dark metal with a bright yellow handle. Big. Hung at his side as he walked.

'Know what I've learned?' said Wallace. 'Life ain't fair.' He raised it overhead. 'Payback time.'

'Darian, no!'

'Might take a few goes. Ready?'

'No!'

'Fuckin' snitch.'

The hammer came down. Once was enough.

Boateng couldn't fault the rendition of Al Green's 'Let's Stay Together' that the singer and his eight-piece band were dropping. Across the table, Etta was clicking her fingers, eyes closed. He wished he was that relaxed. Normally Boateng loved coming to the Hideaway; he and Etta had been regulars at the Streatham nightspot since their third date. A small candlelit place where, no matter how many years went past, they could still own the dance floor. Dinner was fantastic, as usual. They'd both ordered a house special: Moroccan tagine with lamb that fell off the bone, washed down with a bottle of red wine. All perfect. Except tonight, again, his mind was elsewhere.

He took a mouthful of wine that was too big, felt it burn his throat slightly.

The afternoon's encounter with Froggy and his crew had left Boateng in the hinterland where excitement and fear blurred. On the plus side, he'd won the young rapper's trust enough to get time alone with him. That had resulted in Froggy – after serious ego massaging and the offer of more cash – agreeing to contact someone in Two-Ten. Despite shelling out six hundred quid of family holiday money for leads that ultimately might come to nothing, Boateng felt that tingle under his skin. He was drawing nearer to the truth about what happened to Amelia. Can't have been more than a dozen guys in the group when it existed. A chance, then, that whoever Froggy would introduce him to might've been the gunman himself. Either that, or could tell him who was. A tiny stab of adrenalin coursed through his belly.

But this produced the obvious question: what would he do with the answer when he had it?

Another large slug of red.

As investigations went, he was making progress. Apart from letting his team down by not giving a hundred per cent to the Wallace investigation, the biggest problem was his freelancing. The Met didn't know about any of it, which served his purposes right now. But it meant that no one had his back. That tall guy with the Puffa jacket in Angell Town had very likely been carrying a pistol today. Next bloke might be packing something too. At this rate, law of averages said he'd see a weapon up close before long, especially if he was asking awkward questions. No amount of fast-talking could help him then. Was it time to protect himself?

Boateng caught the waiter's eye, signalled for another bottle.

Were these morbid thoughts only about security, or something more... proactive? He hadn't explicitly considered what he'd do if he came face to face with Amelia's killer. Follow his training, right? Minimise personal risk and maintain cover. Gather solid evidence and present it to the relevant murder squad, despite question marks over trust. Logical advice from his right brain. Left brain told him to get creative. He'd read psychology research on how common it was to have violent fantasies of retribution against an attacker. One of many normal processes after a trauma. How many times had he imagined beating that man to death with raw, bloodied knuckles? Slowly choking the life out of him, another favourite. Boateng allowed these dark daydreams to come, sometimes even cultivated them as a safety valve for the frustration of his powerlessness. For almost five years they'd just been abstract. Now, meeting his daughter's murderer was steadily becoming a possibility. Of course, he knew reason would get the better of his emotions if that point of confrontation ever arrived. Wouldn't it? The image of his hands gripping the killer's neck returned, squeezing with all his strength—

'Zac!'

Etta was standing before him, her red dress hugging her full figure. She nodded towards the stage. The guitarist had struck up the riff of Horace Brown's 'Things We Do For Love'.

'Come on,' she smiled. 'Don't break your promise.'

Enough thinking. Boateng gulped down the rest of his wine, took her hand and stepped onto the dance floor.

Time for another shufti out back.

Spike had been watching the front of the building solidly all afternoon and evening. Knew there was a rear door, but it was accessible only via a fifteen-foot wall from a locked car park on the other side. Had to pick one entrance, and front was more likely. Plus he had cover to be there. Have to be Spider-Man to get in the back way. Half an hour ago, Spike had climbed over carefully – didn't want to do an ankle – and checked on Parker. Couldn't hear much, but some light spilling from the studio into the corridor at the rear suggested he was inside. Probably still dancing like a muppet. Spike had returned to his recon position at the front. Earlier, he'd clocked everyone else in and out of K Studios. It was now 10.15 p.m., and by Spike's calculations, Parker was the only one left in the building.

He returned to the rear yard, peered in the window. Same dim corridor. Same hint of sound from the studio. But there was something new this time: small dark patch on the floor by the doorway, catching light. Spike knew blood when he saw it.

He took out his shove knife, slipped it down the side. Had to work hard – the door lock was heavy. After a few attempts it clicked open. Music grew louder but no alarm tripped. He had a feeling what he might find.

Spike drew his Sig and entered. Crept towards the light, pistol raised. Corridor was clear. Blood trail ran inside the studio. Spike followed it around the doorway.

Parker was strapped to a chair, head forward, great big claw hammer sticking out of his noggin. Eyes shut. Finger on the floor. Jesus. Like something out of one of them torture-porn films. Not the worst he'd ever seen, mind.

Spike approached, aware he might already be contaminating the crime scene with his own fibres and DNA. Pulled his bike snood up over mouth and nose. Bent level with Parker, pressed a knuckle to his arm. Still warm. Touched the carotid artery, waited ten seconds: nothing.

Parker's eyes opened.

Spike recoiled. Not expecting that. Poor fella wasn't long for this world. Chance for some intel though. He got closer.

'Where's Darian Wallace?'

Parker stared ahead, gave one laboured breath.

'Oi. Can you hear me? Where is Wallace?' He cocked the hammer back on the pistol. 'Tell me where he is and I'll do this quick for you. Make the pain stop.'

Parker seemed to register the words; one eye flickered. Tried to say something. Sounded like 'Gaaa'. Pure gibberish.

'What?'

Blood dribbled from his mouth. 'Cara... van.'

'Caravan? Where?'

Parker gave one long breath, his gaze fixed. That was it. Little bastard had died before he could say any more. Spike de-cocked the pistol. Was Wallace living in a caravan? For now, he needed to get out of here before anyone else showed up. Spike spent three minutes erasing any trace of his own presence, closed the rear door behind him.

Wallace had maybe a fifteen-minute head start. Spike had a motorbike.

Someone would find Parker's body in the morning.

CHAPTER TWENTY-THREE

Sunday, 25 June 2017

Boateng had a serious feeling of déjà vu.

Early start on a weekend. Tape across the building frontage, white suits moving inside, camera flashes. Chair, restraints, blood on the floor. Hammer embedded in the victim's skull. But it was Southwark this time, and the dead man wasn't a pawnbroker. Like Harris though, he was on Wallace's list.

Trent Parker.

The other difference was Jones. Although they had both attended the scene in Deptford last weekend, this time she was like a different officer. Boateng could see her confidence had grown in just eight days on the case. Her shock subsided quickly and they began analysing together, Boateng letting her lead. Malik and Connelly had come too and were outside interviewing the dance studio manager and night security guard. With Volz on her way, they got started.

'What d'you reckon?'

Jones stared at the body, spoke through her mask. 'Restraints and hammer, like an execution. Planned in detail. Cut a finger off as well – only one this time. Clean, probably same kind of mechanical blade used on Harris. Could've been a punishment, or maybe the killer wanted information. Got to be Wallace, right?' She turned to Boateng. 'We knew he was after Parker.' There was guilt in her voice.

'Did everything we could. Told him he was in danger, offered protection twice. His right to refuse it.' That was accurate, but Boateng still felt the pang himself, the weight of personal responsibility, followed by a burst of frustration at Krebs's refusal to sanction the surveillance he'd recommended on Parker. The hangover wasn't helping either, further sapping his minimal energy reserves. He'd been in the Hideaway with Etta while this was happening, drinking and dancing. If he'd worked harder, could this death have been prevented? The young man had been arrogant, offensive, a thief. But he didn't deserve to die. And no one should have to endure this end. Now there was another kid without a dad, parents without a child. 'I know it's worse,' he told Jones. 'When you've met the victim, seen them alive.'

'I'm OK.' She paused a beat, gathered herself. Scanned the room, traced an arc with her finger from the door into the studio. 'Let's say it's Wallace then. He knows Parker's in here alone, could've been watching him. Comes in the back way, less chance of being seen, overpowers Parker somehow. Maybe that was the bruise on his face. Same as the blunt force trauma on Harris's head. Then he ties him up, chops off a finger, kills him with the hammer, leaves.' Her eyes flicked around. 'We think Wallace wanted to find Ash too, right?' Boateng nodded. 'What if the finger was about that? He took one digit off Parker but four from Harris. Maybe Wallace stopped torturing Parker because he gave up what he knew. That means he might have some connection to Ash still, even if the man's off the grid in every other respect.' Before Boateng could respond, she called over to the SOCOs: 'Did you guys find a phone on Parker?'

'Yup,' replied one, pointing. 'In the bag over there. Was plugged into the stereo.'

'We get full analysis on that,' said Jones to Boateng, 'it could tell us about Ash. Call log, texts, emails. Cross-reference with known numbers and look for anomalies. A mobile that's on and off, remote, or doesn't move much. The odd one out. Cell site data might even take us to Ash. Which is probably where Wallace is heading next.'

Despite the grim scene and his own negative emotions, Boateng managed a smile. In two minutes she'd mastered the disgust any normal person would feel then used deduction and inference to produce a credible operational lead. He could see why she was one of the fastest-promoted officers in the Met.

'Good work, Kat,' he said. The corners of her mask rose as she took the compliment.

Malik appeared in the doorway. He couldn't help glancing at the body. 'Manager's in a right old state. One of the lads had to go get her another cup of tea. I've said no one's to let her in, don't want her to get an eyeful of this.'

Boateng frowned. 'The manager hasn't seen him? As in, she didn't call us?'

'Nope. Says the place is closed on Sundays.'

'OK, back up a second.' Boateng raised his hands, looked from Jones to Malik. 'Then how come we're even here?'

'Sorry, boss?' Malik looked confused.

Jones answered. 'Homicide Assessment Team called it in. Lambeth lot.'

'Yeah. But how did they know Parker was dead? Studio's got no windows. And no other staff came this morning to open up. Follow me.' He led them out to the courtyard and across to a picnic table, where a man about Zac's age sat smoking. His receding hairline was visible despite his shaved head. Stubble across his face and neck, above a loosened tie, made it look like he hadn't slept in days. A ridged brow and prominent jaw fixed his expression in a scowl. That didn't change as Boateng approached and introduced himself.

'DCI Dave Maddox,' he replied.

'From?'

'Lambeth MIT.' He took a big drag on the cigarette, stared down his crooked nose at Zac as if the encounter was already an imposition.

'Thanks for calling us, sir. Appreciate you checking the link to our case off a night shift.' He received a grunt of acknowledgement. 'Your people first on the scene?'

Maddox exhaled a big cloud of smoke towards them. 'Southwark patrol car was, they belled us.'

'Where'd the original tip come from then?' Boateng smiled, making an effort.

'Anonymous call to the Crimestoppers line.' He stubbed out the fag, stood up. He was taller than Boateng would've guessed from his slumped posture at the table. Six four, built like a rugby player. 'No name or number, before you ask. Details are in the email.' Without offering a hand he turned, walked away.

'Thank you, sir,' called Boateng after him. Shook his head. Maybe Krebs wasn't so bad. His thoughts quickly returned to the mystery call. Could Wallace have alerted the police to a murder he'd committed? But what did that mean? Letting his guard down perhaps, or playing a game?

Malik clapped him on the shoulder. 'Don't worry, boss. If you acted like that we'd tell you quick sharp.'

'Cheers, Nas.' He saw Connelly jogging towards them. 'And Pat has full permission to Taser me.'

'What did you say to that fella?' asked Connelly. 'Face like a bag of dead rats.'

'Never mind.' Boateng stared after Maddox a second. 'What did our security man have?'

'I think you'll like this, Zac.' The Irishman's eyebrows jigged. 'He's got a hidden camera showing someone leaving via that little car park behind the studio at 10.04 p.m.'

'Wallace?'

'Probably. Then a second figure going in and out ten minutes later.'

Boateng and Jones exchanged a look of disbelief.

'Gets better,' continued Connelly. 'Second one's armed – nine-millimetre handgun by the look of it.'

'Our anonymous caller?' suggested Jones.

Boateng nodded. 'You're on fire today, Kat. And I'd be really impressed if you can tell me who he is.'

Nothing. Sweet FA. That's what his search last night had achieved. Spike felt like he'd been down every street in south-east London, hunting for Wallace into the early hours. No trace. So he'd gone home, brewed up and re-examined the background stuff from Patey's contact. Tried to make sense of Parker's last word. If Wallace was out for revenge, who was he after? He'd done the pawnbroker and the dancer, and the cops would be all over Fletcher's place – if she wasn't in protective custody already. Who was left? Harvey Ash: the muppet with no known address. Spike did the obvious with two plus two and realised it was probably Ash he was looking for in the caravan, not Wallace. Sent a WhatsApp message asking the insider to confirm it.

After a couple of hours' kip he was back on the motorbike.

Needles in haystacks though. Wished Parker had given him better intel before croaking. By 11 a.m. he'd already been to two London caravan sites. Shown a photo, given the story about a dead relative and some inheritance. Offered money. But nobody knew anything, no one had seen Ash. Just had to check all the caravan parks one by one, that's what the colonel would expect. But Spike had the feeling time was running out. He was grasping at threads to find Wallace. If he screwed up again it might be his last chance to earn eight hundred quid a day working for Patey.

Not to mention nailing the cocky little bastard he was hunting. Money and respect.

Spike walked slowly down the close in South Bermondsey, paralleling the railway line over the fence. This place was one of four official traveller sites listed by Southwark Council. Sort of place you might find someone living in a caravan. But they didn't look like a bunch of pikeys. More brick housing than caravans. People had even stuck up hanging baskets for decoration.

Taking out the photo, he approached a chubby young woman with bleached hair hanging laundry off a line. Forced himself to smile. 'Hello, madam.'

'Top o' the morning' to ye,' she replied flatly.

He unfolded the paper, held it out. 'I'm looking for this man.'

'Bailiff?'

'Nothing like that.' He kept grinning. 'I represent a solicitor's firm, tracing relatives who've been left money in a will.'

'Lucky folk.' She studied the image a second. 'Well, I haven't seen the fella.'

'Are you sure? There's a fee in it for anyone who has.'

'I'm sure.'

'Is there anyone else around here I could—'

'Who're you?' The voice behind him was deep, aggressive.

Spike wheeled round, clocked the man. Tall geezer, heavyset. Huge scar on his jaw. Couple of knuckles missing: a fighter. And clearly pissed off. Bloke didn't wait for an answer, stepped towards him. 'What business've you talking to my wife here?'

Be nice, he told himself. 'I was just asking—'

'Asking what?'

'Leave it, Jimmy.' The woman had stopped pegging clothes. 'The man's no bother, he's from a lawyers'.'

'What's he doing in my yard then?' Big lad's body was tense, ready for drama. 'You've no right to be here. Tell your lawyers they can piss off.'

'It's not about us,' said the woman.

'You keep out of it.' He jabbed a finger at her. 'I'm speakin' to him.'

He played it through in his mind: man takes another step forward, Spike's left hand lifts the shirt at his back, right grabs Sig from belt, left comes around into cup and saucer grip, double tap – boom-boom – two rounds in the chest. Dropped. Less than a second start to finish. Even drawing would be enough to stop this guy acting a silly bollocks. Not so hard now, are you? Spike loved that moment when someone giving it all the chat saw a weapon and realised they weren't the man any more. But if you draw, gotta be prepared to use it. And he wasn't, at least not here, with a witness standing right next to him. Woman already said she hadn't seen Ash. Sounded like the truth. Best option now was a tactical retreat. Let this bloke think he's got the upper hand.

He backed off slowly, hands spread. 'You're right, my mistake. I'll be on my way.'

There were more caravan parks to check. He'd do the other three traveller sites then head south to Crystal Palace.

Boateng had made excuses about needing to go back for a briefing with Krebs, leaving his team to continue wrapping up with the SOCOs and on-site interviews. Said he'd see them at the office for coffee, doughnuts and operational planning in two hours. Enough time before the pre-arranged meeting in Brixton to hit the bank and empty his personal savings account of another two thousand pounds. Definitely the end of his plan to take Etta and Kofi on holiday to South Africa. He felt like the bank teller could see his betrayal. At that moment, he hated himself. Tried to ignore the heavy feeling of shame and concentrate on why he'd got the cash: Agyeman.

Off shift, his doorman pal had told Boateng to come over to Block Workout in Brixton. The rugged outdoor gym was a maze of kit for body-weight training, against a backdrop of bright colours and heavy basslines. Tractor tyres, oil drums and kegs for lifting lay strewn around, more stacked at the side. At 10 a.m. on a Sunday the place was heaving and he found it harder than usual to spot the giant Ghanaian amongst the crowd of hulking athletes. Agyeman was doing dips on parallel steel bars, thick arms repeatedly pushing up with muscles visible that Boateng wasn't sure he even possessed.

Agyeman spotted him, finished the set. Dropped down, ripped off his gloves. They slapped palms. 'Strict form,' grinned the big man. 'That's the secret.'

'I'll take your word for it.' Boateng wasn't much in the mood for banter. He'd thought very carefully about what he was going to ask. Considered it from all angles. Repercussions for himself, for Agyeman. The doorman had already done him a favour to locate Optikon, whose introduction to Froggy meant Boateng was close to meeting someone from Two-Ten proper. His feeling of vulnerability had crystallised into a desire for protection. That's what he told himself.

They wandered over to the high perimeter fence, stood alongside a brick wall. Boateng briefly felt as if the cartoon faces on its street-art mural were watching him. Kept his voice low. 'I know I've asked a lot of you, Sammy, but there's one more thing I need.'

'Name it.'

'A gun.'

Agyeman emitted a high-pitched laugh, clapped him on the shoulder. 'Zac! Please, you're talking crazy.'

'Nine-millimetre pistol, ideally a Glock. And a box of ammunition.'

'Are you on drugs?'

Boateng produced a wad of fifty-pound notes. 'I've done my homework. Here's two grand.'

The smile faded as Agyeman realised he was serious. 'What the hell are you thinking?' He sucked his teeth, pushed Boateng's hand away.

'I need to be safe where I'm going,' replied Boateng. Wasn't sure if he believed himself. 'You've helped me enough already, so you can tell me to piss off. Wouldn't want to cause any trouble for you.'

'Why don't you get a replica? People can even make those with 3D printers these days. They look good. If we just ask—'

'Sammy.' Boateng jabbed the money at him. 'It's got to be the real thing. Can't go into another situation like I did before without backup.'

'Then take me along with you.'

Boateng gestured towards his bulging arms. 'Sometimes that's not enough. Anyway, I can't put you in danger. I'll take that risk myself, but I won't bring it to anyone else. It's your call if you want to do this for me. No problem if you don't.'

Agyeman was silent.

'Look, Sammy, I can't trust my colleagues. I've got to bring this guy in alone. I can't live knowing that I walked away when I was so close to finding Amelia's killer. The man who took my daughter from me. I'm not about to let him take me down too.'

The big man gave a long breath, fixed Zac with a stare. 'Tell me the truth. When you find this man, are you going to kill him?'

Boateng kept eye contact, swallowed. 'No,' he said quietly.

'Swear?'

'I swear.'

Agyeman nodded, made a discreet beckoning motion with one hand. Zac handed him the cash.

CHAPTER TWENTY-FOUR

'Alright, guys.' Boateng strode into the office, clapped. The action was as much to marshal his own focus as to get the team's attention. He had to be back in the zone now, put aside his conversation with Agyeman. All the way home he'd thought about it, tormented himself. Was there another way to achieve his aim? A safer approach with greater chance of success? There was no denying that when Agyeman accepted the money, he'd got a buzz. Boyish excitement of which he was instantly ashamed. It piled on top of guilt at the lies he found himself telling to everyone now. If he carried on ruminating like this he'd go insane. Had to find some distraction, concentrate on the matter in hand. He cleared his throat. 'Gather round. Thanks for cancelling your Sunday plans, whatever they were.'

'Just a lazy morning speaking the language of love to my French beans,' replied Connelly. 'Best way to make 'em grow.'

'Not sure I wanna know, Pat. Great work this morning by everyone.' Jones passed him a coffee and he nodded his thanks. Malik and Connelly wheeled chairs around. 'If you thought last week was tough, we've got two murders on our hands now. You can expect to see Parker in the news pretty soon – Wallace's face out there again too.'

'And gone from the headlines by tomorrow morning.' Connelly slurped his mud-brown tea.

'You're a cynic, Pat,' said Boateng.

'Not me, boss, I'm an optimist. I'll take a beating for two-and-a-half rounds and still believe I can knock the other fella out. It's just the way news is these days. Story's up there for five minutes then gets replaced by some celebrity's arse.'

'Never know. We might catch a lead. Krebs is all over the media stuff anyway. She's briefing the press now. How's your optimism helping with the facial recognition? Any luck?'

Connelly shook his head. 'Nothing so far. I'll keep trying, work outwards from the murder scene last night. General CCTV too.'

'OK.' Boateng turned to Jones. 'How about Harvey Ash?'

'All our previous database searches drew a blank. But there might be something in Parker's mobile. We've got a quick-and-dirty from forensics on his phone. Nas and I have run the numbers already.' She smiled at Malik, who did his best to look modest. 'Eliminated all but one. Unregistered mobile called three times by Parker since Wallace got out of prison but not before that. Our guess is it's Ash. We know they colluded to put Wallace away; makes sense they'd be in contact the last two weeks.'

'I agree. So what's your plan?' He already knew, just wanted her to reason through it.

'Request cell site data, find Ash from above.'

'I know he's meant to be a large fella,' said Connelly. 'But that's a long shot.'

Jones shrugged. 'So's a public appeal.'

'True.' Boateng didn't need convincing of that. Scratched his jaw. It was the best lead they had right now. 'Know how to do the form?'

Jones nodded. 'I put one through in Cyber Crime.'

'OK. Start filling it out and I'll work on Krebs. She's gonna complain about the cost, always does.'

'Grand a pop, right?' Malik reached for a doughnut.

'Yeah, not to mention there already being a list long as your arm of requests from terrorism cases. And it's a Sunday. I'll do my best but we might be back of the queue.'

'Back?' exclaimed Jones, wide-eyed. 'The guy's a double murderer! Ash is probably his next victim. And it's back of the frigging queue?'

'Middle then.' He took a swig of coffee, amusement at her incredulity fading quickly as he wondered what his own cell sites might reveal about the little private investigation he'd been running over the past week.

'Boss is right, Kat.' Malik spoke through a mouthful of doughnut. 'Sounds weird but murder isn't top priority. I mean, not like anything's gonna go bang, is it?'

Jones wasn't smiling. 'It might.'

Wallace peered in the caravan window. Couldn't see much, but looked like no one was inside. This is where the friendly old dear said 'Danny' was staying. He took out the new hammer he'd bought that morning from the elderly Pakistani man. Stuck its claw in the flimsy door lock, popped it open. Glanced around. No one paying attention. He stepped up and in.

Empty.

Place was tiny, cramped. Wallace could barely stand up straight. How did such a fat man survive in here? He scanned the interior. Little cooker in the corner, some cupboards, bed down the other end. Door leading to a toilet stuck diagonally to fit in. The solitary folding chair made him smile: that could work. Ceiling wasn't high enough to swing a hammer but there'd be another way. He began searching for information. Found a handwritten receipt for the caravan pitch made out to 'D. Ellis'. Must have a fake ID or something. A security shift rota for Limes Avenue business units, Penge. 'Ellis' appeared every day or two. Wallace found today's date. Sunday, 25 June: Ellis was on night shift, 7 p.m. till 7 a.m. on Monday. It was about three in the afternoon. So where was he now? Probably at the shop buying all the pies.

Wallace slumped into the chair, pulled his bag up close. Felt his limbs relaxing. A wave of tiredness came over him. How much longer could he keep going like this? Began to wonder if life wasn't easier on the inside. He was sleeping in a garage, unwashed and stinking, shitting in public toilets, hiding from everyone. And this was supposed to be freedom. Maybe it didn't matter if he let Ash get away with his betrayal... Immediately, Wallace scolded himself for being a pussyhole. Stick to the plan. It was nearly done, then his new life would start. Just a couple more jobs to do. But he had to stay awake, otherwise it'd all be over. Falling asleep meant getting caught. Not to mention the same old nightmare that would surely come for him, like it did every time he shut his eyes now. The Grim Reaper with his pistol, the agonising trigger-pull.

Reaching into his holdall, he took out the angle grinder. Turned it over, examining the diamond-tipped blade. He'd got rid of the messy one he'd used on Parker, dropped it in a drain. This one was clean, shiny. Wallace flicked a fingernail against it. Maybe he could just wait here for Ash to come back.

He sank further into the chair, closed his eyes. Started drifting.

A child's squeal outside snapped his head up. How long had he been asleep? Then another sound: footsteps. They were too heavy for a kid. And getting closer.

Time to move.

'Sit down.'

Spike motioned Harvey Ash toward the chair. Fat bastard dropped into it, canvas creaking under his bulk. Clutching the carrier bag of groceries like a muppet. His top lip quivered, gaze fixed on the pistol.

'Put the bag down. I'm not here to hurt you,' said Spike. 'I want Darian Wallace. Tell me where he is.'

'I don't know.' Ash's cheeks were flushed, his breathing shallow. 'Who are you?'

'Oi, I'll ask the questions.' Spike pulled the Sig's hammer back with his thumb. It made a satisfying click against the caravan interior's silence. People always shat themselves when they heard that sound. Muppets didn't realise you could still fire without doing that. Or that doing it didn't equal a shot. They just thought the noise meant a round was coming their way. Though sometimes it did, obviously. 'Where is he?'

'No idea. I swear, mate.'

He could almost feel sorry for this sack of shit, trapped in a pathetic life, looking over his shoulder for a man he must've guessed wanted revenge. 'You know he's coming for you.' Statement, not question.

Ash didn't reply. Just whimpered.

'In fact, he might've already been here today.' Spike de-cocked the Sig, nodded left. 'Door was unlocked when I came in. You leave it like that?'

Ash shook his head, cheeks wobbling.

'He knows you're here. You hear how the last two died?'

The fat man swallowed. Spike gripped the pistol in his right hand, fished out a card from his jeans with his left. 'Got a phone?'

Ash dipped his head. 'In my pocket.'

'Leave it there. This is my number.' He tossed the card into Ash's lap. 'I'll be close by. Get a hint he's around, you dial it quick sharp. I find him, you get some decent cash. That's what this was all about, wasn't it? Money.'

Ash studied the eleven digits. Nothing else printed.

Spike tucked the Sig back into his belt. 'Plus, I might just save your life. That's worth a call isn't it?'

'Budge up.'

Zac perched on the bed, one leg over the side. Next to him, Kofi sat propped against a pillow. They opened the battered book of Anansi stories. 'This was Grandad's,' Zac explained. 'Traditional folk tales from Ghana. Remember?'

'I like Anansi. He's an African Spider-Man!' Kofi mimed shooting webs from his wrists with accompanying sound effects.

Zac riffled the pages, flicked over a few more and held out the book. Kofi began reading aloud. It took Zac several seconds to realise what he'd chosen: the story of Anansi and Brother Death. Psychoanalysis would've said the selection was anything but random. Now as Kofi read, the tale took on a new light. Anansi the spider goes into an old man's house again and again, helping himself to food and drink without permission. One day he brings his daughter to the old man and leaves her there to cook. When he returns, the girl has vanished. Only then does Anansi understand that the old man was Death, and he has taken his daughter. He flees and Death chases him to his own home, where it begins to capture the other members of his family in a sack one by one. All the while, Death says to him, 'I want you.' Zac's mouth felt dry as Kofi reached the end: the spider and his family escape thanks to a trick he pulls, but at too great a cost. Anansi lost his daughter and nearly sacrificed his son, too.

Zac knew he was gambling with big chips. He'd taken risks already – with his career as much as his physical safety – and he'd asked Agyeman to risk prison time acquiring the gun, but it hadn't yet occurred to him that his obsession might put his family in harm's way. He didn't believe in prophecies, but maybe this was a warning from his unconscious.

'He cheated Death, didn't he, Dad?' Kofi giggled. 'Anansi thought he was going to die and then he escaped!' He slapped the page in delight.

Zac stroked his son's hair. 'It was a close-run thing though.'

'Why did Death come for him?' Kofi shut the book.

'Because Anansi was arrogant and doing something he shouldn't have been.'

They sat in silence for a moment.

'Death came for my sister, didn't he?' Kofi's voice was quiet.

'Yes.' Zac put an arm around his narrow shoulder. 'He did. But we never forget her.'

'Was she doing something she shouldn't have been?'

'No, she wasn't. Someone else was.'

'Who?'

'I don't know.'

Kofi considered this. 'Where is she now?'

Boateng stood, bent down and tapped his own temple. 'In here.' He kissed his son's forehead then touched it lightly. 'And in there.'

'Mummy says she's in our hearts, too.'

'Yes, she is.' They hugged, holding one another tight. 'Sleep well, son.' Zac squeezed his hand, then turned to leave.

'Dad?'

'Yes?'

'Will Death come for us too?'

Zac returned to the bedside, held his boy once more. 'No, he won't.' The words felt empty.

Downstairs, he fired up the tablet and went to YouTube. It wouldn't be long now: Froggy could come through any day. Had to know who he was up against. If the Anansi story had made him pause for thought, it hadn't shaken his drive. Like it was too late to pull out, even if he hit the brakes. He clicked and scrolled down videos posted by Froggy to his own channel. Watched three or four, repeating one where guys appeared in the background, faces covered. Hit pause to stare into the masks. Were these the young men who killed his daughter?

'Hey, baby!'

Zac was so absorbed he hadn't heard the front door. Etta slung her bag and keys down on the table, beamed at him. 'Mum and Dad were in a good mood tonight, they only mentioned my brother's spectacular list of life achievements four or five times.' Rolled her eyes. 'Whatcha doing?'

'Nothing. Just about to watch *Match of the Day*.'

She took the kettle over to the sink, frowned. 'It's June, Zac. Even I know that's not Premier League season.'

Damn. 'Yeah, it's internationals.'

He quickly cleared the last hour's history and switched off the screen. Stood and embraced her, kissed briefly. As they pulled apart he could see Etta was still looking at the tablet, her smile gone.

CHAPTER TWENTY-FIVE

Monday, 26 June 2017

'Zac!' Etta called down the stairs.

'Mm?' Sounded like he had a mouthful of food.

She pulled on the Paul Smith suit jacket. 'Have you done his lunchbox?'

'Mm.' Wasn't clear what that noise meant.

'Make sure you put the carrot sticks in for him.'

'Mm.' Equally vague. Better see what was going on.

Her boys were in the kitchen. Big one making sandwiches on the side while shovelling in toast. Little one at the table, bent forward drinking from his cereal bowl. 'Kof! What've I told you? Use your spoon.'

'Sorry, Mum.' Bowl and spoon clattered to the table.

About to intervene further, Etta checked herself. Remembered her mindfulness class at work: breathe, notice, let it go. 'Be a good boy today, OK? Work hard.' She kissed Kofi on the head then touched Zac's arm. 'See you tonight, love.'

He pulled a face. One that normally excused bad behaviour. 'Maybe.'

'What do you mean?'

'Work.' Zac shrugged. 'The usual right now.'

She frowned. 'You're picking him up from school though?'

'Yeah, but once you're back I might have to go out again.'

'Come on, Zac.' Frustration rose but she told herself to chill. What was all this about? He'd been so weird lately, creeping around, hiding things. She knew the Met had frozen overtime on all but critical cases, yet her husband was working 24/7. And it seemed like something had changed in Zac recently. Part of him felt out of reach from her. They'd been through so much together, for better and worse, tackled it as a team. Over the past week, though, his behaviour had become erratic, secretive. Last time he acted like that – a year ago – it turned out he was planning a surprise weekend in Berlin for their fifteenth wedding anniversary. But there were no big dates coming up except for Ammy's passing. More than that, she'd caught him out a couple of times: uncharacteristic omissions rather than clear lies.

Zac was a sharp guy but he'd become distracted, unfocused in the last few days. She'd even seen it at the club on Saturday night, when normally he loved that place. He'd drunk too much, wasn't into it when they danced. Was there something else going on? A few years back, one of her best friends found her husband cheating, the awful cliché of a younger female colleague. Etta didn't have any reason to think he was being unfaithful, no evidence suggested that. Even so, there was this Jones woman he'd started working with in the past couple of weeks, Zac had talked about her in glowing terms...

Stop. Notice that thought. Come on, surely this was just paranoia talking. It was her Zac. She trusted him. And they could talk about anything, couldn't they? Not knowing was starting to get to her though, and the frustration returned.

'What's going on?' she demanded.

'What do you mean?' he said through a mouthful of toast. 'Nothing.'

'You're acting weird.' She was aware Kofi was listening.

Zac shook his head. 'You're imagining things.'

'Don't tell me what I'm thinking,' she snapped, then checked herself. Took a breath. 'Look, do whatever you need to do. I'll be back at seven.'

'Thanks, love.' He didn't look up. Just crammed more toast in his mouth, cut the sandwiches.

She'd confront him about it properly when the time was right. Without Kofi there, and with more tangible evidence than just his odd behaviour.

Eyes level with the ground, Wallace lay prone between two thick bushes and scanned the park's horizon. Someone who wasn't Ash had come to the caravan yesterday afternoon. Wallace had got out just in time, caught nothing more than a glimpse of the guy before legging it. After that near miss, he'd gone back to the lockup to sleep before returning here at 5 a.m. and taking up his current position at first light. Ready for Ash to come off the night shift. He'd risked using the angle grinder for a second, sliced branches off a tree further back to cover himself. Confident he was pretty much invisible now to anything except dogs snouting around for a place to shit.

Trap laid, he just needed the prey to arrive. Initially that sparked a familiar thrill. But it had worn off in an hour and Wallace found himself losing concentration, dozing again. The nightmare had jolted him awake. Thought he might've made a noise at the gunshot ending, but if so he reckoned nobody heard. That was a couple of hours ago, just after dawn, and the park had been silent.

The rota said Ash was working night shift in Penge till seven, so the fat boy should be back around now. If anything, he was late. What must it be like to know you were about to die? Of course, Ash wasn't aware of that yet, not in a real sense. Unlike

Parker, when he'd seen the hammer raised two nights ago. Ash would be in the same position soon, strapped to the flimsy chair with plastic ties, his melon head an easy target. That brought a smile briefly.

Wallace needed to occupy his mind. He'd already run through the plan in detail three times, the last things he had to do. Daydreamed about a new life in Europe. Once he'd got the cash he could even relocate somewhere warm – Jamaica, maybe? Felt like a turning point, a chance to start again.

As the waiting continued, Wallace found himself going back over certain decisions he'd made. A lot had been motivated by money. Drug dealing after he left school, small robberies to start off and then the safe deposit box job. But cash wasn't his sole objective. He wanted respect too.

That was why he killed.

Money came and went but your name was everything. It outlived you. It was you to people you'd never met; it shaped others' decisions across space and time. Life had taught him by his mid teens that you don't let anyone push you around. Meet force with more force. Someone throws a punch, crack 'em over the head with your belt buckle. Someone snitches on you, dead them. Simple rules.

But there was one thing that nagged him. What about the people close to those you killed? Did the effect on them matter? Might make you think twice about revenge if it did. He imagined his own mum before she'd lost the plot, how his death would've destroyed her, eaten away till there was nothing left. He'd done that to people, and for what – his name? Did his name mean anything to the guy who came at him in prison with a switchblade? Course not. So what good was—

There he was.

Ash appeared from behind some caravans, waddling towards his own. He rubbed both eyes. Looked exhausted, like a wildebeest that's been chased by a lion in one of those documentaries on Africa. Before the lion rips its head off. Rage swelled within Wallace at the thought of this flabby joker plotting with Parker to take him down. Who did those snakes think they were dealing with?

Wallace inspected his holdall. Plastic ties ready. Rotated the safety cover off his angle grinder and returned it to the bag. Hammer in hand, he began to slide himself out from under the branches – a crocodile creep forward. Ash had his back turned now, fumbling in his pocket for keys. Payback time.

Stop.

A middle-aged man wandered in from the right, all cheery smiles and greetings to Ash. Had a kid behind him on a tiny BMX with stabilisers. Guy was waving some kind of electrical cable, pointing to it and asking questions. Ash stared at it like a moron then flapped a hand at his caravan and invited the guy inside.

Wallace watched the kid circling on the bike. Pushed himself back into the bush on his forearms.

He could wait a bit longer.

Private number.

Boateng stared at his mobile on the office desk. Already working out where to escape if it was Froggy using another line, he swiped the screen, picked up. 'Hello?'

'It's Maddox.'

'Oh, hi.' Must've got the number through switchboard. Boateng wandered across to the window. 'How are you, sir?'

'Knackered. Anyway, I wanted to apologise for yesterday. You lot were trying to work out what was going on and I didn't do you any favours. Duty night shift plus other stuff. Bastard twenty-four hours. You know how it is sometimes with the Job.'

'Yeah, I do.'

'Look, I was out of order not helping you guys more.' Maddox gave a throaty cough. 'Sorry.'

'No need to apologise, sir. We've all been there.'

'How's the hunt for Wallace going?'

'Not much further on. We're trying to find the other bloke implicated in the burglary back in 2014, Harvey Ash. Reckon he could be the next victim and we want to get to him first. Except he's vanished. And the public appeal hasn't turned up anything on Wallace. Our other long shot is CCTV and facial recognition around his last known whereabouts. But…' He trailed off, sighed. Articulating it, the probability of success now seemed pretty damned remote. 'When someone's got no regular network and doesn't want to be found, it's tough.'

'Tell me about it. Well, I'll let you get back.'

'The struggle continues, as my old man used to say. Appreciate the call, sir.' He rang off, frowned at the mobile.

'Boss!' Malik was waving him over, jabbing the monitor. 'We've got a result off the phone company.'

Boateng marched to the desk, where his team was studying a map overlaid with clusters of tiny triangles.

Jones glanced up. 'Number's most active in two spots. One's industrial units in Penge, likely he works there, so the other one's probably his home. Crystal Palace Park. Resolution's good enough to see it's this bit.' She circled a grey area among the green with her biro. 'Google Maps says it's a caravan site. Makes sense, doesn't it? No council tax or utility bills, stay off the electoral register.'

'Sneaky bastard.' Boateng shook his head. 'Alright, which borough?'

'That part's Bromley,' said Connelly, leaning over the back of Malik's chair. 'Although if you stand in Crystal Palace park you can chuck stones into Lewisham, Southwark, Lambeth and Croydon. Assuming you've got enough rocks. Though why you'd want to do that…'

'Thanks, Pat, we don't want to piss off the locals. Nice work, guys. When was it last pinged?'

Malik clicked and scrolled through a window full of digits. '7 a.m. at the industrial park. What d'you reckon boss, early shift or late?'

'Could be either. Kat and I will head to the caravan park, you two check out the industrial estate.' Boateng rapped knuckles on the desk. 'Let's go.'

CHAPTER TWENTY-SIX

Time's up.

Wallace had waited nearly half an hour. Bloke had gone inside, emerged at the caravan door ten minutes later with a cup of tea. Chatted away to Ash like they were old buddies while the kid cycled around. Eventually he'd walked off, holding a different extension lead, with more waving and thanks, taking the boy with him. Jesus. They were so friendly it made Wallace feel sick. But now they were gone and Ash was alone.

He had to act quickly – the park was getting busier. Wallace manoeuvred forward out of the bushes and stood up. Shook off stiff limbs, flexed his fingers. Picked up the holdall and walked over to Ash's caravan, checking side to side. Listening. Switched the bag to his left hand, pulled out the hammer in his right. Heartbeat quickened slightly: he was the Grim Reaper again.

Now he was right outside and could hear Ash's movements within, the caravan creaking as his bulk shifted around. Sounded like he was cooking. 'Course he was, fat bastard. Wallace reached for the door handle.

'Danny Ellis's pitch is just over here, officers.'

Instinctively Wallace dropped, rolled under the caravan. Footsteps approached and he saw three pairs of shoes outside Ash's door. Just two metres away from him, maybe less. Large Crocs with hairy legs, a pair of plain black lace-ups under dark grey suit trousers and smaller, flat-heeled leather ankle boots below jeans. Two men and a woman. A male voice said thanks, they'd take it from here, and the Crocs departed. He recognised the voice from that time watching in the park. Boateng.

They banged on the side and politely asked for Mr Ellis. Door opened and after a brief exchange the shoes rose and disappeared. Began moving around above his head, heels tapping on the floor. The cheap unit swayed under the weight of three people and for a second Wallace thought it might collapse on him. He took a moment to think. Could he slide out and attack? Three birds with one stone. Stop Boateng and his sidekick investigating any more, remove the risk of them blocking his escape to France. And take out Ash. He'd have surprise on his side and they'd be trapped.

He gripped the angle grinder, stroked his thumb across the blade.

Boateng looked down at the portly younger man in front of him. He'd automatically sat in the chair as if expecting an interrogation. Like he knew he'd done something wrong before they'd even said why they were there. The sausages he'd been frying were getting cold.

'Harvey Ash,' stated Boateng.

The guy flicked his eyes to Jones and back. Trying to work out if this was a good cop, bad cop routine and if that meant the woman was on his side.

'That's your name,' Boateng continued. 'Or at least it was until a couple of years ago.'

Ash said nothing, simply nodded. His cheeks wobbled.

'Given us quite a runaround, this name-changing business. You're in trouble, you understand that?'

'Yes,' whispered Ash.

'Not with us, of course. Do you know Darian Wallace? Don't play games.'

'I did.'

'Seen him recently?' asked Jones.

Ash swallowed. 'No.'

'We think he's looking for you,' said Boateng. 'Not sure if you follow the news much out here, but he's already put a hammer through two skulls in the past ten days. One of whom you know, I believe. So, Detective Sergeant Jones and I would like you to come back to Lewisham with us. We'll look after you while we find Wallace, and in return you'll tell us everything you know about the guy.'

'Do I have to?'

'It's probably in your interests to help us find him.' Jones leaned back on the narrow counter.

'Am I under arrest?'

Boateng smiled. 'No. So it's up to you whether you accept our offer or not. Could always spend another day here, visit us tomorrow…'

'I'll come. But…'

'Yes?'

'You're not the only ones asking about Wallace.' Ash pivoted with difficulty, plucked the little card from under a mug on the counter next to Jones. 'Some bloke was here yesterday, he left this.'

Boateng and Jones exchanged a look. 'We want to hear all about him too. Come on.'

'Can I take my sausages?' Ash pointed to the frying pan.

Boateng suppressed a smile, blinked slowly. 'Go on then. But no grease on the car upholstery.' He threw open the door, stepped down. Something felt different. He stood still a moment, tried to work out what. Shook his head; probably just the fresh air after Ash's stuffy caravan.

Walking back to the car, Boateng checked his mobile. Damn! Must've missed the text from Agyeman while they were driving over. He stabbed the screen. Heart leapt in his chest, the fatigue he'd felt all day temporarily lifted.

Got what you wanted. Am at home now. Pick it up soon as.

'You alright, boss?' Jones's face tightened with concern. 'Anything important?' Ash had stopped too, watching.

Boateng realised he'd frozen, mobile held in front of him. 'No,' he replied, pocketing the phone. 'Just my wife. I need to go and see her once we've taken Mr Ash to the station.'

One hour later, Boateng was sitting in Agyeman's flat. The big man slid the shoebox across his kitchen table. Boateng hesitated, then pulled it towards himself with both hands. Even without lifting he could tell there was more inside than just the size nine Nike trainers stated on the label.

'Your change is in there too.' Agyeman gestured at the box. 'Call the trainers a gift. You could do with some more exercise,' he grinned.

'Sammy,' began Boateng. Didn't know what to say next. Stared at the orange cardboard. Flipped up its lid, carefully took out the shoes. Paused, glanced at Agyeman. The doorman nodded. No one else was home and they couldn't be observed: his friend's gigantic frame was blocking any view in from the window. Boateng slowly peeled away layers of tissue paper.

The dark grey pistol lay next to a small ammo box, atop some of the fifty-pound notes he'd given Agyeman at Block Workout. Boateng recognised its angular shape; almost any police officer would. He read the barrel engraving: *GLOCK 19 AUSTRIA 9x19*.

'Serial's been removed,' said Agyeman proudly. But Boateng knew that wasn't enough to avoid identification. Not only could chemical techniques recover a firearm's unique number, but the rifling in its barrel also bore a signature: one left on any round fired through it. That enabled ballistics experts to match a slug to its weapon, crucial in prosecutions. Great for investigators: such evidence had been decisive in two convictions during Boateng's career. But now he was seeing things differently. Those features had become means to link him to an unlicensed gun and any related incidents. His request had been a trade-off: older weapons had fewer elements susceptible to forensic scrutiny, but they were rarer and harder to obtain. Sometimes unreliable too, depending on how they'd been looked after. Glocks were among the most widely used 9 mm pistols in the world. Boateng knew it wouldn't be hard to get hold of one in London. Whoever sold this to Agyeman probably got it off a supplier smuggling from Europe, jacked the price up a hundred per cent and passed it on without much thought to its use. He didn't want to know the history of this particular gun. It looked new, at least.

Reaching cautiously, as though it might scald him, he picked up the pistol. Pretty light, a plastic frame. He racked the steel slide, confirmed it was unloaded. The action was smooth and he felt a pulse of excitement. Last time he'd fired a handgun was seven years ago. Boateng had been given a session on the range by Troy, his old mate from basic training at Hendon, who had worked in the Met's firearms unit. Hadn't been the most accurate back then, and what skill he had developed under Troy's brief tutelage was perishable anyway. He didn't feel confident hitting much with it other than at close range. But at least it had been a Glock he'd shot on that occasion with Troy, albeit the larger 17 model. Another reason he'd stipulated the brand.

Hold on.

Boateng caught himself. He was thinking about firing a handgun. Step back a second. What did that mean? Most likely nothing – the chance of him actually using it was tiny. But not zero. Take it into a situation and you could never guarantee the outcome. At two extremes lay terrible possibilities: killing someone, or being killed. He'd long been an opponent of arming UK police as standard, arguing it would just up the ante and increase illegal gun demand. He'd debated the pros and cons with Troy over a pint more than once in twenty years of friendship. Now he was holding a pistol which he could go to prison just for possessing. If he was caught, Etta and Kofi would be on their own, his son growing up with a convict for a father. Like so many of the young men he'd come across through his work. He'd pitied them, wondering at the relationship between their criminality and the fathers' time inside. And that wasn't the only risk. What if he lost control of the pistol in a struggle? Troy had told him that several scenarios in the Met's firearms training involved stopping an attacker from taking your weapon. Let that happen and, well… He took a deep breath.

'Are you sure you want this, Zac?'

Boateng didn't reply. He just stared at the pistol in his hand, no longer taking in its manufacturing details or physical properties. He was only considering what it represented. Danger, yes. But also power. The ultimate threat in service of his obsession – getting to the truth about Amelia. Something there seemed to be no other way to achieve. He'd always rejected the idea of carrying a weapon himself. If it had to be done in London, leave it to specialists like Troy. But things had changed in Boateng's world, and he was no longer sure his original argument held. That daydream of beating Amelia's killer to death flashed back, only this time he was armed with the Glock. He quickly replaced the pistol, tissue paper and trainers. Put the lid back on, moistened his lips.

'Thanks, Sammy. I promise that nothing from this will come back to—'

'Just be careful, OK?' The big man's jaw set tight.

Boateng nodded. Took the shoebox and left without another word.

No comms from the muppet.

Ash hadn't been in touch for a day, so Spike decided to make another visit to the caravan park. He'd spent the morning checking homeless shelters for Wallace. Been up Vauxhall, St Mungo's at Tower Hill, New Cross. Asked around, shown the photo. Offered cash and ten per cent lager. Plenty of takers, zero intel. Had to give the prick some credit: Wallace knew how to stay off the map. Lucky for him it was summer – made it easier to sleep rough, move at night, whatever he was doing. The whole thing reminded Spike of the escape and evasion phase for SAS selection. Sent off on your Jack Jones and tracked for days by men and dogs. A mutt had got Spike in the end, smell gave him away. Should he have used a dog for Wallace? No, they couldn't track in cities like out in the woods.

Curtains were closed on Ash's caravan. He did night shifts, obvs. Door? Locked. Spike banged on it. Nothing. Again, harder. Still silent. Slapped the side where he knew the bed was.

'He's gone out, you know.' Spike turned, saw an old boy standing there. 'Mr Ellis.'

'Oh, right. D'you know where?'

'Nope.' The man smacked his lips. 'But he walked off with the two people who came to visit him.'

'Two?' Couldn't be Wallace then. Spike fished in his jeans for twenty quid. Did the story about the dead relative, handed over the note. 'What did they look like?'

'One woman with a ponytail, younger. Then a black fellow, bit older.'

Had to be the coppers. 'When?'

'About two hours ago.'

Bollocks. Spike grunted thanks to the old geezer and walked back to his motorbike. Ash was with the police, Parker in a body bag, Wallace nowhere, and he'd run out of ideas. Much as it hurt his pride, he had to go back to the insider. Better that than Patey. Made the call via WhatsApp.

'Yes?' said the voice.

'It's me.'

'I can't talk now. What do you need?'

'Something to go on.' He paused, made himself say it. 'I've run out of options.'

There was a cough down the line. 'We don't know any more than you now. So your best chance of finding our man is to follow us. Stick with Boateng.'

Spike couldn't hide his irritation. 'Can't you get anything else?' he snapped.

'You have everything there is. Boateng's the best person to follow, he's closer to it than anyone.'

'Got it.' Spike rang off. Gobbed on the ground. Sat there a minute, thought. No other way now, Patey's contact was right. He made a new operational plan. Gun it home on the motorbike, brew up a tea and get on the database. Find out where this Boateng lives and works. Leave the bike, take the wagon back into town, then clap eyes on him. Hurry up and wait till Boateng located Wallace then bam! SAS. Speed, Aggression, Surprise. Couple of nice stun grenades, few shots overhead. Hit 'em hard. Coppers would still have thumbs up their bums by the time he'd extracted with Wallace in the boot of his car. There was no threat from the Old Bill, the best they had was Tasers. And when the flashbangs went off they wouldn't have a clue which direction to fire them anyway. Spike grunted a laugh. Maybe he should've done this all along, saved himself a lot of nause.

CHAPTER TWENTY-SEVEN

Jones looked up as Boateng entered the office. 'Is she OK, boss?'

'What?' He looked confused, distracted.

'Your wife. Weren't you just—'

'Yeah, yeah, she's fine. Medical stuff. You good to go?'

Jones scooped the manila file off her desk, nodded. She'd put together everything they'd dug up relating to the safe deposit box burglary back in 2014. They were hoping it could jog Ash's memory, rake up something that might resemble a clue to Wallace's plans. She'd watched Ash sweat the whole way to Lewisham station in the back of their car, poor guy: dark circles at the armpits of his T-shirt. How much of that was the rising summer heat and how much guilty conscience wasn't clear. She did feel sorry for him though. Couldn't be much of a life, sleeping on your own in a caravan, working nights in security at industrial units. And that's before you factor in Darian Wallace and his angle grinder.

'I thought you could lead,' said Boateng. 'You know more than any of us about the safe deposit job.'

'Sure,' she replied, heart beating slightly faster. Stay calm, follow the training. She didn't want to get it wrong, damage her chances of being asked in future. She hadn't needed to do many interrogations in Cyber Crime. But maybe that was life in the MIT: whatever came up, you just got on with it, until eventually you did know what you were doing.

'Where's Pat?'

'Dunno, boss. He was around a few minutes ago.' She riffled through the pages, checked all her notes were there, anything that could be useful. Grabbed a biro. And a backup one.

Connelly jogged across to them, clutching his mobile. Jones thought how light on his feet he was for someone more than twice her age. 'Sorry about that.' The Irishman smiled briefly. 'Had to take a call.'

'Can you sit on the other side? Kat's in charge.' Boateng pocketed his own phone.

'Grand.'

Boateng led the way to the little interview room, held the door open for her. Inside, Ash was sprawled on a cheap metal chair, sweat patches still growing. Jones saw the light go on as Connelly flicked the switch from behind the observation mirror. She placed a polystyrene cup of water on the table in front of Ash. 'Here you go, Harvey. Or do you prefer Danny?'

He downed the drink, slapped the cup down. Still looked scared. 'I'm definitely not under arrest?' Glanced between them again, checking for disagreement.

'No,' she answered, taking a seat opposite him. 'But you can call a lawyer if you'd like.'

'I'm alright.' Ash wiped a hand across his face.

Boateng stood against the wall, arms folded. It was his idea she lead, but Jones felt like she was the one under scrutiny.

She started the CDs recording, did the introductions. 'So, Harvey. Can you tell us everything you know about the robbery of Capital Securities on Holbein Place in 2014, please? The safe deposit box vault where you were employed.'

'I…' Ash hesitated, pulled the T-shirt away from one armpit. 'All I know is that the place was raided. Two guys accused of it. Parker got out, Wallace went to jail. Half of the stuff they nicked was still missing when I stopped working there.'

'What role did you play?'

'None.'

'The alarm was disabled. From the inside.'

Ash shifted in the chair, scratched a man boob. 'Can I have some more water?'

'Perhaps DS Connelly can—'

'Stop the recording, Kat.' It was Boateng. 'We'll get Mr Ash his drink.'

Following procedure, she announced the interruption, paused the machine, shut the file and scraped her chair back. No one else moved. Boateng was staring at Ash, arms still folded. 'Go on.' He nodded.

Ash spread his hands on the table. The backs of them were dimpled with fat at the knuckles. 'It was Trent's idea. I promised to help on condition that if it all turned to shit he wouldn't name me. He kept his word. Wasn't till later I found out that psycho Wallace was in on the job too. If I'd known that I would've…' His head slumped.

Jones leaned forward. 'What happened after the vault job?'

'Parker and Wallace each took half. Supposed to hide it for a year then gradually sell the stuff on, bit by bit. Twenty per cent of the cash was gonna be mine. But Parker messed up, couldn't wait. Money problems. So he took some gear to the pawnbroker and then, well, you lot got him.'

'What about Wallace's stuff?'

'Far as I know it's still out there, somewhere. Sooner he gets it and fucks off the better.' The last words were bravado. People in his position often tried to show they weren't scared, even if their body language said otherwise.

'Where could he have hidden it?' Jones asked.

Ash shook his head slowly. 'Somewhere personal, I guess, that only he'd know.'

'How much are we talking about? Physical size.' She made a sliding scale with both hands.

'Depends how full the deposit boxes were. About four big holdalls' worth total, so two each, maybe.'

'And you've no idea where it might be?'

'I'd say wouldn't I, if I knew?'

She studied him. 'Tell us about that number on the card.'

'Another psycho. In my caravan when I come back from the shops yesterday. Had a gun aimed right at my face. He thought Wallace was coming for me. Wanted a tip-off, said he'd pay me a grand and protect me.'

Boateng might have some ideas but Jones was stumped. Who would be looking for Wallace? A former enemy? They weren't sure what he'd done between leaving school and robbing the vault. Seemed the sort to piss people off. 'Describe him to me, please, Harvey, in detail.'

Ash shut his eyes. 'White bloke about six foot, kind of skinny but looked strong. Wiry, you know. Had a scar in his cheek, like a hole that'd been patched up. Short brown hair, stubble.'

'Could you tell where he was from? How did he sound?'

'British, English, whatever. Like maybe he was from round here.'

'Anything else distinctive about him?'

'Only his watch,' Ash sat up, animated for the first time. 'It's just, I know a bit about nice watches. I'm into them – good investments, yeah? He had a Breitling. Big thing, special edition too. SAS one. You had to be in the regiment to buy them back in 2005, limited numbers, you know? Some guys obviously stuck 'em on eBay, got four, five times as much. But he didn't seem like one of those pretend soldiers who buys all the gear second-hand off squaddies. Military fantasists. Geezer broke into my caravan and pulled a pistol on me calm as you like. He'd obviously done it before.' Ash paused, pushed out his lower lip. 'Reckon he was the real deal.'

Jones tried to think clearly. If Ash was right, that'd narrow the identity of the man pursuing Wallace to less than a thousand names, even fewer once you factored in the physical description. Maybe just one man if the scar was rare enough. Should they get on to the Ministry of Defence? More immediately, it meant they were dealing with a pro. Was he a hired specialist? Why track Wallace? It didn't sound like your average criminal payback. She tapped her biro on the desk. Think. Boateng didn't say anything. Then it came to her.

'Was there anything stolen from the vault that was particularly valuable?'

'All of it, that's why it was in the boxes.'

'You'd imagine so. I'm not talking about monetary value, Harvey. I mean something more… significant.'

'No. Don't think so. I don't know what was in the boxes. Some people there used to talk about dodgy stuff, a personal cocaine stash or—'

Jones silenced him with a hand. 'What about after the theft? You still worked there, right?' Ash nodded. 'Did anyone who owned a stolen box make a particular fuss about what they'd lost?'

'A lot of 'em. People who had heirlooms and that nicked, family stuff.'

'But compared to the cash value or whatever. Anything stick out?'

Ash rocked the chair back, narrowed his eyes. Was silent a few seconds. 'There was one, actually, now you mention it. Receptionist told me some MP kept ringing up the boss. I remember it cos normally they've got secretaries and that, haven't they? But she personally called every day after the robbery. I thought it was weird – her stuff was only two thousand quid, nothing special. And you reckon someone like that'd have too much else going on to spend time checking up.'

That buzz passed through her, a mini shockwave. The thrill of something new that might be crucial. A logical connection. The ex-SAS guy looking for Wallace, an MP obsessing over a small item he'd stolen…

Boateng's phone went off. Jones watched his expression change as he saw the screen.

'I have to take this,' he blurted, already half out the room. Heard him say 'Roy' as he answered the call. Then the door closed behind him.

She hoped Zac was OK. For a guy leading a double murder investigation he had a lot of other stuff going on.

Wallace lay supine on the floor.

The day's heat had turned the lock-up into an oven. But being stuck here with the door shut was preferable to spending time outside where he could be seen. He knew he needed to let go of Ash – the Five-O had him now. Three people who broke the street code were on his list, and he'd done two of them. That didn't count Jas grassing last week. Initially the rage had got the better of him, winding up until he'd sliced a big gash in the breeze blocks with his angle grinder. After that it ebbed away, leaving him less certain of his purpose. When he was back in prison, the objective had been clear: take out the snitches that sent him down. Protect your name with extreme force. Had to be done. Harris, Parker: fine. But with Ash he'd failed. And it didn't seem to matter that much.

Maybe he should add Fletcher to the list. Go back and make her understand why betrayal has to be punished. Hat, sunglasses, head down, walk to Camberwell as darkness came over London. Take the angle grinder. But he found himself thinking about Reece, the 'lickle man', left without a mum or dad. Something crystallised when he saw Boateng playing football with his son.

Revenge isn't isolated, a single hit. It spreads its tentacles out, coils around people who don't deserve it, haven't done anything wrong. He could choose to leave Jas alone, then Reece would have a parent as he grew up. Like Wallace had his mum. The youngers like Reece and Neon needed to be given chances, not dragged into feuds about reputation that had nothing to do with them.

Once he had 1.5 million quid's worth of stuff in bags and he got to Europe, he could buy a different identity, a new existence. One where maybe he wouldn't ruin any more lives. But for that he needed the jewels.

It was time to get them back.

Derek flopped down into the armchair, cracked open the can and gulped down a few mouthfuls. Christ, it felt good, drinking cold beer at the end of his shift. Every day in his black cab was longer now. Had to grind out each tenner, competing against these Uber guys, even with tourists in the West End. And his lock-ups weren't bringing much in either; demand for them seemed to have dropped off. Except for the bloke with the tattoo under his eye, he paid two ton upfront. Might be more where that came from. He belched, breathed out slowly. Things would pick up, he just had to cut down his spending. Mortgage, running the cab, football season ticket. It all added up. Pints were a fiver these days. Seemed like life got more expensive while he earned less and less.

He reached for the remote, put his feet up on the coffee table. Swigged his lager. Zapped from a reality show to *Eggheads* then a sitcom. All crap. Hit ITV London news. Might as well see what's going on.

When the face appeared on his screen, Derek dropped the can. Spilled beer on the sofa. Didn't curse or mop it up. He just nudged the volume higher.

It was the guy from his lock-up.

Darian Wallace, they were calling him, not John. Funny that. Charged with a murder, wanted in connection with another. Bloody hell. No wonder he was hiding in a garage. Derek had known the story about his car was bollocks. Wasn't going to lie though, the cash had been useful. Obviously the coppers had no clue where he was or they wouldn't be putting it out on the news. He grabbed a pen, scribbled the anonymous tip-off number. The right thing to do was call it in. But he knew John or Wallace or whoever he was had cash, he'd seen it. Notes he wouldn't need in prison. Perhaps he'd visit the lock-up, see how much the guy had. What he'd be willing to pay for Derek to pretend he hadn't seen the news. He smirked to himself. Then he'd call the cops anyway. Was he scared? Been in enough scraps himself over the years, some with weapons. That was part of the deal when you were old-school Millwall, practically royalty when it came to football hooliganism. He'd gone against top boys from other teams and some of those lads had definitely done people in. Alright, that was back in the nineties, but he still knew what he was doing. He'd take some protection along just in case. One young bloke cornered in a garage? Derek fancied his chances, murderer or not. Most likely the guy would just pay up.

He finished the rest of his lager. Noticed the slight tremor in his hand as he crushed the can.

CHAPTER TWENTY-EIGHT

Baked beans.

That was what Etta found on the hob when she returned home. Zac hadn't even bothered getting bread out for toast. Her husband was poking a saucepan, transfixed by the steaming orange contents. More evidence of something wrong: Zac loved cooking; he was great at it. Secretly, Etta preferred the days when she took Kofi to school and worked later, because it usually meant coming back to a feast from Chef Boateng. The chilli, spice and palm oil-laden aromas of West African dishes would fill the kitchen, drawing her in. But not this evening, clearly.

She dropped her keys on the counter. 'You alright?'

'Yeah.'

'Kofi in bed?'

'Yeah.'

'Did you go to the supermarket?'

'No.'

Etta pulled the clips out of her hair, shook it loose. 'It's not twenty questions, Zac.'

'Eh?'

'You're allowed to say more than just yes or no.'

'Sorry.'

She put on some toast; at least now it would vaguely resemble a meal.

The only sounds as they began eating were the scrape and clip of cutlery. She tried to lift the mood by talking about her plans for them to visit Greenwich Park at the weekend, take a picnic. Maybe call some friends, see if they were free. Offered to play football with her boys. But Zac's responses remained terse, monosyllabic. His mind was somewhere else entirely, not 'present', as her mindfulness teacher would say. She'd known him to withdraw during the most intense cases; occasionally it was his way of dealing with pressure. Normally he could compartmentalise, separate home and family off from the dark places of work. Not this time, evidently: the division was between them.

She placed a hand on his forearm. 'I meant what I said before. Whatever it is, you can talk to me. We'll work it out together.'

Zac raised his head and met her gaze for a few seconds. His eyes wide, searching, enveloped by tiredness. Lips made tiny movements with no words. Then he looked down again, prodded the beans.

'I can't help if you don't tell me what's going on.' Her tone was tougher.

'There's nothing going on,' he replied slowly.

'Obviously there is, since you're out all hours now and even when you're here it's like the room's empty.'

'It's the case.'

She slapped the table. 'Bullshit.' Surprised herself with the aggression.

He pushed away the plate. 'I've got to go.'

'Hey! You can't just run away, whatever this is. Where are you going?'

'I can't tell you.'

'Why not?'

He strode to the door without looking back.

'Zac!' she screamed after him.

Etta sprang up, tipping her chair over, raced out. Saw him grab flat cap, jacket and an orange shoebox in the dim hallway before the front door slammed. Footsteps echoed on the tiles, fading to nothing. She stood there, suddenly feeling alone and scared and angry all at once. How dare he treat her like this? Nineteen years together and in that moment they were strangers. Her throat thickened, face tight as she held back tears. She turned to the photo of a young Zac in uniform staring out from the wall. Without thinking she lashed out at the frame, shattered the glass. Instantly regretted it and stooped to pick up the shards, grateful none had cut her.

She went back into the kitchen, took the tablet. Swiped till she found the Glympse tracker app. Eighteen months ago she'd made Zac install it after he misplaced his mobile twice. At the time he'd been embarrassed, claimed he didn't need it. He hated any challenge to his practical skills. But she'd persisted, volunteering first then convincing him to follow with the argument that it would be useful in emergencies. This wasn't what she'd had in mind, but it definitely qualified. She tapped the icon, scrolled through. There he was under 'Favourites', so the app was still on his phone. Since they were already connected, there was no need to send a location request. It'd be automatic if she selected his name. One tap would show exactly where he was.

She shut down the app, pushed the tablet aside. Maybe a part of her didn't want to know, rejected stooping to tracking her own husband covertly. She just needed to talk to him. Etta massaged her eyes with the heels of her hands. Then topped up her wine glass and trudged to the living room to see what was on TV.

Wallace emerged from the trees, crept towards the cluster of headstones. Darkness in the countryside was deeper, blacker than the city. Fine by him, he needed cover. Not that it really mattered, there was no one within a mile and his only company was a hooting owl.

As night fell he'd taken a train from Waterloo to the village of Cobham in Surrey. Walked down lanes and across fields, finally reaching the specialist Silvermere cemetery through the woodland.

Didn't take him long to find the grave. It looked like many others, the standard package. Small marble memorial stone and surround marking the plot, grass neatly tended. Eight hundred quid well spent. Given what had happened, it was one of the smartest investments he'd ever made. Wallace set down the holdall, removed a folding spade from inside and squatted down.

He traced his fingertips across the single word chiselled into the marble: *BLAZE*. At four quid a letter, that was all the information he needed. He'd been fond of the dog, got some wins with him on the track in racing days. Had his ear tattooed to stop anyone nicking him. But no way he'd have paid that kind of cash, not to bury an animal. It was unbelievable how much people spent on sticking their pets in the ground here. When you were dead you were dead, simple. In London, Wallace would've dropped Blaze in a canal with a sack full of stones when his time came. No big deal if the same thing happened to him. We were all worm food ultimately; it was your name that lived on. Or so he'd been telling himself for years. Prising the headstone up and hefting it aside, he drove the spade tip into soil, began digging.

Forty minutes later he struck the coffin. Sweeping the earth away, he saw its wood hadn't degraded much. Probably couldn't say the same for the corpse inside. Wallace took a screwdriver from his holdall and set to work. Recoiled as the lid came off: smelled like a kitchen bin left in a sauna. Fur had sloughed off the bones, most of it decayed but some still recognisable. He pulled on industrial rubber gloves, lifted limbs and ribcage out. A single bullet hole in the top of the skull. For a second he froze while a film played of the skeleton with its slow trigger action. Then he snapped back and dumped the skull to one side, peeling off the gloves. Unscrewed the coffin's floor panels piece by piece. Removing them, he could just make out two slim, silver flight cases in the gloom.

Wallace reached down to the handles, hoisted them up. Laid the cases carefully on the grass, popped the combination locks and peered inside. Sealed cloth bags lay among foam padding. Reckoned each case was around half a million quid. Maybe more after a couple of years' inflation. The other third of his share was in a backup spot; he'd get that tomorrow. He stuck both flight cases in the holdall, heaving it onto his shoulder. Considered putting the grave back together. Then decided against it; he was leaving anyway. Let the local feds work it out, see if any of them were sharp as Boateng. He snatched a final glance at the pile of bones and set off towards the trees.

Susanna Pym couldn't sleep. She squinted to bring the alarm clock's neon digits into focus: 01:03. None of the usual sources of night-time wakefulness were bothering her: no urban foxes screwing each other to death, no snoring from her flabby husband, no impending parliamentary debates. It was lack of results in the search for her pendant – memory stick, more precisely – that kept her brain whirring. Slipping out of bed, she grabbed a packet of cigarettes and some perfume and crept into the guest bathroom. Cracked the window and lit up. Her own bloody home and still she couldn't smoke freely – other half would give her grief for it. Strange that although nicotine was a stimulant, it somehow soothed her. That was addiction, she supposed. The problem she'd never quite shaken. At least it wasn't cocaine these days. Not often, anyway.

A whole week had passed since she'd met Tarquin Patey in the Oxford and Cambridge Club. His crack team of operatives had found bugger all in that time. Had it been a mistake to give the police officer's number to Patey for his inside info? People like him probably had their own contacts. But it could help, and the officer would have no idea that they were searching for her memory stick; he didn't even know it existed.

She needed that stick back. Her future hinged on it. The intention in recording her conversations with the police officer was to have some protection, some leverage should he try to expose her. He was a cocky sort and a few years ago – over several whiskies – she'd managed to get him talking about his 'business'. Sidelines to his police work. With typically male bravado he'd shown off about his contact with a heroin importer, his ability to get hold of weapons, even a kidnap and ransom he'd organised. To Pym's shame, her acquiescence to his demands over the years meant she might even have contributed to one or two of these awful exploits. But at least she had them on record.

Her thoughts travelled over the reason for all this nonsense. Would she be better off if the policeman were removed altogether? She would be free from his demands, from the risk of her career disintegrating, free to make her way to the top. It didn't feel like being blackmailed, perhaps because he offered her favours as well. Things the police didn't normally do. The embarrassment of a speeding ticket gone; a full and proper investigation when her home was burgled; a stalker warned off in no uncertain terms. She'd benefitted from her devil's pact.

It was a chronic problem rather than an acute one. Sometimes those are the worst though, eating away at you slowly until it's too late, and you haven't even realised the end is coming. Did Patey's firm offer that kind of service, removal of a tumour or tapeworm? She'd bet they did. But that was a different game altogether, one she wasn't ready to play. Not yet. So, she'd just have to give them a little longer to find her memory stick. And hope that the police didn't get there first.

Pym stubbed out the cigarette and sprayed herself with perfume. Then she went back to lying in bed, wide awake.

The old BMW with blacked-out windows pulled into Benedict Road, parked up under an overhanging balcony and killed its headlights. Boateng watched from the back fence of Stockwell Skatepark. He'd got there early, spotted the vantage point and taken up position. At 1 a.m. the skatepark was quiet, a few youths sprawled on the undulating concrete passing a joint and cognac bottle between them. This was the location Froggy had given him on the phone. Said a guy called Mamba who drove a 'bimma' would be there at midnight. No one else with a BMW had come or gone since 11 p.m., so this was probably him. Froggy had only supplied two other details to Boateng: first, the interview would cost five hundred pounds; second, Mamba had been in Two-Ten.

Since the call he'd been unable to think about anything else, practically ignoring Jones, Ash, the Wallace case, even Kofi and Etta. Especially her: she was most likely to try stopping him. Walking out on her earlier had been inexcusable. But shame wasn't the only feeling. Boateng had the premonitory sense that this could be one of those points in life where a decision is made by reaction rather than reason. Despite the week's worth of tiredness that clung to him, his pulse was racing. He had to calm down. He checked his outside jacket pocket for the money. Then reached inside the left breast, felt the Glock's hard frame. Handle facing up and out towards his right hand. Just in case. Self-protection, he reassured himself. Pulled the zip up to cover it and began walking.

Approaching the vehicle, Boateng caught the hum of bass reverberating from within. Took a deep breath, knocked on the driver-side window. It dropped smoothly, releasing wisps of tobacco smoke into the night air. A black face turned in the gloom, features highlighted by white and green lights from the stereo. A cigarette butt flicked past him.

'I'm Roy.'

Dark eyes studied him before the head jerked towards the passenger door. Boateng climbed in. 'You Mamba?'

A grin spread slowly across the face. 'My man said five hundred.' The voice was baritone. Boateng caught a whiff of booze.

'Two fifty now, the rest when we finish.' He produced a roll of notes, handed it over. 'That's how I work, I'm sure Froggy told you that.'

'Whatever man.' Mamba tucked the cash into his shirt pocket.

'Can you tell me about Two-Ten?'

'Everything stays here, get me? No recording.'

'Nothing.' Boateng spread his hands. 'Look, I don't even know your name. Where did "Mamba" come from anyway?'

'Black Mamba,' the guy smirked. 'Ask the ladies about that one, yeah?'

Boateng played along, chuckled. 'So how did the group start?'

'We was raised together in Brikky, all lived in the same ends. You get to know certain man, trust them more than others.' Mamba lit another cigarette, tip glowing as he sucked and blew two jets from his nostrils. 'Started to run on the road together, usual stuff. Shifting weed, few stick-ups, moved on to crack. Sy had linked up with some Jamaican mans that imported the raw stuff. We was making two grand a day. Bought anything we wanted.' He gestured to his shirt and jeans. 'Gucci, Louis V, Rolex, Dom Pérignon. Life was good them days.'

'Was? What happened to you guys?'

'Sy happened, man. Tore us apart.' Boateng let the silence hang, pulse thumping at his neck. 'He starts seeing this girl out of Peckham. I said it was a bad move, you know how Peckham-Brixton beef goes. But he did it anyway, cos Sy was Sy. Didn't nobody tell him what to do. Then one day she broke up with him. They always did in the end, he used to slap 'em around and that. Sy couldn't deal with it, started losing his shit. First he was making mistakes with the gear, missed an appointment with the Jamaicans. Took me weeks to smooth it over. Then he found out some guy was banging his girl and that was it, man.'

Boateng's body was rigid. 'Who was the guy?'

'Man called Dray.'

Boateng's mouth felt dry, he swallowed, moistened his lips. 'Draymond King?'

The eyes narrowed. 'You know him?'

'No,' replied Boateng quickly. 'Read about it at the time though.'

'Sy planned the hit. Got himself tooled up with a new piece, a nine mil. Killed Dray at the newsagent but took down two other people with him. Shop owner and a little girl, man. Both innocent.' Mamba shook his head, dragged deeply on the cigarette. 'That was wrong. Just…' He tailed off.

'Go on.'

'Me and the others couldn't really trust him after that, the man was a loose cannon, get me? That's when it started to fall apart. That day in Peckham. A year later it was every man for himself, some of us had joined new crews. I did my own thing.'

'What about Sy?'

'Guess he did too. Mans drifted apart, innit.'

So close. Boateng took a chance. 'Who was Sy?'

He sensed the body alongside him stiffen. 'Why d'you need to know that? I've told you, he was just Sy.' Another drag, jets through the nose.

'What was his real name?'

Mamba sucked his teeth. 'Man, fuck you, get outta my car. This shit is over. Matter of fact, gimme my other two fifty first.' He pushed the central locking button, a thunk resounding from the doors.

Boateng steadied his breathing. 'OK, sure. No problem,' he said quietly, reached to his pocket. 'Sorry, it's just—'

The flat of his right hand hammered into Mamba's neck before he lunged with the left, grabbing his wrist in a lock, pressing the burning cigarette tip into Mamba's skin before the guy squealed, dropped it. Boateng pushed back to his seat, reached inside the jacket. Mamba made to move forward, froze when he saw the pistol trained on him.

The younger man raised hands, spoke carefully. 'Just chill, yeah?'

'Unlock the doors. Now hands on the steering wheel,' barked Boateng. 'What's his name?'

'C'mon, man, please,' he whispered, voice catching.

'His name?' growled Boateng.

'Don't do nothing crazy—'

He racked the slide.

'Wallace.'

Must have misheard. 'What?'

'Darian Wallace. He's inside now for robbin' some safes.'

Boateng felt like the floor was dropping away, sensation in his limbs draining. The car interior blurred, his head falling along with the gun. Became aware of hands on his own, pulling, wrenching. The Glock jammed into the armrest between them as his focus returned, Boateng's finger squeezing the trigger under Mamba's grip until the bang smacked him round the ears, the air a single high-pitched tone of confusion. Boateng twisted his body left, bending Mamba's arm and forcing him to let go before crashing a right elbow into his face. Whipping back round he trained the muzzle on Mamba, whose nose was streaming blood.

'No more games,' shouted Boateng, almost unable to hear himself over the tinnitus. 'Describe him.'

'He – he's light skinned,' Mamba spoke quickly. 'Half Scottish, half Jamaican. So we used to call him Scotland Yard, S-Y, Sy, yeah? Got a tear inked under his eye after the hit on Draymond, cos of the girl. Said he didn't mean to kill her, it was just a stray, but that don't matter now.'

Just a stray. Boateng ground his teeth, lips trembling. *Hold it together.* He needed one more piece of information. 'How do you know for sure Wallace did the newsagent murders?'

Mamba sniffed at the blood trickle. 'I was there, man, I rode the motorbike.'

Accessory to murder. Amelia's murder. Boateng's finger curled on the trigger, taking slack off its mini safety catch.

'I didn't know anyone else died till I saw it on the news.'

Tone from the gunshot still buzzing in Boateng's ears; things seemed to slow down, his own heartbeat a bass drum. His control was slipping.

'I swear.' Mamba's face contorted. 'Please.'

He could pull the trigger now, it would be so easy. Eye for an eye. This guy had helped Wallace take Amelia from him, from their family. Dimly aware he was shaking, Boateng found his breath quickening, limbs tensing. Just let go. Follow your instinct, to hell with the consequences. His forefinger tightened a fraction more.

Then it was like he came to, finger easing off the trigger. Boateng wound up and smashed the pistol butt into Mamba's face with a satisfying crack. His left hand reached forward, took the money from Mamba's pocket. 'Give me your keys too.' Keeping eyes and gun fixed on him, Boateng reached back, popped the door handle. Slid along until his shoes touched asphalt, stood and replaced the pistol in his jacket. Dropped the keys, turned and sprinted past the skatepark into the night. Didn't stop running until his thighs ached and lungs burned. Only then did his tears come. He wiped them on trembling hands. Realised his entire body was shaking.

CHAPTER TWENTY-NINE

Tuesday, 27 June 2017

'What's wrong, Dad?'

'Hm?' Boateng looked up from the kitchen counter.

'Are you cutting onions?'

'No, I'm making your lunch. Come on, finish those corn-flakes.'

'Normally you cry when you cut onions.'

Boateng pinched the bridge of his nose. 'I'm not crying.'

Kofi giggled. 'Liar.'

'Oi!' he snapped. 'Don't be so cheeky. Something went in my eye, that's all.'

Boateng wiped both hands over his face. Last night's encounter had left him a physical wreck. Hadn't slept much, thoughts chasing each other, looping round, incessant. Now his body felt light, disconnected. Adrenalin-sapped yet still on high alert. Drawing the Glock on Mamba had been instinctive. In that moment, his desire for the truth had overpowered reason and once it happened, all bets were off. Ordinarily he'd trust his self-control, coolness under pressure that the Job trained you for, demanded. But he hadn't been in control for those few seconds while his finger curled on the trigger. Like it wasn't him pulling it. Knew that both he and Mamba were lucky to escape in one piece; he'd fired a shot in the struggle, for God's sake.

Physical danger aside, there was Etta. If he'd woken her last night when he returned at three, she pretended to be asleep. They hadn't touched in bed, an invisible barrier bisecting the mattress. She left for work early without speaking to him. Each new secret he kept from her – and every lie to cover them up – chipped away at the trust built in their relationship over almost two decades. There had to be a limit. Felt like either an explosion was coming or this slow, inexorable drift away from each other would continue past the point of no return. That didn't bear thinking about.

But what could he tell her? He'd finally discovered who killed Amelia, after nearly five years? That he'd achieved this by breaking the law he was paid to uphold, behind his colleagues' backs? Worse still, that at least one officer had impeded the original investigation. What would it do to her to know all that?

Of course, he was taking information at face value. Night Vision's story about Draymond King, Mamba's account of the shooting – either could be mistaken, lying or have a hidden agenda. And yet, it made sense. Facts that added up, had plausibility. Most murders in London were solved, so perhaps someone in the Met did help Wallace one way or another. And he'd never considered that Amelia's killer would be in prison for a different crime. Maybe those two features explained the lack of new leads despite his regular inquiries, and the case ultimately being shelved. Then Harris had been murdered in Deptford and ten days later Boateng was here.

These logical operations of his brain were jabbed by raw emotion. Some of the helplessness he'd felt for years was gone, now he knew. But there was still unprocessed grief at Amelia's loss. Flashbacks to her lying there, the red stain growing on her yellow dress as he tried and failed to revive her. Anger at the man who did this, murderous rage from a place deep within that most of us pretended didn't exist. He'd experienced those sensations for years, ebbing and flowing, but the last ten days had brought them back centre stage. All of it could now be directed at Wallace.

Next question was what to do about it. For a few seconds last night, he'd considered pulling the trigger on Mamba. Something had stopped him, the last tendrils of self-control. But with each day that passed, pressure rising and sleep escaping him, that resistance was diminishing. If it was Wallace in his gun sights, would he give in to that brutal, base desire?

'Are you going to be Batman again tonight, Dad?'

Zac started. 'What?'

'You know, when you go out at night to fight baddies. Like last night. And the other nights.' Kofi's eyes widened. 'Must be a lot of bad guys out there.'

Looking at the boy, Boateng softened. 'True. Sometimes they're hard to find.'

'But when you do find them…' Small hands mimed shooting. 'Po-pow!'

'It's not like that, Kof.' Normally. His son was right about one thing though: he was going out again tonight. In the absence of legitimate channels, he had few intelligence-gathering options on Wallace. He needed to see Night Vision again.

'Hang on, yeah?'

Three bolts scraped, two locks turned. Decent security measures; Wallace was pleased about that. Only last year a similar establishment in London had been robbed of a hundred grand's worth of stock. This place was off the radar, but even so. His hostess took one confirmatory glance through the crack with large darting eyes. A chain fell slack, the door swung open and she walked away. The woman was mid twenties, petite, with bare sinewy arms and a shock of hair like Sideshow Bob. Wallace followed her inside, grimacing as the fetid odour of corpses hit him for the second time that day. He wasn't squeamish, but decaying flesh still made him want to throw up; maybe she'd got used to it. Turning death into art was Stella Winberg's business. At least, some people called it art. More like a horror show. Scanning the cluttered studio for his item, Wallace clocked some monstrous hybrids. An erect black cat with no forelimbs, crow wings spread from the flanks, a bird's tail in place of its own. The four-headed white rat climbing out of a lab beaker. Most grotesque was a fox's head mounted on four pairs of dog legs so it looked like some giant furry spider. Drawn closer, he gazed into the lifeless eyes.

'Sorry it's a bit like Fort Knox,' called Winberg across the studio. 'Gotta have bolts and stuff, otherwise the animal rights lot'd be in here torching the place.'

'Wouldn't want that.'

She noticed him staring at the creature. 'If you like the Arachnofox, check out what I'm doing here.' The young woman gestured to the bench behind her. 'Working title's "See No Evil". What d'you think?'

Wallace stepped across. One squirrel had impaled another using a knitting needle while a bystander third theatrically shielded its eyes. In some ways, taxidermists saw life at its most honest: that any animal was nothing more than skin, bone and a ton of blood and internal organs. This woman was good at what she did. Twisted too, or maybe just immune to gore. Spotting a crucified bat up on a shelf, labelled 'Stigmata', its mouth contorted into a scream, Wallace began to feel creeped out. Wasn't a pussy; just something about being surrounded by reanimated dead bodies that made him want to finish the transaction. Get back outside in the fresh air. He recalled his reason for coming here in the first place. Logistically it would've been simpler to go to London Taxidermy, round the corner from Wimbledon greyhound track, but they were pros running a business and the bullet hole in the dog's head would have raised suspicion, not to mention the stuff he'd wanted put inside the animal. After a bit of searching he'd found Stella Winberg, an independent artist operating out of a unit behind the Bussey Building in Peckham, who referred to herself as a 'rogue' taxidermist. A recce of the studio had convinced him her morals were sufficiently flexible to accommodate his request. And her income sufficiently low to need his patronage.

'Have you got what I came for?'

'Yeah, course. Been looking after her for you.' She pointed to the corner. Wallace dragged the big cardboard box out. It was heavy. Knelt and took a penknife from his pocket, cut the tape. 'So, where you been?' she adjusted the vest top under her apron.

'Away.' Obviously she hadn't been watching the news. He opened the flaps, checked inside. Bambam was lying on her stomach, paws extended ahead. Fine dark grey fur was perfectly preserved. Smaller than her brother Blaze but with the same sleek face. Wallace pointed to the brass winding key protruding from the bullet wound in the top of her skull, turned to Winberg. 'What's that?'

'Soz, couldn't resist putting something in the hole. She's a beauty. Bag's inside the shell, like you wanted. Made it from a polyurethane cast with wire support. Strong as hell.' She bent down, gave a coy smile. 'What's in it then?'

Wallace leaned forward, their faces inches apart. 'I didn't pay you a grand to ask questions.' His thumb stroked the penknife blade. Her smile vanished but she didn't seem scared. Oblivious rather than brave. He tried lifting the box. No way he could get this thing on the bus, not without drawing a lot of attention. 'You got a car?'

'Yeah.'

'Give you fifty quid to drive me and the dog to my storage spot.'

'Alright.' Winberg's response was instant. The trade in mutilated animals hadn't picked up while he was inside then. 'Now?'

Wallace nodded and she grabbed a bunch of keys, began removing her apron. He sheathed the penknife, hoped she didn't get any more inquisitive.

Jones arranged her briefing notes. It was past three, but Boateng didn't look ready for the meeting yet. She scanned the office, wondered briefly if she'd got the time wrong, missed some unwritten rule. Normally her boss was all over it, ready before them. His gaze was fixed on Wallace's mugshot, in the centre of the large whiteboard. Boateng just stood staring at their target through puffy eyes, arms hanging limp. Looked exhausted. Hadn't touched the coffee Malik made in his favourite mug. She'd expected the MIT to be stressful, but this looked like something more.

Malik and Connelly pulled chairs over, Connelly insisting on a steaming mug of tea despite the afternoon's warmth. The Irishman was explaining the phrase 'trot a mouse' to Malik, referring to tea so dark and strong the little creature could walk across it. At least the other two thought there was a meeting as well.

She cleared her throat gently. 'Are we starting, Zac?'

'What do you want now?' he snapped.

Wow. Didn't see that coming. Normally he was so chilled. 'I was just asking about the meeting,' she said, more tentatively. 'Um, are you OK?'

'Sorry,' he muttered, rasping a hand across chin stubble as he sat down slowly. 'Yeah, let's start.'

Jones waited for instructions that didn't arrive. 'Shall I update on the mystery man first?'

'You've got a new boyfriend?' Connelly grinned, and she rolled her eyes. Should've seen that coming. Before she could think of a reply, Malik cut in.

'Shut up, Pat.' He scowled. 'Let her speak.'

'It's not you, is it, big man?' Connelly winked.

'Piss off.'

Malik was sweet, she liked him. Fit, too. And he seemed keen. Should she...? Jones wasn't sure about dating a younger guy. Particularly one she sat opposite all day in the office. On the other hand, Malik had a lot more going for him than the losers she often seemed to draw: drunken lads on nights out with her mates, friends of friends who flaked and bailed, or blokes off Tinder who never matched their descriptions. It was a source of ongoing embarrassment to her that in a city with five million men she couldn't find a decent boyfriend. The working hours didn't help, and maybe the job title put some guys off. Perhaps that was why most police ended up getting together with each other, single or not. For now she was determined to keep her love life out of work. Nonetheless, she gave Malik a little smile.

'Ash came in earlier and checked security footage from outside the dance studio,' Jones said, glancing at her notes. 'Reckons the guy who goes in after Wallace could be the same man that broke into his caravan. I've contacted Ministry of Defence on the basis of his SAS theory, gave the description and year we think he served at Hereford. They shut it down immediately, said the identities of Special Forces personnel were secret even after they've left the regiments. When I told them it was a murder inquiry, they asked if he was a suspect. I had to say no, just a possible witness. They didn't budge.' She paused. No reaction. 'Boss?'

'Great,' replied Boateng.

'No, it's not.' She frowned. 'We don't have a clue who he is.'

Boateng seemed to wake up, focus. 'Sorry, I mean, good work following it through. I'll go back to Krebs, get her to take it up the hierarchy for us.'

'Don't hold your breath,' said Connelly. 'Military look after their own.'

'At least it's a lead,' said Boateng. 'I'll take anything right now. Bringing Ash in kept Krebs happy for a day, but we met an hour ago and she bollocked me for not knowing more about Wallace.' He shook his head.

Jones felt for him, taking the flak. 'But Ash didn't have anything to give except his intel on the soldier.'

'That's not how she sees it.'

Connelly broke the silence. 'Nas and I were down in Crystal Palace this morning, spoke to a bunch of people. Found an old fella that lives near Ash's pitch. Once his false teeth were in, he told us a man matching the soldier's description came by yesterday looking for Ash. Backs up the story. Nothing else though.'

Boateng bit his lip, nodded slowly.

'It's not all doom and gloom,' offered Malik. 'Something just came in from Surrey Police. Get this. Animal cemetery in Cobham had a grave desecrated last night. Manager said they'd never seen anything like it. Massive greyhound coffin dug up, broken open, bones just chucked on the side. Staff couldn't get hold of the owner, so reported it straight to police. Lucky for us, Guildford's finest had nothing else to do, so they put the owner's name through the national system and found it flagged by us.' He leaned back, smiled. 'Darian Wallace.' Malik snapped his fingers.

Boateng sat bolt upright. 'His share of the safe deposit box stash, has to be. Hidden in a grave. Of course.' Hands gripped his knees, eyes darting around. 'It's been done before.'

'Hatton Garden raid, couple of years ago,' said Jones. 'Guy used his father-in-law's grave. Didn't dig up the body though.' She was chuffed at recalling the fact, but Boateng didn't acknowledge it. Just sat still, said nothing.

'What do you reckon that means, boss?' ventured Malik.

Boateng spoke quietly. 'It means I don't have much time.'

'I?' Last Jones checked this was a Major Investigation *Team*.

'We.' He glanced at her. 'We haven't got much time. He's probably going to flee the country. No reason for him to stay here any longer.' Boateng numbered off on his fingers. 'We've had Wallace's picture on telly and in the papers last few days, so it's risky for him to be out much. He can't get to Ash since we've

stuck him in the hostel round the corner to keep out the way.
And it sounds like he's got the loot now too.'

'Should we brief UK Borders again?' suggested Jones.

'Definitely. Pat, see if Wallace crops up on any train station
cameras coming back into London from Surrey. Might tell us
where he went.'

Jones raised a hand. 'What about the MP? Ash said it was a
woman. That narrows it down to around two hundred possibles.
I can cross-reference with the safe deposit burglary report from
2014, find the match. Could go and speak to her?'

'Just don't expect her to tell the truth,' added Connelly.

Boateng wrinkled his nose. 'Krebs is not going to like your
theory about her tasking some kind of hitman to go after Wallace.
Doesn't get more political than sticking an MP on our suspect
list. We'd need better intel before doing anything. Hold off on
that for now.'

She bit her lip. Trusted his judgment but still felt deflated.

Noticing, Boateng managed a nod. 'Keep the ideas coming
though. Let's focus on Wallace and how we think he's going to
leave.' Clapped his hands. 'Alright, back to it.' As the others
moved away, he returned to examining Wallace's mugshot.

Jones approached, touched his arm gently. 'Seriously, are you
OK, Zac?'

'Fine.'

'You just look, you know, really tired.'

'Thanks.'

'I didn't mean—'

'Appreciate the concern, but don't worry about me.'

'Look, if there's anything you need me to do with the investigation, I don't mind staying later or whatever. Without overtime,
just until—'

'Thanks.' Boateng cut her off again. He swivelled back to the
mugshot.

She noticed his fists were balled. Jones went back to her desk, glanced over again at him. Her boss's behaviour was weird, uncharacteristic. Maybe just stress. Jones admired his sense of responsibility, but still, he was being a bit of a dick.

CHAPTER THIRTY

'Hello?' a voice crackled through the speaker.

'Takeaway for number fifteen. Think their bell's broken.'

A buzzer sounded and Boateng pulled open the heavy front door. Didn't want to stand outside Lockwood House at 11 p.m. explaining over intercom who he was to Night Vision or anyone else in his home. He'd rung eleven flats before someone let him in.

Calling on Clarence Thompson was a long shot, but he had few alternatives. Might only be a matter of hours before Wallace vanished, gone forever. Boateng had considered levelling with his team about what he'd discovered but couldn't bring himself to reveal the extent of his duplicity. Perhaps he was just making excuses for what he really wanted to do: find Wallace alone. Get face to face, hear him confess. And then… he didn't know. Try to keep control. Thompson was about the only ally he could think of in that quest; Agyeman would help, but he'd done enough. Boateng knocked on the door, stepped back as he heard footsteps inside and locks turning.

'Yes?' The chunky middle-aged woman in a loose green dress looked him up and down. 'Whatcha wan' this time a night?'

'Sorry to disturb you. Can I speak to Clarence please? I'm a colleague from the Post Office.' Paused. 'It's a personal matter.'

The lady sighed, as if this were a daily occurrence. 'Wait 'ere.' She shuffled inside and moments later Night Vision appeared.

'What you doing?' he whispered. 'You can't be here.'

'I know. Need to speak to you alone.'

Thompson hesitated, narrowed his eyes. 'Come on.' Closing the front door, he directed Boateng down the corridor to an empty stairwell of bare concrete. 'What d'you want?'

Boateng bit his lip. No point messing around. 'Look, Clarence, when we spoke before, I wasn't straight with you.'

'What fed ever is? Your money was good though.'

'I'm not working with Nathan. When I asked about Draymond King, it wasn't because I had an interest in him.'

'What then?'

'My daughter died that day. In the shop.'

Thompson met his eyes as if to verify the statement, then simply nodded.

'So we want the same thing,' said Boateng. 'To find the guy who did it.'

'If I knew who it was I'd have popped him myself.'

'I do know.'

Eyes bulging, Thompson's jaw set hard before the words burst out. 'Fucking tell me. I'll go there right now,' he shouted, jabbing a finger in air.

Boateng held up his hands. 'There's nowhere to go, he's AWOL. The killer's called Darian Wallace, from Two-Ten crew. Went by the street name Sy back then.'

'Heard of him. Bastard.' Thompson ground his teeth, body tensing.

'Listen to me.' Boateng spoke calmly, voice low. 'Draymond was targeted because of a woman. She'd dumped Wallace and started seeing him instead, so Wallace decided to kill him. Somehow he got away with it, then went to prison two years ago for burglary. Did his time, came out and murdered two of the people that sent him down. Now I think he's trying to leave the country. Can you help me find him?'

'How?'

In truth, Boateng didn't know, but he had to project authority. 'Wallace is hiding somewhere. But no one's truly off the radar. There'll be contacts he's visiting from the past, could be business or just people he's saying goodbye to. Try to think of places he could be, ask whoever you need to for information. Come back to me with anything you get, quick as possible.'

Thompson nodded slowly, relaxing. As a trained source from his Trident days, he'd understand the role of intelligence in carrying out an operation. This was no different. 'Then what?'

Boateng drew aside a coat flap, revealed the Glock in his belt. After last night's incident he'd emptied the ammo; this evening it was just to show Thompson he meant business. 'We'll take it from there.' Still didn't know what would happen when he did find Wallace, but it was important to give the impression that executive action would be taken. Didn't want Thompson going alone if he did somehow locate their target.

'Damn, you don't mess around. I'm in.'

'Obviously I'll pay, too, if the intel's good.'

Thompson blinked slowly, shook his head. 'No need, man. This is for Dray. I'll start now.' They exchanged numbers, slapped hands and the younger man returned to his flat.

Descending the concrete steps, Boateng realised he should've got a description of Nathan off Thompson, and cursed silently. That could wait; the priority was Wallace. Crossing the central yard area towards his car, he spotted a group of three young men on the path ahead. They were huddled in dark jackets, faces hidden. A squat, muscular dog stood between them, its chain leash taut. Looked to Boateng like a pit bull: a banned breed in the UK. Legit to own one with a special exemption, but this wasn't the time to be inquiring after its provenance. In daytime on normal work routine he'd be over there asking questions. Now he kept his flat cap lowered, picked up the pace as he arced past them.

'Yo!'

Boateng carried on, head down.

'Hey! Where you goin' so fast, man?' They began walking across to him. 'Gonna introduce yourself? This is our manor and we don't know you.' The pit bull was already slobbering, pulling forwards. Some fighting dogs were trained to be aggressive with strangers. Boateng kept going, realised he was encircled and stopped, glancing around.

'Hold up.' One cocked his head sideways, wagged a finger. 'I know his face. Seen 'im on TV, innit? You know who this is?' He looked at the others. 'A fed man. Five-O.' They closed in on him. 'These ain't your ends. So what you doing here on your own?'

'You must be thinking of someone else.'

'Bullshit, he's a fed.'

'Man don't live 'ere, that's for sure,' said another. His companions chuckled. 'Who you after?' The dog began a low growl, front paws lifting off the tarmac.

'You meetin' a snitch? Or you bent?'

They were between him and his car. Boateng considered the options. He couldn't tell if these guys were armed. The Glock in his belt was literally an empty threat. Drawing on them might work if no one called his bluff, but that was a last resort. Only real thing he could do was hit them over the head with it. And worse, nobody knew he was here. His mouth went dry. Could they be reasoned with?

'Say something, cuz.' Each man stepped closer and he could see drool on the dog's jowls. 'Stand up for yourself.'

'OK. I'm off duty, alright? Got a relative here. On my way home,' Boateng replied quietly, began walking again.

'Whoa, slow down.' One blocked him off. 'Who's your relative?'

'Look, I make a call and half of Kennington Station will be down here.'

They laughed together. 'They don't come around these streets, man, it's not safe. Plus you ain't got no backup. That's not how you lot roll when you work. I'll ask you again, who's your relative? Cos you know what? My little brother come runnin' to tell me there's a man pressing every buzzer outside the block. No one visiting a relative does that. So what the fuck you doing here?'

Nothing for it. Boateng reached back for the Glock, but as he lifted his jacket the punch from behind hammered into his kidney. Pain shot through his back but he lashed out, caught something solid then lunged forward. Grabbed at clothing, threw the guy blocking his path into his mate and ran. Sprinted away, willing his legs to move faster. Could see the car about fifty metres off but a scrabbling noise made him turn. Drawing his pistol he saw the young men in pursuit flinch, but saw too late the pit bull in mid-air, launching itself at him. Boateng was knocked to the ground, head crashed into tarmac, but he kept hold of the gun. Dog was on top of him now, all noise, slobber and paws as he fought it off. Then a vice closed on his forearm and Boateng howled. The animal bit deeper, jaws locked on his sleeve. He pitched over but the dog's teeth clamped down, pain spreading through his arm. Boateng rolled, saw the men advancing towards him. Two had drawn weapons he couldn't make out. Quick. He shook his arm but that only hurt more. Smacked the pit bull's head with the pistol butt. It pulled away for a second then attacked again, biting harder and into the flesh of his hand this time. Bellowing, he writhed on the ground, trying to twist and kick out at the beast, couldn't get an angle. The men were closer now and Boateng could see a large kitchen knife glinting beneath the street lights. He spun again onto his back, the dog bounding on top of him. Fighting through agony, knew he had to get his arm free before—

A shot echoed between buildings and the pit bull's body went limp on his chest. The men froze then began stepping back, scanning balconies and rooftops. Boateng wrenched his arm free, heaved the dog away. It'd been shot clean through the skull, inches from him. But no exit wound. What the hell? Didn't matter. He scrambled to his feet, bolted. Still disorientated, horizon pitching as he made the final few yards to his car, popped the doors. Glanced back: his attackers had already disappeared. Boateng shoved the gun in the glove compartment. Noticed his left sleeve was drenched with blood. Hand shaking, he jammed the key in, revved and pulled away with a screech of tyres.

Etta couldn't believe what she was seeing.

'I've got to go, Mum.' She hung up immediately and stood as her husband lurched into the kitchen, blood all over his jacket. 'Oh my God! Zac, what happened?' She rushed over, helped him into a chair.

'I'm sorry,' he croaked. 'I've been such an idiot. Damn!' Boateng winced as she rolled back the sleeve.

She shuffled closer, inspected his left arm. Touched the skin, blood slick on her fingers. 'What the hell is this?'

He gulped. 'It's a dog bite.'

'We have to get you to hospital.'

'No, it's OK, if—'

'It's not OK, Zac, you've got to get that cleaned up, checked for rabies. How on earth did it happen? Were you at work? Why didn't your colleagues take you to A & E?' The questions tumbled from her without pause for answer, each angrier than the last. 'I'm calling an ambulance.' She snatched up the phone.

'No.'

'What?' she shouted, incredulous.

'Listen, Etta. I— I'm so sorry.' He reached out, touched her arm with his good hand.

She met his gaze, recognised the sadness. But the fear she also saw there was something her husband rarely displayed. She fought back her own frustration at him. 'What've you done?'

Zac took a couple of breaths. 'I know who killed Amelia.'

Etta's mouth opened but no sound emerged. She let go of him, slumped back against the chair. When she spoke several seconds later, her voice was quiet yet firm. 'I'm going upstairs to get the first aid kit. Then you'll tell me exactly what's happened, from the start.'

He nodded.

When she returned and began cleaning the wounds, Zac relayed the whole story to her: Scotland Yard's informant vault, Night Vision, Agyeman, Optikon, Froggy, Mamba and Wallace. His Roy Ankrah journalist cover, the money he'd doled out for information. How he'd planned to spend those savings on a holiday for them. And how a pit bull had torn into him tonight before some guardian angel saved his life. All done solo with no backup. It was almost too much to take in, too fantastical to believe. She listened to the whole thing without interrupting her husband. At last there was an explanation for what had been going on these past ten days. It wasn't an affair. But it was egoism and poor judgement and recklessness. In some ways that was worse: lies as well as putting his career in jeopardy, his life in danger. After disbelief her next reaction was anger, rising quickly. She didn't hold back applying antiseptic into his cuts, her fingers taut and trembling.

'What the hell were you thinking? Selfish bastard. How could you be so, so—' She searched for adequate words, spat them at him. 'So fucking stupid?'

Her husband didn't respond, dipped his head in shame.

'You lied to me, Zac!' She jabbed his chest, left a bloodied fingerprint on the jacket. 'Do you know how I felt? I was scared. Thought you were...'

'Didn't know what else to do.' He shook his head, eyes moistening. 'Started out as almost nothing and before I knew it I couldn't stop. I didn't want to tell my colleagues because of what Thompson said about the cover-up, or whatever it was. If one of my own got in the way of that investigation...' He shook his head, lips tight. 'I'll—'

'You'll what?' She unwrapped another antiseptic wipe, dabbed the wound. 'Take the law into your own hands? This whole thing is madness. Just—' Etta held up a hand, but instead of more words a dam of tears burst and she wept, shuddering next to him.

He laid a hand on her back. 'I'm so sorry, my love.'

She could feel him sobbing gently too, his broad shoulders shaking, and pulled herself into him. 'You're a fool, Zachariah Boateng. A damned fool. But I love you.'

His head bowed, touched the top of hers. 'And I love you,' he whispered.

They held one another a minute. Eventually she raised her head, the fury dissipating. 'So, you've discovered this. What's your plan now?' She took a roll of bandage and scissors.

'Find him.'

'Not on your own.'

'Course not.' His reply was instant.

She studied him. 'You can't go on like this, Zac. You've got to own up, tell people. Longer you leave it, the worse it'll get. Even if you personally find this guy, imagine what a defence counsel will make of your freestyling in court. And the others can help you catch him. After all, he's the target of your team's double murder investigation. Use their resources.'

'I'll bring him to justice, I promise, I—'

She tutted loudly, anger welling again. 'I don't want this *me, me, me*, Zac. It's not all about you. Forget your ego for a minute. I lost a daughter too. Remember that. Not one day goes by I don't feel her absence. The girl I gave birth to, breastfed, nurtured.

Nothing's been the same since that day. Like a piece of me's gone
forever. I still feel it now, same as every day since she died. I'm not
losing a husband as well. Kofi's not losing a father, do you hear
me? He's scared enough as it is that one of us might just vanish
from his life, like his sister did. You and your team can bring
Wallace in, make him stand trial, then we can live knowing the
monster who murdered our daughter is locked up for life, not
that he cost our family more…' She tailed off, swallowed. 'OK?'

He bit his lip, blinked agreement.

She reached for her phone, opened the minicab app. 'Right
now you need a doctor to look at your arm.' He made to speak
but her glare cut him off.

With an injury like that there was no point trying to be a hard
man. The dog bite had looked gross. Absolutely gopping, claret
all over the place. The copper needed to screw the nut: sort
himself out and get a medic. Instead, he'd driven home like a
maniac, stumbled inside. Not come out since. Maybe the missus
was patching him up. And perhaps he didn't want to explain to
anyone what he was doing alone on the estate in Kennington
when he got attacked.

Spike watched the Boateng residence from across the road.
Checked his watch: 12.23 a.m. He'd parked up, killed the ignition
and cracked a window. What was this Boateng bloke playing at?
He'd let three muppets get a step on him, drawn a sidearm, not
fired it, then almost got mauled to death by a mutt. If Spike hadn't
been there, either the dog or those street kids would've done him
in. Lucky he only had to shoot the animal. Human injuries were
a lot harder to explain away, especially to the colonel.

During surveillance earlier today he'd briefed the boss on his
plan to let the coppers lead him to Wallace. Patey wasn't pleased,
but recognised they didn't have a lot of options left. Fat lad in a

caravan was being looked after by the Met and their insider had produced sod all else by way of leads. What did they mean by Boateng being 'closer to it' than anyone else? Some sort of connection between him and the safe deposit heist. Boateng hadn't investigated it at the time, so maybe it was a personal link to Wallace. Spike had googled his new assignment and found a ton of articles. Detective Inspector Zachariah Boateng had enjoyed a decent career spanning murder investigations, missing persons, kidnaps and drug work. Could be that his path had crossed Wallace's sometime then, but there was no record of that on the Met system. One news story stood above the others though: his dead daughter. No one ever caught for it. Was that what Patey's person in the Met was referring to? Perhaps Wallace brassed up Boateng's girl in the newsagents five years ago. But if the case was never solved, how could the insider know that? All the nause was making Spike's head hurt. Whatever way you looked at it, one thing was obvious: people were out to get Boateng. And he didn't seem that great at handling himself. So better keep him safe until he located Wallace.

A taxi pulled up outside the house and Boateng emerged a minute later, clutching his left forearm. Wife hugged him for ages on the doorstep and they kissed. Soppy bollocks. Then Boateng got in the back of the car. Spike followed them until it turned into Lewisham hospital. Finally he was getting a medic to sort him out. Nothing else likely to happen tonight then. Time for Spike to drive home and get his head down for a few hours before the hurry-up-and-wait routine started again tomorrow morning. He'd be ready.

CHAPTER THIRTY-ONE

Wednesday, 28 June 2017

'Dad, what happened?'

Kofi froze, spoon mid-air, eyes wide. Etta watched her zombified husband lurch towards the kettle, flick it on. He eased himself painfully against the kitchen counter and inspected the bandage on his left wrist. In A & E he'd been given two stitches for the puncture wound plus a rabies shot. Doctors said there appeared to be no tendon or joint damage: a lucky escape. They didn't know the half of it. Despite that good fortune, her husband still looked as if he'd been ten rounds in a boxing match or ten minutes in a bar brawl.

'Were you fighting the bad guys?' their son persisted.

Zac snapped out of his trance. 'This?' he held up the bandaged arm, grinned. 'You should've seen the other guy.'

'Wow!' exclaimed Kofi, glancing at Etta to gauge the reaction.

Both her boys knew she didn't like them joking about violence. 'Zac...' The single word was usually enough to remind him.

'Not really, Kof, sorry.' He chucked a teabag into his 'World's Best Dad' mug, a title she wasn't convinced he still merited. Zac looked away as he added the boiling water. 'It was just a little accident at work, I'm fine though.'

The kid gave a whine of disappointment.

'Your father's got to be more careful,' explained Etta. 'Like I've said to you, Kof, never run off without telling someone where you're going.' She caught her husband's eye. 'Sometimes the same goes for grown-ups.'

Derek left it till midday before he began walking to the lock-up. He'd get this errand done then jump in the cab for a late shift. Had to psych himself up a bit, going alone. Back in the days when he ran with the football firm at Millwall, being around the other lads after a few pints was enough. Mob mentality, they called it. That was years ago. But he could still turn on 'Old Derek' if necessary, when a customer was taking the piss.

Before leaving the house, he'd reached to the back of the odds 'n' sods drawer and pulled out his old brass knuckleduster. Just in case. Didn't expect any trouble though. Wallace might be wanted for double murder but he wasn't a moron. A few choice words from the older man and he'd see sense. It was like collecting tax, that's all. And he definitely needed it; just that morning two new bills had dropped onto the doorstep.

Derek took out his mobile and called the number. No harm in having some backup. If everything went according to plan, he'd be at home with a cuppa and a pocketful of cash before the Old Bill arrived at his garage. He could just claim ignorance when they asked about Wallace. Or identify himself as the source and maybe even blag a reward off them too.

His call was answered on the third ring. 'Hello, Crimestoppers. How can I help?'

'Yeah, I wanna report the location of a murder suspect…'

No good keeping his head down. DCI Krebs had already spotted Boateng and was striding towards his desk. Wasn't long before her six-foot frame was looming over him.

'DI Boateng,' she said, using his formal title in front of his team. 'What's your progress on the Wallace murders?'

'Ma'am. Other than the SAS lead…' He let the words hang.

Krebs shook her head quickly. 'No joy there yet.'

'We've had one other development. DS Connelly?'

'That's me. Facial Recognition had a hit on Wallace from yesterday evening, halfway down Old Kent Road. Target was walking south-east, holding a bag.' The Irishman jerked his thumb at his laptop. 'I've been collating CCTV footage to track his movements before and after. Got him going into King Rooster for his dinner but we lose him either side of it when the coverage drops out. Our working theory is he's holed up somewhere nearby, eatin' his chicken.'

Krebs planted her hands on the desk, leaned in. 'So what's your operational plan?'

The brief silence was interrupted as Malik's desk phone rang and he reached across and answered it.

Boateng cleared his throat. 'We continue searching CCTV for other signs of him and deploy surveillance on Old Kent Road. If he's been to King Rooster once, chances are he'll go back. He's obviously not worried about being recognised there.'

'Time to up the media coverage,' stated Krebs. 'We need to show London we're doing all we can to catch this man. He's clearly psychotic.'

'Psychopathic.' Boateng couldn't resist correcting her. 'I don't think he's lost contact with reality at all, but I reckon he is capable of killing someone without losing much sleep. Believe me, that's scarier.' He reached for a cup of water, bringing his left hand above the desk. If Krebs was going to take issue with his psychological profiling, she was distracted by the bandage.

'What happened to you?'

'Oh.' He rotated the injured wrist. 'Damned dog in the park last night. Didn't like my football skills.' He forced a smile as the others chuckled. 'Five hours in Lewisham A & E getting stitches.'

'Well, if we see you foaming at the mouth we'll know who to blame.' Krebs's attempt at humour fell flat. She smoothed her bob cut. 'Right then. Back to work, everyone. Keep it up. Remember, efficiency. We all have to do more with fewer resources.'

'Er, sorry to interrupt, ma'am.' Malik was still holding the phone. 'Anonymous tip's just come through Crimestoppers. Member of the public says he knows Darian Wallace's exact whereabouts. Location's a lock-up garage off Old Kent Road. Could be a load of rubbish like the rest of—'

'Shit!' Boateng slapped the desk harder than intended and his team stared. Much as he wanted to, there was no way to go solo. Best he could hope for was some recon and the chance to come back after work. A story about extra surveillance was already forming in his mind. Golden opportunity to nick the suspect presenting itself to the lone officer on detail… quickly followed by a darker tale, arriving to find Wallace shot, his enemies having finally caught up with him. Despite what he'd told Etta, his personal quest was still on. And his anger was as visceral as ever.

Boateng stood. 'Location tallies with Pat's hit on facial recognition. That's good enough for me. Arrest warrant's been issued so we're ready to go. Let's keep it low-key. Two unmarked pool cars to go check the place out then we'll radio in for borough units. Don't want to spook him.'

'Er, DI Boateng.' Krebs had folded her arms. 'Surely after the previous two attempts to nab Wallace you'll be waiting for Armed Response or Tactical Support? You can't risk him getting away again.'

Boateng hesitated. If only she'd come in twenty minutes later, they'd have been gone. Just had to sell his plan on her terms. 'Staking the garage out could help us gather intelligence on anyone assisting Wallace,' he began. 'That's more arrests. And even better, we might learn where his jewellery stash is hidden. Lots of happy customers if we get that stuff back. Great publicity.'

Krebs frowned. 'Unlike you to think with a PR hat on, Zac. Don't take that the wrong way. You've got a point though. Mount the surveillance with your team. But wait until armed backup is available first, then deploy.'

'But with respect, ma'am, if they're on another job it could be hours. We may not have that kind of time. Do we really need them? There's no reason to suspect Wallace has a firearm.' Boateng realised he didn't know if that was true.

'Well, I'm not having another innocent man Tasered or mayhem in a public place slapped on social media. You'll do this one by the book.'

Boateng bit his lip. Bollocks. 'Ma'am.'

Wallace turned the memory stick over in his hand, examined it under the bare light bulb. The device looked ordinary. He'd found it inside a big piece of jewellery that must've got bumped about in transit. The back had come loose. No markings, no clues, no means of checking what was on it. Maybe he could head to a call shop nearby, some of them still had PCs you could rent, with USB drives…

Or not.

Probably a waste of time; he'd guess it was encrypted. He'd investigate later. Main thing right now was getting out of London. Still, the question gnawed at him: who hides a memory stick inside silverware then puts it in a safe deposit box? Either someone very paranoid or a person with big secrets. Perhaps both.

A sudden bang on the metal of the garage door sent adrenalin shooting through him.

Wallace kept still, silent. Could they see in broad daylight that he had the bulb on? Another slap came on the garage door.

Someone who could put force into it. The lock turned and Wallace shielded his eyes as sunshine slanted in. Squinted to focus.

The old man.

'Alright.' He stepped inside, shut the door behind him. He was big, solid. Seemed to fill the space. 'Come to talk about your rent.'

Pocketing the memory stick, Wallace shifted his body to block the holdalls behind him. 'I've paid it.'

'Yeah, but I'm talking about an extra fee.'

Wallace already knew what was coming. He said nothing.

The old bloke moved towards him, one hand fidgeting in his trouser pocket. 'I thought you and I might come to some sort of understanding. What with your position and all.' He sniffed. 'I want a thousand quid.'

'Or?'

'The coppers are gonna be round here quick sharp.' Derek coughed. 'So?'

First reaction: pay the man. Could give him a grand's worth of stuff, hard-to-trace items he could sell on. But no guarantee it'd shut him up. Pay an extortionist today and he's back tomorrow wanting more. Or calling the cops anyway. That's how they operated, these people. Parasites. The familiar sense of injustice was already kindled. Being taken for a mug. Wallace felt the rage ballooning, making his limbs stiffen, teeth grind. So close to the end, and now this pussyhole was trying to fuck him over. Who did the old prick think he was dealing with? Wallace pictured his dad for a second. He wasn't having this. One more name had just been added to his list. He blinked, slowed himself down. Smiled.

'OK,' he conceded. 'Grand, yeah?'

Derek stepped forward. 'Should do the trick.'

'Or something worth a grand you can ship on?'

'Fine, long as it's not marked.'

Wallace turned, knelt. Unzipped both holdalls, displayed the contents of one to Derek. The older man stooped, reached towards a Rolex as Wallace put his hand in the second bag. The angle grinder whirred to life and Derek looked up in time for the blade to plough into his face, opening a cheek, biting into bone and out again. At first he made no sound, just stared at the tool. Wallace slashed the whining disc hard across his throat. A jet of blood hit him, another sprayed upwards and within five seconds the old man's lifeless body was on the floor, leaking crimson expanding into a pool around his head and shoulders.

The lock-up was silent except for Wallace's slightly accelerated breathing. He could hear seagulls screeching outside. Chucked the angle grinder back in his bag and stood there looking at the corpse. Blood everywhere. Couldn't stay here now. Only question was how much time remained. He patted Derek's pockets. Knuckleduster in one, mobile in the other. Wallace took out the antiquated handset, scrolled through its calls. Clocked the last number dialled. He'd seen it before. Grabbed his copy of the *Evening Standard* from Friday, flicked to the article and found it. Crimestoppers anonymous tip line. Thirty minutes ago.

Wallace scanned the garage, chucked a couple more items into the holdalls. Swapped the bloodied T-shirt for another one, pulled on his hat and sunglasses. Knew he hadn't got everything but there was no time to waste. Cracked the garage door, peered through. Nobody there. Hefted both holdalls outside. Closed the big metal slab behind him, locked it and set off into the warm summer afternoon.

'Armed police!'

The Enforcer smashed into the top of the door, snapping open the lock. Two officers moved in on either side, hoisted up the metal, while three more covered the garage, Heckler & Koch MP5 guns trained on the interior. Boateng could see from five metres back that the figure wasn't Darian Wallace. From the amount of blood on the concrete he could also see that whoever it was had long since died. He pulled on the basic kit to enter: gauze mask, gloves, overshoes. Told his team to stay put.

It'd taken two hours for Armed Response to come off another job, during which time he'd nodded off twice in the car with Jones, exhaustion getting the better of him for a few seconds. Krebs had insisted on regular updates during their surveillance. When no one came in or out of the garage for a further three hours and the firearms lads were bored, complaining about being needed elsewhere, she made the decision to send them in. He'd voiced opposition by radio, still quietly hoping to be able to send his colleagues home one by one until he was alone. But given the lock-up's contents, it was the right call to enter. Assuming this dead man was the source of the Crimestoppers intel – and it was legit – logic suggested Wallace had killed him and fled.

Boateng stood at the perimeter of pooled blood. Adult humans had about five litres inside them, though to look at this poor sod you'd think it was twice that. Open neck wound indicated a severed artery. The unidentified man's limbs were already curling slightly with the first stage of rigor mortis, so they were about five hours too late. About the same time since they got the Crimestoppers call. Who was he? That'd become clear soon enough. If Wallace had been here the lock-up could offer a clue to his next move. He'd obviously left in a hurry. Rubbish everywhere: toilet roll, fast food boxes, a plastic Coke bottle filled with what looked like piss.

After taking a good look at the gore, the Armed Response boys had left and were conferring outside, clearly planning to move on. Boateng signalled his team to join him beside the body and they stepped carefully through. Jones suppressed a small gag but stayed put. Connelly shook his head, crossed himself. No humour this time.

'Who do we think he is?' Malik didn't take his eyes off the victim.

'The source?' suggested Jones.

'Maybe.' Boateng swept a hand around the lock-up's cramped interior. 'Let's check all this stuff.'

'Should we wait for the SOCOs?' asked Malik.

'Normally, yes. But this is a live manhunt, could be actionable leads here. Look for anything that tells us where he might've gone. Nas, grab some forensic bags from the car.'

'Boss.'

Boateng squatted in the far corner, began sorting the detritus of Wallace's hidden existence. An old *Evening Standard* lay over a dark shirt reeking of body odour. Lifting the garment, his breath caught. A mobile, plugged into the single socket, charging. Boateng glanced over his shoulder. Jones and Connelly were facing away, absorbed in discussion. Malik hadn't returned. He took up the device – airplane mode. The simple handset had no PIN. Shielding it with his body, he opened the call log and toggled it to outgoing only. Just two numbers, both mobiles.

Cognitive psychologists have found most people can remember seven digits, give or take. Boateng knew he could manage a whole phone number, but two? Impossible. Could choose one, but what if the other was a better lead? He heard the car boot thunk outside, footsteps. Had to risk it. Took out his own mobile, selected its camera. Snapped a photo of the outgoing calls screen and dropped it back in his pocket. Closed Wallace's mobile again as Malik approached, and held it out.

'Get this bagged up and sent to the lab, will you, Nas?'

The young man cocked his head. 'Might take a couple of days to get anything back.'

'I know. But if it's going to be evidence we need to do things by the book. Like Krebs said.'

Malik took the phone. 'Boss.'

Dickhead.

Wallace bashed the heel of his hand into his skull. Why did he lose control with the old man like that? Surely there was an easier way of dealing with the situation – didn't need to kill him. The guy probably had a wife, kids, family, mates, whoever. A life ended in seconds over a Rolex watch or two. Then again, if he'd paid him off, the feds still might've come round; wasn't clear what Derek had told Crimestoppers. So perhaps he had made the right choice, if you could call it that. Happened so fast, like his unconscious had taken over. Survival instinct or hardwired violence? Maybe he was fooling himself that moving countries and starting again would make a difference. If that rage was in him, like it was in his dad, perhaps he'd never escape it. Magma seething under rock, always there, waiting for a fissure to erupt.

Wallace sat among dense trees below the bridge at Deptford Creek, Thames water lapping against the brick wall below him. Just had to wait a few more hours. Then he could get away from all this shit.

But before that, there was one last person to see. He'd made a promise.

CHAPTER THIRTY-TWO

Zac cracked open the beer, took several big gulps then held the cold bottle against his forehead. He had to think. Checked his watch: 8.36 p.m. Another slug of beer. Mounted the stairs, reasoning that his sax might help. Etta was out at her Wednesday gym class, and Kofi was staying at Neon's. His son was spending a lot of time there recently, but Zac was glad to have the space tonight.

He lifted the King Zephyr sax, set his fingering and began some warm-up exercises. Any chance of staking out the lock-up was blown once the firearms team had gone in. Out of desperation he'd even bought dinner from the King Rooster chicken shop on Old Kent Road, hoping vainly his target might return. Pathetic. He felt completely impotent. Wallace could be anywhere now. Maybe already gone.

Worse still, when presented with the chance to action a lead at the murder scene, he'd recorded the mobile numbers for himself. Lying by omission to his teammates. That wasn't how it worked. You had each other's backs, and he should be setting the example to junior officers. If what he'd done today came out in the wash, disciplinary proceedings were guaranteed. Directorate of Professional Standards would trace it all, unpick his movements, tug on every thread until his covert investigation unravelled entirely. It'd cost him his job; he might even go to prison. Is that what Amelia would've wanted? Zac took his lips off the sax. Reached for the bottle, drained it. Closed his eyes a minute. Eventually he opened them, moistened the mouthpiece again.

Slowly, he began to play – a lilting, melancholic tune that pretty much summed up his state of mind. That fool's errand last night could've got him killed, and in the cold light of day what chance did Night Vision have of finding anything? He wasn't an active informer any more and his old contacts had probably vaporised. But Zac didn't know who else to ask.

His own leads were somewhat better, but hard to action. He'd googled those two numbers from the garage. Had to do it on his own laptop, couldn't risk a trace of his search on the work system. One was listed on the website of an artist in Peckham, whose speciality seemed to be dismembering and recombining animals. Perhaps that was a dead end – no pun. Something to do with Wallace's greyhound? More interesting was the other mobile, dialled three times in six days, most recently this morning. Linked online in classified ads to a boat skipper based in Kent. Surely the escape plan.

Zac knew what he *should* do with the information. What he *wanted* to do was another matter. A little voice was whispering, telling him how good it would feel to give in to the rage and put a bullet through Darian Wallace's head. With the fuzz of tiredness in his brain, he couldn't think clearly enough to counter the idea. Started to improvise on the sax, louder and faster, blues turning to pure frustration.

Behind two closed doors, downstairs in the kitchen, his mobile rang. 'N Vision' flashed across the screen before voicemail kicked in.

Wallace knocked on the door, pulled his hood down, took a half step back. Didn't want to seem threatening. The latch clicked and behind a taut chain he recognised Neon's mum peering out. 'Hello, Shanice, how're you doing?'

She gave a long, slow breath, looked him up and down. 'What do you want, Darian? You not bring no trouble to my house.'

'Course not,' he grinned. 'Just came by to see Neon, that's all.'

'It's nine thirty. The boys are in bed.'

Boys. Someone else with Neon. The Boateng kid?

'I don't mean no harm, Shanice, just thought I'd say goodbye to Neon.'

'I watch the news, you know. You're a wanted man.'

Wallace nodded, leaned forward and dropped his voice. 'I didn't kill those guys, you have to believe me. You know how it is once you get a criminal record – everyone judges you. Certain people tried to set me up. Including the police.' He could see she was less sure of herself now. 'That's why I have to leave. Don't want to, you know how my mum is.' The woman's lips pursed in acknowledgement. 'Neon's like a little brother to me, helping him was probably the best thing I've ever done with my life. I know it's late, but can you let me speak to him? Please. I wanna give him some advice. Keep the lickle man on point with his maths, yeah?' He gave a small laugh, held eye contact.

She smiled too and slipped the chain off. 'Alright. Only a few minutes though, you understand?'

Wallace climbed the stairs, heard the noises of video game football before he'd reached the top. Easing the bedroom door open, he stepped in and closed it behind him. Neon was under his duvet, game controller in both hands, face tight with concentration. Battling him on screen was the Boateng kid, sitting up inside a sleeping bag on a roll mat spread across the floor. Both boys froze when they noticed him, like a ghost had appeared.

'Keep going,' he told them, gesturing at the TV. 'Two minutes left in the half.' Did he ever have carefree days and nights like this, where the result of gaming against your mate was the most important thing in life? What a luxury. Watching the clock tick towards forty-five minutes on screen, Wallace wished for a moment that he could just stay here, be part of this world. Have another chance. He wanted to tell these kids to make the most of what they had. Listen to their teachers, the good ones anyway. Do their homework. Go university if they could get the money.

'You came back, Darian,' said Neon when the time expired.

'Yeah, wanted to see you, innit.'

'Are you going away again?'

Wallace pursed his lips, nodded. 'Got to.'

'Will you come and visit?'

He blinked. 'Dunno.' Why was he getting emotional? Pussy-hole. Just say bye-bye and get out. There was a boat coming for him any time. 'You know, Neon, gots to make the right choices as you grow up. Otherwise you have to keep running and hiding, and that's no life. Get it?'

The boy looked confused.

'Don't make the mistakes I've made. You understand? Don't mess up like me.'

Even as he said the words, a small voice nagged him about the Boateng kid. The same voice that told him he was owed because of what happened in his family. The same voice that told him drug dealing, robbery, burglary, violence were all fine. Even murder; if people got in your way, put them on your list. The world and most of its people were out for themselves, so why shouldn't he be? Why lie down and get crushed by the stronger, tougher ones? You had to be the predator, ahead of the competition. A lion stalking the grassland, feeding on the weak. Or else you were the gazelle getting its throat ripped out. That was life. And right now this voice told him to ditch the sentimental talk and focus on Boateng's son. Here he was. The perfect insurance policy for his getaway. A gazelle at the edge of the pack.

Boateng had played his lungs out. He'd been up there well over an hour. Lost himself in the zone. He remained in that zombified hinterland – too wired to rest, too exhausted to make progress. And still no inspiration on what to do next. Trudged downstairs to get another drink. Remembered the ten-year-old whisky his mate Troy had given him a couple of years back. Too smoky for Etta, so he normally drank it alone. Now seemed ideal. He reached to the back of the kitchen cupboard, pulled out the bottle. Poured a generous measure. He took a first sip and felt the warmth spread around his mouth and throat. Despite the quality he was considering downing the rest when his mobile chirped. Missed call? Checked the screen, saw Thompson had rung him an hour ago. Damn. He dialled immediately.

'It's me. You called.'

'Yeah.' Sounded like Thompson was in a factory. 'I'm at work, gimme a second.' Receding noise suggested he was navigating to a quiet spot.

'Have you got something?' Boateng couldn't conceal the urgency in his voice.

Pause. 'Probably not. Dunno.'

'Bollocks,' he muttered. More disappointment. Shouldn't have got his hopes up. 'So why did you call?'

'Easy. I'll get to that. Tried everything I could think of, yeah? I'm talking blanket social media coverage. Messaged everyone I knew that might've known him, friends of friends and whatnot. Sent messages all night long.'

'And?'

'Nothing.'

Boateng's heart sank again. Why was Thompson bothering to tell him? Every communication between them carried a risk. Perhaps he should've been tighter on his instructions.

'Then I changed up my tactics,' continued the young man. 'Wallace was in Pentonville prison, right? So I belled my man who was locked down there too. He knew someone who knew someone. Called in a favour or two. Eventually I get on the phone with a guy that's still inside.'

Boateng knew that, although banned, mobiles were common in most prisons, smuggled in by visitors or drones over the walls. 'Go on.'

'He was the guy that used to do laundry shift with Wallace. I figured since they spent hours together every day for like, months, he might know more about the man than anyone outside that used to see him. Up to date, you know?'

'Good thinking.' Boateng was impressed with the initiative; he wouldn't have been able to generate leads on his target from inside Pentonville. 'What'd he say?'

'Wallace was damn smart, did everything the screws asked, on his best behaviour the whole time. That's why his sentence got reduced, innit?'

'I know. What else?'

'Come on, man, let me tell my story.' Thompson chuckled. 'So the laundry guy says they used to talk about this and that, plans for when they got out, how many days left, usual stuff.'

'And?'

'He told me Wallace only cared about two people in the whole world. Didn't give a damn about nobody else. One was his mum. She's in a care home down Croydon – she'd had a stroke and started losing her memory. He wanted to take care of her, move her somewhere nicer, pay the bills, you know? So I was thinking if we locate his mum, Wallace is probably gonna go there and then bam! We got him. I've started making some calls to the homes. Do you know how many there are in Croydon? Hundreds, fam.'

Boateng felt like throwing his phone at the wall. All that for something they already knew and had discounted. 'We've traced her. She… never mind. Might as well—' He stopped, the fog in his mind clearing for a second. 'What about the other person?'

'Just some kid he used to teach maths. Like a mentor or whatever. Wasn't his son or nothing.'

'Who was he?'

Thompson laughed. 'Boy had a mad name. Neon.'

CHAPTER THIRTY-THREE

Boateng popped his car's central locking, slid into the driver's seat. Reached across, pulled out the pistol. Glancing up his street and checking the mirrors for passers-by, he quickly reloaded the clip with 9 mm rounds from the ammo box. Gloves made sure he left no prints on the casings. He'd wiped the whole thing down earlier too. Filled a mag, inserted it, but didn't rack the slide: a bullet in the chamber risked accidental discharge, like in Mamba's car the other night. If the gun did go off, it would be deliberate. His numbed brain started attempting to work through a 'heat-of-the-moment' defence as he stared at the pistol. Snapping out of the trance, he stowed his weapon in the door pocket and gunned the engine, tearing off towards Neon's house. Drove like a madman, overtaking at every chance, slamming the horn to any dawdlers.

He parked down the street from the Grant residence in Honor Oak Estate. Tucked the gun into his jacket and crept towards the front door, scanning the pavement, open spaces, shadows. Wasn't sure what he expected to find at the tiny flat in Spalding House. Realistically nothing except the Grants and his own son. Best he could hope for was something to help close the net on Wallace. Still, a small part of him hoped the murdering bastard might actually be there. With surprise on his side, Boateng would confront him and make the arrest. Reassured himself that was the plan. But if Wallace had laid a finger on Kofi…

No answer when he knocked on the door. Maybe Shanice Grant didn't hear him. Surely not asleep already? It was only ten fifteen. Boateng knocked gently again. Eventually movement came from within and she appeared, rubbing her eyes. Opened the door fully once she saw him. 'Zac, is everything alright? Must've dozed off in front of the telly, y'know? Didn't expect to see you until tomorrow mor—'

'Is he here?' whispered Boateng, right hand inside his jacket.

'Kofi? Of course, he's in Neon's bedroom. They should've put the light out by now, I told them—'

'Not Kofi. Darian Wallace.'

She swallowed, glanced upstairs.

Boateng clapped his left hand on her shoulder, spoke quietly through gritted teeth. 'Is he in your house?'

Shanice bit her lip.

'Up there?'

She nodded.

He drew the pistol into a cup-and-saucer grip, moved in towards the staircase. Above him the first floor was all darkness. Put one foot on the bottom step, which groaned as his weight shifted to it. Boateng froze. He mimed quiet to Shanice, motioned her to kill the hall lights by the front door. Then he directed her back inside the lounge, where the TV murmured, a burst of laughter followed by applause from a studio audience. Eyes adjusting to the gloom, he edged up the stairs, back to the wall. Hoped Wallace hadn't heard their exchange, that he'd assume the creaks were simply Neon's mum heading up to bed. Heart thumping quickly as he reached the top, everything was still.

Boateng had been here enough times to know the basic layout. Three small bedrooms and a bathroom. Neon's door off the landing was ajar, and he approached slowly. Aiming his pistol into the gap, he eased it open with his foot. Saw Neon lying in bed, duvet twisted around him. Moonlight spilled through thin curtains onto a TV and little desk. One slow breath and he kicked the door, rounding it with pistol raised.

Kofi's sleeping bag lay empty on the roll mat.

Telling himself to keep calm, Boateng pushed the bedroom door to, shook Neon gently. 'Where's Kofi?' he asked the bleary-eyed kid.

'Uh?'

'Neon! Where is he? Kofi.'

'Dunno.'

'What about Darian Wallace?'

The toilet flush outside cut through their exchange. Boateng stepped back, covered the bedroom door with his pistol sights. Lowered a flat hand to Neon, who lay still. Soft footsteps approached. The door creaked open and Boateng felt his hands start to tremble as it swung inwards. Held his breath.

'Dad!'

Kofi stood in the doorway, his features picked out by light from the window. Boateng exhaled heavily, lowered the Glock. Beckoned his son in. 'Both of you need to tell me right now: where's Darian Wallace?'

The two boys broke their stares at the gun, exchanged a guilty look.

'Come on!' he hissed.

'He left,' replied Kofi. 'But we don't know where he went.' The kid frowned, cocked his head. 'Is he a bad guy?'

Ten minutes later, Boateng was sitting in front of the TV, using a video game controller to navigate its web browsing history. Neon had told him about Wallace's previous visit, his demand to use the machine. Boateng inferred it was his means to obtain online information with minimal exposure. Amazingly his list of pages was still there. Had Wallace been too rushed to delete it, or too confident? Perhaps he didn't know the process. It wasn't straightforward on a games console; Boateng had to pull up a

YouTube video to help him find the archive. All this cost time in which Wallace would be putting distance between them. But he knew that haring off into the night wasn't the way to find his quarry. He needed intel.

As Boateng read, Neon recounted Wallace's parting advice on making the right choices in life. Then he'd said a serious goodbye. Probably meant he was planning to leave very soon. Maybe even tonight.

Scrolling down the sites visited, Boateng noted extensive research that made sense of one number he'd discovered on Wallace's mobile. Vessel and engine types, ports in France, examination of maritime message boards. Wallace had looked for boat skippers and followed up with background searches on some of them. He'd also accessed a tide calculator for North Woolwich. The UK Hydrographic Office data had been examined for several days, but only tomorrow's results were cross-referenced with a weather forecast. A further search of locations around Docklands appeared to focus down on Trinity Buoy Wharf. Boateng's thoughts raced as he pieced it all together, willing his brain to work more efficiently. The boat skipper's phone number, the tidal and weather data, the potential departure site at East India Docks, the goodbye to Neon. His best guess was that it all pointed to one thing: Wallace was planning to escape in the early hours of tomorrow morning.

He told the two boys to go back to bed, kissed Kofi goodnight and went downstairs. Didn't know what to say to Shanice Grant about letting Wallace into her house, he'd deal with that later. Had to get to East India Docks right now. Maybe he was already too late. Briefly considered calling it in, or even sending a text to Connelly, Jones or Malik. Dismissed the idea quickly without further exploration. 'No time' was the reason he gave himself.

Driving away from Honor Oak Estate towards the main road, heading east, Boateng twice glimpsed another vehicle behind him.

The same dark saloon on two quiet streets with no other traffic. Checked his rear-view mirror again on the main road but saw nothing except the snaking red and white lights of night traffic.

Passing the sign for Blackwall Tunnel to take him under the river, he floored the accelerator.

Things were getting a bit tasty.

Spike struggled to keep up without making it obvious he was in pursuit. The copper was driving like a lunatic. Less chance he'd spot the car behind, at least. Heading north towards the river, the O2 arena loomed up ahead like some giant spacecraft. Boateng's dark green car was six in front.

Emerging from Blackwall Tunnel, the copper hooked a left onto the A13 before quickly circling back south again. Spike stayed with him as the road twisted around the River Lea and it became obvious Boateng was aiming for a spit of land off the docks. The solo mission, urgent driving and random location meant the geezer probably knew something important. Could be a false alarm. Could be Wallace.

Spike slowed, watched the copper as he turned into the road leading to Trinity Buoy Wharf. Bunch of giant warehouses. Killed his lights, spun the car round and parked up a hundred metres away from Boateng's wagon. Made sure his nose was facing out for a quicker getaway after. Old habits.

The wharf was dark and quiet, a low traffic hum the only background noise. Spike retrieved his bag from the boot, slung it over one shoulder. Needed high ground. He scanned the buildings, mostly big units of corrugated iron and shabby brickwork. Saw the red glow above of Bow Creek lighthouse. That'll do. Pulled on his motorbike face mask.

Scaling the drainpipe and scrambling up the pitched warehouse roof, Spike used the iron ladder to reach the lighthouse dome's top deck. Clocked the camera. Bollocks. Considered taking it out before concluding no one was likely to be watching at ten past eleven on a Wednesday night. Sabotaging it would only draw attention, set off an alarm somewhere. If he kept low and still, any mug looking probably wouldn't see him directly beneath it, all black gear at dark o'clock. Worth the risk for his 360 view.

Spike took out the Diemaco sniper rifle, screwed on a sound suppressor, extended its stock and bipod, settled into the prone position. Flicked on his night scope. The world became a grainy circle of greens, white and black. Not much wind tonight, that was good. He'd tested the rifle last week with his usual home-made hollow point rounds, zeroed the sights for around 150 metres, got a nice grouping. Boded well, although not for Wallace.

Or the copper, if necessary.

Unpaid overtime. The worst kind. Still, Jones didn't have other plans tonight. She'd done a good gym session this morning, and after they'd discovered Wallace's newest victim in the lock-up garage, working on their main case seemed like the most useful thing she could do right now. She had been tempted earlier by the cinema trip her flatmates suggested, it'd be a great way to switch off, but Boateng would appreciate the help here, and it seemed like he was under a lot of pressure right now. That was understandable: the buck stopped with him on Wallace. Well, technically it stopped with Krebs, but Jones suspected any failure would rapidly slide off her and hit Boateng.

Maybe that was just the way you got on in the Met, and Krebs was certainly doing well. And Jones would be lying if she said she herself hadn't been strategic to get to DS in only five years. But letting others take the blame was something else… Would it ever come to that for her? Dad wouldn't have done that. He always said you needed to be able to 'look yourself in the mirror and know you did the right thing'. But how did you know what the right thing was? She'd discovered that reality was often more complex than her Dad had made out, though his moral compass never seemed to waver. Neither would hers, Jones resolved: whatever her career ambitions, she liked and respected Boateng too much to let him take sole responsibility for failure on this case. That's what kept her in the office at 11 p.m., crunching data. Her boss was probably home with his family, putting a boundary around the Job, hopefully getting a few hours to relax. Good for him. She admired Boateng's work-life balance. Which was why she'd agonised over interrupting his evening.

Jones had retrieved the log off Wallace's phone before it'd gone to the lab. Figured there could be something urgent on there. Bit weird that Boateng wasn't fussed and had asked Malik to bag it up before they'd done a quick-and-dirty on the SIM. She'd used her initiative: actioned the request immediately then followed up with a call to the mobile company's contact. A sweet, geeky guy she used to chat to back in her Cyber Crime days. Told him what a legend he was, asked him very nicely if there was any way he could possibly run the billing data before leaving for the night. He'd obliged.

Wallace hadn't done much with the phone: he was obviously savvy about using it, leaving traces. But one number stood out, called six times in the last few days. Jones had hit the online research from all angles in the past couple of hours and worked up the profile. Steve Miller, a forty-six-year-old boat owner from Kent who chartered his vessel out for day trips. Police National Computer said he did two years for smuggling cigarettes from France with his brother in 2009. She felt her excitement grow as Wallace's plan crystallised, and with it the realisation she had to tell Boateng. Now.

No answer from his mobile. Jones left a message saying she needed to speak to him now. Tried again five minutes later, same result. Texted, no reply. Went to the intranet spreadsheet of Lewisham MIT staff, called his home.

'Hello?' A woman's voice.

'Er, is this Zac Boateng's home?'

'Who is this?'

'I'm DS Kat Jones, I work with your husband. Could I speak to him please? Sorry to call so late. It's urgent.'

A brief snort came down the line, then a moment's silence. 'I thought he was at work. He's not with you?'

'Not that I know of.'

'And it's urgent?'

'Yes.'

'About his current case?'

'That's right.'

Boateng's wife clicked her tongue. 'You're in Lewisham now?'

'Yup.'

'I think you'd better come over.'

Etta had been feeling great. Sweated buckets at circuit training, jumped in the shower and headed for dinner and a drink with Jennie. Nattered away to her old mate, swapped funny stories about their kids. Hoped she'd return to find Zac at home, and with Kofi at Neon's house for the night, perhaps they could even…

But he hadn't been there. She'd assumed he was still at work till this Jones woman called. Zac's younger, female colleague. Who was attractive, as Etta had suspected. Whom she'd briefly worried was getting it on with her husband, until he'd fessed up to the real problem. And who was now standing in their kitchen saying the same thing as her: I thought he was with you. They faced one another across the flagstones.

'Zac told you he was at home?' asked Etta.

'Yeah, said he was hoping to have an early night for once. That was about seven.'

Etta folded her arms. 'Do you think he's gone after Darian Wallace?'

'Alone?' Jones frowned. 'Why would he do that?'

Etta hesitated. She was reluctant to breach Zac's confidence, but after the dog attack and God knows what else he'd done, she was concerned. For his safety if she did nothing; for his career if she did something.

'If I tell you what he told me,' she began, searching the young woman's face for a signal of trust. 'Do you promise to keep it to yourself?'

Jones swallowed. 'OK.'

Etta took a breath. 'Darian Wallace murdered our daughter.'

'What?' exclaimed Jones. 'How? I mean, sorry, how do you know?'

'Zac said a gang member who'd driven the motorbike away from the shooting confessed to him.' Etta fought to muster her self-control but could feel tears coming. 'He even thought someone from the Met was involved with shutting down the inquiry at the time.'

'Oh my God. Why?'

'He wasn't sure.'

'How did he find this out?'

Etta flexed her eyebrows. 'He's been doing some freelancing…'

Jones nodded. 'Explains why he hasn't seemed himself at work. I've been worried about him.'

You've been worried about him, thought Etta. Try being married to the guy.

'Think he wants to find Wallace on his own?' asked Jones.

'I know my husband. He was full of anger about Amelia's murder for years. I was too, at the beginning, but for me it shifted over time to something else, to sadness. Zac held on to the anger much more. He's pretty bloody stubborn. And he's been taking some risks recently.' Etta gave the true account of his dog bite, Jones's eyes widening in shock as she spoke.

'Any idea where he might've gone?' asked Jones.

Etta reached for the tablet, tapped and swiped across. Opened Glympse, held it up for Jones. 'If we find him with this, can you go look for him?' She was trying to sound calm, knew she wasn't pulling it off. 'Just make sure he's OK?'

'Of course.'

'Without involving your other colleagues? Please.'

Jones held her gaze for a moment, then nodded.

CHAPTER THIRTY-FOUR

About a hundred metres off, the hooded figure walked to the jetty, carrying two large holdalls, which he placed at his feet. He faced away, watching the river, but Boateng knew instinctively who it was.

Darian Wallace.

It had been only a few hours since they found his latest victim in the garage. Three days tracking him for Parker's murder, eleven for Harris's. And 1,803 for his daughter's. Not to mention the shopkeeper and his intended victim that day, Draymond King. Five years. Boateng just hadn't known who he was looking for until a week ago. Now all his searching came down to this moment.

He stayed in shadow alongside a warehouse, crept closer. Drew the pistol from his jacket with trembling hands. Needed to breathe and be calm, even if he was past the point of no return. Pictured Amelia's bright eyes. Her grin, the little gap in her teeth. Felt the rage swell. How close would he have to get – twenty metres, fifteen maybe – before he could start firing straight into Wallace's back? Same as he'd done in the newsagent that day. Justice. An untraceable gun, no witnesses; he could just melt into the night and never be caught…

He was about fifty metres away now, treading silently, heel to toe in trainers, watching his footing for anything he might step on that could make a sound. The figure remained motionless. Boateng clenched his teeth, continued. Thoughts chased around his brain: about his team, backup, Etta and Kofi. Was Wallace armed? Could he bring him in alone? Then a darker scheme: what if, during arrest, Wallace struggled and happened to produce a Glock which—

No, he told himself.

You're not a killer. You're not like him. You're better than that.

Still, he placed a finger on the trigger.

Forty metres.

Wallace had taken Amelia's life, denied her a future. Robbed their family of a daughter. Surely only his death could atone? Boateng wouldn't have agreed with such a principle until the day she died. He'd have argued that the law was there to deal with anything, its measures proportionate to the crime. Until she was murdered in cold blood. Only then did an eye for an eye begin to seem reasonable.

Thirty metres.

He had to make a conscious effort to move slow, quiet. Nice and easy. Soon he'd be in the open, with no cover from buildings. Much as the cauldron of fury stoked since Amelia's death demanded he empty an entire clip into Wallace with no further debate, he had to know. Had to confront him, hear it from his mouth. Only then could he decide what punishment was required. In the shelter of a final doorway, Boateng activated the voice recorder on his mobile, tucked it into the breast pocket of his coat. Took one slow breath. Then moved out quickly.

'Freeze!'

The figure turned, saw the pistol, recognised Boateng. Cracked a smile. 'Wondered when you'd find me.'

'Take your hood down slowly. Hands where I can see them.'

Wallace did so as Boateng approached. He was close enough now to look into those eyes, the teardrop inked below one. Close enough to smell his body odour. Close enough to fire and hit the target.

'Six murders,' he growled. 'At least. People who had families, friends. Lives destroyed by you. They all mattered. One more than the rest to me. Amelia Boateng.'

'I know,' Wallace said quietly. His jaw set.

Boateng's heart pounded against ribs. 'Did you do it?'

No reply.

Raised his voice. 'Did you do it?' One more step. 'Did you kill her?'

They were five metres apart now.

Wallace closed his eyes. 'Yes.' Neither gloating nor dismissive, just fact. He even sounded relieved.

Boateng squinted through his pistol sights, the rear-side luminous green dots lined up over Wallace's chest. 'Why?'

'That prick King had it coming. But I didn't mean to hurt your daughter.'

Boateng took up slack on the trigger's safety. The anger was growing, spreading through him. Three metres.

'I'm sorry,' said Wallace. Seemed like he meant it.

Tears pricked at Boateng's eyes, his top lip quivered. Keep it together. 'Why wasn't it investigated properly?'

'Have to ask your mates about that.'

'Bullshit.' Boateng took another step forward. 'There must've been forensics, shell casings, something. A ballistics match. Why was nothing done?'

Wallace held eye contact, sighed. 'If I tell you, d'you promise to let me go? I've got a new life here.' He gestured to the holdalls. 'Boat coming any minute. Yeah, I was the one who pulled the trigger that day, but your daughter's death was an accident, you get me?'

'One you caused.'

'OK.' Wallace spread his hands. 'I accept that. And I'm sorry, for real. Never meant for that to happen.' Gestured vaguely to his face. 'It's why I got this teardrop. I suffer for what I did, believe me. Madness, nightmares and shit.'

'*You* suffer?'

'Alright, alright. Look, all I'm saying's the man you want is the one who sold me the nine. One of your lot. Same guy that made sure I never got caught. Not for that, anyway.'

Boateng blinked rapidly. 'You're saying a copper sold you the gun that killed my daughter, then protected you afterwards?'

'To protect himself.'

'What was his name?'

Silence.

'Name.'

Wallace tilted his head, let his arms drop. 'Promise?'

Boateng bit his lip, hesitated. 'OK. Tell me his name.'

'Called himself Kaiser.'

'Kaiser?'

'You know, like an emperor or some shit. I don't know his real name. Swear down.'

The pistol grip slackened slightly as Boateng tried to process the information, any significance of the nickname.

Didn't see the angle grinder until it screamed at him like a giant hornet. Boateng snatched at the trigger but only got a dry click. Nothing in the chamber. The whining blade came at him again and he blocked it with the pistol. Glock and angle grinder both clattered to the concrete and Wallace was first to dive on the gun.

Boateng piled on top of him, limbs flailing, connected with two punches. Wallace held firm, Glock in one hand so he couldn't rack it to load a bullet. Boateng tried to get him in an armbar but Wallace writhed underneath. Managed to hook one elbow round Wallace's neck, squeezed hard, but it wasn't enough. Had to keep his other hand on Wallace's left wrist and the Glock. The younger man's right elbow was pounding his ribs. As Boateng shifted to get more body weight on the pistol, Wallace swung a hammer fist straight into his balls. Boateng's body crumpled, he felt sick. Then came the blow to his temple and he rolled over, stunned, his vision a blur of light. Heard the slide rack above him.

Wallace had the gun.

Spike watched the whole thing. Bloody shambles. How the copper got closer and closer, talking too much, till Wallace whipped out some bit of kit, smacked the pistol from his hands. Cake and arse party they'd call that in the regiment. He couldn't risk firing while the pair of them were rolling around on the floor, too much chance of hitting the wrong guy. So he let it run, thought Boateng would come out on top, cuff Wallace. Then Spike goes in, bosh, nabs the holdalls, thank you very much. But after a scrap on the deck the young bloke was stood over him, aiming with one hand. Round up the spout. No messing around now. Spike reckoned he had a single shot to change the outcome of this situation.

Crosshairs alighted over Wallace's chest. Aim for the torso at this range, bigger target. Steady breaths. Hit the exhaling point they call natural respiratory pause, where movement is minimised.

Smoothly pulled the trigger.

The flash from Wallace's muzzle half-blinded Spike. What the hell? When he looked through the night scope again Wallace was on his back, still holding the pistol. No question though, he'd fired it before getting brassed up. Were they both dead? Couldn't tell.

Spike collected his shell case, slung the rifle in his bag, climbed down.

Time to finish the job.

Wallace didn't know what happened.

One second he was in control of the situation; next he was hit by a freight train. Back slammed into concrete, chest started burning. Touched the top of his left pec, felt warm liquid. Held it in front of his eyes: dark. Had to be blood. His own. Jesus. He gasped, tried to make sense of it. Did the nine backfire? Could someone else have shot him right as he pulled the trigger?

Lifting his eyes, he saw Boateng a few metres away. Motionless. Like with the old guy in the garage, Wallace's survival instinct had just kicked in, and he'd fired the nine at Boateng before even thinking about it. Now he could make out dull footsteps through the tinnitus, but didn't know from which direction. Forget the backfiring theory. A third person was here. Probably whoever took him down. Shit.

Turned his head, saw the Glock just out of reach. Glanced at Boateng again. The fed didn't move. Footsteps were louder now. Wallace twisted onto his side, howling at the chest pain. Scrabbled towards the gun, fingers outstretched.

A boot came into view, kicked away the pistol. Wallace looked up at the figure, head to toe in black, ski mask and everything. Like a goddamn ninja. Then the boot crashed into his face. Felt like his jaw exploded. Wallace spat blood and a tooth, agony screwing up his eyes.

'Remember me, sunshine? You're a slippery little bastard.' His voice was muffled by the balaclava but Wallace recognised it: soldier guy from the greyhound track. No way. How'd he found him? 'Still got that thing you stole, ain't ya?'

Rhetorical question. Wallace said nothing. Try to think. Ringing in his ears was starting to fade. He hawked up more blood, pressing just below his collarbone with both hands now.

'In those nice bags, is it?' The man dragged them across and knelt, began searching through with gloved hands. 'Stay where you are, Darian, unless you wanna end up in the river. Won't float too well with that hole in you.'

Wallace registered the low hum of a boat engine in the distance. Getting nearer. Think. Seconds ticked past. Come on.

'This the one?' Soldier-boy brandished the emerald pendant, gave it a little shake like a Christmas present. Prised off the back, swiped around carefully. 'Where's the memory stick?'

'Uh?' So that's why a pro had been after him.

'The memory stick.' Ninja cocked his head. 'Don't play silly buggers this time.'

'What you talking about?' It was still in his trouser pocket from the lock-up. Wallace pressed harder on the gunshot wound. Felt like something was trapped in his chest. Engine was close now.

Got it.

'That boat's coming for me,' he gasped.

'You taking the piss?' The guy pulled some scope thing out of his shoulder bag, looked through it across the Thames. 'The RIB?'

'Yeah.' He coughed, spat. 'Let me get on and I'll tell you where it is. Deal?'

Ninja-man sniffed. 'OK.'

Wallace began hauling himself up, dimly aware the guy was fiddling with a shoulder bag. Eventually he stood, legs unsteady but working. Lungs felt tight. But he wasn't dead. Couldn't believe it. He could actually walk. Lucky escape, bullet must've—

The jab and crackle felt like his ribs were being clamped in a vice then shaken by a pneumatic drill. Wallace sucked in air as his legs were swiped from under him. Ninja was leaning over, holding a small black box. It sparked between two prongs. Stun gun.

'Where is it?'

Silence.

Another stab and the rattle surged through him again like a wild animal. When it stopped, Wallace realised a damp patch was growing at his crotch.

The guy tutted. 'You've pissed yourself. Want some more?'

Wallace shook his head, wheezed.

'So where is it?'

'Pocket.' The reply was instant, involuntary.

'Good lad.' Hands patted his jeans with swift, controlled movements and alighted on the tiny stick, removed it. Scrutinised the item. 'That's the one, mate. Only two places it could've been since you're gonna take that boat. In them bags, or on you.' The ninja wrapped the memory stick and pendant together in cloth, put the package in his bag and walked off into the shadows alongside the warehouse. In a few seconds he'd vanished like a nightmare.

Wallace gripped his wound again, felt it still oozing blood. Could smell the reek of his own piss. Humiliated, outsmarted, injured. He'd need medical treatment soon. But he still had the stash. And a means of escape. Maybe he could pull this off. Strained his neck to see. The vessel drew in alongside the jetty, its engine loud and rasping before being cut as it moored.

Snatching a final glance back at Boateng's lifeless body, Wallace rolled over and began dragging himself to his feet. Towards the holdalls discarded by ninja-man. Towards the boat that would take him to France.

Towards his new life.

CHAPTER THIRTY-FIVE

Thursday, 29 June 2017

Etta had urged her to keep going, head for Trinity Buoy Wharf at the docks: the last known location of Boateng's mobile. She was monitoring it from their home in Brockley while Jones drove Etta's car – until the signal had gone and Glympse informed Etta the mobile could no longer be found. This worrying news had made Jones drive even faster, reassuring Boateng's wife via the hands-free that she was almost there.

Turning into the docks, a car passed her on the corner. Too dark and quick to get a good look at it. Standard five-door saloon. Glanced in her rear-view: one occupant. Could be relevant but she had to continue. Rounding the bend, Jones recognised Boateng's car among a handful of vehicles. Stationary, no one inside. She parked behind it, climbed out. Started running towards the river. As the road bent and looming warehouses gave way to a central square, she needed no further directions.

Boateng was lying on the ground. He wasn't moving.

Her run became a sprint.

First thing she saw up close was the blood around his shoulder. There was some on the ground too. Jones knelt next to him, fought back rising panic, wiped clammy hands on her jeans. Tried to think clearly; DR-ABC, they were taught at Hendon.

Danger: a quick scan showed a figure moving towards the river with difficulty, dragging something. Could be Wallace. Had to let him go for now.

Response: she shouted Boateng's name. Nothing.

Airway: she tilted his chin, no blockages.

Breathing: leaned over his face, waited.

Still nothing.

Then air on her cheek, barely perceptible. Adrenalin shot through her.

'Zac! Come on.' As the flow of air increased, she sat back to give him space. He opened his eyes, stared at her, momentarily confused. 'Can you hear me?' she called.

'Kat,' he said quietly. 'It's Wallace, he—'

'You're bleeding, Zac, and right now I'm helping you. She tore off her leather jacket, wrapped the sleeves tight round his shoulder. He gasped as she pulled hard, checked the blood flow. 'OK, I'm calling it in.' Punched 999 into her phone, hushed his protests. Gave her rank, name and badge number, said she needed an ambulance for one injured officer and local units for a possible suspect. Calmly stated the location. Then hung up.

Examining the wound, she could see what looked like a bullet's entry point in his jacket on the left side of his chest. Felt behind it, touched several hard, jagged objects. Gently lifted the jacket flap. His mobile, shattered. Bullet must've ricocheted off it and out through his shoulder. Damn sight better than entering his lungs.

Boateng began to move, shifted his legs. Slowly pushed up onto his good elbow, breathing easier now.

A noise made her turn.

The stooped figure was still pulling his holdall towards the jetty. He froze a second, looked right at her, shifted his gaze to Boateng, turned, staggered on. Then collapsed.

Jones didn't know what to do.

'Go!' croaked Boateng.

She looked from her boss to Wallace and back. 'But I've got to make sure you're stable, I—'

Boateng managed a nod in Wallace's direction. 'He needs your help.'

Jones checked her improvised tourniquet once more then ran to Wallace. He was passed out between two large black holdalls, blood on the decking where he'd fallen. Ahead on the jetty a boat was cranking up its outboard motor. Surely the ex-con skipper hired by Wallace for his escape. She bellowed 'Police!' at the craft and an engine roared before it pulled out, accelerated away downriver. Jones stayed put. Maritime might catch him if she could call soon enough.

Jones stared down at Wallace, the man who had caused so much pain, carnage and misery. Not just in the last two weeks but for years. The man who'd murdered Boateng's daughter. If she did nothing he'd bleed to death before the ambulance arrived. She hesitated. Thought about her Dad. Do the right thing. Looked back at Boateng. He watched her, gripping the makeshift bandage in his other hand. She stood over Wallace as the regular movement of his ribcage slowed.

Then she knelt and began to stem the blood flow from his chest wound.

Jones directed the first medics to Wallace, who needed them more. While they tended to him, with another vehicle on the way and maritime units alerted, she returned to Boateng. Kept her voice low.

'Etta told me everything. About Wallace, about what you've found. You should've brought us in. Trusted us.'

'I wasn't thinking right.' He shook his head, grimaced. 'Didn't know who to trust.'

Her look said that wasn't OK.

'I'm sorry,' he added.

'I know why you did this, Zac. But it nearly killed you. Then what would it have been worth?' She checked over her shoulder before continuing. 'That handgun over there.' She jerked her head across to the warehouse. 'Whose is it?'

He turned awkwardly.

'You know what I'm talking about. The thing that did this to you.'

Boateng seemed to be weighing his answer carefully. 'Mine,' he said quietly.

Jones knew what this meant: five years minimum sentence, job gone. She blew out her cheeks, scanned the scene, hoping his pistol would disappear. Knew she could make it disappear. She thought a second before asking.

'He fired on you?'

'Yeah, I got too close, he took it off me and—'

'OK. You leave any trace on it?'

Boateng shook his head. 'Maybe just where we fought over it.'

'So Wallace has prints on the gun, residue on his clothes. Ballistics will confirm the angles. Just your word against his on whose weapon it was.'

Her boss stared back at her. Might've been surprise on his face.

'Look, I'm not saying I think it's alright. It's just…' She didn't know how to express it. 'That would be…'

'Justice.'

'Right.'

He managed a half-smile.

'So you've got about two minutes before the rest turn up and everyone from the ambulance driver to the commissioner wants to know what happened. You'd better get a story about why you were here alone.'

Boateng nodded. 'Kat, I don't want you to have to lie if—'

She silenced him with a hand. 'You can trust me.' Knew she had the right reasons. Just hoped it wasn't the wrong choice.

A siren rose in the distance.

The chink of cutlery and babble of conversation wafted around the Grand Divan at Simpson's-in-the-Strand. At 7.30 a.m. the ornate room was packed with businesspeople and Savoy hotel guests. Susanna Pym finished reading an article – to which she hadn't really been paying attention – about some or other new obstacle to Brexit. PM wouldn't be happy about that. Mind you, she'd be even less joyful if that memory stick was out in the open, and she had to explain why one of her ministers was accused of colluding with a corrupt police officer. Pym threw her *Daily Telegraph* across the huge table, sipped her coffee and speared a piece of sausage. She'd chosen one of the old chess booths down the side of the room, facing the door. Keeping an eye out for her guest. Hoping he'd be the bearer of good news. Perhaps four refills of coffee hadn't been the best way of coping with her nerves. She could already feel the heart palpitations. And she was craving a cigarette. Needless to say, no bloody smoking in here either.

Pym was considering another coffee in lieu of tobacco when the tall slim figure in his well-cut suit appeared at the doorway. He beamed at the maître d' then marched over to her. Slipped into the booth, placed a small bag on the table. 'Good morning, Under Secretary,' he boomed.

'Keep your bloody voice down.'

Tarquin Patey half raised his hands in apology. Smiled and slid the bag towards her. Pym stopped chewing mid-mouthful, dropped her knife and fork, reached for the bag. Inside was a case. Her eyes flicked up to him as she opened it, extracted the pendant, turned it and prised off the back. Closed her eyes, sank back into the booth's cushion. 'Thank you,' she whispered. The large emerald sparkled in chandelier light. 'Must say I'd begun to doubt you.'

'My chap is nothing if not tenacious.'

'Tell him I'm grateful. Without mentioning my name, obviously.'

He bowed his head. 'Goes without saying.'

She felt the mood lift, her whole body relaxing. Realised she'd been tensing her neck and shoulders for half an hour. Patey sensed the change. Nodded at her full English.

'Not a great advert for a health minister, is it?' He arched an eyebrow.

She stared at the plate, flashed a grin. 'They used to call this Seven Deadly Sins, now they've renamed it the Great British Breakfast. I prefer the original title. Life's too short to eat bloody chia seeds. Why deny yourself simple pleasures, I say.'

'Couldn't agree more,' he drawled, and gave a low chuckle.

She laughed too. Imagined his charm had worked on many women over the years, especially at the rate soldiers had affairs.

'Any, er, how would you put it – collateral damage?'

'None of consequence. A couple of gunshot wounds, non-fatal. And your thief's back in custody, apparently.'

'Gunshot wounds?' Pym hadn't meant to say it so loud. 'This isn't bloody Afghanistan. The police tend to investigate that sort of thing here.'

'Be rather disappointing, as a taxpayer, if they didn't.'

'I'm not joking.'

'Trust me.' Patey made a small chopping movement with his hand. 'They won't find anything. My man's seen to that. He's rather adept at covering his tracks. I'll spare you the details.'

That sounded comforting, but Pym's concern remained on her face. 'I don't want to have to speak quietly to the Home Secretary about it.'

'I'm sure that won't be necessary.'

'Good. Did you use that number I gave you?'

'I believe my chap spoke to him once or twice for some relatively low-level tactical information. A couple of updates, that's all.'

'Your man didn't mention the memory stick?'

Patey looked disgusted. 'Of course not. That's confidential client information.'

She scrutinised him, nodded. 'And nothing else tying it to me?'

'Absolutely not. Worst that could happen once the police get through an inventory of the stolen goods is that yours is among several items from the vault that weren't either seized or returned. If it comes to that, you can always shrug your shoulders and claim the insurance.'

'I already have.' She twitched a smirk, relaxed again. Order was restored. Three years' agitation over. Her little secret would remain just that. Unless the demands of DCI David Maddox turned to all-out threats and it became a matter of survival. She gestured to the stick. 'Main thing now is to get this locked away somewhere.'

'Might I recommend a vault with more trustworthy employees?'

She gave him a withering look. 'Thank you for the sage advice, colonel.' She took a slice of toast from the silver rack, bit in with a crunch.

'Well.' Patey steepled his fingers. 'I won't keep you from your breakfast. Do let me know if you or any of your' – he searched for the word – '*friends* have similar issues they might require assistance in resolving.'

She dipped her head in acknowledgement. 'Shall I make an announcement in the Commons, see if anyone's interested?'

Alarm flashed across Patey's features for a second before they both forced a laugh. Enough deniability to keep both of them safe from any possible inquiry into those gunshot wounds. And enough tangible association to bind them together in secrecy. Or mutually assured destruction, to give its proper name. She seemed to be making a habit out of those relationships.

Empty eye sockets stared at him.

A hollow skull; pale bones that could move unaided. A gun muzzle trained on his forehead, the slow trigger-pull.

Wallace awoke at the bang, eyes immediately darting around the room, trying to orientate himself. Was he dead? No, he could feel his own body, move his limbs. Saw the large plastic tube coming from his mouth, two red socks poking out the end of the bed sheets. Clocked the heart-rate monitor to his left reading eighty-five; saline drip to his right. Recognised the whole set-up from his mum's stroke. Hospital. Pulled the pale green robe down at the neck, registered thin black spikes projecting from under his collarbone. They were too close to focus on, looked like stitches. Surgery, for a bullet wound. Shit. He remembered the night before, the ninja and his electric shocks. The blood flowing as he staggered towards the boat, seeing Boateng move, the woman arriving. Then darkness crowding his vision until he must've blacked out.

The room was neat, clean and only large enough for a single bed. One of those places they put the most difficult patients: infectious, delirious, violent. People with enemies. One of his mates had been isolated in a room like this when he got stabbed back in the day; police thought someone might come in and try to finish him off. Fed on the door, an alias in the ward register. Wallace assumed the same would be true now. Craned his neck to the doorway, felt the tube pulling in his throat. Through the crack he could see sturdy boots planted, plain dark trousers. Five-O.

Damn.

Wallace sunk back into his pillow. He was screwed, again. Where had Boateng got his information from? He checked back mentally. Maybe they'd traced activity on the mobile he left in the garage. Blamed himself for that slip. But how did they know about the docks? Had to be the Internet record – Neon, via the Boateng kid. He tried to hold back the fury. It can't have been Neon's fault, he knew not to tell. Could've been Miller with his boat, a stooge for the feds. But more likely Boateng junior. Once Wallace was out of here he'd find out for sure. And do the thing he knew best. Take revenge.

He thought a second.

Kofi. Yeah, that was the kid's name.

Wallace let the rage seep away for now. It was only a matter of time. He couldn't say the name out loud with a tube down his throat, but replayed it over and over in his head until it became a synonym for payback.

Kofi Boateng. A new name on the list.

CHAPTER THIRTY-SIX

Sunday, 16 July 2017

They strolled in warm sunlight along the path up by the Royal Observatory in Greenwich Park, drinking in the view over London, the Thames flowing sedately between the Old Naval College and Canary Wharf's glinting skyscrapers. Kofi ran ahead, dribbling his football. Given the number of people around, Zac had encouraged the lad to work on 'close control'. Etta held his right arm, the one that didn't have a bullet wound in the shoulder. He'd been discharged from Lewisham hospital after three days, doctors telling him once more how fortunate he'd been that his mobile had altered the round's trajectory, missing his lung. Stitches had come out a couple of days ago and there was some mobility in the joint now. His bruises were fading too.

'How're you feeling?' asked Etta.

He shrugged, winced a bit. 'Fine, pretty much back to normal. Still can't quite hold the sax, but that'll—'

'I mean about Amelia,' she said, cutting him off gently. 'It's five years on Friday.'

He kicked a stone off the path. 'OK, I guess.'

'Only OK?' She studied him as they walked.

'Yeah, only OK. You?'

'I'm coping, I think. Main thing is that we talk about how we're doing, you know? Tell me about "OK".'

Wallace had been remanded in custody after his discharge from Queen Elizabeth Hospital in Woolwich. Surgeons removed a 5.56 mm hollow point which had mushroomed in his chest. The type of ammo used by Special Forces. Zac didn't think there was much chance of tracing the sniper – the MoD had been no further help and the inquiry was with a local MIT now anyway. Krebs had called it 'speculation' that this was the same person who'd threatened Harvey Ash in his caravan and ordered them to prioritise other cases.

The first hearing date had been set for Wallace to have charges read: the murders of Ivor Harris, Trent Parker and Derek Howell. There was no record of his confession for the newsagent shootings in Peckham Rye Park on 21 July 2012. Wallace now denied having anything to do with it, and with Boateng's mobile in pieces, no evidence existed to the contrary. Given the nature of the killings he was accused of committing, Zac and his team were confident of getting the murder charges to stick. He'd receive three life sentences: probably a minimum of thirty years before consideration for parole. Not a bad result in a business where lawyers tied you in knots until the best you could hope for was a verdict of manslaughter to put your suspect away: fifteen years on paper, six to eight served. That never felt like enough. But neither did thirty years for Wallace.

'I wanted to bring him to trial for killing Amelia,' he replied eventually. 'Get the closure she deserved.'

'You know the way you got his confession would be considered inadmissible. His brief would plead it was only given under duress, and in the absence of other evidence…' She let the sentence hang unfinished.

Zac dug hands into his pockets. 'Absence of evidence isn't evidence of absence.'

'You don't need to tell me that, I'm a solicitor. But the jury can only go one way without proof. You wouldn't even have enough to charge him.'

'But where was the evidence? Five years ago, I mean. That's what I want to know.'

'Time to let this go, Zac, move on. We know who did it and he's behind bars. The rest is vanity, box-ticking. We should focus on Amelia, not Wallace. You're lucky to still have a job.'

Boateng turned away, pissed off. Because he knew she was right. He swallowed his pride and told her so. He was fortunate to have avoided disciplinary proceedings. He and Jones had stuck to the story about the Glock belonging to Wallace. He'd denied it, of course, but he denied everything else too. Forensics tied Wallace to the pistol and it became no more than a footnote in the case they were putting together. The angle grinder found at the docks was a match to the wounds on Parker and Howell, where Wallace had made less effort to cover his tracks. Connelly and Malik thought they should push for attempted murder – of a police officer – to be added to the list of charges against Wallace, but that fell into the 'harder to prove' category and Boateng had vetoed it given the strength of their other cases.

Explaining his presence at Trinity Buoy Wharf had been trickier. Had to have a quiet word with the Grant family on that. Neon's mum had been terrified that charges would be brought against her for aiding and abetting a fugitive. She told the police that Wallace had intimidated them into it, on Zac's advice. Coupled with his statement that the Grants had volunteered information on Wallace's Internet use to Zac that night, they were off the hook. He still faced a bollocking from Krebs for not calling in help earlier at the docks, but he cited urgency in tactical decision-making and the boss was getting applause from her superiors, so basically everyone was happy. The trade-off for all that was a feeling of unfinished business. He kept thinking about Wallace's words that night: *The man you want is the one who sold me the nine. One of your lot. Same guy that made sure I never got caught.*

They went on in silence awhile before he spoke. 'I have to find this Kaiser. If he's one of us – if he's police – I can't let that go.'

'What did I just say to you?'

Zac stopped. 'Could you live with it if a colleague of yours was involved in Amelia's death?' He looked at her, but she was searching the crowd for their son.

'Kofi!' she shouted. 'Don't get in people's way! Come back to us.'

Zac waited for her answer. It didn't come.

'You're a good man.' She squeezed his arm. 'But you're damned stubborn.'

He gave a small laugh. 'I prefer dogged.'

'Inflexible,' she countered.

'Single-minded.'

Etta gave him a playful punch. 'There are more than fifty thousand people in the Met. Human nature and the law of averages says there'll be a few rotten apples in there. You guys have a whole department whose job it is to pick them out. It's not your responsibility, Zac, there have to be some limits. Take it to the DPS.'

'But they won't listen to me, cos—'

'You haven't got any proof. So, you can bang your head against a brick wall for another five years, or you, me and Kofi can get on with our lives together.'

He glanced across to see their boy dribbling back towards them, tongue protruding in concentration. He turned and kissed her. 'Sounds good to me.'

'Which option?'

'Both.'

Etta smiled, shook her head. 'Come here,' she said, pulling him into a hug. Kofi ran over, flung his arms around them. 'Just don't go putting yourself in danger for the sake of your own ego, do you understand me, Zachariah?'

'Would I do that?' He cracked a grin.

Kofi looked up at his father, squinted into the sun. 'Can we play, Dad?'

Zac flicked the football up into his hand, nodded at the park below. 'Course we can. Let's go.'

'Yes!' Kofi snatched the ball off him and dribbled away, shouting something about beating his dad again.

Zac and Etta watched their boy run ahead. She slipped an arm through his and they began walking together.

A LETTER FROM
CHRIS MERRITT

Thank you for choosing to read my debut novel, *The Murder List*.

Much of the plot was inspired by real events. As a psychologist in the NHS I've worked with both victims and perpetrators of crime. Hearing victims' accounts of trauma and loss prompted me to write this book. But I also wanted to tell the perpetrators' side of the story, trying to understand what leads to crime. No matter how serious the offence, people act for a reason. Knowledge of those motivations can help us reduce crime and rehabilitate offenders. I'm confident Zac Boateng would agree with me, most of the time…

A sequel featuring Zac is coming later this year. If you'd like to receive information about upcoming novels in the series, plus other news and events around the books, then please sign up to my mailing list here:

www.bookouture.com/chris-merritt

You can unsubscribe from the updates at any time and your email address will not be shared.

Please also feel free to connect with me on Twitter or through my website, where you can find blogs and articles I've written about psychology. Some of my research links to themes in the novel – like trauma and risk-taking – so please take a look if you're interested to learn more.

Finally, if you liked *The Murder List*, it would be fantastic if you could leave a review. This lets me know what elements of the book worked best, and I can use that to help craft future stories. It also encourages others to buy the book and discover Zac Boateng for themselves.

I would like to thank you again for your support, and I hope that you enjoy the next book in the series, due for release soon!

All best wishes,
Chris

 @DrCJMerritt

www.cjmerritt.co.uk

ACKNOWLEDGEMENTS

There are so many people who helped this book to develop from the idea I had four years ago. Firstly, my sister, Steph – aka S. J. Parris – for encouraging me to write and tell stories. My parents, for reading all the early drafts and supporting me along the way. My girlfriend, Kate Mason, the most brilliant first reader anyone could hope for: never afraid to tell me what she thinks, and pretty much always right. Thanks to my editor, Helen Jenner, and her team at Bookouture for transforming my manuscript into the finished product and sharing their great ideas. It's been a pleasure to work together. To my agent, Charlie Viney, for seeing some potential in 2015, working with me to develop the characters and my writing style and doing it all with such good humour. To others who helped me by reading and commenting on early drafts: Charles Cumming and Frank Tallis. And to Mark Billingham for his encouragement when success didn't happen overnight.

In terms of subject matter, I'd like to thank Amy Gorman and other ex- and current members of the Met Police for sharing their experiences of the Job. Thanks to Naana Agyeman for her account of the Anansi folk tales and other aspects of Ghanaian culture during the time we shared an office at King's College London, and to my old colleague in Lewisham NHS, Lawrence Odelola, for introducing me to the gospel according to jollof! When researching gangs and gun crime in London, I was helped by Dr Rhiannon Lewis at Wandsworth Youth Offending Team, and found the work of Tony Thompson, Graeme McLagan and Tom

Gash very useful for further background information. Professor Fred Hickling shared his wisdom on Jamaican gangs when we met in Cape Town. Finally, thanks to some gentlemen who shall remain nameless for their stories from the SAS.

Lightning Source UK Ltd.
Milton Keynes UK
UKHW02f2012100518
322432UK00011B/746/P

9 781786 813947